SLOWLY, ANNIE TOOK HER CLOTHES OFF UNTIL SHE STOOD BEFORE HIM IN ALL HER GOLDEN NAKEDNESS.

"Come here," he said softly, and smiled when she walked unselfconsciously and gracefully toward him, her eyes wide and luminous as they looked anxiously into his.

Tentatively she reached out and traced the prominent lines of his chiseled face and grinned impishly at seeing them soften. She stood between his muscular thighs and strained against them, but he put her at arms's length, running his eyes and large hands down her.

"'Tis time to teach you the savoring," said Loch as he laid her against the pillows and started divesting himself of his clothing. Annie stretched like a cat and watched him, smiling mischievously. . . .

Books by Aleen Malcolm

THE TAMING
RIDE OUT THE STORM
THE DAUGHTERS OF CAMERON
KENLAREN

KENLAREN

Aleen Malcolm

A DELL BOOK

Published by
Dell Publishing Co., Inc.
1 Dag Hammarskjold Plaza
New York, New York 10017

ISBN: 0-440-14456-6

Printed in the United States of America
First printing—August 1984

KENLAREN

PART ONE

Lightly she whipped o'er the dales,
Making the woods proud with her presence;
Gently she trod the flowers; And as they gently
kissed her tender feet
The birds in their best language made her
welcome, Being proud that Oriana heard their
song.

—BEN JONSON

Prologue

In the beginning there was Lady Rebecca Forsythe. Actually she was not really the beginning, for down through the ages, towering above the common throng, was a noble family who managed by hook or by crook to retain their title and lands by direct descent despite changes in thrones, allegiances, religion, and very possibly sterility.

Sir Hendrick and Lady Amelia Forsythe were vastly relieved at the birth of a son after the disappointment of producing five daughters, Lady Rebecca being the third. Lady Amelia was vastly relieved because she no longer had to dutifully submit to an act she found unholy, unpleasant, unbearable, and positively disgusting. Sir Hendrick was vastly relieved because he much preferred to perform with applauding bed partners and because he now had an ally in his castle full of females.

The five Forsythe daughters were raised genteelly as befitted nobility and were taught all the correct customs that would mold them into conforming wives for earls, dukes, barons, and, hopefully, higher peers of the realm. Profoundly and fanatically religious, Lady Amelia kept her daughters so pure and virtuous that the eldest, Lady Mary, decided to marry Jesus and be a nun. Sir Hendrick actually lit some candles in the chapel and thanked God, as the herculean task of marrying off five daughters was dashed expensive and interfered with his playtime in town. He managed to marry off his second daughter, Lady Rachel, to the decrepit widowed duke whose lands marched side by side with his to the south, and he betrothed Lady Rebecca to the baron to the north, thereby greatly increasing his family's holdings. Now, Lady Rebecca's fiancé had a very unsavory reputation—something to do with small boys and whips—but as he was a baron and a Catholic, Sir Hendrick and Lady Amelia ignored the rumor, ascribing it to jealous tongues. Indeed the baron was older than Lady Rebecca's own father, but he was nowhere near as ancient as Lady Rachel's decrepit duke, stated Lady Amelia when Rebecca tearfully objected. Besides, the weeping girl was an incurable romantic and needed a strong hand and perhaps a whipping or two to bring her down to earth.

Lady Rebecca had always dreamed passionately of Sir Galahad, Sir Lancelot, King Arthur, and Young Lochinvar galloping out of the west, east, north, and south to carry her off to castles in the sky. Despite her mother's dire warnings and her betrothal to the neighboring baron with the whips and small boys, Lady Rebecca fell in love at first sight. She stood tragically on the ramparts of Forsythe Castle, a gentle breeze ruffling her long hair, staring dreamily and sadly over the rolling countryside as the hunt raced across the verdant hills . . . and there *he* was, the epitome of all she had ever read, dreamed, imagined, and fantasized. Tall and strong, the sun glinting through his auburn hair so his head appeared surrounded by a halo of fire like a god. Hunting plaid and kilt streaming in the wind. Mounted on a chestnut stallion. Oh rapture! To a delicately raised romantic young English girl, the sight of this braw Scot evoked unnamed yet forbidden emotions. His strong bare knees and thighs caused her own legs to entwine in a very improper fashion, and when he had galloped out of sight she sank down breathlessly as a pulse hammered in an aching but unmentionable part of her body.

Five days before her marriage to the baron with the unsavory reputation, Lady Rebecca Forsythe eloped with David Gunn—a Scottish barbarian, a Protestant, a mere nobody—and thereby became the first to very publicly thin and taint the noble blue blood of the Forsythes in more than four hundred years.

Rebecca was declared disowned, dead, and unmentionable. To her sister Sarah, who was forced to marry the baron in her stead, she became an object of intense hatred when the rumors of little boys and whips turned out to be surprisingly accurate and somewhat understated. To her sister Rachel, married to the decrepit duke to the south, she became the object of consuming jealousy, and to her younger sister Naomi she became a cautionary lesson. To her eight-year-old brother Robert, stifled and bullied by the castle full of religious women, Rebecca became the most exciting, mysterious ray of sunshine amidst the boring, stultifying gloom of childhood. Luckily at eleven he was sent away to public school, where his totally female environment was exchanged for a totally male one as traditionally befitted a member of his class.

Little did the Forsythes know; little did poor David Gunn know; and even less did Rebecca know. She found herself a farmer's wife. There were no maids to dress and undress her. There were no servants to be summoned to do her every whim, except the cook, a toothless witch who cackled and stirred a large black cauldron. In short, there was nothing romantic after the anticipation of the elopement. In fact, to her delicate little nose, the farm stank, David stank, everything stank.

Oh, the first night was vaguely romantic. Rebecca was still so blindly in love that she didn't notice the odor of the farm animals . . . she didn't notice anything. She kept her eyes tightly closed and was only conscious of the hammering of her heart and other unmentionable pulses as David masterfully carried her over the threshold and up the stairs to their bridal chamber. She was near swooning in ecstasy as David gently undressed her. She lay gracefully panting, bathed in a rosy haze, enjoying the most exquisite fantasy she had ever conjured in her entire life as he caressed her milk-white breasts and kissed her heartshaped lips. As David's passion rose, however, romance flew out the window and Rebecca found herself impaled in a beastly nightmare.

Nine months to the day of that honeymoon night, Rebecca was delivered of lusty twin boys, Duncan and William. The toothless hag reluctantly left her black cauldron to act as midwife, much to Rebecca's terror. David was ecstatic, forgiving and forgetting the preceding months when his hopes of marital bliss had been shattered by his seventeen-year-old bride who locked herself in the bedchamber all day and locked him out of it all night. When it had become evident she was breeding, he gave in to her petulant demands and pampered her—even hiring her a maid and showering her with romantic gifts. Rebecca lay on a chaise longue in the very best parlor like a suffering heroine, swooning and vomiting at the crude farm smell of her solicitous husband. He submitted to even more of her demands by scrubbing himself raw and entering the house through the servant's entrance.

For David it was like being a bachelor again except for the addition of the twin boys, who tumbled up somehow with the help of the witchlike crone, as their mother hadn't the remotest interest in them except from afar. She'd stare mistily out of her parlor window and see them as poetic cherubs.

When the twins were about four years old, David demanded his marital rights. He was, after all, a normal, healthy male. Rebecca ignored his rappings at her locked parlor door; she read romantic poems at the top of her voice to drown him out. David, who had imbibed heavily, kicked down the door and ravished her on the floor. Rebecca loved it. The dominance thrilled her. There was no tearing pain ripping her in two like before . . . but a golden pulsating ecstasy that lifted her to great heights. She clutched Young Lochinvar to her straining breasts, then opened her eyes to the reality of the crude farmer with whom she had so rashly eloped.

Rebecca's strange mind took a new twist and poor David was soon worn out. He toiled as a farmer from dawn to dusk, and from dusk to dawn he toiled as Sir Lancelot, Galahad, and Young Lochinvar as Rebecca closed her eyes and wove her fantasies. Once more, to her great distress and even greater puzzlement, Rebecca found herself pregnant.

After their son Michael was born, Rebecca's romantic, addled brain put two and two together and she surmised the cause of pregnancy. Once again her door was locked;

her husband found simpler women with less demanding appetites.

The boys grew, David toiled and Rebecca read, fantasized and felt neglected, so therefore she behaved like a petulant princess. David was furious with his wife's new behavior. She ordered expensive gowns and accessories as well as a barouche so she could trot about the countryside pretending to be any number of tragic, beautiful heroines looking for her Prince Charming.

When the twins were seven and Michael two, David summoned up his courage to put an end to his wife's extravagance. That night Rebecca, in an expensive flowing gown with flickering taper in hand, was pacing the parlor lost in a romantic reverie. David, fortified with whiskey, strode in to take the bull by the horns and ended up writhing with her on the floor, his appearance neatly dovetailing with her fantasy.

Oriana Rebecca Gunn was a living, squalling monument to the very last coupling of David and Rebecca. Dr. Murdock (hastily summoned by the maid, Maude Potter, because the child's birth coincided with the Beltane Sabbat so the toothless old crone was prancing somewhere in the moonlight and unable to deliver the impatient baby) dolefully shook his head as he informed the young couple that there could be no more children. Rebecca locked her mind away with her heroes, never really facing reality again. She lived in her pretty parlor like Rapunzel in her tower whilst her husband grew more and more dour and humorless, and her four children grew in the kitchen, barns, and fields. Sometimes when the moon was full she dressed in gossamer and rode about in her ghostly barouche in search of phantom lovers . . . and sometimes there could be heard the swish of fairy wheels up the Gunn's drive bringing Sir Galahad, Sir Lancelot, and Lochinvar.

So in the beginning there was Lady Rebecca Forsythe who brought shame and tainted the illustrious Forsythe blood.

Chapter 1

The very honorable Sir Robert Forsythe, feeling extremely virtuous at having performed his filial duty by visiting his family seat for a long two days, arranged with his valet to have his portmanteau packed in preparation for his return to London. He sighed at the thought of the city with its various drinking, sporting, and gaming clubs that used to amuse but now merely served to fill empty hours. He shuddered at the thought of the boring patterns of society functions, where pushy mothers paraded their simpering darlings, hoping to lure wealthy and preferably titled sons-in-law. He grinned and absentmindedly stroked his cheek as he mused upon one of the young ladies in particular, a not-so-simpering, and decidedly-not-sweet young miss who had sharply slapped his face after a very passionate and promising kiss that still seemed to be imprinted on his well-formed lips.

"Iona Montgomery," he whispered aloud as he closed his eyes and pictured her seventeen-year-old taller-than-fashionable figure.

"I beg your pardon, Sir Robert?" enquired his valet.

"Carry on, Wilkes," he directed, leaning back comfortably as his diminutive manservant adeptly stropped a cutthroat razor.

Robert was leisurely shaved, manicured, bathed, and dressed. He purposefully allowed his valet to take his time in hopes of avoiding the uncomfortable and unnecessary torture of kneeling on the cold sharp stones of the family chapel before breakfast. While the gesture would please his mother, the Lady Amelia, the past two mornings of such supplication had been more than enough to atone for his carnal pleasures. Even carnality itself had begun to seem boring, humdrum, and decidedly predictable, he mused, as his cravat was tied in the latest careless fashion by his faithful valet.

"Was ever a man so cursed? he lamented, thinking of his four fanatically religious sisters—one, praise God, safely ensconced in a convent, a small mercy as his mother's devoutness more than made up for the absence.

"I beg your pardon, Sir Robert?" asked Wilkes standing back and appraising his handiwork. Robert just grunted. Yes, his father had the only sensible idea: he was happily housed in London with a voluptuous young mistress and he made dutiful pilgrimages to the castle only during the hunting season, Christmas, and a very occasional Easter. At Forsythe Castle even Christmas was not the festive celebration it was supposed to be—it was merely an excuse for an unbearable escalation of religious observances—and the crucifying pain of Easter didn't bear thinking of. With a shudder Robert shrugged into his coat and dismissed his valet.

Judging the time to be ripe, Sir Robert descended the gray stone steps hoping the breakfast hall was vacated so he might partake without the interminable grace that usually congealed the eggs, toughened the lamb's kidneys, and left him with no appetite. Halfway down the stairs he became conscious of loud voices and shrill screams of hysteria. Not willing to be subjected to breast-beating, martyring, or the like, he quietly walked into the gallery overlooking the great central hall, and secure he was well-hidden, stared down at the scene below.

Two tall, auburn-haired youths in rough farm clothing stood hiding their awkwardness and apprehension by keeping their heads proudly raised. Robert gasped aloud at their identical faces. With regret he tore his eyes from the handsome boys and looked to the source of the anguished cries and sobs. His mother, Lady Amelia, stood like a Valkyrie, her features as cold and hard as the gray stones of Forsythe Castle. She seemed to be ignoring the pitiful sight of a slender, long-haired woman who groveled on hands and knees, weeping and clutching the hem of her skirts.

"What the hell!" hissed Robert irreverently, totally bewildered by the proceedings.

"Mama? Mama? Forgive me, Mama? Don't send me back! I'll be good, Mama! Stop the roses bleeding, Mama, please, and I'll be good!" promised the distraught figure.

"Could it possibly be the notorious Rebecca?" wondered Robert excitedly, his breath catching between his teeth as the object of his curiosity raised her tear-wet face. He saw that despite her advanced years of thirty-four or five, she was as beautiful as he remembered.

"Stop the roses bleeding, Mama?" begged Rebecca, weeping. Robert smiled dreamily as he acknowledged that she was even more tragically romantic than he had imagined. He was brought back to reality as his mother uttered a word he had never supposed she knew.

"Bastards!"

There was a shocked cry of protest from Lady Amelia's three other daughters who clustered nearby, clutching each other, repelled by their wanton sister writhing at their mother's feet.

"See what sin has produced! See the sin of her loins!"

"Mama!" gasped Rachel.

"Mama!" gasped Naomi.

"Ooooh!" gasped Sarah. "Loins!" she sighed while blushing.

"There you see the wages of sin!" proclaimed their mother with a fervent gleam of savage enjoyment in her eyes as she pointed quellingly at the two boys. "There you see the blighted, twisted, and unnatural fruits of filthy copulation!" she cried majestically.

"Mama!" breathed her transfixed chorus of good daughters, who dutifully left their neighboring castles at the crack of each dawn to attend early mass in the Forsythe chapel. The identical youths stood as one, their amber eyes pinned to points above their grandmother's head, where row upon row of Forsythe nobility stared down unmoved by the dramatic scene.

"Take this pitiful creature to the chapel, Brother Paul," ordered the pious Lady Amelia, and a sackcloth-garbed man shuffled forward. The auburn heads of the youths moved as one as they watched their demented mother clutching and scrambling at the coarse robe of the bent old man who led her away. Even when she was out of sight, their eyes remained focused on the dark passage that seemed to swallow her up, and they stood listening to her pathetic childlike voice spiral back, bouncing and echoing off the hard cold stones until there was stark silence.

"Well?" Lady Amelia's harsh voice shattered the stillness. "What do you want?" The boys stared silently. "Our strayed lamb is back in the fold where she belongs, and we owe you nothing," she ranted, unnerved by the steady eyes of her grandsons. "Oh, I pray there are no more of you . . . no more products of my wicked daughter and that black-souled satan who seduced her!"

The twins turned as one, and walked out of the castle without acknowledging their grandmother's imperious voice, which ordered them to remain where they were until dismissed.

Robert watched them go feeling a mixture of emotions. He was slightly appalled at his mother's callousness but it was to be expected. Amused at her language, he never imagining the word *bastard* could slip past her teeth, but most of all Robert was fascinated by his handsome, proud nephews. He descended the stone stairs three at a time, ignoring his sisters, who squawked and clucked like a brood of chickens on seeing him.

"Robert, you missed it. You should've seen. 'Twas terrible! 'Twas Rebecca!" Robert, eager to be after the twins, gently extricated himself from the many plucking hands. He kissed his mother on the forehead, and informing her he was on his way back to London, strode out, ignoring her commands that he stay.

At the stables he ordered his horse saddled and he paced impatiently as he waited.

"What were they driving?" he demanded of an ostler.

"Funny old-fashioned lady's carriage, sir," answered

the lad, giggling. "They didn't 'alf look a sight in their 'ob-nailed boots driving that prissy thing."

"Excuse me, your honor, but her ladyship begs for your presence," stammered a footman, out of breath.

"Tell my mother you missed me," said Robert curtly. "Riggs, what the blazes is taking so long? Where's my horse?"

"Be right there, sir," came a voice from the dark interior of the stables.

"But, your lordship, sir, it has to do with your sister, the Lady Rebecca, sir. There have been some occurrences that I don't think you're quite aware of. . . ." ventured the harassed footman.

"Don't be impertinent! I am quite well aware of this morning's occurrences," replied Robert testily. "Ah, about time, Riggs," he barked, swinging himself into the saddle and kicking his fresh horse into a gallop. He nearly knocked over the hand-wringing footman, who was sure to be humiliated by the Lady Amelia when he returned without her son.

It was a beautiful warm morning in May. Flowers bloomed in profusion, visited by multicolored butterflies and busy, droning bees. Robert, oblivious to the beauty of his surroundings, nevertheless felt the gray, cold oppression of his family home fly from him as he rode at breakneck speed, disturbing the pastoral tranquility. Flocks of peacefully feeding birds exploded into the deep blue sky, chattering their fear and indignation, while a gaggle of grazing geese flapped, hissing and honking, necks outstretched at his intrusion. The dust from the dry baked earth, churned up by his horse's iron hooves, dulled the fresh, vibrant colors of the tulips and daffodils in the cottage gardens.

Of the funny old-fashioned carriage there was no sign. Robert was not surprised, for he supposed his stoic nephews had waited until clear of the cold, pious stones of Forsythe Castle to unleash their fury by whipping their poor horses and putting as much distance as possible between them and their grandmother's insults. Of the little he knew, his sister Rebecca having been unmentionable for eighteen years, he surmised the boys would head north—their errant sire was rumored to be some blackguard of a Scot—so he cut across the country to intercept the much-traveled north road.

As he rode he had to admit to himself that despite their rough appearances, he had a grudging respect for the boys' forebearance and restraint. They had displayed an innate pride, a dignity that denoted breeding, as they stood with their auburn heads held high. He laughed to himself remembering the look of apoplectic indignation on his mother's face when they had turned on their heels and quit the castle. What type of man was this Scot who'd let his sons face such a scene, a responsibility that was his own manly duty, Robert now wondered as he reined at the crest of a hill and scanned the winding road below him.

A cloud of dust heading north caused him to smile with satisfaction before digging in his heels and chasing after. As he drew near he saw the cause of the stableboy's mirth. The outdated barouche, barreling along precariously, would have seemed more appropriate in a park carrying a pair of sedately promenading, black-bonneted old ladies instead of two muscular farm youths. Robert galloped alongside, noting the identical, angry young faces.

"Would you mind slowing down a trifle, I should like to talk to you!" he yelled, trying to be heard over the rumbling wheels and thunderous hoofbeats. The twins made no sign they had heard or seen him for several minutes. Finally the barouche slowed down but still kept a brisk, steady pace, and neither youth looked at him.

"Would you mind awfully stopping for a moment so we might converse?" ventured Robert. He was at a decided disadvantage as long as he had to watch the road and keep a safe distance from the light carriage, which tended to sway extremely dangerously from side to side. Without a word and still not looking at him, the twins pulled the carriage to a halt.

Robert felt at even more of a disadvantage as the youths sat and stared straight ahead. He hadn't a clue as to how to start the conversation he had initiated. Why had he followed them, he wondered. He felt awkward and ridiculous, and he was furious at being made uncomfortable by two callow farm boys.

"If 'tis money you're after, we have none," intoned one of the twins with a soft Scottish burr.

"Do you know who I am?" demanded Robert roughly.

"Don't look like no hightoby I've ever seen," remarked the other twin still without looking at him.

"I am no highwayman, I am your Uncle Robert," he pronounced. To his intense irritation they didn't even blink, they just sat resignedly as though barely tolerating his presence. "I am your mother's brother, Sir Robert Hendrick Forsythe."

"What do you want of us?" demanded one of them after an insulting silence. Robert frowned and fidgeted, causing his highly strung inbred horse to prance nervously. Why had he chased after them? It seemed more than just a welcome diversion from his very predictable existence; something about the identical youths intrigued him.

"I should like to know you," he confessed.

"We have no wish for that!"

"And I can't say that I blame you, after the godawful reception your grandmother gave you. Look here, I am frightfully sorry and all that. Isn't there anything I can do for you?" he added, not so much out of altruism but curiosity. He had fantasized about his errant sister all his childhood and was determined to see the romantic retreat the barbaric Scot had transported her to.

"We dinna need anything from you or yours," replied one of the twins curtly. He whipped the horses and they continued on their way.

"Mind awfully if I accompany you?" shouted Robert.

"Canna stop you," was the cryptic reply. The twins resumed their breakneck speed, the spiderlike barouche in danger of collapsing into a pile of delicate cobwebs at each rut in the road. After a few miles they slowed down to a more moderate pace. Robert had a shrewd suspicion that they had been trying to lose him by wearing his horse out, but they must have realized their inferior animals were more likely to drop first, and so had changed their plan.

All day they traveled, passing every inviting inn, and eating and drinking their own provisions as they took turns with the reins. Robert's stomach, which had been denied breakfast, growled constantly, but seeing they had neither the breeding nor the good manners to share refreshment, he just gritted his teeth and kept his eyes straight ahead until they had finished chewing.

The sun was setting blood red into the horizon as they crossed the border from England into Scotland. They had passed through the spectacular Lake District at a steady, bone-wearying plod. Robert comforted himself that there was no way they could travel all night; surely the darkness would soon stop them.

"They must have cat's eyes," he swore later as the pace did not lessen. He picked his way blindly, trying to follow the carriage.

His head and back aching, Robert dozed, letting his horse plod as he would, resigned to spending all night in the saddle. He raised his head groggily when he noticed light bouncing sporadically through what he assumed to be trees in the darkness. So intent was he on trying to make out the twinkling ahead that he was unprepared for a sudden joyful cry.

"Yoo-hoo!" A small fleet shape materialized out of the blackness, causing his weary horse to rear in fright. Robert, nearly unseated, fought to calm the animal.

"Who's that who canna control a puir beastie?" gurgled a young voice.

The sharp clatter of his horse's shod hooves on hard cobblestones jarred through Robert's tired body as they entered a yard. He saw the symmetrical squares of warm light and realized thankfully that they were at the end of their journey. The door was flung open and light streamed into the darkness as a boy of about twelve carrying a lantern hurried out.

"You did it? Was Mama happy to be there? What are our grandparents like?" he chattered wildly.

"Hush your face, we've company," growled one of the twins, flinging the reins to the boy. Robert dismounted stiffly and tied his horse to a tree as the twins climbed down from the barouche and stamped the cramps from their young legs. A fourth, even smaller child clung like a monkey to one of their backs. As they entered the house, Robert was aware of the flash of eyes straining to see him. He stood at the doorway looking in at the large warm kitchen.

A small, tousled auburn head peeked over one of the twin's broad shoulders.

"Who's the fancy man, Will?" asked a young husky voice.

"I'm your Uncle Robert. May I come in?" he responded, angry at having to ask. Hadn't Rebecca taught any of them the social graces?

"Suit yourself," was the terse reply. Hardly a welcome. He entered, and not being offered a seat, threw convention to the wind and sat in a large comfortable chair.

"Down you get now," said the twin who'd been called Will, swinging the lithe child from his back. "Go and help your brother Michael wie the horses."

"No, I won't. I dinna care to. He can do it hisself," returned the child pertly standing in front of Robert to stare openly.

"Do as you're bid or go to bed," growled one of the older boys, advancing on the disobedient child.

"But I dinna want to miss a thing and Michael maun be done by now unless he's a slummock."

"Dinna use such words!"

"Sorry, Duncan," the child apologized hastily, seeing the anger in his eyes.

"So you are Duncan and your brother is Will. How can one tell you apart?" asked Robert.

"'Tis easy," crowed the vivacious child. "Will has a little mole below his right ear."

"Do as you're bid," ordered Duncan angrily, grabbing the tiny lad roughly.

"But Michael's already finished, see? There he be," exclaimed the child, trying to wriggle out of Duncan's firm grasp. Michael entered and stood silently staring at Robert, who was beginning to feel quite intimidated, sitting while the tall brothers stood. He slowly rose to his feet, thankful that he stood as tall as the twins and was broader of shoulder. He extended his hand.

"I think we should introduce ourselves properly. I am Robert Forsythe," he announced, but none of the brothers clasped his hand. He stared at his wall of nephews, seeing the resemblance of each to the other, and realized his mother's fervent wish—that there be no other products of the unblessed union—was unanswered. How long Robert stood staring at the row of stony faces with his hand outstretched, he had no idea. He felt like an idiot, and his pulsing rage disspelled his weariness. He was just about ready to explode and slap the insolent young faces, when a small grubby hand clasped his, pumping it up and down. Bemused, he allowed the youngest to affect the introductions.

"This is Duncan, he has nae the mole under his ear. And this is Will . . . and this Michael and I am Oriana Rebecca Gunn but you can call me Annie."

"Annie?!"

"Aye, Annie. Hae you nae heard on it before? That's strange as there's four Annie's in the village. Old-Annie, Young-Annie, Annie-at-the-Mill and Daft-Annie who's got gley eyes like this," and the child demonstrated the cross-eyed affliction of Daft-Annie.

"You're a girl!" blurted Robert in amazement, staring at the small child in boy's clothes.

"Aye, sad isna it, for I'd much rather be a boy like my brothers," answered Annie frankly.

"And what Annie are you known by?" Robert asked.

"Wild-Annie Gunn," returned the child proudly.

"How old are you?" Robert guessed her age at about seven.

"Nine. I'm sma for my age. I'm the runt of the Gunn litter. How old are you?"

"Twenty-five," he replied after a pause, rather taken aback by the child's audacity. His other sisters' children would never have been so impertinent. Yet he suddenly realized he didn't much care for his other nieces and nephews. They were anonymous, blending into the gray stones of the Forsythe family with their conformity.

"That's old! Older than Will and Duncan even," proclaimed Annie with great satisfaction.

"What is it you want of us?" asked Will.

"I think questions should wait until we've eaten," Duncan interrupted with a meaningful nod indicating Annie, who was all ears.

"Och, Duncan, I saw your look. 'Tis not fair to hae secrets from your own wee sister," she protested.

"Oriannie Rebecca Gunn, we are dropping on our

feet. Don't you hear our bellies growling?" Will cajoled, swinging her off her feet and over his shoulder.

"Is he—the uncle—going to eat wie us?" asked the child, pointing a rude finger. Robert found himself holding his breath for the answer as hunger pangs shot through him and saliva ran freely into his mouth.

"If he has a mind to," answered Duncan tersely, seating Annie in a chair about the large kitchen table.

"Mrs. Wilson went to one of her important gatherings. She says she will be back in a day or so but she made three dinners to last and says I'm old enow to make breakfast and decide which of the three dinners to serve first," Annie informed them without taking a breath.

"So, what's it to be?" asked Michael.

"Bread and scrape and a boiled kipper." Robert felt his hunger ebb away, and Duncan laughed seeing his distasteful expression.

"Shame on you, Oriannie Gunn," chided Duncan humorously.

"Dinna smell like kippers to me," joined in Will.

"No, 'tis shepherd's pie wie the leftover mutton from Sunday, so fetch it from the oven as 'tis too hot and heavy for me," she ordered imperiously. Robert frowned as he saw his mother mirrored in the small tyrant.

Thankful, Robert sat down to eat. It was refreshing to dine without ceremony, just one course of the savory farm fare with plenty of homebaked bread and ale to accompany it. Replete, he pushed his chair back from the table and stretched his long legs as he surveyed the room. He guessed them to be in the servants' part of a manor of quite considerable size—compared to the Forsythe's castle, a mere hovel—but obviously no small farmhouse judging from the size of the kitchen.

He glanced at Annie, whose eyelids drooped though she forced herself awake with a start every few seconds. She was an enchanting child. Her small pointed elfin face was dominated by enormous wide-spaced amber eyes and a riotous mop of vibrant gold-streaked auburn hair.

"Bed, Annie," order Duncan.

"No!" shouted the child, instantly wide awake and alert.

"Aye, and right now," Will insisted as Duncan walked purposefully around the other side of the table to cut off her escape route, and Michael fleetly prevented her disappearance under the table.

"No! I want to hear about our mother and everything," she screamed, fighting free of Michael only to be caught firmly by Duncan, who tossed her like a pillow to Will.

"Aye, and you will tomorrow," reassured the twin, easily carrying her up the stairs despite her frantic struggles.

"You can put me to bed, William Gunn, but I willna stay there. I'll steal out and listen to what you dinna want me to hear. And if you lock my door I'll just climb out of the window and maybe slip and bang my head and be dead! And if you bar the shutters I'll scream so loud and bang on the floor you'll not be able to hear yourselves think!" ranted Oriana Rebecca Gunn.

"She certainly keeps you busy!" gasped Robert as the monologue receded up the stairway.

"Aye," was Duncan's laconic reply.

"Where's your father?" Robert ventured after a long, tense silence.

"Why?" Duncan countered as Michael quietly sidled out of the door to the yard.

"Why why? Surely 'tis a legitimate question?" exclaimed Robert impatiently.

"Legitimate?" echoed the youth sarcastically, raising an eyebrow.

"Dash it all! You know what I mean!"

"I do?"

"Surely to ask the whereabouts of your father is not a breach of anything personal. It seems a logical, sensible question under the circumstances," responded Robert with great irritation as Will strode noisily down the stairs.

"Why?" Duncan repeated. He stared pointedly at his twin, who looked about the room trying to locate Michael.

"Because, dash it all, it should have been your father at Forsythe Castle facing my mother!" Robert was insulted by the sign language that excluded him as Duncan answered a query in his twin's eyes with a nod toward the door.

"We did what had to be done," answered the youth, turning back to Robert.

"Well, I think it was deuced cowardly to have two raw boys do his dirty work for him!"

"We are not raw boys but *men*, and our mother is not 'dirty work,' " replied Will with a dangerous glint in his eye.

"By Jove, of course not, that is not what I meant at all by dirty work. Dash it all, she is my sister, you know. And I am not disputing that you are men, but you are that barely. How old are you?"

"We will be eighteen," Duncan replied.

"I'm near thirteen," Michael volunteered, sidling in through the open door of the yard. No one responded.

"Well, I don't hear the threatened crashes and screams," Robert said with a smile, breaking the tense ticking silence and staring at the ceiling.

"Och, that's probably because she's lying low, planning to sneak out when she thinks we've forgotten about her," returned Will, preferring the change in the conversation.

"And that being very possibly the case, I suggest we wash up the supper dishes and not talk until she gets bored and falls asleep," said Duncan gruffly as he stacked dirty platters. Robert sat at the table watching the three brothers busy themselves with what he considered menial servant's work—and female servant's work at that. He stared at Michael who worked silently, his young face closed and set but his eyes shifting uneasily as though he were intimidated by his two tall older brothers. Catching the boy's eyes appraising him in turn, Robert smiled, but Michael averted his gaze and scampered into the dim recesses of the scullery.

Robert sat sipping the raw whiskey and wondering exactly what he was doing in this rough Scottish kitchen when all he really wanted at that moment was for his valet to pull his boots off, draw him a hot, scented bath, and help him into a soft, comfortable bed. He gasped and chuckled when Will quietly reached behind the settle and picked up a small bundle of clothes.

"By Jove! I didn't see her sneak in!" Robert exclaimed

as Annie was cradled and carried back up to her bed. "It's amazing! Not only did she creep in, but right into the middle of the room!"

"Aye, that's Wild-Annie Gunn for you," Michael said wistfully. "She's as silent and fleet as a wee mouse. And to see her climb you'd think her a squirrel. Swims like a salmon too," he added as an afterthought.

"Strange accomplishments for a female," remarked Robert dryly.

"Aye," agreed Michael.

"We've done our best," Duncan's tone was quite defensive.

Robert frowned. "You've done your best?" he repeated.

"Aye," Will answered, entering from the stairs. Robert stared questioningly at the twins. They suddenly seemed very young and vulnerable, glaring at him as though daring him to criticize their baby sister. He smiled with new satisfaction as he realized he had an almost parental feeling of benevolence for his young nephews even though not ten years spanned their ages. He pulled himself up to his full height of over six feet and puffed out his chest, infinitely preferring his present position to his usual one of being the youngest, nagged and bullied by an army of older sisters and his mother.

"I cannot believe my sister Rebecca approves of her nine-year-old daughter running wild and dressed as a boy!" he declared.

"Our mother neither approves nor disapproves," replied Will bitterly.

"Where's your father?"

"'Tis not your business!" Duncan spat.

"It most certainly is," Robert stated firmly, banging his fist on the well-scrubbed table and thoroughly enjoying the effect as the three young faces lost their truculent composure. "I happen to be one of your closest relatives and you are minors in the eyes of the law."

"We are nearly eighteen," protested Will.

"Nearly legal," added Duncan.

"When?"

"Six months," Will replied sheepishly.

Michael looked from one twin to the other, his young face showing panic. "What happened? Didn't all go well with our mother? Won't our grandmother care for her? Won't our grandfather take care of Annie and me?" he cried.

"Hush your face!" snapped Duncan. "We dinna need help from any!"

"Where's your father?" demanded Robert once more.

"Gone more'n six months ago," replied Will reluctantly after a long pause, during which he had seemed to be having a silent struggle with his twin.

"Gone?" puzzled Robert. "Good Lord! Surely you don't mean . . . er . . . demised?" Michael gasped and backed away, his freckles standing out on his suddenly ashen face as the twins looked at each other with consternation. "Demised? Deceased? Departed? Dead?" strove their uncle, not knowing the extent of their vocabularies.

"Nay! Nay!" screamed Michael. "He's not dead! He's gone to . . . to . . . to Africa to find gold on the Transvaal. . . . Wittersrand, right, Duncan? Right, Will?" he implored. They nodded numbly, confirming his story. "So, will our lady grandmother take Annie so she can learn to be a gracious lady? Will she buy you commissions in a cavalry regiment?" His eyes burned in his thin face with a strange fervor. "Will they send me to school so I can go to university?" His tone grew fearful when he received no answer from his brothers.

"Nay! Our grandmother called us bastards and dinna want to know about any of us," shouted Duncan. "She called our mother a sheep and us the sins of her loins!"

"No! No!" sobbed Michael, shaking his head wildly from side to side, his amber eyes wide and haunted. "We're not bastards, are we?" he whimpered.

"Nay, our parents were married in the church in the village," reassured Will.

"Any marital union unblessed by the Holy Roman Church to my mother just doesn't exist. So even though she is incorrect, in her eyes you are all illegitimate. Unfortunately, now Mother will probably bully poor Rebecca into having the marriage legally annulled. That is why your father should be handling these sticky affairs instead of gadding about the Transvaal."

"Our father will not be back," Duncan stated.

"And from what I saw of my sister's condition, I doubt if she will be either," added Robert, wondering how his nephew could prophesy his father's future actions with such conviction. "What are you going to do?"

"That is our business," returned Duncan, meeting Robert's eyes challengingly. Robert rubbed his chin thoughtfully, looking from one young face to the other. Despite the rough facades and truculent expressions, the twin boys were young—still children despite their assertions of manhood. They were afraid. He smelled and sensed it in the air and he was determined to shatter their composure. He felt anger emanate through him when he realized that the two seventeen-year-olds had more responsibility than he had ever had in his whole life. Suddenly he felt as though their positions had reversed. He felt stupid, rough, and callow . . . useless and effete.

"It is not just your business!" he replied. "What of your small sister?"

"She is well fed," Duncan said with anger. "And she has gowns but she willna wear them!" he added defensively.

"It seems that Michael would like to go to university one day?" parried Robert. "What of schooling?"

"Michael can read and write Latin and French," boasted Will.

"And German," added Michael eagerly.

"Go to bed, Michael," growled Duncan and the boy backed away and hid in the shadows by the stairs.

"And you two would like commissions in a cavalry regiment?" queried Robert mildly. The twins avoided his eyes. "Well?"

"There's a lot in life we wish for but can never have!" hissed Duncan.

"Deny yourselves because of some foolish notion of pride!" retorted Robert. "But don't deny your sister! What future do you see for her? What will she ever be besides a wild little hoyden? What dowry does she have? What is she equipped for?"

"What was our lady mother equipped for?" snarled Duncan. Michael shrank further into the shadows, alarmed by the bitter intensity of his brother's cry.

"I was barely eight years old when my sister eloped with your father. I saw her for only a scarce few minutes this morning. So I don't profess to know what she was equipped for. However, I have four other sisters who are very well provided for, have well-connected, wealthy, titled husbands, and belong to families who are respected by society. I do not think it unreasonable to allow Oriana to have the same options in life," he stated, his voice and manner pompous. Briefly he wondered why he was so concerned about his rag-mannered, rebellious little niece.

"How? I canna see our wild Annie being welcomed into that cold pile of stones by our lady grandmother!" challenged Duncan scornfully.

"There are many schools for young ladies, and there are governesses. I could be her guardian and oversee her education," Robert improvised, unable to believe his own ears as he heard what he was saying. He stared suspiciously at the crude mug of raw whiskey that he held. He scarcely knew the wild, ragged brat, and here he was offering to raise her. The little he had seen and heard of her so far made him doubt that any school or governess could curb her very unruly tongue.

"Are there schools for me?" whispered Michael timidly from the shadows.

"It has been a long day," intoned Duncan after making an angry gesture that sent Michael scurrying hastily up the stairs. "Aye," concurred his twin.

His brain seething with loose ends and unanswered questions, Robert was silently ushered into a spartan bedchamber. The bed was unmade but had a supply of clean linens folded neatly on top. Never having made a bed in his life, and having no inclination to learn, he didn't try. He became so exhausted pulling off his own boots for the very first time that he fell asleep fully clothed, his blond head dangling over the side of the hard bed.

Chapter 2

Bright sunlight flooded through Robert's closed eyelids. He thrashed around trying to cover his head with the nonexistent blankets in an attempt to cocoon himself from the rude assault of day. He roared sleepily for his valet, threatening him with a long list of tortures for not drawing the draperies, when a gurgle of delighted laughter caused his eyes to fly open. There was little Annie Gunn grinning between the painful dots of light. He closed his eyes quickly and rolled onto his stomach, allowing the memory of the previous day to flood his fuzzy brain. His eyes reopened and he stared in horror at the mattress devoid of sheets, then reared back and looked with disgust at his wrinkled, slept-in clothes. Feeling itchy and dirty he prayed that no parasites had sought haven on his sleeping person.

"There wouldn't be a chance of a bath, would there?" he asked hopefully of the child who perched on the washstand.

"A bath! In the morning before you've got dirty?" she exclaimed. "There's the burn to swim in and the pump in the yard. I'll pump for you and scrub your back if you like," she offered with an appealing eagerness.

"No, thank you," declined Robert hastily, not having the slightest intention of performing his ablutions in front of all and sundry with a nine-year-old urchin in attendance. "I think I prefer a ewer of hot water." He pointed at the large jug next to her on the washstand.

"There's hot water downstairs on the hob," she informed him before leaping off her perch and prancing out of the door. "And you'd better be telling me what you'd like for breakfast or it'll soon be time for lunch."

"Wait—you've forgotten the ewer!" cried Robert as the child disappeared empty-handed. The elfin face popped around the door, the brow furrowed with puzzlement.

"I forgot what?"

"The ewer. The pitcher," explained Robert, pointing to the jug.

"I did not! What would I be needing that for? I'm clean, 'tis you who needs to wash." With that the saucy child scampered off.

Robert swung his long legs off the bed, closed the door decisively, and searched the room for a commode or chamber pot to ease his painfully full bladder. No such convenience being in evidence, he opened the window. From the cobblestoned yard below, Annie waved merrily. Robert stretched and pretended appreciation of the orchard beyond, where the trees proudly ruffled their clouds of pink and white blossoms, and beyond that, like patchwork, the neat fields of different blends of green stretching and diminishing in the morning haze. He closed the window, pulled on his boots, and descended the stairs to the kitchen. A clock chimed the half hour and Robert saw to his amazement and disgust it was only six thirty.

"What'll you be having for breakfast? I'm cook because Mrs. Wilson—"

"Has gone to one of her gatherings," Robert interrupted, not eager for a long monologue at such an ungodly hour of the morning.

"Important gatherings," corrected Annie. "So what'll you be having?"

"What everyone else is having."

"They had theirs hours ago. You're a right slug-a-bed!"

"'Tis just six thirty, nearly the middle of the night," protested Robert indignantly.

"Now, there's plenty of eggs, and gammon, and shepherd's pie from last night. Oh, and I can fry up some leftover haggis if you've a mind." Robert did not have a mind, unused to eating before eleven or noon each day; also, the mention of fried leftover haggis churned his stomach sickeningly. He shook his head, wondering how to approach the indelicate subject of an outhouse with a nine-year-old female. In his pious gray home there was never a mention of bodily functions, especially with the opposite sex. In fact it hadn't been until he was well-nigh grown that he learned, to his complete amazement, that females actually had the same bodily functions, his own mother and sisters seeming much above such baseness.

Robert strode out to the yard followed by the persistent Annie, who waved a large skillet.

"And there's porridge, 'tis a bit stringy and slimy as it has been sitting awhile, and cheese and pickled onions, and a nice bit of tripe left from the supper before last," she continued.

"I am not the least bit hungry, Oriana. I am in dire need of privacy," he stated firmly. The girl frowned with complete bewilderment for a moment and then without batting an eyelash stared down at the front of his tight riding britches. Her face lit up with understanding.

"'Tis the privy you are needing! Well, why didn't you say so!" she exclaimed without a trace of embarrassment. Robert stood in shock, unable to fully comprehend what was taking place. "Go through the orchard and follow your nose," she directed, waving the frying pan and wrinkling up her own small nose in illustration. Robert, finding her directions much too literal and himself unprepared for such base aromas, walked even deeper into the orchard, where he was finally able to relieve himself, observed only by a strutting rooster and his harem of clucking hens.

Not yet awake enough to subject himself to more of Annie's ebullience, he walked around to the front of the house. Standing back he was able to appreciate its beauty despite the years of obvious neglect. Elizabethan in architecture, the graceful manor stood well-placed amid tall elms on a knoll. A herd of cattle grazed on what had once been a well-manicured lawn. The expanse of grass sloped gently, encircled by a wide carriageway and encompassed by majestic, though tarnished, wrought-iron palings to which were tethered several goats. He strode up the driveway to the impressive front door. Finding it locked, he peered through the windows into formal rooms, the furniture protected by dust covers. Picking his way through an overgrown rose garden, he found himself back in the cobbled yard next to the stables.

"Did you find the privy?" inquired a small voice as Annie seemed to pop up from nowhere. Robert nodded curtly, not wishing to resume the previous discussion. "You were a very long time. I've been waiting for ages," she complained.

"I took a walk around the house. It must have been beautiful at one time, when the grounds were kept up."

"When the grounds were kept up? They're kept up. Every field is sown," stated Annie indignantly. "We've barley, wheat, mangle-wurzels . . ."

"Why don't you live in the main part of the house? I looked through the windows but couldn't see much. The glass hasn't been washed for years," Robert interrupted.

"We're comfortable where we are. We don't need more rooms to take care of."

"Show me the rest of the house?" he asked.

"Why?" spat Annie, backing away from him as though afraid.

"Why not?" probed Robert, curious about her reaction.

"I want to show you outside things, not stuffy inside ones."

"There's plenty of time for both."

"How long are you staying?" inquired the child, relieved to be off the subject of the house. Robert hesitated. He really should be leaving, as he couldn't bear to stay without a change of clothing.

"It depends," he evaded.

"On what?"

"Many things. Will you show me the house?"

"I dinna want to go back in there," cried Annie.

"Why?" Robert was quite surprised at the genuine terror in the child's voice.

"'Tis full of ghosties and bad things. At night I hear the dead tossing and turning, creaking up the big staircase."

"Probably the wind or mice," Robert said to calm her.

"Maybe," answered Annie. "But at night when 'tis dark and I'm sleepy I dinna think so."

"Well, 'tis not night now and you certainly aren't sleepy," her uncle challenged.

"No, I dinna want to . . . I canna . . . I canna!" Robert stared at Annie's drawn white face as she backed away from him in terror.

"What happened in there to make you so afraid?"

"Nothing! Nothing!" she shouted defiantly, taking to her heels and disappearing into the orchard. Robert stared after her. His good judgment told him to get on his horse and leave this crude side of his family immediately before he was firmly embroiled in all their problems. He had followed the boys merely to satisfy his curiosity and while away some boring hours, and surely he had done so. But what had he discovered? Four children living in the servants' quarters of an Elizabethan manor. Whose manor was it? Theirs? Or did the boys lease it and work the fields much like the tenant farmers on his own family estates? Why was the child so terrified? Deciding the brothers had invented bogeymen and the like to keep the mischievous girl from the owner's property, and determined not even to attempt all the other unanswered questions, Robert stood and stretched, wondering where to locate his not-too-hospitable hosts. It was time he took his leave. He felt a sadness and realized tne romantic memory of his sister Rebecca was tarnished, and he wished he'd been less impulsive and had left it intact. No wonder she had returned sobbing and begging to be allowed home. Who wouldn't, cooped in the middle of nowhere, forced to live without comforts in the servants' quarters of a simple farm? How had she stuck it out for all those years? He couldn't imagine Rebecca—or any of his sisters for that matter—cooking, cleaning, laundering, or the like. Yet the only servant besides the children themselves seemed to be the unseen but much talked about Mrs. Wilson.

Robert, unused to saddling his own horse, entered the stables with that purpose in mind only to find his horse gone. Each of the ten stalls was empty and his saddle was thrown over one of the partitions, so he assumed whoever had taken his horse was riding bareback.

"Oriana?" he bellowed between cupped hands as he stormed out into the sunlit yard. "Oriana? Oriana Gunn?" he called, but there was no answer or appearance. Furious, he stalked through the orchard, scattering numerous chickens that flapped and squawked, and headed toward the fields he'd seen from his bedroom window, hoping to find his nephews. The land was flat and the waving green grain too high to see beyond. He cupped his hands at his mouth again.

"Halloooo! Halloooo!" he roared, then waited for a reply. Nothing. Cursing, he paced the muddy, rutted track that skirted the fields. All he wanted was to leave the god-forsaken, miserable place immediately and return to his nonthinking indolent life in London. But how, without a horse? The only blessing he could find about the whole experience was that the brothers hadn't taken him up on his rash offer to be the undisciplined brat's guardian. But they might unless he could hastily quit the place before they came to such a decision.

"You lost again?" inquired a merry voice. Robert scowled at the small, grinning child who stood in rolled-up trews, barefoot and ankle-deep in a muddy puddle.

"Where's my horse?" he roared.

"In the pasture wie the others. What are you all fashed up about?"

"Get my horse!" Robert demanded. Annie stared at him and made no move to obey. "Did you hear me?"

"Aye, I'm not deaf."

"Then do as you're told!"

"You are very rude," stated the child emphatically.

"I'll have none of your impertinence, young lady!"

"'Tis you who's impertinent!" returned Annie, standing her ground with her amber eyes flashing. Robert's fury hammered in his chest, wrists, and temples. For a moment he was speechless.

"How dare you!" he thundered, grabbing her by the straps of her overalls and lifting her off the ground. For a long moment Robert glared into the small rebellious face that he held inches in front of his own, and then reason flooded in. What was he doing? How could he expect civility from a child who hadn't even been taught the bare rudiments of manners? Annie noticed the look of blind rage ebb from her uncle's face as he put her down and turned away contemptuous. She stared at his broad back for a moment and then turned away herself. Robert, catching the movement from the corner of his eye, was determined not to be deserted again.

"Where are you going?" he demanded.

"'Tis no business of yours."

"Haven't you been taught any manners at all?"

"Manners?" queried the child, totally bewildered.

"Yes, manners!"

"We're not at the table and I'm nae talking wie my mouth full or reaching across your plate wie out excusing myself," protested Annie. "And I hae nae belched!" she added.

"Do you respect you elders?"

"Aye, if they deserve it," she returned.

"What can one expect!" Robert exploded, turning his eyes to the heavens but unable to find an answer. His blind rage had returned. "'Tis no wonder my poor sister washed her hands of you and returned home," he muttered angrily.

"Because of me?" asked a small voice. Robert felt an uncomfortable emotion suspiciously like guilt at hearing the pathos in the vulnerable voice. "She went away because of me?" Annie repeated, pulling on his sleeve like a worrying puppy.

"Well, dash it all, if you were answering back and dressing like you are . . . and running wild, having no decorum, no discretion or etiquette. Well, your choice of subject matter alone is enough to curl one's hair! No well-bred, gently raised female should have to . . . Well, I mean to say it must have been deuced difficult for her . . ." blustered Robert lamely.

"But she didn't ever see me, did she?"

"What on earth do you mean she didn't ever see you?" Robert was totally taken aback.

"You mean she did? I would pretend she did but I thought it was just pretend. Sometimes I watched her through the keyhole. Och, she was so beautiful like the Fair

Ellen and the Lady of the Lake, like a princess from the stories she read."

"How could she read you stories if she never saw you?" demanded Robert triumphantly, positive he was being played with.

"I'd listen outside her door and she *did* know I was there! All this time she knew I was there," sang Annie joyfully. "What did she say about me?" Robert stared down at the expectant little face not knowing how to answer. "She said all those horrible things about me, didn't she?" returned the girl mournfully, when no response was forthcoming. "Well, I dinna care! I dinna want to be a lady anyway!" she shouted, rebellion covering the sorrow that brimmed in her eyes.

"She said nothing of the kind. I didn't even speak with her," confessed Robert.

"But you said she went away because of me?"

"Actually I said *maybe,*" he corrected himself.

"You dinna!"

"I absolutely refuse to stand here having an argument with a nine-year-old brat!" retorted Robert. "Get my horse and I shall be on my way post haste!"

"But you said you were going to stay and we'd have lots of time to explore and I did all my chores," protested Annie.

"I have changed my mind!"

"You dinna like me, do you?"

Robert stared down at her with amazement. It had never occurred to him to like or dislike any child, especially one of so inferior a class.

"It's a pity because I like you even if you do get all stuffy like a hubbly-Jock, hubbling and gobbling and giving your orders and getting angry and supposing me to know why when you don't even say why," chattered Annie, walking away from him. Robert was astounded. Nobody in his whole life had ever talked to him in such a manner. Who did she think she was?

". . . and saying all sorts of untrue things about my mother and you making it all up because you dinna even speak to her . . . and saying you'd be staying awhile when you're really leaving . . . and not being able to get your own hot water or saddle your own horse or unsaddle it but leaving it for Michael to do when he has all his own work," she continued as she stormed away. Without knowing why, Robert followed, his feet leading him as he strained his ears to hear her long list of unbelievable complaints about him.

"I feel meikle foolish defending you!" she said balefully, turning on him.

"Defending me?" echoed Robert.

"Aye, defending you! You should've heard them at breakfast talking after you. Lily-white hands like a woman—a prissy woman that dinna know work! How you sat last night letting them clean up after you like they were your servants. Looking down that long bony nose of yours. You may be older and hoity-toity and everything, and your fingernails might be cleaner, Uncle Robert, but we work hard and are proud. Leastwise, my brothers are proud," she finished lamely.

"You're not proud?"

"If I was a boy I'd be."

They walked in silence along the dirt path that ran between the orchard and the fields of grain. Robert felt oddly content, purged, and as was his nature he didn't pause to wonder why. He appreciated the delicate scent of the apple and cherry blossoms, the soft harmony of the birds and bees, and the squelching of mud beneath their feet.

"Is it too late for some breakfast, Annie?" he asked ruefully, breaking the quiet solemnity between them.

"You're not leaving then?" she crowed. Her face was vibrant with excitement.

"Why does it matter to you so much whether I stay or not?" Robert asked, bemused by the feeling of happiness he felt at her joyful reaction. Nobody in his existence had ever cared very much where he was unless it inconvenienced them in some way. Oh, he had several mistresses through the years who professed great excitement, but that was mainly for jewels or clothes and not really his presence, he thought cynically.

"I get lonely. Everyone is always busy so nobody has much time for me," Annie answered matter-of-factly. "Besides, you're handsome when you smile and I like you even if you don't like me."

"Despite the fact you are without a doubt the rudest, most improper female I have ever encountered, I do like you. I have no explanation for the fact either," laughed Robert, feeling carefree. He stopped suddenly, seriously considering his sanity, knowing he shouldn't be feeling elated under the circumstances. Annie giggled and tugged at his hand, pulling him along impatiently.

"You'll help me find your breakfast, 'tis one of my favorite tasks. I was saving it so you could help me," she declared as they entered the orchard. She broke free of his clasp and disappeared into the high tangle of wildflowers and grasses that climbed the brick wall dividing the field from the blossoming trees. A great squawk arose from the large white hen, which flapped her wings in Robert's face making him recoil in distaste. Despite his first misgivings, however, Robert found great enjoyment in hunting for eggs. His childhood having been devoid of Easter's brighter side, he let himself go and make up for the deficit now by calling out triumphantly when he spotted a nest with four large speckled ones.

"I'm winning, I've found more than you!"

"They dinna count if they're rotten," chortled Annie, picking one up and feeling its coolness.

"That's not fair," protested Robert as the child threw one of his eggs at the trunk of a tree.

"See, 'twas bad. Go smell the stink."

"I can smell quite adequately from here," declined her uncle, trying to balance the dozen or more eggs he cradled in his untucked shirt tails. He breathed deeply of the cherry blossoms to counteract the foul odor.

"First we maun gie MacTavish some," pronounced Annie as they made their way to the kitchen.

"MacTavish?" echoed Robert.

"My ferret."

Robert eyed the ferret MacTavish, who eyed him back with little beady evil eyes.

"Isn't he fine?" proclaimed Annie, deftly picking up the teeth-baring, hissing vermin behind the head.

"Looks rather dangerous," remarked Robert, thinking a small lap dog or kitten would be a more appropriate pet.

"He is. Och, he'd love to bite me again, wouldna you,

MacTavish?" she crooned affectionately as she held the venomous face inches from her own.

"Not a very friendly pet."

"He's no pet; he catches rabbits for the pot," informed Annie, putting two small eggs and the ferret back into the cage. "I tie a long string about him and set him down a warren and when I hear the scream I pull him up."

"Amusing pastime for a young lady." Robert winced at the relish with which his young niece pronounced the word *scream*. "MacTavish has his breakfast—now what about mine?"

"Do you know how to cook?" asked Annie as she deftly broke six eggs into a bowl and whisked them with heavy cream.

"No."

"You don't even know how to cook," mourned the girl and Robert squirmed uncomfortably. Then, at the realization that he was feeling shame at such a deficit in his character, he grew indignant.

"Of course I don't know how to cook. I am a man," he muttered.

"Will and Duncan are men and they know how. Michael's not nearly a man and he knows how."

"I have a cook so it is quite unnecessary for me to do so."

"We have a cook, Mrs. Wilson, but sometimes like right now she's not here. What do you do when your cook is ailing or goes visiting?" asked Annie, pouring the beaten eggs into the skillet.

"I have many cooks."

"Well, what can you do?" inquired the talkative child.

"Many things," answered Robert tersely.

"Such as?"

"Well, I can ride."

"Everyone can do that. What do you do for a living?" Once again Robert found himself feeling very uncomfortable.

"Well, in my position in life I really don't have to do anything except be the only son, and at the death of my father I'll take over his estates and responsibilities," he explained hesitantly.

"You mean you have to wait for your father to die before you have anything to do?"

"Not quite. I have to learn all about running the estates. Know who takes care of what. Actually it mainly involves hiring competent people to do the work and then hiring someone else to see that it is done correctly," he said, wondering why he was explaining such things to a nine-year-old.

"Then you'll have to hire someone to see to that person and another to see to that person. . . ."

"That's right," Robert interrupted, certain the child would repeat all day if allowed to go on.

"Seems to me 'twould be best to do the work yourself and then you'd know it was done right," stated Annie sagely as she piled scrambled eggs on a plate.

"Running one very large castle, two town houses, as well as three country estates with a total acreage of five square miles would be well nigh impossible for one person. And 'tis not proper for a female to discuss business, especially at breakfast."

"You must be very rich," sighed Annie, cutting thick slices of homebaked bread. "We were rich once before I was born . . . before my brothers even. My grandfather Gunn lived very high off the land . . . gambled all his money away. My father was an only son . . . that's why he couldn't be a soldier and he really wanted to be one. Will and Duncan want to be soldiers too. I wish I could be a soldier. Would you like to be one?" Robert nodded, his mouth too full to answer. "But you canna because you're an only son?" Robert nodded again. "But you have sisters?" continued Annie, and Robert continued chewing and nodding. "So if you were to die like a hero on the battlefield, your sisters could look after your castles and land. So you could be a soldier and be useful after all, couldn't you?" stated Annie triumphantly. Robert neither nodded or answered, but kept his eyes on the plate of eggs and ate methodically as he wondered what future lay in store for inquisitive little Oriana Gunn.

After he finished his meal Robert leaned back in his chair and watched the little girl wash the skillet and plates.

"Well, as I helped you collect the eggs, surely it's time

that you showed me the rest of the house," he suggested idly, his keen eyes pinned to the slight back that went rigid as her hands stopped wiping. "What is there to hurt you? The sun is shining and I'm tall and strong." he cajoled upon receiving no answer.

"Shadows of memories and the like. Bad, wicked things that I canna explain."

"Then show me where the key is and I'll go brave the bad, wicked things alone."

"I'll go wie you," Annie burst out impulsively.

"'Tis not necessary, though I'd welcome your company," responded Robert softly, noticing her obvious fear.

"Has to be faced!" stated the small child, leading the way, her thin back braced like a warrior. She led him through the kitchen, past several other rooms that he guessed to be pantries, root cellar, scullery, and the like, though he wasn't completely sure, not having any familiarity with the working quarters of any house. She stopped in front of a tall double door.

"I dinna think 'tis locked unless from the inside. Gie it a push," she whispered, stepping behind him. Robert pushed and the doors swung open. He strode into a large central hall off which were several formal rooms and a broad handcarved stairway that swept upstairs in a graceful arc. All the doors stood open except one. Annie stared at the closed door apprehensively.

"Shall we start with that room?" Robert suggested, following her gaze.

"No. Here is the library," she exclaimed quickly, pulling him toward another room, which was well proportioned with floor-to-ceiling bookcases housing just a few scattered volumes. Above the ornate mantelpiece a portrait of an auburn-haired man scowled down.

"Who is that merry chap?"

"'Tis my grandfather Duncan Gunn," giggled Annie nervously. She looked behind her as though expecting ghosts to pounce out. "He was the laird of all around here, even the village, but he wasna very prudent. He had lots of wives but they all died having babies. I think there were five," she chattered, twisting her fingers.

"What, wives or babies?"

"Wives. Not all at once because I dinna think that's allowed. There was only one baby who lived . . . my father. I suppose that's why my grandfather wasna very prudent and drank a lot—losing all those wives and babies in this very house."

"That could tend to make a man imprudent," agreed Robert solemnly, peeping under the dust covers at heavy, fine furniture, the oak dulled by neglect.

They looked into the drawing room, a small music room, a large dining room and a small dining room, and a long conservatory, where more ancestors scowled down.

"Not a very friendly-looking lot, were they?" he remarked, trying to elicit a smile from the white-faced, frightened girl.

"They dinna have much to be very friendly about. They lost most of their land to the English. Originally they came from the highlands to the north."

"Let's explore the room across the hall?" suggested Robert.

"All right," said Annie grimly, gripping his hand very tightly. Robert stared down at her set little face.

"'Tis just another parlor, I wager."

"'Tis my mother's room. 'Tis where she always lived. 'Tis the most beautiful room in the whole world. 'Tis fit for a princess. My mother is the most beautiful woman in the world, isn't she?" demanded Annie, hanging back, loath to touch the door. "This is where I would sit and she'd read me stories," she added, sitting on a small hassock to one side of the door. "She was Queen Guinevere and the Lady of the Lake, and Lancelot and Lochinvar came to see her. They loved her. I heard them loving her."

"She lived in there?" asked Robert after a shocked pause.

"Aye, in there," replied Annie, staring at the door in alarm. "I dinna think she'd like us to go in there. What if she's come back and is there and we disturb her?"

"Did your father and brothers live in this part of the house with her?"

"No, just my mother lived here. We lived where we do now. Except Father, he had a bedroom upstairs until he went away."

"How did she eat? Who took care of her?" probed Robert.

"Her maid, Maude Potter. Great ladies have maids, you know. Mrs. Wilson would cook her food and Maude Potter would serve her," chattered Annie. She filled with dread as Robert's hand turned the embossed metal door handle. "No, dinna go in there!" begged the child.

"Dammit!" swore Robert, finding the door locked. "Where's the key?"

"I dinna ken," sobbed Annie. "We maun not go in there. . . . We could die."

"What?" ejaculated Robert. "How on earth could we die?"

"I think others did," whispered Annie, feeling very sick, her face turning a wan greenish color. Robert stared down at her face and recognized the symptoms of someone about to empty his stomach. Without thought he picked her up, and, sliding the bolts back on the large front door, he opened it and rushed into the fresh air.

Annie retched and retched, oblivious to everything as she tried to rid herself of the terror that stalked and the cloying redolence of roses that filled her. Robert held her upside down with his face averted, trying to hold on to his own recently eaten meal as his elegant rumpled clothes and hessian boots were liberally splattered.

"What the hell as I doing?" he groaned, looking down at the small dejected child and his own bedraggled state. On the overgrown lawn they were surrounded by curious cows and goats, and several chickens strutted by and gave them withering looks. Robert pulled himself up to his full height of six feet plus an inch or so, trying to muster as much dignity as he could under the circumstances, unaware that he was standing in a generous mound of manure.

"I'm sorry about your fancy clothes," hiccoughed Annie woefully.

"So am I," returned her uncle, equally woefully.

Chapter 3

Will, Duncan, and Michael leaned wearily on their rakes and hoes, appreciating the sight of their elegant uncle, stripped to the waist, sluicing himself under the pump in the yard.

"What happened to you?" inquired Michael, gazing at the elegant riding britches that were liberally splattered with some foul-smelling material. "Och, those handsome boots," he mourned.

"I was sick on him," confessed Annie, who had been pumping energetically.

"What scared you?" demanded Michael as the twins stomped into the barn to put away their tools. "Did you frighten her? She only upchucks when she's afraid."

"He dinna scare me," shouted Annie, still looking wan and peaky.

"Strip off your clothes—you smell," ordered Michael, and to Robert's consternation and utter amazement, Annie stripped herself naked and stood obediently under the pump.

"'Tis your turn to pump now," she ordered her uncle as Michael followed the twins into the barn. Robert gaped down at the skinny naked girl, noticing she looked nothing like the undressed females he was accustomed to. Bemusedly he pumped the handle, showering the brave child with freezing water.

Dressed in borrowed rough farm clothes, Robert sat

at the luncheon table, not feeling particularly hungry. Annie, her auburn hair still dripping, and dressed in clean overalls and shirt, listlessly piled the table with what looked like the leftovers from a week of meals.

"What made you sick, Annie?" asked Duncan sternly.

"Nothing," she replied, avoiding his eyes. He reached out and grabbed her small face, forcing her to look at him.

"It was my fault," confessed Robert. "I insisted she show me the rest of the house. 'Tis a beautiful house—well, it would be if it were taken care of. There are some excellent pieces of furniture," he rambled uneasily, feeling the hostility in the air.

"What did you see that made you sick, Annie?" asked Will.

"Nothing! Nothing! Honest! The door was locked. . . . I dinna see anything at all!" shouted the child, going alarmingly green again. Robert's eyes narrowed as he stared around at the intense young faces.

"Hush yourself, 'tis all right," comforted Will, pulling the child onto his lap and holding her tight. "'Tis all right, Oriannie Rebecca Gunn," he crooned, stroking her damp auburn curls. The boys ate silently and stolidly, ignoring the child, who had fallen asleep on her brother's lap. Robert watched them curiously.

"We've work to do, so you'll not mind doing the cleaning up," said Duncan tersely, standing and stamping out into the yard.

"I'll stay and take care of Annie," volunteered Michael.

"Nay, you're needed in the fields. Our Uncle Robert wants to be her guardian; let him tend her," growled Duncan. He thrust the sleepy child into Robert's arms before pushing his younger brother before him and following his twin out of the house.

Robert sat staring at the mess of food and dirty plates that littered the table, with his arms about the girl, who wiggled like a puppy getting comfortable before relaxing back into a sound sleep. Idly he buried his face in the child-soft, sweet-smelling hair as he questioned his sanity for about the tenth time that day. He, Robert Forsythe, son of Sir Hendrick of that noble and illustrious family, was sitting in a kitchen holding a female child whom he had just bathed, and how he was about to embark on the menial task of washing dishes and stowing food in a pantry. He sat, expecting to feel waves of fury and disgust, but to his surprise found himself feeling more alive than he had ever felt before. Whistling cheerfully, he put Annie on the settle and set about clearing the table.

Annie was awakened by several crashes, and she opened her eyes to the wonder of her uncle trying to wash the plates. She smiled at the picture he made in her brother's farm smock open to the waist, as his chest was broader than either of the twins'.

"We'll hae no dishes left," she gurgled.

"Then I'll buy you some more," he said with a grin, feeling very happy and carefree. "How do you get these platters clean?"

"Rub them wie some sand and soap," informed Annie, padding over to him. "My belly feels better," she added.

"Young ladies do not have bellies, Oriana," Robert explained, deciding this was a good time to start her education.

"Then where do their babies grow when they're breeding?" asked Annie.

"I beg your pardon!" exclaimed Robert.

"If they've nae a belly, where does the baby grow after they've rutted?" repeated Annie patiently. Robert sat heavily.

"Rutted?" he echoed in shock.

"Aye, rutted?"

"Oriana Gunn, you should not be knowing about such things at your age. Or at any age for that matter," Robert muttered.

"Why?" puzzled the child.

"Animals rut; gentlefolk do not," he informed her coldly, trying to terminate the subject.

"Will and Duncan do," volunteered Annie confidentially. "Really they do. There's a woman at the Pig and Whistle, on the Dumfries road."

"That's enough!" hissed Robert. He drank a long quenching swallow of ale.

"Uncle Robert? How do gentlefolk have babies if they don't rut like us common folk?"

"Help me put the food in the pantry," Robert ordered sharply as he tried to think of what school for young girls would possibly take his niece with her too-forthright way of speaking. He would have to install a governess at the manor house, he decided, but first it needed an army of workmen to set it to rights. Plans for the house's restoration ran through his mind as he briskly swept the floor, stirring up a choking cloud of dry, powdered mud. Annie snorted and rolled her eyes heavenward before sprinkling sawdust.

"What are you throwing on my clean floor?" grumbled Robert, not understanding her action. Annie shook her tousled head in exasperation at his ignorance before wresting the broom from him and indicating he should scrub down the table.

"Want to go for a ride wie me?" she asked him when the kitchen was spotless. Robert surveyed the sparkling room with satisfaction, feeling extremely accomplished and pleased with himself.

"I should like that."

"First we hae to catch the horses and you have to saddle yours," giggled Annie, clasping his large hand and pulling him into the courtyard.

"I should like to see the village," stated Robert as they rode side by side across the pasture. Annie's open sunny expression hardened, and for a moment Robert thought she was going to dig in her bare feet and gallop away from him, but after hesitating she nodded sullenly. "Is there something about the village I should know?" he asked, puzzled by her reaction. Annie didn't answer for a while but stared straight ahead to where Robert could see the church spire above the trees.

"They say bad things about us," she suddenly blurted out.

"Who?"

"Near everyone," she answered with a shrug. "You'll see."

Robert and Annie rode slowly into the picturesque sleepy village that consisted of a dozen or so thatched cottages, a church with a graveyard, and two taverns set about a central green complete with pond, where ducks swam followed by their young. A couple of old men dozed in the afternoon sun outside the taverns, and children played in the cottage gardens surrounded by vibrant, fragrant flowers. Cats and dogs lay curled in sleep under the shade of stately oak and elm, and busy birds and bees flew and flittered with the many butterflies.

"Seems a pleasant enough place," remarked Robert but Annie didn't answer. She kept her gaze straight ahead, eager to be gone as she felt the eyes that stared from behind the lacy curtains in the cottage windows.

"Rebecca Gunn's whoring's done. Rebecca Gunn's whoring's done," chanted a young voice from behind a privet hedge.

"Rebecca Gunn's whoring's done," chimed in several other giggly voices. Robert frowned as the malicious, high voices slashed through the sleepy tranquil afternoon.

"Silence! " he roared imperiously, riding toward the source.

"Dinna bother," said Annie, reining her horse and watching her uncle scatter the laughing children. Once more she breathed deeply with exasperation at her Uncle Robert's naive foolishness as a large mucky clod of questionable origin struck him full in the chest.

"Rebecca Gunn's whoring's done!" now piped from several directions. Robert wheeled his horse about and rode ruefully back to his niece, who sat proudly, her small face showing nothing but disdain.

"She wasna a whore. They were her lovers, Lochinvar, Sir Galahad, and the like," she stated solemnly before digging her small heels into her horse's firm sides. Robert frowned, trying to understand the malicious rhyme and his niece's reference to the literary heroes. He watched her dignified retreat, debating whether to follow her or pursue his original plan of examining the church register. He gazed down with distaste at the foul-smelling splatter on the front of his borrowed farm smock and shrugged, then stared speculatively at the church and rode slowly toward it. A brief flutter of layers of lace at the adjacent parsonage window caught his eye and he waited, knowing whoever it was would again peer out to satisfy their curiosity. Sure enough, several seconds later the curtains were parted and a prim, pinched face peeked at him from behind a potted geranium.

"Good afternoon, madame," he boomed stentoriously, and the head popped back into the dark recesses of the room. He tethered his horse to a flimsy rose trellis and strode up the crazy pavement toward the front door. His hand was raised to grasp the brass knocker and hammer when the door flew open and a birdlike woman trembled before him. Her unhealthy lavender-tinged face crinkled as she recoiled from his odiferous, soiled clothing.

"I am looking for the parson, my good woman," he pronounced quickly, seeing her backward movement and not wanting the door to be slammed in his face. The vicar's wife teetered in the doorway, seduced by his cultured tones and yet repelled by the raw farm smell. "This," he stated ponderously, indicating the offensive mess, "was foist upon me by some malicious children."

Still the vicar's wife hovered, not knowing what to do. It was obvious that the tall blond young man was gentry and should be conducted in to her very best parlor, but how could she when he was so soiled? She wrung her blue-veined hands nervously before extracting a cologne-scented handkerchief from the layers of clothes that hung on her gaunt body. With it she covered her nose.

"My husband is in the churchyard," she finally chirped all in one breath, fluttering her hands in some vague direction before again sniffing into her handkerchief.

"Forgive my appearance, madame," Robert apologized firmly taking her hand and bowing as he brought it to his lips, which curled mischievously. He idly wondered how long the wretched woman could hold her breath against the malodorous stench that assailed her pinched nostrils.

"My husband doesn't brook disturbances when he's composing his Sunday sermon," she gasped painfully.

"But I have need to examine the church registry," he drawled, availing himself of her other hand so she could not inhale the eau de cologne. Nearly swooning, the woman couldn't answer but turned a very interesting shade of purple and butted her head frantically toward the church. Robert smiled charmingly before releasing her hands. He chuckled as she fell back into her house with unladylike haste and slammed the door. He strained his ears and grinned broadly as he heard her thankful gasp. Whistling nonchalantly, he strode back up the garden path.

"Wild Annie dressed in breeks, hold your nose cos she reeks! Wild Annie dressed in britches, she is one of satan's witches!" Once more the shrill malicious voices cut through the heavy afternoon air. Robert frowned seeing Annie sitting stoically upon her horse as about her pranced several children. Her small back was ramrod straight and her exquisite little face was set on sneering lines as though she didn't even deign to acknowledge their base existence.

"What's that dried-up prune's name?" he asked casually, nodding toward the hastily drawn lace curtains.

"The vicar's wife?"

"Yes, what's her name?" asked Robert impatiently as Annie turned an alarming shade of green and he suspected she was about to be violently ill again.

"Nevins," whispered Annie, trying to stem the wave of inexplicable panic that flooded through her at just the mere thought of the name Nevins.

"Wild Annie dressed in breeks, hold your nose cos she reeks. Wild Annie dressed in britches, she is one of satan's witches," chanted the strident voices.

"Let's go home," begged Annie in a small voice, still holding herself straight and proud. Robert nodded, deciding to confront the Nevinses and the church register another day when he was alone and dressed more imposingly. He wheeled his horse and they rode side by side through the seemingly serene village followed by a hate-filled chorus.

"Gunn, Gunn, your days are done! Gunn, Gunn, your days are done!" Robert put his flaxen head to one side as if to hear more clearly; it seemed deeper adult voices had joined the strident children. Annie longed to dig in her heels and gallop swiftly away from the spiteful chanting, but an innate sense of dignity made her walk her horse in a relaxed, unhurried gait until they were out of sight and sound of the village. Then, giving a wild whoop, she urged her horse into a furious pace so she could race out the humiliation.

Robert galloped across the open moorland neck in neck with his niece, who rode bareback with bare feet. He grinned across at her elfin face before putting back his head and bellowing with laughter at the pure unadulterated freedom he felt for perhaps the first time in his life. Turning to the child again, he gazed fondly at her golden face haloed by the glinting auburn curls and marveled at her resilience and ability to put aside the hurt and humiliation of barely an hour before.

"We'd best get back to put tea on the table," gurgled Annie. "I'm going to teach you to cook drop scones!"

Once more Duncan, Will, and Michael stood agape at the kitchen door watching their elegant uncle, bare to the waist and liberally smudged with flour, dropping batter onto a hot griddle as Annie sat on the table directing.

"Wash yourselves for tea," ordered the little girl imperiously and the youths sheepishly shuffled back to the pump in the yard. Robert looked at her with admiration.

"If you're not very careful, young lady," he said in a thoughtful tone, "you could become just like your grandmother!"

That night after helping clear the supper dishes and wash the plates, Robert stretched out in a comfortable chair with a generous mug of whiskey. Annie perched on the arm of the chair and fought to keep her eyes open. Her uncle grinned, ready to reach out an arm each time she swayed and was in danger of falling to the hard, stone-tiled floor, but she always jerked herself awake and stared indignantly with eyes propped wide, daring anyone to say she was sleepy. There were many questions Robert wanted to ask but he bided his time, not wanting Annie privy to this conversation. Finally the small girl toppled gently onto his broad chest, and wriggling about to get comfortable as though he were a piece of furniture, she dropped into a sound sleep. Robert filled with an aching tenderness as he saw that one of her small hands possessively clutched the borrowed shirt he wore.

Will took the sleeping child from him and carried her

up to her bed, leaving Robert to feel strangely bereft at the loss of her relaxed warm body. He sat silently until the youth returned.

"Annie took me to the village today," he informed the twins. "Was not a very cordial reception," he added harshly. Neither Will nor Duncan responded, though they stared long and hard at him before dropping their eyes and drinking deeply of the burning spirits. "I want some answers," he demanded.

"Ask," shrugged Will, picking his teeth in an effort to appear at ease, when all he longed to do was go to sleep and thereby avoid all the questions.

"Rebecca Gunn, your whoring's done?" quoted Robert.

"Stop it!" shouted Michael, covering his ears.

"Just silly jingles," dismissed Will. "You maun pay them no mind, Michael."

"There's more about our Annie and her britches," stated Michael.

"Sticks and stones," answered Will with another shrug.

"Gunn, Gunn, your days are done!" repeated Robert. "Is that a threat to your property or your lives?"

"Neither," laughed Duncan harshly. "It is but the silly prattle of ignorant people. Our family used to own as far as the eye can see in every direction. Our grandsire was laird and that is all it refers to."

"Are you positive?" asked Robert.

"Aye, are you?" joined Michael. "Maybe they want to hurt us," he added fearfully.

"Och, stop your girlish whining and get to your bed!" snapped Duncan, causing the younger boy's face to blush with embarrassment.

"Go and see if your sister sleeps," suggested Will in an effort to temper his twin's harshness as Michael sullenly climbed the stairs.

"What happened to my sister's maid?" demanded Robert breaking the brooding silence that ensued after the boy's boot steps creaked overhead.

"Our mother is no longer here, and has no intention of returning, so has no need of a servant," retorted Duncan after a shocked pause.

"Nevertheless I should like her name and address in case my sister had a fondness for her," stated Robert firmly, looking from one youth to the other. "I want some answers and also the key to my sister's room," he added authoritatively. Duncan and Will exchanged guarded looks as their uncle poured himself a generous portion of whiskey and casually stretched his long legs. The silence lengthened, measured by the ponderous ticking of the clock. A furtive creaking on the stairs caused them all to look to the shadows.

"It canna be Annie or we'd not have heard a peep," growled Will as Duncan strode purposefully toward the stairs, glad of the diversion.

"I canna sleep," protested Michael's high voice as he stepped into the room.

"You have nae tried," snapped Duncan. "Well, it is late and there's much to be done early tomorrow," he said, stamping out into the moonlit night to relieve himself before bed. Will thoughtfully watched him go before following. Robert listened to their booted feet recede into the night, knowing they needed to talk between themselves.

"Go to your bed, Michael," he said softly to the small slumped figure on the bottom steps of the staircase.

"I hate the night. I hate the darkness and the shadows. I hate the ugliness and screaming," pronounced Michael.

"Ugliness and screaming?" repeated Robert casually.

"Aye, ugliness and screaming like spitting cats. Howling and crying . . . but Duncan and Will says it's just bad dreams . . . bad dreams like Annie gets."

"What do you see in those bad dreams?" probed Robert curiously.

"Canna see, it is too thick and black. I just hear and feel. Feel cold, snaky shivers prickling my skin. Hear the sound of fairy wheels . . . swishing, humming, and the tinkle of happy laughter and pretty voices. But then it's twisted into ugly curdling screams and my heart would race and my head would ache and the screams wouldna stop," recalled Michael.

"Just bad dreams," growled Duncan at the open kitchen door. "'Tis no wonder you canna have proper rest at night! You dinna get to your bed on time! Get to bed!"

he ordered harshly. Michael hesitated as though to disobey and challenge his older brother, but then his thin shoulders slumped and he turned and dejectedly climbed the stairs.

Robert watched Duncan sit back at the table and pour himself a drink as Will could be heard in the yard sluicing himself with cold water from the pump. Once more the seconds ticked by measured painfully by the deep metronome of the clock as neither spoke but waited for Will to enter. Robert assessed his nephew's young face in the warm glow of the lantern light, noting the premature lines from worry and manual labor out in the natural elements. The hands that nervously clutched the whiskey tumbler were cracked and callused, appearing more like worn leather than like adolescent flesh. Will entered, humming tunelessly beneath his breath, and he sat heavily with a long sigh expected more of an old man than a seventeen-year-old. Robert poured him a drink and the three sipped in silence.

"Our mother was not in her right mind," stated Duncan suddenly.

"That much I have ascertained," replied Robert.

"Jealous, ignorant people will say anything," offered Will.

"Why whore? Why witch?" probed Robert ruthlessly.

"Madness frightens many, so they find their own names," Duncan stated, evading the issue.

"And that's all you have to tell me?" Robert snapped angrily.

"Aye," returned the twins as one, and Robert knew they had made a pledge of silence to each other.

"Where's the key?" he asked wearily.

"'Tis late. I'll find it and gie to you on the morrow," answered Duncan. Robert nodded before standing and stalking out into the fresh night air. The moon was full as he strode around to the front of the house. He leaned against the ornate wrought-ironwork of the gates and gazed at the attractive manor perched under the stately trees on its grassy knoll. It really was a pity that it had been so neglected, he mused as several curious cows lumbered up to him, swishing their tails and noisily chewing the ever-present cud.

Robert breathed deeply of the crisp night air before walking back to the rear of the house ready for his bed. It had been barely twenty-four hours since his arrival and he felt an entirely new man. It didn't occur to him to think how or why he felt so; he just did, and he accepted it. He entered the back door and painfully barked his shin in the impenetrable darkness, as the twins had doused all the lanterns. Blindly he felt his way to the stairs, making a tremendous clatter as he knocked over countless things and swore furiously.

Finally, much bruised, he found his way up the stairs and fell thankfully across his bed, moonlight flooding across his face. He smiled ironically at having light now when he had no need of it before getting up and attempting to cover the bed with the neatly folded bedlinens. He stood back and frowned at the untidy results but shrugged, preferring a rumpled bed to sleeping on the rough ticking for a second night. After he completely stripped he climbed under the light blanket, expecting to fall asleep immediately, but a little elfin face disturbed his serenity. He tossed and turned, uncomfortable with the visions his mind's eye conjured of Annie harnessed and groomed until she was as cold and gray as the stones of Forsythe Castle and its occupants, devoid of all her sparkling vibrancy.

He lay on his back, going over the events of the strange day as the spiteful jingles repeated in his brain.

"Rebecca Gunn, your whoring's done! . . . Gunn, Gunn, your days are done!"

Robert sat up and leaned against the headboard, trying to still his seething mind as Michael's dream and Annie's terror joined with the malicious jingles. What did it all mean? A furtive creak on the stairs prickled the hair on the back of his neck and he quietly slid out of the tall bed, pulled on his borrowed britches, and crept on to the landing. He frowned as he saw the strange distorting light from a taper. Then an immense shadow in a flowing robe dominated the back staircase. For a moment Robert's blood froze and he imagined he saw a ghost, but he forcibly shook his head and padded on bare feet after the strange apparition.

Little Annie Gunn in a long white nightshirt, candle

in hand, walked slowly and carefully down the stairs. She crossed the kitchen toward the door that divided the servants' quarters from the rest of the house. Watching her intently, Robert gasped as a heavy hand came down on his bare shoulder.

"Dinna wake her or you could stop her heart!" hissed a voice, and Robert turned, grabbing Will by the throat.

"You nearly stopped my heart, pouncing on me like that," he whispered. "You mean she is walking in her sleep?" he asked with amazement. Will nodded. "Does she do it often?"

"Hush," hissed the youth. "Go back to your bed. I shall see to my sister."

"No," replied Robert firmly, pushing the youth aside and tiptoeing down the stairs after the tiny figure. Will hung back for a moment and then followed the two through the stately double doors to the formal part of the house. Robert stood side by side with his nephew, watching Annie as she seated herself on the little hassock outside her mother's room.

"Och, Young Lochinvar is come out of the west, through all the wide border his steed was the best," sang the little girl in a sweet piping voice, sending shivers down both listeners' broad backs. "And save his good broadsword he weapons had none. He rode all unarmed and he rode all alone. So faithful in love and so dauntless in war, there never was a knight like Young Lochinvar."

Robert frowned as the child recited each verse of the Walter Scott poem about Lochinvar and the fair Ellen, and he noticed that tears poured unchecked down Will's young face. When she was done, Annie stood and opened her mouth in a silent scream. Robert recoiled as he saw the expression on her face. He had never seen such fear or pain. He reached out his arms to gather her to him but Will dragged him back into the shadows as the girl solemnly made here way through the double doors to the kitchens and up the backstairs to her small bedchamber.

Will and Robert sat together at the scrubbed kitchen table after Annie had been firmly tucked into her narrow bed and the taper blown out. They had stood in the doorway looking at her peacefully sleeping face in the moonlight before quietly creeping away.

"Does that happen often?" asked Robert.

"Now and then," shrugged the youth evasively, and his uncle snorted with impatience.

"Do you ever give a direct answer, dammit!"

"Now and then," he retorted. Robert stared angrily into his very young face and saw a stark vulnerability that belied the impudent words. Instinctively his hand reached out and grasped the work-callused hand of his nephew. "I am sorry," apologized Will, wishing desperately he could confide in his uncle. "I canna tell you . . . I canna," he faltered. His amber eyes bore into those of his uncle with a kind of mute desperation. Robert nodded silently, not knowing what to say. "I suppose wie all these goings-on you have no wish to take care of Annie and Michael," the boy said after a long silence.

"I'll take care of Oriana and Michael," promised Robert, remembering the stark terror he had seen imprinted on the beautiful child's face. "And you and Duncan too," he offered magnanimously.

"We are men and have no need of your protection!" stated a rough voice from the stairs, and they turned to see Duncan.

"Annie walked in her sleep to our mother's room again," explained Will in defense as the twin stared accusingly at him. "I have told our uncle nothing, but I think it best that she should be away from this house wie the memories," shouted the gentler twin heatedly.

"What memories?" pounced Robert and both the identical faces set stubbornly, mouths firmly closed. "Then she shall stay here and I shall hire an army to get this house restored to its former glory . . . and install a competent housekeeper—"

"We have Mrs. Wilson," Duncan interrupted.

"You'll have maids, manservants, tutors, governesses, and whatever else it takes to turn Oriana Rebecca Gunn into an acceptable member of society," he declared with more optimism than he felt. At the same time he wondered yet again at his sanity.

Once more Robert stripped and climbed into the high hard bed hoping to sleep, but again he tossed and turned as the malicious rhymes from the village meshed with the immortal lines of Sir Walter Scott. In less than one day and night he had lost his carefree, irresponsible existence and had appointed himself guardian to a nine-year-old hellion and her twelve-year-old brother. He shook his aching flaxen head in disbelief as his heavy eyelids drooped and sleep finally claimed him.

Chapter 4

The next day dawned gray and overcast. Robert opened his eyes to a morose little girl sitting on the washstand staring balefully at him.

"Do you know what time it is?" she demanded angrily. Robert closed his eyes and shook his head. "Seven thirty!" she pronounced in outraged tones. Robert groaned and buried his head under the pillow, yearning for several more hours sleep, but Annie rhythmically drummed her heels on the resounding wood of the washstand until her uncle reemerged. He resignedly rolled on to his back, yawned, and sleepily regarded her.

"Something's going on," she stated emphatically. Robert yawned again, waiting for her to continue, but all that did continue was the irritating drumming of her hard little heels.

"What?" he finally asked.

"Strange things," she answered.

"What strange things?"

"If I knew that," Annie breathed indignantly, "I wouldn't be sitting here wasting my time watching you snoring away!"

"I certainly do not snore!" retorted Robert, wrinkling his nose at an acrid smell of burning. "I sincerely hope that isn't my breakfast," he said.

"They're burning my mother's things," she replied

sadly, rubbing her nose so he wouldn't see the tears that prickled her eyes.

"What!" ejaculated Robert, throwing off the covers and then hurriedly pulling them back up to his neck when he realized he was naked. Annie frowned at her uncle's strange, strangled cry. She sniffed, wiped her eyes on the back of her hand, and regarded him suspiciously.

"What is the matter wie you?" she asked, noting his heightened color. "You think I've not seen a naked man before?" she said crossly, realizing the cause of his discomfort. Robert choked, unable to say a word in response to this candor. "All men are the same, aren't they? Except for hair color and size or the like," she added, her hard heels still drumming the hollow door of the washstand. Robert breathed deeply and shook his head in despair.

"Oriana Gunn, I would appreciate it if you allowed me some privacy," he stated coldly. The girl hunched her shoulders, cocked her auburn head to one side, and frowned at him contemplatively.

"You're nae going to piss out of the window, are you?" she asked.

"Out!" thundered Robert.

"Chase me out," dared Annie, knowing he would stay in bed clutching the covers about his neck until she left the room. "Och, yer a funny mon," she sighed, and jumped agilely off the washstand. She stood with her small hands on her skinny hips, shaking her head in disbelief before stalking out the door and slamming it. Robert waited, listening, not trusting the wild child to resist leaping into the room as soon as he swung his legs to the floor. Cautiously he swaddled the covers about his waist and reached for his borrowed britches. He stood at the window looking out at the dreary day. The clouds hung low and threatening and the smoke from a bonfire drizzled across the drooping blossoms in the orchard.

Annie sat dismally at the kitchen table, her small chin propped on her fists. Robert stopped in amazement at the sight of the tears that streamed down her forelorn little face. The wicked minx of a scant five minutes before was now a picture of abject misery.

"They are burning all her pretty things," she sobbed.

"I tried to stop them but they locked me out." Awkwardly Robert patted her tousled auburn curls before striding to the double doors that divided the house. He shook them angrily but they were securely locked. He hammered on the solid wood and roared.

"Duncan? Will? This is your uncle. Open the door!" he ordered. He strode angrily back to the kitchen and found the door to the yard was also securely bolted from the outside.

"'Tis no use—we're locked in here. They've even shuttered the windows. I could go out of the one upstairs but I've already had one skelping this morning. I dinna want another," sniffed Annie, trying to stop her flood of tears and succeeding only in muddying her face.

"A skelping?" questioned Robert.

"Aye, Duncan hit me harder than he's ever done before and he shook me and shook me like I was . . . I was . . . I was . . ." sobbed Annie as her tears resumed. "And all you did was sleep!"

Robert was nearly knocked off his feet as, with a great wail of misery, Annie dove into his stomach and wrapped her skinny arms about his waist, drenching his borrowed smock with a fresh torrent of tears.

"Is there any breakfast?" he asked after a while when her sobs had lessened.

"But canna you stop them?" hiccoughed Annie.

"How?" replied Robert, feeling less than a man.

"But you're older and bigger and their uncle," she begged. "You maun stop them!" Robert shrugged uncomfortably as the rasping sounds of the rusty bolts being drawn back heralded Duncan and Will's entrance. The twins stood sullenly in the doorway, the gray of the overcast sky and smoke behind them mirroring their moods and sooty faces. Annie flew at them, biting, kicking, and screaming.

"I hate you! Hate you! Hate you!" she cried, and Robert frowned as the youths didn't defend themselves from her savage attack. He pulled her away and tried to contain her raging fury. Annie aimed one more kick, shrugged free, and flew out of the door into the wet yard. Listlessly Duncan sucked an ugly bite where the girl's strong young teeth had broken the skin. Robert slowly sat and regarded his two nephews.

"Where's Michael?" he asked after a long pause.

"At the market in Kirkcudbright. He'll be back at nightfall," replied Will.

"Why didn't you send Oriana with him?" demanded Robert.

"She wouldna go!"

"Am I right in assuming that the door to my sister's room is now unlocked . . . and the room is empty?" he asked coldly.

"Aye," replied Duncan rebelliously. Robert nodded before striding out into the yard. He lifted his face to the light rain, wishing the unpleasant burning smell would wash away. He surveyed the smoldering bonfire for a clue but the twins had done their work well, so, thoughtfully, he walked around to the front of the house. Although several goats were still tethered, no cows browsed on the lawn. The large front door stood open. He entered and frowned at the chickens that roosted impudently on the graceful curved banisters.

Annie sat dismally on her little hassock, staring into the bare room where her mother had woven her fantasies. The room was empty. A carpet had evidently just been removed, its place marked by a symmetrical border of dust that skirted the room.

"It was the most beautiful room in the world," stated the child.

"Describe it to me," suggested Robert softly.

"I canna! I never saw it!" she screamed before rushing out so that the chickens flew squawking in all directions. Shaking his head in bewilderment, Robert entered the vacant room. A space of pleasant proportions, it had three large windows overlooking the rolling front lawn. The walls were covered with a delicate rose-patterned print, which in places had been ripped forcibly from the lath and plaster. Robert ran his well-manicured hands over the exposed places able to determine that the paper had been very recently removed. The twins had been quite thorough, he observed ruefully. They had eradicated all trace of the woman who had lived there for many years.

"What did you hope to find?" asked Will gruffly from the threshold, where he had stood watching his intent uncle.

"Actually, I'm not exactly sure," replied Robert blandly. "Maybe a sign . . . even a faint perfume of my sister Rebecca who dwelt in this neglected manor for eighteen years. Maybe a reason for the intense hostility toward this family that I witnessed in the village. Maybe an answer to Oriana's night terrors and Michael's bad dreams. But you and Duncan have left nothing," he finished acidly.

"Let the dead rest in peace," begged Will.

"Which dead?" returned Robert sharply.

"My mother . . . aye, mother," stammered the youth.

"My sister Rebecca is not dead!"

"She might as well be," stated Will sadly before turning on his heel and quitting the house. Robert watched him stride hurriedly across the soggy lawn, then pensively he walked up the gracefully curving staircase to the second floor. He stared without emotion into each of the shrouded bedchambers, noting the thick layer of undisturbed dust that covered everything in eight of the nine well-furnished and carpeted rooms.

"Aha!" he uttered triumphantly, opening the door to the ninth room and raising an eyebrow at bureau drawers that were crookedly open and empty. A wardrobe door stood ajar, exposing a vacant interior. Robert ran an idle finger across the dusty washstand, recognizing there the familiar sharp outlines of removed toiletries. He stooped to retrieve a well-worn shaving brush that had rolled into the shadows by the bed and located a stone whiskey jug that was peeking out of the hanging folds of the draped counterpane. He rubbed the dry bristles against his fingertips, smelling the lavender scent of shaving soap as he wondered what sort of man would go gadding off to Africa in search of gold, burdened down with all his possessions save his wife, his children, and his shaving brush.

"There's nothing here!" stated a bitter voice. He turned to see Duncan in the doorway.

"It appears your father forgot his shaving brush . . . and his boots," remarked Robert, reaching under the bed and displaying a pair of sensible farm shoes with dried mud generously caked to the worn leather.

"Could be anyone's," Duncan lied after a long pause. He tried to shrug nonchalantly but just seemed agitated and nervous.

Robert sighed with vexation as he wearily walked down the stairs, his nose and eyes itchy from the dust. Together he and Duncan squelched morosely across the soggy lawn, oblivious of the rain that sheeted down relentlessly. The goats, however, complained bitterly and pulled against their tethers, while in the distance could be heard the hissing, honking, and squealing of geese and pigs.

"Where's Oriana in this infernal weather?" Robert asked harshly just for something to say, using speech as a release of the irritation that churned within him.

"She can take care of herself. She has the sense to get out of the rain when she has a mind," retorted Duncan truculently. Suddenly Robert felt disgusted with the whole lot of them. He wished there were some magic that could miraculously transport him the nearly four hundred miles or so to London. What in God's name was he doing in the barbarous border country of Scotland anyway? There was probably no great mystery here. It was obvious that his poor demented sister Rebecca had finally cracked under the pressure of living with four totally undisciplined children and a boorish farmer husband, who had probably absconded with the maid . . . which in turn must have caused vengeful Rebecca to take a lover or two, which caused the villagers to spout malicious gossip.

They entered the kitchen in silence and sat dejectedly at the table, their heads dripping and darkening the bleached wood. Duncan poured two mugs of nearly black tea, which Robert estimated had been brewed several hour before, from the stewed bitter aroma that rose from the tepid contents. The youth rudely shoved one of the mugs toward his uncle so that it slopped messily.

"Is there a coach to London from any point about here?" Robert asked abruptly.

"One a week from Kirkcudbright."

"How far is that?"

"About six or seven miles as the crow flies."

"What day of the week does it leave?" continued Robert, trying to curb his impatience.

"Monday," was the curt reply. Robert cursed beneath his breath and got up to look out of the door at the rain that poured persistently from the sky, shining the rounded cobblestones of the yard. He leaned against the door jamb, staring broodingly over the wet farm buildings and finding nothing at all appealing in the ducks that waddled proudly with their uniform lines of tiny fluffy ducklings. Four days to go, he seethed, after estimating it was at least Thursday or maybe, unfortunately, Wednesday, but unable to inquire of his nephew which day of the week it might actually be.

"So you're eager to return to London?" Duncan challenged in derisive tones.

"I am!" stated Robert, turning to face the youth.

"What about Annie?"

"I thought you just informed me that she could take care of herself?" snapped Robert sardonically.

"Then you're withdrawing your offer of guardianship?"

"You don't see fit to trust me with information about *my* sister. Why should you trust me with *your* sister?" retorted Robert angrily.

"We are protecting our sister," pleaded Will, entering from the yard, the rain pouring off his lean, gawky body.

"Dinna beg!" snarled Duncan harshly. "Did you find Annie?" His twin silently shook his wet head so that the water sprayed in all directions.

"I thought you said she had enough sense to get out of the rain?" repeated Robert cynically. A disturbing image of her muddy, tear-wet face flashed into his mind. He shook his head to dispel the picture as he remembered her savage attack on her brothers and the way she had kicked and bitten ferociously enough to draw blood. "How's your hand?" he asked gently. Duncan looked down at the angry teeth marks and shrugged. "Does she get so unbridled often?" The twins stared at him blankly, worry etched on their identical faces.

"Change your clothes, Will. I'll find her," said Duncan, shrugging an oilskin over his already drenched clothes.

Robert and Will watched him bend his auburn head against the driving rain as lightning cracked, rending the sky. Will ripped off his sopping smock and roughly rubbed his wet hair with it before throwing it into the corner. Robert sat back, seemingly relaxed, and watched the rangy youth pace about like a pent-up wild animal. Will was the more malleable of the two, he mused, as the thunder rumbled threateningly overhead, shaking the house.

"I might have lily-white hands that have never done a hard day's work, but dash it all, that doesn't mean I am a complete idiot," he drawled carefully.

"Meaning?" asked Will cautiously.

"Meaning I'm not blind and deaf. Would you have me believe the viciousness inferred in the village?" strove Robert.

"Believe what you will," replied the youth dully.

"Believe my sister is a whore?"

"Your sister is my own mother," answered Will with heartrending simplicity, his eyes brimming with tears. Robert felt brutal shame well with his nephew's tears. Here he had been digging, determined to root out the truth about his sister, without a thought of what emotional harm he might be doing to her two sons who had shouldered such awesome responsibility. He felt embarrassed and guilty now, seeing the youth's display of tears, remembering the admirable stoicism of the twins when they had faced their grandmother's insulting acid tongue. Feeling at a loss, he took a very large swig of the rancid tea and swallowed the tepid liquid painfully, feeling the sourness coat his teeth and burn his empty stomach.

"Uncle Robert, we'd nae blame you for leaving. It is our mess," stated Will gruffly when he had scoured the scalding tears from his cheeks and composed himself.

"My offer still stands. I shall take care of Oriana and Michael," said Robert firmly after clearing his throat noisely. "But I need to return to London for funds and other trifling necessities. By the way, are there competent workmen about that I could hire to set the house and grounds to rights?"

"They'd nae work here," laughed Will shortly. "They

hate the Gunns. Besides, they think Kenlaren haunted," he added.

"Kenlaren?"

"Aye, we are the Gunns of Kenlaren," pronounced the youth, his brimming eyes belying the cocky grin on his handsome young face. "The only reason we have Mrs. Wilson to be our cook—and housekeeper, now that she's no longer needed as a nurse—is because she's thought to be a witch."

At the mention of *cook* Robert's stomach growled hollowly and he wished the woman would fly through the storm on her broomstick and cook up a savory repast.

"Is the village also called Kenlaren?" he inquired, and Will nodded silently without ceasing his pacing. Outside, the storm raged, the sky as dark as night although it was barely noon. "Does Oriana disappear often?" he asked conversationally after a long, boring silence of nearly half an hour's duration.

"Not disappear exactly. But she's not used to being accountable to any except Mrs. Wilson. Most days she's off on her own for hours upon end . . . and sometimes she stays away when she's been upset. She dinna know our mother and we let her hae her fancies. Mrs. Wilson felt she should be strong and free." Will chattered on distractedly, still pacing.

"What do you mean she didn't know your mother?" probed Robert, wanting to hear about the strange living arrangements from someone other than Oriana.

"Mother never spoke to us. She lived in the main part of the house, as you already know," replied Will as the thunder rolled and the lightning cracked.

"Never spoke to any of you?" exclaimed Robert, surprised. He had assumed it was only Oriana who was kept from her mother.

"She spoke to Father, I suppose. Well, if they dinna talk they certainly did other things, as we are the proof," replied Will. Robert nodded, thankful that the children all bore the Gunn stamp of amber eyes and auburn, sun-streaked hair. With all the talk of his sister's loose morals it was a small miracle, he mused. "Och, I hope Michael took cover wie the wagon or we'll be having mildewed grain," worried the youth, walking backward and forward across the kitchen until Robert was ready to forcibly seat him.

"If I take responsibility for Oriana and Michael, what will you and Duncan do?" asked Robert as time ticked by and there was no lessening of the storm nor sign of the small girl or the other twin.

"I dinna ken," shrugged Will, unable to think as he moved restlessly about, peering through the teeming rain for sight of his brother and sister.

"Follow your father to Africa in search of gold?" laughed Robert, trying to lighten the tense waiting.

"What?" puzzled Will. "Oh . . . och, aye . . . maybe," he added.

Once more silence fell, so Robert rummaged through the pantry helping himself to bread and cheese. He munched, wishing his nephew would relax and stop pacing. Suddenly Will tensed his head to one side, listening. Robert stopped chewing and followed his gaze, his brow creased with puzzlement as he wondered what the youth had heard. In several lithe strides Will crossed the room and reached behind the door to the wine cellars. Robert's mouth gaped open with amazement as he saw Annie pulled out and suspended from her brother's strong hands. Her small face was flaring with fury like a spitting kitten's.

"Did you know Duncan is out there in this storm looking for you?" clipped Will, his rage whitening his nostrils.

"Guid! That'll teach him to shake me like a rat and beat me!" spat the child viciously.

"How long have you been hiding there?" asked her brother.

"Long enough, William Gunn, long enough!" she jeered, kicking out at him in an effort to get free. Will assessed her bone-dry hair and clothes and his heart sank, knowing the child had been privy to the whole conversation. What had been said, he worried as he set her away from him, took a slicker off the peg, and shrugged it on over his bare chest. He strode silently out into the storm to find his twin, his mind mulling over the conversation he'd had with his uncle.

Robert gazed down at the rebellious child as he

chewed the dry bread and cheese thoughtfully. Annie stood waiting for him to remark scathingly on her behavior, and when he didn't, she grinned impishly and helped herself to a hunk of cheese. She perched on the arm of a chair, watching him pensively as she chewed.

"Now I suppose you'll change your mind and not take care of me," she remarked.

"Don't talk with your mouth full!" snapped Robert, his own mouth full of the unappetizing stale bread. Annie opened her mouth to object but then closed it again with an obedient nod. Robert blinked with surprise. Annie got up and poured two mugs of dark ale when she saw him swallow painfully. He nodded curtly and drank deeply, and they finished their meal in silence. Robert noticed that despite her previous defiance her eyes kept straying apprehensively to the door, watching for her twin brother's return.

"Are you expecting Duncan to thrash you again?" he asked, and she nodded white-faced, her eyes appearing even larger in her small face. "Well, you certainly deserve it!" he said firmly, feeling rather sorry for her although he was furious at having worried about her. Annie glared at him reproachfully, as if he were a traitor.

"Have you ever hit a wee defenseless bairn?" she asked.

"Of course I haven't , but I have had no occasion to." This wasn't completely true, as there had been many times he had wanted to do violence to some of his sisters' snotty little prudes.

"Would you, if you had the occasion to?" she persisted.

Robert was saved from incriminating himself when the twins stamped angrily into the kitchen. Annie hid her fear and braced herself, facing her brother Duncan with a mutinous look. He picked her up roughly and plunked her down on the kitchen table, keeping his hands on her small shoulders.

"Oriana Rebecca Gunn, I was worried sick about you!" he hissed, his voice tight with fury. He gave her violent shakes to punctuate his words.

"Why? I'm just a wee pest who stops you from traveling about the world seeking gold!" spat the little girl fiercely. "I know you dinna want me! I know I am in the way! You dinna want me about any more than our mother and father did! Well, I dinna care! I curse you, Duncan Gunn! And you, too, William Gunn! I'll hae Mrs. Wilson weave a spell to make your man-tails shrivel and wither!" she threatened. "And I'll summon Satan!" Robert raised his eyes to heaven, realizing that soon this unprincipled little hellion would be his responsibility. "Aye, and the Black Leonard will make your bollox drop off and you'll be libbed like the hog we're fattening in the barn!"

"Enough!" roared Robert, unable to believe his ears. "That is more than enough from you, young woman! Get to your room before I thrash you myself!" Annie gaped at him in surprise, trying to estimate the cold fury that emanated from her usually mild-mannered uncle, then she slithered off the high table and scampered up the stairs to her room. The twins and Robert exchanged stunned looks, all of them unable to believe her obedience. They waited with bated breath for a scream or crash, but all in the house was tranquil. Robert preened arrogantly, feeling in control and very important.

"She just needs a firm hand," he stated pompously, half expecting the golden-haired imp to reappear with another list of unmentionable dire threats.

"Well, we did our best," chorused the twins. "Now 'tis your turn, Uncle Robert." Robert felt a sharp premonition of disaster but he kept his blond head high and a nonchalant, bemused expression on his face. He even smiled parentally at the two boys, who looked young and relaxed, as if the weight of the world had been lifted off their shoulders, until he realized where the burden had been squarely placed.

"When does Witch Wilson return?" he asked, still trying to seem jaunty and unconcerned.

"Tomorrow perhaps. Her black sabbat's surely over by now . . . the moon's on the wane," offered Will cheerfully.

"There's work to do in the barn," announced Duncan, hastily changing the subject.

"I'll give you a hand," announced Robert, not willing to deal with the comment about black sabbats, and feeling cooped up with an excess of energy to expend. The twins exchanged noncommittal glances, which put Robert's hackles up, but he strode cheerfully beside them, trying not to look at his damaged hessian boots, and determined to pull his weight no matter what he was asked to do. Stoically he raked the fetid straw, his stomach churning at the base odor, knowing his nephews were testing him. To his great surprise, after a short while he was unaware of any stench but felt alive and fit, as though he had just had a good workout at the fencing academy. He whistled merrily as he raked, casting an appreciative eye over several very good-looking horses, and he idly wondered why the twins hadn't used the superior horseflesh for the long, rugged trip south to Forsythe Castle.

"They're not ours. We're boarding them," volunteered Will when he saw his uncle's evident curiosity. Robert frowned, noting the lie in the boy's hasty tone. His eye saw a quick movement as Duncan impatiently kicked his twin.

"Boarding?" gurgled an irrepressible voice, and Robert stared up to the hayloft and into Annie's dancing amber eyes.

"I am not interested!" he roared, suspecting horse stealing and not sure how he would respond. "Oriana, get to the kitchen and cook something more palatable than that abominable luncheon," he ordered, and once more the young men exchanged stunned looks as the rebellious child obeyed, albeit gracelessly.

Robert and the twins worked steadily side by side for several hours and then stepped out of the dim barn into the mid-afternoon. Only distant rumbles of thunder and a faint shimmering on the horizon remained as traces of the storm. The sun shone, steaming the wet earth, and the blossom-laden trees dripped steadily. The three of them breathed appreciatively of the sweet-smelling countryside as they walked toward the pump, stripping to the waist as they went. Robert flexed his muscles as he sluiced the crystal-cold water over his head and torso, delighting in the strong virile feeling that filled him. He was alive, in charge, and undeniably male . . . like a strutting rooster in the farmyard. This was such a different sensation to what he experienced in the female-dominated Forsythe Castle.

A delicious smell wafted to the young men and their mouths filled with saliva as they walked to the house, anticipating a sumptuous meal. Robert stopped in his tracks, though, as a tiny, beady-eyed woman stabbed a bony, bent finger at him.

"Come here, my wee witch-wife," she wheezed. "Is this the mon?" Annie, her piquant vivacious face liberally smudged with flour, scampered out of the kitchen.

"Aye, that's my Uncle Robert, who's going to teach me how to be a great lady and he's going to turn Kenlaren into a gracious home like it was before in great-grandfather's time. And you are going to be the housekeeper and boss about all sorts of fancy maids and the like . . . and he's going to take care of Michael and me. Right, Uncle Robert?" she chattered excitedly.

"And where is wee Michael-mine?" asked Mrs. Wilson sharply.

"Kirkcudbright . . . to the market," answered Duncan. Robert waited patiently for the gnarled old crone to acknowledge him, but she pointedly ignored him as she bustled back to her kitchen and stirred the large black cauldron suspended over the hot embers.

Robert pushed his chair back from the table and laced his hands contentedly over his full stomach.

"Isna Mrs. Wilson the best cook in the whole world?" rejoiced Annie expansively.

"That was absolutely delicious," concurred Robert, recalling the savory pie with a crust so light it melted as soon as it entered the mouth.

"Aye, there's nothing like a squirrel pie to fill a working man's belly," cackled the old hag.

"Squirrel?" exclaimed Robert.

"Aye and I killed them wie this," boasted Annie, pulling a homemade catapult from her pocket. "I got five rats too. Big ones like this," she added, exaggerating the size with her small hands.

"I say, they weren't by any chance in the pie too?" gasped Robert, his full stomach churning and beads of sweat breaking on his top lip.

"Of course," stated Annie innocently. She tried to

keep a straight face as her twin brothers burst into delighted laughter at the dismay evident on their uncle's arrogant features.

"Get along wie you, you wee kelpie," chided Mrs. Wilson fondly, seeing the greenish tinge on the English lord's face and not wanting a mucky kitchen floor. "You ken we're saving those fat juicy rats for the next black sabbat." She placed a steaming apple pie on the table with a large bowl of clotted cream. "Och, lost your appetite, yer lairdship?" she chuckled as Robert strode hurriedly into the fresh air, declining the rich dessert.

Chapter 5

The following morning Robert dressed in his own clothes, thankful they had been passably cleaned and pressed by Mrs. Wilson, and rode into the village of Kenlaren intent on speaking to Vicar Nevins. This time there were no jeering voices; he was greeted with deferential bows, curtsies, and politely doffed hats. This time Mrs. Nevins all but fell over herself as she ushered him into her very best parlor to serve him tea from her very best silver service. Unfortunately for the trembling woman, Sir Robert pompously declined the tea, which smelled decidedly of polish, and demanded to see her husband.

"Someone died," explained the harassed woman.

"As long as it is not your husband, which I would find dashed inconvenient, I haven't the slightest interest, madame," he answered rudely, as befitted his upper class breeding.

"But . . . but . . . he's delivering the eulogy . . . at the funeral," stammered Mrs. Nevins as the tall young man impatiently paced about her cluttered parlor, his sweeping cape threatening to cause great destruction to her precious knickknacks. Robert's keen eyes noted the value of the assorted porcelain shepherdesses and bone china cats and he frowned, wondering how the Nevinses could afford such expensive albeit ugly ornaments.

"What do you know of my sister?" he asked abruptly after a long pause. The nervous woman had been incessantly sniffing and stirring her tea so that the spoon clicked against the thin bone china, setting Robert's teeth on edge.

"Your sister?"

"Rebecca Gunn née Lady Rebecca Forsythe?" he answered, and then stared with absolute fascination at her sudden paroxysm of twitching contortions as she slopped her tea so her gown clung to her skeletal legs. Why on earth was she so agitated, he wondered, hoping she didn't have a communicable affliction.

"We . . . we . . . were once friends," she stammered, trying to regain some of her former composure. "I am Lord Biddle-Botham's daughter, you know," she added, preening piteously.

"*Were* once friends?" repeated Robert, aghast. "Are you informing me that you are now enemies?" He raised an arched eyebrow as he remembered all the snickering jokes about the "Piddle-Bottoms," as they were irreverently referred to by members of his circle.

"Enemies? Of course not . . . no . . . no," struggled the frazzled woman. "It was not like that at all . . . not at all. There was no occasion . . . your sister married to a savage Scot. She was too, too refined. I fear the crudity of farm life quite despoiled her."

"Crudity? Despoiled?" repeated Robert in outraged tones, further disconcerting the woman.

"I meant destroyed . . . destroyed not despoiled," stuttered Mrs. Nevins. "She was not born to baseness."

"Born to baseness! Explain yourself, madame," ordered Robert severely, thoroughly enjoying himself.

"Baseness? Farm life?" she strove, waving a thin blue hand, which clutched a lace-edged handkerchief. "Earthiness?" she added, trying to explain delicately.

"Earthiness?"

"Raw animal . . . er . . . um, crudities?" struggled the poor woman, blushing with embarrassment.

"What on earth are you talking about?" demanded Robert.

"Your sister, Lady Rebecca."

"My sainted sister born to baseness? Earthiness? Raw animal crudities?"

"Oh, my goodness, no! She wasn't well . . . up here,"

said Mrs. Nevins, tapping her head pointedly. "Confused . . . up here, if you know what I mean?"

"Madame, I haven't the slightest idea what you mean!" thundered Robert, deriving malicious glee from her acute discomfort.

"Oh, my gracious!" wailed the woman.

"Do you mean to tell me that you, a fellow member of the English aristocracy in this inhospitable, barbaric country, failed to extend welcome and companionship to my sister?"

"Oh, I did, I did, of course I did," wept the vicar's wife. "But I have a position to maintain. I am a part of the church. My husband is the curate and I could in no way associate with . . . with . . . such . . . goings-on!"

"What goings-on? " demanded Robert relentlessly.

"Sir, I am a refined woman of delicate sensibilities!" gasped Mrs. Nevins.

"And I, madame, am a man of very little patience!" he returned quellingly. "How ever long does it take to bury someone?" he ejaculated after a tense silence.

"I beg your pardon!" squealed the hand-wringing female, backing away fearfully.

"Your husband, madame. Obviously I am not going to receive a coherent answer from you!" he said witheringly, and resumed his pacing, aware that the woman shuddered each time his cloak brushed the fiddly array of Limoges china. "What of the children?" he barked so suddenly the frail ever-moving hands dropped the delicate cup and saucer.

"Children? Children?" she repeated, staring with dismay at the floral shards at her feet.

"Duncan, William, Michael, and Oriana?"

"What of them?" she asked fearfully.

"Surely in your most responsible position as the vicar's wife you had dealings with my sister's children? Baptisms? Bible classes? Schooling? Guidance? Especially as you were aware that my sister was unwell . . . up here," he stated, tapping his head in imitation of her previous gesture. "As you so articulately put it?"

"Oh, my gracious," lamented the woman.

"What about a wedding?"

"A wedding? Whose?"

"Lady Rebecca Forsythe to David Gunn?" replied Robert shortly.

"If they were married at all it was by the blacksmith at Gretna Green," spat the little woman with obvious relish, losing her frail, frightened demeanor. Robert sneered triumphantly into her malicious, gleaming eyes. "Well, that's what was said," she added defensively.

"By whom?"

"Everyone from here to London. It was common knowledge in all the best circles that she had eloped."

"So you are stating categorically that there is no record of my sister's marriage in the church register?"

"No record of births either," crowed the woman. Robert stared down at her, speculatively sensing there was more going on than he could put his finger on. Had his mother beaten him to this place, he wondered. He kept his gaze on the lavender-faced woman.

"So you're one of Piddle-Bottom's litter," he mused aloud, remembering the long line of Biddle-Botham girls, each uglier than the next. "Your poor father spawned even more daughters than my own. You must be the eldest by a great many years," he remarked sweetly. Mrs. Nevins's face blotched with anger.

"That must be Mr. Nevins now," she snapped huffily as they heard the sound of a back door closing quietly. "Edgar?" she shouted harshly. There was a pregnant silence, as though poor Edgar waited to see if he could escape, then came a low, mournful sigh.

"Yes, Emily," he called dutifully. A skinny-legged little man with a rotund paunch, he edged into the room reluctantly and stared with surprise at Robert. "Oh, dear! Oh, dear," he muttered, rubbing his small hands together and blowing on his fingertips.

"I am Sir Robert Forsythe," Robert introduced himself.

"Forsythe? Forsythe? Oh, dear . . . of course," murmured the vicar, hurriedly pouring himself a drink.

"Edgar, it is still morning," reproved his wife.

"If that's brandy, I should appreciate one," stated Robert.

"Lady Amelia must have sent you," said Vicar Nevins hopefully as he handed Robert a drink, not noticing his wife's frantically shaking head. Robert made an unintelligible snort of assent as he sipped the brandy, then he raised his eyebrows at its very superior quality. "And how is your good mother? Haven't heard from her for years, have we, Emily? But, by Jove, that was a very generous contribution she made to our modest church."

"Mumsey is quite well and quite religious," answered Robert, his voice laced with irony.

"Very devout woman," agreed the vicar. "For a papist," he added as an afterthought.

"May I see the church?" Robert was eager to extricate the chatty little man from his shrewish wife.

"Edgar?" trilled Mrs. Nevins shrilly as she shook her head and fluttered her hands.

"Yes, Mrs. Nevins," he answered with a weary sigh, frowning at her strange facial grimaces as she tried to warn him. "Are you all right, my dear?"

"I am faint," she improvised. "Very, very faint."

"Then lie down, my dear. I won't be long. I just want to show our young friend the stained glass window his mother donated," said the vicar cheerfully as he ushered Robert out of the cluttered cottage. The young man grinned as he heard a loud thump. Either she had fainted or thrown something in frustration, he mused.

"Well, here we are," proclaimed the vicar, proudly opening his arms toward an enormous gaudy window that was quite out of proportion in the tiny village church. "Your mother donated it—anonymously of course. Not quite the thing for a papist to donate such a priceless work of art to my modest Presbyterian kirk," he chortled. Robert shook his head in disbelief, unable to give credence to the gharish blood and thunder he gazed upon. "Quite takes one's breath away, doesn't it?" Nevins rhapsodized as Robert gaped, robbed of all speech. "Satan cast from heaven," explained the vicar, pointing to the upper right corner. Every conceivable torturous death was depicted, from being crucified to being boiled upside down in oil. A small brass plaque under the window stated cryptically R.F. BORN 1858 DIED 1875.

Again Robert dolefully shook his head as he wondered if his mother would similarly dispose of him when she discovered his actions on behalf of Rebecca's children.

"Who was R.F.?" he asked, somehow reluctant to believe the merry little elf of a man guilty of destroying church records for the glory of a gory stained-glass window. He watched in surprise as the reverend Edgar Nevins's benign expression hardened until he resembled a grotesque goblin. "Is something the matter?" asked Robert, feigning bewildered innocence at the vicar's metamorphosis. "Ah, there is something so inspiring and awesome about the pure holiness of churches," he said expansively, smiling warmly into the venomous expression of the little man, who had turned an interesting grayish-green. Nevins now reminded him of one of the stone gargoyles that decorated the chapel in Forsythe Castle.

Robert rode away from the kirk in the village of Kenlaren in awe of his religious mother's busy bitterness and the Nevinses' grasping greed. He was so furious, he determined to make amends not only by restoring the Gunn manor to its former glory but also by making it the showplace of the county, where he could loudly and publicly exclude Lord Biddle-Botham's sanctimonious daughter. He laughed aloud and kicked his horse into a brisk canter, impatient to put his plans into action. As he rode toward the town of Kirkcudbright his mind was awhirl with colorful and exciting ideas. He would buy commissions for Duncan and Will into a most prestigious regiment; tutor Michael so he could eventually go to the university of his choice; and, best of all, turn Oriana Rebecca Gunn into the most cultured, exquisite debutante the world and century had ever seen. Robert sang joyfully at the top of his voice, feeling more stimulated and alive than he had ever thought possible. It was one of the first times in his twenty-five years that he wasn't bored.

Annie's amber eyes widened as a sleek curricle, led by a magnificent pair of matched grays, bowled into the yard.

"Och, Uncle Robert . . . you look . . . so bonny!" she gasped, staring up at the handsome blond man who lounged nonchalantly, resplendent in sparkling new clothes with a hat perched at a rakish angle. "Och, Uncle Robert, where did you ever get such . . . er . . . fineness?" she gasped.

"Me or the horses?" laughed Robert, leaping down carefully, not wanting to soil his new britches with farm mud.

"Both."

"'Tis the best I could find in Kirkcudbright," replied Robert with a grimace. He was unused to wearing ready-made clothing and all too aware of the inferior material and cut. "As long as I'm not seen by my London colleagues, I shall keep my reputation. The horses are another matter altogether," he added, grinning his appreciation and patting their arched necks.

"Did you steal them?" asked Annie innocently.

"Certainly not!" returned Robert, remembering the two horses in the Gunns' barn. "Are those two suspicious mounts still housed here?"

"Will dyed them," she informed him cheerfully.

"Dyed them!"

"Aye, they're now black. Duncan'll take them back over the border to sell soon."

"Hush your mouth, Annie," growled Duncan, striding into the yard in time to hear his sister's incriminating words. "I take it from the horses and carriage that you are on your way?" he asked his uncle.

"You're going now?" Annie exclaimed before Robert had time to answer.

"I shall be back within two weeks, and I hope by that time there will be no horses of different colors or the like," he replied, the steely look he shot at his twin nephews a direct contrast to his weak joke.

"Can I go wie you?" begged Annie.

"Not this time, but I'll take you for a little ride before I go," responded Robert, seeing the disappointment in her eyes.

"I dinna want you to go. You won't come back. You'll get busy with all your fine fancy friends in London and forget about us," predicted Annie. Robert frowned down at her, feeling uncomfortable, as though the child knew more about his character than he did himself.

"I'll be back, Oriana Gunn, and when I return you'd better be prepared because there are going to be a lot of changes. No longer will you live in the servants' quarters dressed like a stable boy, but you will learn to be a well-mannered young lady," he said quietly.

"Sounds terrible," returned the irrepressible child, looking disgusted.

Duncan, Will, Michael, Annie and Mrs. Wilson watched Robert leave. Michael and Annie ran alongside the carriage waving.

"Well, he certainly knows how to handle those grays," said Duncan grudgingly.

"Knows his horseflesh too," agreed Will. "You think he'll return?" he asked after a long pause as they all kept their eyes on the curricle until it was just a distant speck of dust. Duncan shrugged. "What do you think, Mrs. Wilson?"

"Canna tell wie the likes of him. Maybe yes, maybe no," she stated, shaking her head and hobbling out of the hot sun into the cool dairy. The twins watched Michael and Annie slowly walking back.

"If he doesna come back?" asked Will.

"He doesna come back," replied Duncan wearily.

"And Annie?"

"I dinna ken," said Duncan, running a work-callused hand through his thick auburn hair. "I think we should continue as if he had never come here," he added.

"Aye, we canna burn our bridges," agreed Will.

The days passed slowly and May turned to June. Annie frowned at the new horses in the barn.

"Uncle Robert said no more of that!" she protested angrily to her brothers. "What if he comes and finds them? He might be angry and not help us."

"We dinna need his help. We managed before without," answered Duncan tersely.

"But 'tis nearly a fortnight, so he'll soon be here," complained Annie.

"Dinna hold your breath, Annie Gunn!"

Annie glared at her brothers' broad backs as they stomped away from her.

"We need the money, Annie," said Michael as he looked down at her from the hayloft. "The farm doesna pay off the debts to the bank."

"You dinna think he's coming back, do you?" yelled Annie, rushing into the bright sunlight and lithely shinnying up a tall oak. She swung onto the roof of the barn where she sat hugging her knees, watching the paths that converged on the manor.

June turned to July, and July to August, and each day Annie sat on the barn roof waiting for her dashing uncle to drive up tooling his matched grays with the sun glinting on his flaxen hair.

"Annie, get yourself down here and help Michael wie the chores," ordered Duncan as he and Will hitched up the heavy farm wagon laden with produce to sell at the Dumfries market. Once a month they made the longer trip to the larger town, where they made payment to the bank, leaving Michael, Annie, and the farm under Mrs. Wilson's care as they stayed overnight.

"Oriana Gunn, did you hear me?" roared Duncan.

"Let her be," said Will gruffly, staring up at his little sister, knowing how disappointed she was that their uncle had broken his word.

"She's getting wilder and wilder," grumbled Duncan, feeling as betrayed and disappointed as Annie. It now seemed he and Will would never be free of the debt-ridden farm and the frightening responsibility of the younger siblings. He savagely jerked the reins, causing the carthorses to lumber forward so suddenly the wagon bucked over the dry, rutted road.

"Slow down," chided Will, reaching out just in time to save a wicker cage full of pullets from being bounced out of the wagon. With a long shuddering sigh, Duncan slowed the horses to a more sedate pace.

Annie watched the wagon slowly trundle out of sight before slithering down the steep barn roof and dropping nimbly to the ground. Her riotous auburn hair was streaked with blond and copper highlights and her skin was a golden brown from the sun. She raced through the fragrant orchard, reaching up and tearing apples from the laden branches before continuing up the lane toward one of the hidden pastures where the horses grazed.

"Annie!" hailed Michael, but she ignored him as she climbed to the top rung of the gate and gave a piercing whistle, holding the apples out to tempt. Two young horses whinnied and approached, bucking their graceful heads. "Och, Annie, not that one!" shouted Michael as his willful sister agilely mounted a chestnut filly and galloped away. "Come back! She's not been dyed yet!" screamed the boy as Annie rode toward the coast on the stolen horse. Michael debated following, but he knew he would never catch her. He shook his head with anger and frustration as he walked dejectedly back to milk the cows, who were complaining loudly about their full udders.

"Has my wee witch-wife taken herself off agin?" wheezed Mrs. Wilson, busy churning the butter. "Dinna fash yourself, Michael-mine, she's a child of nature. There's them that take care of their ain. She'll be back when she's good and ready."

"She took one of the unchanged horses," tattled the boy.

"So she took one of the unchanged horses?"

"Duncan'll skelp her bum!"

"If'n Duncan lays one hand on my wee-an's backside, I'll lay my spurtle aboot his ears."

"You never stick up for me like that," complained Michael sulkily.

"Och, is that the green-eyed monster I hear eating up your innards?" scolded the crone.

"Maybe the constables will catch her and put her in gaol," remarked Michael as he rhythmically pulled at the docile cow's teats and squirted the milk noisily into the pail.

"She'll be as right as rain. The de'il takes care of his ain," cackled the old woman merrily.

"I think I should go after her," said Michael.

"I may be a witch but I canna and willna milk twenty cows, do yer ken!" screeched the old woman. "Let her be. She doesna ride where there's folk. She keeps to the wild places and rides through the tidepools by the sea."

Wearing just a pair of tattered britches that barely came below her knees and held up only by one strap that crossed her suntanned back and belly, Annie raced the stolen horse across the sand and through the cobwebby remains of the ebbing tide. She loved the smell of the salty breeze that cooled her hot cheeks and streamed her streaked auburn mane.

Lochiel Montgomery reined his horse on the steep cliff edge and stared down at the small racing figure on the sand below. There was something about the gait of the chestnut filly that he recognized. Thoughtfully he kneed his mount into a brisk gallop, intent on intercepting the golden rider.

Annie heard the thunder of hoofbeats nearing and she dug in her small bare heels without looking behind her. She thrilled to the race as she bent low over the graceful arched neck of her horse, straining when she sensed the unknown competitor draw level, urging her horse to find an extra ounce of wind. She gasped as she was plucked easily from the horse's back, and she fought for breath as she was roughly thrown across a pair of hard, lean thighs. The pace and thunder of hoofs slowed to a stop and Annie was rolled over so that she stared up panting into searing black eyes, which were staring back from under the most diabolical thick brows. Lochiel Montgomery marveled in the perfection of the child's sunburnt little face.

"Let go of me!" demanded Annie when she could get her breath.

"Where did you get that filly?" demanded the dark man. Annie felt a sharp pant of fear shoot through her as she remembered Michael's words when she had galloped away. She stared up at the satanic face that blocked the sun, and she struggled to sit up, but a strong hand stopped her movement.

"I found her," she lied. "Is she yours?"

"What's your name?" he demanded.

"Rob Roy MacGregor," she responded glibly. The hawklike face softened slightly, but only very slightly. She tried to grin engagingly, hoping to broaden the faint trace of amiability.

"What is your name," repeated his steely voice, dashing her hopes of leniency. Annie decided it was time to button her lips, so she pressed them together and refused to answer. "Then I shall take you to the nearest constabulary and charge you with horse stealing." Annie tried to keep her face still and not show the panic that pounded her heart. She closed her eyes, unable to bear the searing intensity of her captor.

Loch saw the rapid pulse beat in the child's neck and nodded his approval of the stoicism that kept the delicate features from exhibiting any fear.

"Well?" he asked softly after a long pause while he waited for the amber eyes to flutter open and peek at him from between the thick lashes.

"Well, what?" returned Annie fiestily.

"What is your name?"

"I told you already."

"Rob Roy MacGregor?" remarked the dark man sardonically.

"Can I help it if my parents have a droll sense of humor?" she asked indignantly, and at that the chiseled forbidding features that had loomed so menacingly softened and he burst into laughter. Annie breathed a sigh of relief as the hard hand relaxed. She squirmed around and slithered agilely to the ground where she stood, her bare feet apart and digging into the warm sand. She stared up at him defiantly without flinching as she frantically tried to think what to do. There was no way she could escape on foot; he could outrace her with the horse. She speculated about the sea—but where would she swim to? Her only escape was the steep cliff. Lochiel Montgomery had a very good idea of the thoughts churning through the youngster's mind. "You'd cut your feet to ribbons," he remarked idly and then he smiled cynically at the look of surprise on the child's face.

"You look like the devil. Can you read minds too?" she retorted.

"Would you like a horse like that one?"

"Of course," she responded witheringly, indicating she thought it a stupid question.

"There are ways to ride such a horse without resorting to thievery," said Loch softly, ignoring her rudeness. There was something about the child's arrogance and aristrocratic bearing that intrigued him, and he was determined to find out more about this lad by offering him a job in his stables.

"I told you I found the horse!" Annie shouted, backing away.

"Aye, but you didn't say where," returned the dark, young man kneeing his mount to slowly follow. Suddenly Annie spun about and raced toward the steep cliff. Loch reined his horse, afraid of panicking the child, who was now scrambling up the sheer rocky incline. Stones and shale showered down as the agile ragamuffin searched for hand- and footholds on the near precipitous bluff.

Annie felt his dark eyes sear into her exposed back as she frantically shinnied up the sharp escarpment. Her nails tore as she clutched at the small outcroppings of rock that scarcely afforded her a fingerhold as her bare feet blindly felt their way. She stopped for breath, trying to calm herself and wishing she could turn to see what the forbidding man was doing. She pressed herself close to the abrasive cliff face and carefully craned her neck, looking above for a ledge, but there was just more of the same perilous sheerness. Suddenly the outcropping she held on to came loose and she slid down several feet, fighting to regain herself despite the terrible lacerations to her hands, chest, knees, and feet.

Loch swore aloud as he swung down from his horse's high back. His curses continued when he discovered his riding boots afforded him little traction, but he was able to climb slowly toward the still child suspended on a narrow ledge. Annie was dazed and in agony. Her whole body felt skinned. She didn't dare to move for fear that she would again start the painful scraping descent.

"Don't struggle or we'll both come a cropper," said Loch softly, his dark eyes narrowed with concern at the bloodstained child. "Can you hold on to me?" he asked. He winced with sympathy as the child turned over small hands to exhibit raw palms. "Foolish lad," he said, lowering himself and reaching up for her. Annie hesitated, looking frantically around as she debated trying to scale the cliff again to get away from the stranger, but as she did so he grasped her leg. She howled as his salty hand stung her raw flesh. "It'll hurt more if you fight me," he said grimly, pulling her into his arms. Annie finally relaxed and allowed herself to be carried down the remaining rocks and over the sand to the waiting horses. She was lifted up onto the back of an enormous stallion, and the man mounted behind before she had time to escape.

"What are you going to do with me?" she asked as the horse cantered across the beach, the chestnut filly being led. The man didn't answer. She tried to swivel around but the effort caused too much pain to her fast-stiffening scrapes.

Annie was terrified, not knowing if she was to be arrested for horse stealing. She had heard all the horrifying stories of what happened to those caught for stealing—gaol, deportation, whippings, and death by hanging. She longed to beg for mercy, to promise anything, but fear and pride kept her mouth firmly closed, and self-survival had her alert to the landmarks they passed so she would be able to find her way home. They rode for over an hour westward along the coast and then due north toward Glenwillie. Annie relaxed, realizing that at least the stranger wasn't turning her over to the constabulary in Kirkcudbright when they crossed the county border into Galloway.

Lochiel Montgomery rode into the courtyard of a stately mansion surrounded by well-kept formal gardens. An old bandy-legged groom with a straw in between his pleated lips grinned at the sight of the chestnut filly.

"Where did you be finding her, your lordship?" he chortled, running a practiced hand down the young horse's legs to check for injury. Annie sat still, waiting for the stranger to dismount. She was braced for rough hands to painfully haul her down.

"How is the filly, Angus?" asked Lochiel as a young girl ran toward them down the mansion's front steps. The old groom smiled and nodded reassuringly.

"Uncle Loch, you found my Princess," cried the doll-like girl with hair in ringlets, dressed in a beautiful while lace dress. "Who's that dirty boy?" she added disdainfully, staring up at Annie. Several other people strolled down the wide front steps as the chestnut filly was led away to the stables. Annie glowered back at these elegant people who stared curiously up at her. She felt like a freak on display at the county fair. She struggled, wanting to dig in her heels and gallop away, but an iron hand stilled her.

"Is that dirty boy a horse thief, Uncle Loch?" piped the clean little girl, who was much the same age as Annie.

"Run along and play, Allison," said Loch, dismounting and pulling Annie down into his arms.

"Did you beat him for stealing my horse, Uncle Loch, is that why he's all covered with blood?" she persisted.

"Come along, Miss Allison," ordered a uniformed woman.

"But Nanny, I want to see Uncle Loch beat the bad boy," protested the vicious little girl. Annie kicked out, trying to get free and not caring how much it stung as she opened the scrapes and scratches and caused fresh blood to well, but Loch held her tightly. He strode around to the back of the house and entered the large, sunny kitchen, which was fragrant with the smell of fresh baked bread.

"And what hae you there?" clucked a robust apple-cheeked woman. "Och, the puir wee lad, hae you any skin left?" she fussed, bustling to the stove and pouring hot water into a bowl. "Set him right there on the table, your lairdship. I'll see to the bairn." Lochiel sat Annie down where the woman indicated, but hardly before his hands left her she had shimmied off the table and was heading for the door. In two strides he caught her and she sank her sharp young teeth into his forearm. He slapped her sharply but she continued fighting tooth and nail, blood liberally covering both of them.

"Stop!" he roared, taking her by the shoulders and shaking her. Annie hung suspended between his hard hands, her chest heaving and her face streaked with blood, sweat, and dirt. "Nobody wants to hurt you," he stated sternly as the buxom woman gingerly advanced with cleaning cloths.

"You should hae that nasty bite taken care of, your lairdship," she clucked, looking at the teeth marks in the strong brown arms that held the child. "I'll see to the bairn. Ned and Jaimie can help me," she added, indicating two large youths nearby who gawked with interest. Loch sensed the child's fear of these two.

"What's going on here, Loch?" boomed a deep voice, and Annie flinched as a stocky man entered and grabbed her chin. "So you are the young horse thief that stole my daughter's filly?" he roared.

"No, Ross, the boy did not steal Allison's horse. I found the filly one place and the lad another. I just brought him back to have his injuries seen to," lied Lochiel.

"Well, I'm sure Mrs. Goodwin can manage without you," said Ross Montgomery. "There're several items I want to discuss with you before you return to Falconhurst."

"I'll be with you shortly, Ross," answered Loch tersely. Annie's eyes narrowed as she sensed he didn't like the heavyset man.

"'Tis all right, your lairdship. Ned and Jaimie'll help me," reassured the housekeeper. Loch again sensed Annie's increased fear as the two large youths edged nearer. "Really, your lairdship, you should have Mr. MacDonald see to your puir arm. What a vicious wee animal!"

"What happened to your arm?" asked Ross, stopping on his way out of the door.

"Boy bit! Boy bit!" slobbered one of the youths, slapping his enormous hands together like a two-year-old. Ross Montgomery shuddered and let the door slam behind him. Annie frowned, noticing the resemblance between the portly man and the two younger giggling and drooling men.

"Sit, Ned," ordered Mrs. Goodwin. "Jaimie-love, help me. Hold the vicious wee beastie while we clean him up." Once again Annie started to struggle as Jaimie lumbered toward her, leering and dribbling. Loch sighed with exasperation and swung Annie into his arms.

"Have hot water sent up to my rooms," he ordered as he strode out, carrying the child.

Annie was deposited on a wide bed in a large well-furnished bedchamber. She lay motionless, staring wide-eyed at Loch and another man who leaned over her.

"Who's the wee squirt?" asked the older man, a tall spry figure. Lochiel shrugged.

"Who are you?" demanded Annie, trying to sound belligerent so she didn't burst into tears.

"I, young sir, am Roderick MacDonald, trusted servant of Lochiel Montgomery, Lord Falconhurst," he informed with a mocking bow. "And you?"

"Would you believe Rob Roy MacGregor?" she answered defiantly, conscious of the tall, dark man named Lochiel, who stood silently assessing her.

"No," was Roderick's crisp reply. His concerned eyes took in the painful scrapes and raw lacerations that virtually covered the whole front of the child. He picked up one of her small hands and clucked sympathetically. "What in heaven's name happened to you, wee-an?" To her absolute horror, Annie felt scalding tears well at his kind words.

"Well, thank the Lord for that, I was beginning to think you were not quite normal," observed Lochiel sardonically as he watched the tears stream, their wetness streaking the filthy little face even more.

"I want to go home," sobbed Annie. "Please, I want to go home."

"Not until you tell me who you are, where you live, and where you got my niece's horse," stated Loch coldly. Roderick frowned at his harsh young master, not understanding his cruelty. He had known and cared for Lochiel Montgomery since birth, twenty-two years, and although the arrogant young lord could be ruthless, he had never witnessed him being deliberately cruel to a child or an animal.

A sharp knock sounded at the door and Annie froze at the sudden noise. Roderick opened the door and several liveried servants entered with a large copper bath and many buckets of steaming water.

"Well, Mr. MacDonald, I am sure you'll manage adequately," said Loch when the door had closed behind the last of the servants. "Of course, it has been many years since you last had practice," he laughed, remembering some of his childhood baths where his poor valet had been drenched. "Don't fret, Rob Roy MacGregor, Roderick MacDonald is excellent with children. He was, after all, my nurse, nanny, and everything else, right Roderick?"

"Right," returned Roderick.

"So behave yourself, Rob Roy, and I shall see you when you're clean and patched." And with that Lochiel Montgomery left the room.

"Well, laddie, 'tis you and me. Into the bath wie you," ordered Roderick, tying a towel about his waist. Annie slithered off the bed.

"I dinna think you're going to like it," she confessed with a strange little grimace, backing away from the steaming bath.

"Aye, it will sting quite a bit, but you look like a braw lad," soothed the valet.

"Lass," stated Annie.

"What?"

"I'm a lass," she repeated, undoing the one strap so her trews fell about her ankles.

"Well, bless my soul! So you are!" intoned Roderick hoarsely when he could speak. Annie stepped gingerly into the water, biting her lips to keep from screaming as the scrapes on her feet and legs stung painfully. She closed her eyes and sat, holding her breath as the agony spread to her stomach and chest. Roderick stood stunned, not knowing what to say, feel, or think at the girl's uninhibited nakedness. Her sharp intake of breath awoke him to the fact that a small hurt child was a small hurt child, regardless of gender. Annie sat holding her raw hands over the water, afraid to plunge them in, and perspiration beaded on her determined little face. Roderick grimaced, knowing how much she suffered.

"You are a braw wee soul," he said gruffly, turning her hands over and seeing the grit and dirt deeply imbedded in her palms. "Into the water wie them." Annie kept her brimming eyes pinned to his kindly face as he lowered her hands into the water.

"Roderick MacDonald, dinna tell him that I'm a lass," begged Annie when she sat wrapped in a large fluffy towel, letting the valet spread a soothing balm over her wounds.

"There, my wee chickie, you're all buttered for the oven," he laughed, refusing to answer her.

"Please, please, dinna tell him," she pleaded.

"You canna ask that of me, little miss," reproved the old man gently.

"Dinna tell him what?" inquired a deep voice and Annie stared with surprise at Lochiel Montgomery where he lounged at the open door. "And why do you call him little miss?" he added when he received no answer from the wide-eyed child. Roderick smiled ruefully at Loch.

"Rob Roy MacGregor is a lass," he stated simply. "Sorry, lass," he whispered gruffly, ruffling the glorious auburn and gold hair that shone like a halo. Loch strode slowly into the room, firmly shutting the door behind him but keeping his ebony eyes fixed on the rebellious little face.

"Surely you are mistaken, Roderick," he intoned.

"There are some things that a mon can be quite certain of, your lordship," returned Roderick solemnly. "And there is no mistaking a naked female body, no matter the age."

"'Tis not my fault!" shouted Annie, fired by the anger in Loch's dark eyes. "I would prefer to be otherwise!" She reached for her trews.

Roderick MacDonald tried to mask his amusement at his young master's incredulous expression as the incorrigible child shrugged free of the towel. Lochiel took an involuntary step back as the naked little girl stood proudly and gracefully despite the cruel lacerations. The healing balm that covered her sun-gold body caught the setting rays and shone, adding a radiance to the perfection of her form. With great self-control, even though a few tears of pain escaped past her thick lashes, Annie carefully stepped into her trews and fastened the one strap across her chest.

"Put her back to bed," growled Loch harshly, seeing the child could barely walk. "Tomorrow we shall decide what we are to do with our small horse thief," he added before slamming out of the room.

Chapter 6

Michael and Mrs. Wilson sat up all night waiting for Annie to return.

"She's going to get it if she's nae home before Will and Duncan get back. She's not been gone so long before," worried Michael.

"Aye, she has too," comforted the old woman.

"Only when she's upset and angry."

"And she's upset and angry now, what wie that fancy uncle of yours breaking her wee heart like that. I never saw the wee witch-wife take such a shine to a stranger as she did to him," ranted the old crone. "Puir wee orphan lass. Michael-mine, go see if the wee-an has climbed in through her bedroom window. Bet she's there, as snug as a bug in a rug while we're down here fashing ourselves silly," she crackled as the boy mounted the stairs. But the small narrow bed was empty. Michael slowly descended, shaking his auburn head.

The night passed slowly, painfully measured by the ticking of the clock and the rhythmic creak of Mrs. Wilson's rocker. The old woman dozed, her fingers crocheting slower and slower, the chair rocking slower and slower until the only sound was the interminable ticking of the clock and a great sonorous snore. Michael watched the old woman start awake at the slightest sound and each time the click of the crochet hook and the creak of the rocking chair resumed with a new fervor.

"Is she home yet?" she almost shouted, and when Michael silently shook his head, she sighed. "I have nae slept a wink. Nary a wink!" she stated defiantly.

"Sun's nearly up," yawned Michael, standing and stretching his lean body.

"Pretty . . . pretty . . . pretty," whispered the old hag as they listened to the dawn chorus swell, each bird competing to greet the new day. "When did you last look in her bed?"

"Just now when you were snoring away," answered Michael truculently.

"Dinna be impertinent, lad! I have nae slept a wink and I dinna snore!" she snapped with asperity, tucking her crocheting away and getting stiffly to her feet. "Now, get about your chores before your brother Duncan gives you the skelping you're wishing for your sister!"

Annie lay awake listening to the dawn's music, too, as the sun lightened the eastern horizon. She was on a small bed in the dressing room that adjoined Mr. MacDonald's bedchamber. Quietly she climbed off the creaky cot, wincing as her torn flesh was painfully tugged. It felt as though her skin had shrunk and she was about to burst out of it. Cautiously she hobbled to the door and peered around it at Roderick, who slept flat on his back, peacefully snoring. Annie tiptoed across the room, thankful for the thick muffling carpet and when she reached the door that opened onto the corridor she slowly turned the ornate handle. It opened with a loud, agonized groan and she froze, expecting Roderick to awaken, but all he did was smack his lips together and mutter something unintelligible before turning on his side and resuming his contented snoring. Annie stepped quickly into the carpeted corridor, glad she was not on the floor above with the forbidding dark stranger, Lochiel Montgomery. Despite her lacerated feet, which left a bloody trail on the delicate yellow carpet, Annie limped swiftly downstairs to the ground floor. Hearing muffled sounds from the kitchen area in the back, she hastily made her way to the large marbled entrance hall, relieved when she reached the cooling agate, which soothed her sore feet. Annie opened the heavy front door and limped down the wide front steps. She nearly screamed in pain as she hobbled across the graveled carriageway toward the stables, keeping close to the shrubbery that ringed the imposing stone house. The sharp grit of the drive embedded painfully in her cuts and she hurried, walking awkwardly on her heels, longing to cross to the soft cool grass but knowing it would make her more visible if anyone were looking out of the windows. Reaching the stables, she sank down in a dark corner to try to remove the most painful of the gravel before deciding what her next move should be. She listened intently but heard only the snorting and chomping of the horses. Quietly she sidled into the stables, glad that the cumbersome doors already stood wide to allow a cooling breeze for the hot animals housed within.

Lochiel's enormous black stallion was in the nearest stall and she stared up at his noble face with awe. She had never seen such a magnificent animal, she decided as she carefully led the huge creature out and, with the aid of a mounting block, managed to haul herself painfully onto the superb horse's high back. She wound her raw hands firmly into the glossy ebony mane and kicked his muscular girth. The stallion sprang forward, excited to be out of the musty closeness of the confining stable and in the clear morning air. Annie hung on and prayed she could control the enormous animal as he cantered up the long driveway. Her legs could hardly encompass his broad back, so despite her scraped knees, she sat with her legs bent like a jockey. Ahead loomed the gatehouse and the closed gates. Forced to change direction, she pulled on the stallion's mane, heading him across the manicured lawn toward the stone wall that enclosed the estate. She took a deep breath and hoped he could jump the high obstacle as she felt his muscular haunches tense to leap. She grinned and crowed aloud with sheer exhilaration as the mighty horse seemed to fly, and then they were free.

Lochiel Montgomery could not believe his eyes. Unable to sleep, his dreams haunted by a vivacious young pixy who elusively darted, one minute seeming to be an enchanting child and the next a sunbeam, he stood at the window watching the dawn emerge. To his astonishment he saw his prize stallion, Dubh, canter proudly down the carriageway and soar over the high stone wall to be lost from view. Frantically he rang the bell summoning his valet as he pulled on his britches and boots.

"What is going on, lad?" panted Roderick.

"That child has stolen Dubh!" clipped Loch, striding passed the half-dressed old man and slapping his riding crop menacingly against his muscled thigh.

"Dinna talk stite! There's none but you can get near that great beastie, let alone ride him!" protested the valet, trying to keep up with his irate young master. "Besides Wee Rob Roy MacGregor is sleeping soundly in my dressing room."

"Did you make sure?" barked Lochiel.

"You dinna gie me much of a chance, summoning me before dawn," yawned Roderick. "How could such a wee scraped-up lassie ride Dubh? 'Tis not possible!"

"I saw her!" replied Loch tersely, his boots clattering across the white marble of the central hall. Roderick frowned at the small bloody footprints there and Loch, following his gaze, snorted as with a curse he wrenched open the heavy front door.

"Och, her puir wee feet," winced Roderick as they crunched along the gravel toward the stables.

"Dinna feel sorry for *her,* Mr. MacDonald!" raged the infuriated young man. "It was *my* horse! Och, I shall find that unprincipled brat no matter how long it takes me!"

Michael stood at the barn door watching the farm wagon slowly trundle up.

"Everything all right?" hailed Will, leaping down and frowning at his younger brother's scowling face.

"Annie rode off on the chestnut filly. I told her not to, but she dinna listen. She's been gone all night," he wailed.

"She grows wilder and wilder," muttered Duncan. The three brothers worked in silence unloading the wagon and carrying the sacks and crates into the barn.

"What if the filly was recognized?" Michael exclaimed, unable to remain quiet after the long night of worry.

"If she's not back by four or so, I'll ride in to Kirkcudbright," returned Duncan shortly.

"Your lunch is ready. A nice pot of mutton stew wie dumplings," called Mrs. Wilson, opening the kitchen door wide to cool the hot room. The fragrant smell wafted into the yard to tempt the healthy appetites of the boys.

Silently they stripped to the waist and sluiced themselves under the pump as their eyes strayed down the lane hoping for sight of their small, wayward sister. Michael straightened up and squinted in the sunlight as he saw the dust rise in the distance.

"Someone's coming," he stated, and the three brothers and Mrs. Wilson stood watching.

"'Tis Uncle Robert," said Will, recognizing the matched grays.

"Well, what do you know, it is himself!" chortled Mrs. Wilson. "I thought he had forgie us all."

"He paid off the debts," informed Duncan.

"All of them?" exclaimed Michael.

"Aye," returned Will as the curricle came to a halt and Robert leapt down with an engaging grin on his handsome face.

"Hah, so ye dinna forgie us, Mr. Fancy-Pants!" greeted Mrs. Wilson irreverently.

"How could I ever forget you, madame," laughed Robert, sniffing the air appreciatively. "I do so hope we're in time for luncheon?"

"We?" asked the old crone sharply

"Wilkes!" called Robert. "Stir yourself, we have arrived!" A small, solemn face popped out of the carriage window. "Wilkes is my man," explained Robert as the small, immaculately dressed man stepped out of the carriage and stared without expression at the three bare-chested youths and the witchlike old woman. "Well, where's Oriana?" asked Robert, looking around.

"Missing," answered Will cryptically.

"Missing?" ejaculated Robert as the tiny valet wrestled with an enormous trunk.

"Are we to stand gossiping whilst my stew curdles?" scolded the wizened Mrs. Wilson. "Michael, help the wee mannikin wie that great coffin!" she added scornfully, looking at the frail Wilkes in his formal clothing.

"I can manage, madame," returned Wilkes.

"Leave it until after luncheon," ordered Robert, striding into the fragrant kitchen. "Now, what is this about my niece being missing?" he asked when he had sat down at the table before a steaming plate of stew and dumplings.

"Set yourself down, wee mannikin," hissed Mrs. Wilson with impatience as the tiny valet hovered uncertainly. Wilkes inclined his head slightly and looked to Robert for confirmation.

"For God's sake, Wilkes, we don't stand on ceremony here!" snorted Robert, his mouth full of the savory fare. "Now, what is this about Annie?" he repeated after his valet had dusted off a chair and sat, correctly pulling at his immaculate trousers so they wouldn't wrinkle. Michael shook his head in disbelief, unable to take his eyes from the expressionless face of the little man, who took a snowy white handkerchief from his pocket and carefully unfolded it before setting it on his knee. Wilkes had never sat at the same table to share a meal with his employer, nor had he partaken of a meal in such crude surroundings before, yet his face showed none of the shock or distaste he might be feeling.

Annie rode east toward the sunrise, knowing instinctively not to retrace the journey from the day before, as Lochiel Montgomery would expect that of her. Instead, she cut straight across the countryside, skirting towns and villages, reasoning that within ten or fifteen miles she would cross the border from Galloway into Kirkcudbrightshire. For the first several miles she was thrilled to be riding the powerful black stallion. She raced across the moors feeling alive and free, laughing aloud at the pheasant and partridge that whirred out of the bracken and heather. As the time wore on and her body ached with fatigue and her scabbed abrasions seized up so fiercely that she didn't dare change position, she thanked the mighty horse she rode but felt no exhilaration, just the need to reach home.

It was well after noon when, hot and thirsty, Annie rode up the rutted lane behind Kenlaren Manor. She blinked and wiped her sweaty forehead, wincing as the salt stung her raw palm, when she saw the curricle in the pump yard. She reined the large horse, not able to believe her eyes. As if in a trance she kneed the stallion so he walked slowly toward the matched gray horses that stood patiently, occasionally swishing a tail at the swarms of flies, or stamping a hoof as they shifted weight. Annie's expression, intense at first as she expected the mirage to fade away into imagination, changed to pure joy.

"Uncle Robert! Uncle Robert!" she rejoiced at the top of her lungs.

Robert, who had sat back contentedly after his third helping of stew and dumplings, leapt to his feet and made a mad dash for the open door, followed by the three boys. Wilkes sat calmly and touched each corner of his mouth delicately with his handkerchief as the old crone, with ladle still in hand, hobbled out into the yard.

Robert and the boys stopped dead in their tracks at the sight of the bloody little girl perched high on the tall back of the great black stallion. Wilkes slowly walked out and raised an eyebrow at the silent tableau. He reached into his breast pocket and removed a monocle, which he affixed to one eye in order to see the object of everyone's curiosity.

"Oriannie Rebecca, where did you get such a horse?" gasped Michael, breaking the shocked silence.

"Och, what a fine beastie, to be sure," chortled Mrs. Wilson. "Are ye sure 'tis not a kelpie disguised as a young horse ready to drown you in the sea? Or maybe 'tis the Nuckelavee!"

"He has two eyes of brown, not one of red fire," answered Annie scornfully, straightening her back proudly as she felt the anger that emanated from the silent twins.

"Get down, Annie Gunn!" ordered Duncan sternly.

"You going to skelp me?"

"Get down!" he repeated, his harsh tone promising no mercy. Annie didn't move a muscle; she just stared down defiantly. Wilkes was nodding thoughtfully as he gazed up at the rebellious urchin, and Annie caught the movement and looked at him in amazement.

"Who the hell is that?" she gasped at the incongruous sight of the immaculate little man with the monocle.

"Get down!" roared Duncan. "And watch your manners!"

"Uncle Robert!" she pleaded to her aghast uncle who stood momentarily speechless, staring with horror at her bare, lacerated chest, belly, and knees.

"Oriana, do as you're told," he said gently.

"I dinna think I can," she replied, lifting her hands to show her raw bleeding palms. "My feet too. I canna straighten my legs."

"Annie, fall off. I'll catch you," said Will gently. Annie nodded, took a deep breath, and leaned to one side so she trustingly toppled into her brother's strong arms. Will carried her into the kitchen and gently set her in a chair.

"Dinna fuss with me," she protested, trying to push him away as he examined her injuries. "I'm starving. I have nae eaten since the night before last."

"You dinna deserve to eat!" stated Duncan angrily.

"Here are, wee-un," crooned Mrs. Wilson, placing a steaming bowl before Annie and peering closely at the scrapes and lacerations. She frowned as she noted a residue of balm adhering to the wounds. "Eat up and I'll make you a herb bath to soothe that puir wee body."

Annie tried to eat without showing the apprehension she felt at the anger that crackled through the room from her silent brothers. She focused her aching eyes on her Uncle Robert's blond head, but his closed, worried expression took her appetite away. Her whole body hurt; she was tired and unable to cope. She pushed her uneaten food away and stood, wanting to be away from the stuffy friction and outside in the fresh air.

"Sit down, Annie!" ordered Duncan.

"I have to see my horse!" she shouted defiantly.

"*Your* horse!"

"Aye, *mine!*"

"I'll see to the horse," said Michael, wanting to get away from the anger.

"Dinna put him in the barn. He needs his freedom," begged Annie. "Can he go in the high pasture?" Michael looked silently at Duncan and Will. Will nodded and Duncan snorted furiously.

"She grows wilder and wilder, ruder and ruder, but always she gies her own way no matter what!" he raged.

"Where did you get such a superb piece of horse

flesh," asked Robert hesitantly, not sure he wanted to hear the answer. Annie looked away, knowing what his reaction would be if she told the truth.

"It does not matter. He is mine!" she stated. *"Mine!"* she repeated vehemently as she heard a high-pitched whinny and the angry stamping of feet. She forgot her sore body and hobbled into the yard in time to see Dubh rear threateningly at Michael, who had tried to mount. "Och, you bad lad, what are you trying to do to puir Michael?" she crooned, approaching the huge animal.

"For God's sake, Annie, get back!" ordered Robert, but Duncan laid a warning hand on his uncle's shoulder, cautioning him to be still and quiet as the girl limped toward the frenzied stallion whose eyes rolled white with fear.

"Och, such a tantrum, Dubh," she chided. She didn't realize she had heard Lochiel call the stallion the Gaelic word meaning black, but thought she had found the name herself. "Come wie me, you big silly," she said, limping toward several bales of hay, which she painfully climbed as the enormous stallion docilely followed her as though he were a pet dog. Once more Wilkes stood in the doorway, his monocle affixed, nodding thoughtfully at the auburn-haired child as she clambered onto the broad back of the horse. "Och, Dubh, what'll I do wie you making such a nuisance of yourself?" she chided as she rode the animal slowly up thc lane to the high pasture, followed by her brothers and Robert.

"She's always had a way with animals," explained Will as they trudged after. "Once when she was a really tiny bairn we found her in the bull pen singing away. We nearly died of fear. Every time we tried to go in to get her out the bull charged."

"How did you get her out?" asked Robert.

"Mrs. Wilson told her it was tea time, and she just said good-bye to the bull and left," laughed Will.

"We should have known right then what a handful she would grow to be," muttered Duncan.

"Let go your anger, Duncan," soothed his twin softly. "Aye, she needs a skelping, but seems this time she has had one," he added as Annie stiffly slid down from the high back onto the stone wall that encircled the pasture.

"In with you, you big silly," Annie ordered as Michael swung open the heavy gate. Dubh cantered around his new surroundings and Annie leaned on the gate, watching him. When she whistled he trotted up and butted her affectionately with his great head. "Now, behave," she said sternly before turning and limping back toward the house. Will picked her up and cradled her in his arms, ignoring Duncan's dark scowling.

"Put her in there," said Mrs. Wilson, indicating a steaming bathtub set up on the floor of the spacious kitchen. "Make yerself useful and help the lass undress, wee mannikin," ordered the crone to the immaculate valet as she turned back to her cauldron, stirring and muttering strange incantations with each handful of dried herbs she threw in. Wilkes turned respectfully to his employer and raised an eyebrow.

"'Tis all right, Wilkes," laughed Robert. "Why don't you walk around? Let me show you the rest of the house."

"No, stay with me, Uncle Robert," begged Annie as Will put her down carefully.

"I'll be here when you've finished your bath," reassured Robert as his intrepid little niece slid out of her trews and stood naked in the kitchen. She turned with a puzzled expression as a strange, strangled cry burst out of the mouth of the dignified valet.

"Are you all right?" she asked, staring at the impassive face.

"Quite all right, thank you, er, miss," he answered with a proper little bow. Robert grinned broadly at Wilkes's very correct restraint. Annie gave her uncle a wan look.

"I don't feel very well," she confessed quietly as tears welled in her eyes.

"You'll feel much better after your bath, I'm sure," he comforted her. "What happened? You look as though you've been dragged through cinders," he observed as she stepped gingerly into the bath and winced.

"Set ye down," ordered Mrs. Wilson. "One of you braw lads pick up the pot, 'tis too heavy for an old lady." She was pointing a crooked bony finger at her black cauldron. Robert obeyed without thought, and again Wilkes's eyebrows rose quizzically although no other expression crossed his face. "Pour it in!" directed the crone.

"Isn't it too hot!" he asked anxiously, causing his valet to nod in approval.

"Nay, 'tis just elbow heat and it'll hae her to sleep in two shakes of a black cat's tail," she chortled softly. Robert poured the heady-smelling brew into the bath water and watched Annie slowly relax. Wilkes coughed politely and the old woman looked up at him with a sharp motion.

"Go show that fancy mannikin of yours what's aboot here," whispered Mrs. Wilson as Annie's eyelids started to droop.

"Don't let her drown," teased Robert half seriously, looking down at the sleeping child whose golden head was pillowed on the old woman's sinewy arm.

"This child of nature?" cackled the crone softly. "Och, you'd be surprised at who watches over this chosen one, yer lairdship."

"Will she be scarred, do you think?" he asked.

"Nay, none go too deep and the herbs will stop any infection. It also looks as though someone else has been doctoring," she answered thoughtfully, her shrewd old eyes scanning the contusions. "Now, off wie you before the mannikin cracks his face wie a frown," she laughed.

"How'll you lift Oriana out?" worried Robert, somehow loath to leave the sleeping child who was clasping his hand so trustingly. A sharp intake of breath caused him to look around to Wilkes, whose very proper and passive expression covered stunned astonishment. He had been Sir Robert Forsythe's intimate servant for seventeen years, and in all that time the spoilt young lord had shown not the slightest regard or concern for any other living thing except perhaps an occasional horse or dog—and then only those of the finest pedigree.

"Michael, would you be a bang-up fellow and show Wilkes about?" asked Robert, still reluctant to disengage the sore little hand that clutched his so possessively.

Wilkes walked very carefully, avoiding the generous mounds of questionable muck and making no effort to keep up with the grubby little boy, who though only twelve years old, topped him by nearly a head. Several geese, curious at the strange apparition of the precise little man, waddled behind, their necks stretched as though to suddenly attack. Wilkes whirled about at them, lunging like a fencer and aiming his Malacca cane.

"'Tis best to ignore them, as they can become very nasty if they've a mind," lectured Michael bossily as the geese hissed. "They could even break your arm or leg. Maybe even kill you." he added gleefully, hoping to shatter the sedate little man's composure as the noisy birds honked loudly. Michael gasped when Wilkes unsheathed a lethal-looking sword that had been concealed inside the cane.

"Not being at all familiar with your northern climes, I came prepared for any event," stated the strange man, suddenly giving a loud shout so that the geese turned tail and ran.

"What do you want to see?" asked Michael, staring wide-eyed at the little valet, who sheathed his weapon and resumed his careful promenade. "The bull? Cows? Goats? Pigs?"

"The main house. As you have no doubt realized, I have no fondness for either animals, birds or . . . small children," he stated cryptically, staring through his monocle at Michael. The boy longed to point out his superior height but was more than slightly intimidated by the meticulous man.

"Why does Uncle Robert call you his 'man'?" asked Michael, leading the way through the overgrown rose garden.

"I am his valet, and when occasion demands, his general factotum," replied Wilkes, drawing himself up to his full height of five feet three inches. He refrained from displaying any irritation as the straggly rose branches clawed his neat clothing.

"You are a servant!" crowned Michael disrespectfully.

"Yes, young man, I am a servant and very proud of it. My family has served the Forsythe family for over seven generations. That is more than two hundred and fifty years," he coldly informed the boy, allowing just a trace of pride to color his words.

"I'll not be a servant to anyone," muttered Michael, leading Wilkes to the front of the manor.

"Yes, yes, yes, Sir Robert was absolutely correct. It is a most magnificent house!" stated Wilkes, clasping his white-gloved hands together and walking backward over the sloping, overgrown lawn to get a better perspective of the graceful—though neglected—manor. He joined his index finger and thumb together to make a frame as he cocked his head from one side to the other, making little sounds of appreciation. A goat bleated loudly, causing the tiny man to forgo his fantasizing and walk briskly toward the front door.

"Sir Robert astounds me! Absolutely astounds me!" breathed Wilkes as he scribbled quickly on a small pad. "For seventeen years I found him typical, ordinary, and predictable. A well-bred young aristocrat . . . bored and boring," he continued, unaware of the incredulous look on the boy's face. He didn't pause in his copious note-taking as he pranced from room to room like a spry grasshopper.

"What are you writing?" asked Michael, looking over his shoulder and trying to decipher the precise copperplate hand.

"Where did you spring from?" snapped Wilkes, staring with distaste at the grubby little boy.

"I've been here all the time," protested Michael, thinking the man even stranger than before. "What are you writing?" he repeated. He scowled at the intense gaze of the valet.

"All that must be done," chirped the man curtly, stepping back and looking critically at the boy's sulky face. "Despite your surliness, there are passably good lines . . . excellent bone structure," he added as he resumed scribbling on his pad. "You have the Forsythe blood . . . and that is a good foundation. As I told Sir Robert, I may be a genius but I am not a magician or warlock, and even I cannot make a silk purse out of a sow's ear." Michael frowned in puzzlement as Wilkes laughed politely at his own witticism. "Luckily, little boy, you have decent bloodlines—at least on your mother's side of the family."

"I have decent blood on my father's side too! He is a

Scottish lord! Sir David Gunn of Kenlaren!" declared Michael hotly.

"Well, my goodness me, that is a small blessing, although a Scottish lord is not of much consequence," muttered Wilkes, still writing busily. "It is certainly better than other ancestors I could imagine. I wonder why Sir Robert didn't mention the fact," he mused. Michael was once more forgotten as the man pranced about scribbling and mumbling excitedly to himself. "Wonderful light . . . well-appointed . . . stately . . . gracious . . . remarkable wainscotting." All these words and more buzzed in Michael's confused ears until he could stand it no more, so he left.

"Uncle Robert?" he called as he entered the kitchen.

"Hush up!" hissed Mrs. Wilson. As Michael's eyes became accustomed to the dark kitchen after the bright sunlight, he saw his uncle cradling his sleeping sister while the old woman spread thick ointments on the angry lacerations.

"Your man is weird!" stated the boy rudely, feeling left out and resentful.

"He's a marvel. He'll have you all organized in no time," replied Robert cheerfully.

"Hush up and take her to her wee bed, and if you wake her I'll hae your hide," scolded Mrs. Wilson crossly.

Sullenly Michael watched Robert carry the little girl upstairs.

"Make yerself useful and empty the water," barked the old lady, digging a sharp elbow into his ribs. Michael angrily bailed out the bath with a bucket and threw the tepid water into the yard, drenching and scattering the chickens. "What do you think Lord Fancy-Pants means about getting us all organized?" she demanded sharply. Michael shrugged. "But I dinna want to be organized, do you?" she rasped. Michael shrugged sullenly again.

Whether they wanted to be organized or not they were; within two days coach upon coach arrived spewing out workmen and materials. The country was agog with all the goings-on at Kenlaren Manor, and merchants for miles about fell over each other trying to sell their wares as Wilkes ordered everything from upholstery fabric to chamber pots.

Masons, carpenters, and painters busily hammered, mixed, sawed, and puttied, transforming not only the stately formal rooms but also the laborer's cottages, returning the large estate of Kenlaren to its former glory.

"Och, beware, my wee witch-wife, for soon it'll be our turn to be painted and patched, primped and polished," lamented Mrs. Wilson as Annie lithely mounted the giant stallion to race him over the windswept moors away from the noisy hive of activity.

Chapter 7

From August nearly to October Annie's head whirled with more excitement than she had ever imagined. She ran from one workman to another, offering to help. She had never been around so many people or had such attention. Wilkes breathed deeply, emitting long, heartfelt sighs but never allowing the despair to show on his face as he watched the girl's hoydenish antics. Michael walked about smiling smugly, enjoying the well-cut expensive clothes that he wore proudly, and attempting to keep them as meticulously neat as Wilkes's. He, too, was happier than he had ever been in his life and he looked forward to the tutor his uncle had engaged to prepare him eventually for university. There were no more backbreaking, messy, menial chores to do, as farm laborers now lived in the restored cottages, allowing the brothers freedom at last. Michael was puzzled, though, by his older twin brothers, whose eyes had shone happily when Robert had told them of their commissions into a noted regiment but who had soon become quiet and remote.

November was to be the magic month. The house and grounds would be finished, Michael's tutor and Annie's governess installed, and the twins off to London to join their prestigious regiment. But as that time approached, the fervent gleam that had shone so brightly in Duncan's and Will's eyes dulled to an uneasy watchfulness. Annie was puzzled by her older brothers' change and hurt when her efforts to cheer them up just caused anger and sullen silence.

Mrs. Wilson thrived in the noisy chaos. Oh, she grumbled mightily and threatened all with dire spells and satanic curses as she stirred her cauldron of soups and stews and kneaded her delicious breads with her gnarled old fingers, but secretly she was in her element among the hordes of working people. What was happening could be for the good, she wavered, keeping a canny eye on the twins.

"Let your brothers be. You're like pestering little gnats!" she scolded Annie and Michael.

"But what's wrong wie them?" protested Annie.

"'Tis just hard to leave what you know. 'Tis a big change. Because of the two of you, the puir bairns hae had no childhood. . .'tis hard to them to let go and see others tending the fields and flocks. They want to go and they want to stay," she struggled to explain.

"It's not just that. There's something else! Something wrong! Like the smell of roses at night that makes me scared and sick to my belly!" retorted Annie.

"Hush up!" snapped the crone. "Dinna prate such stite."

Robert traveled back and forth, spending a few days at Kenlaren only to be driven away by the discomfort and noise. But to Wilkes's surprise his young master, despite his copious grumbles, could never stay away for more than a week. Robert drove up in late September and Annie raced barefoot beside his curricle, yelling at the top of her lungs.

"Wait until you see, Uncle Robert! Every room done! 'Tis like a palace for a princess in one of mother's stories!" she hollered, not noticing the thin elderly woman who rode with her uncle up the driveway to the front door.

"Why aren't the grounds finished!" demanded Robert, frowning at the tangled rose garden as he held out his hand to help the vinegar-faced, black-garbed woman alight. Wilkes stood next to Mrs. Wilson and they both dolefully shook their heads for the first time in agreement as they hoped the woman wasn't Sir Robert's choice of governess. "Miss Primrose Mint, this is Oriana Rebecca Gunn," introduced Robert.

Annie stared up at the woman, recognizing the expression of disgust when Miss Mint recoiled as though she were regarding something foul and infinitely beneath her.

"Och, Uncle Robert, she's not to be my governess, is she?" Annie exclaimed with great chagrin. Robert frowned warningly as the girl backed away, afraid of the sour-faced woman's venomous expression.

"Oriana, come back here at once!" roared Robert, extremely irritated by the long, tedious journey with the boring woman, by his undisciplined niece's rudeness, and by the bedraggled state of the gardens surrounding the manor.

"No!" shouted Annie before disappearing into the tangled greenery. Mrs. Wilson, meanwhile, was trying to concoct an incantation to drive the formidable governess away.

"Wilkes!"

"Yes, sir," intoned the valet, politely stepping forward and bowing slightly to Miss Mint.

"Please show Miss Mint to the drawing room and see she is furnished with some refreshment," ordered Robert coldly. "Then return and inform me why the grounds are still in the same appalling state as when I left a week ago!" Wilkes bowed and led the tall thin woman up the front steps and into the manor, where he rang for two maids, who arranged Miss Mint's comfort.

"Well?" growled Robert to his manservant as Wilkes tripped lightly down the front steps looking calm and unflustered.

"Your nephews, Duncan and William, chased the gardeners away with shotguns," informed the valet mildly.

"Shotguns?"

"Shotguns."

"That's preposterous!" shouted Robert. "Well, isn't it?" he asked when Wilkes didn't say anything.

"If you say so, sir," answered the valet dutifully. "Sir?"

"What?" he barked.

"May I step out of line for a moment?"

"Out of line? Of course not!"

"Very well, sir," sighed Wilkes.

"Well, I will, yer cowardly little mannikin," rasped Mrs. Wilson. "What are you trying to do to our wee lass?"

Robert shook his head, not able to comprehend the old woman's fury. "Bringing that dried-up old virgin to teach our Annie!" screeched the old crone.

"Miss Mint was the only governess who answered the advertisement I placed with the agency," retorted Robert furiously. "Her credentials are exemplary!"

"I dinna care what her credentials are. Her heart is hard! There's not a drop of life or earthy lust in that bitter old maid!" ranted Mrs. Wilson.

"Maybe Oriana Gunn needs a bit of hardness!" returned Robert furiously, scanning about for a sign of his rebellious niece and ignoring the old hag's highly improper reference to "earthy lust."

"Och, 'tis no guid, Lord Fancy-Pants, you'll nae see the wee witch-wife until that old bat has flown!" she stated, and she grinned toothlessly before hobbling back to her kitchen to brew a potion to hasten the governess's departure. "A wee something to curdle her bowels," she plotted, rubbing her bony hands together with relish.

Sure enough, not hide nor hair was seen of the wild child for several days. Five minutes after the ailing Miss Primrose Mint, bent double with agonizing stomach pains, had been driven from Kenlaren, Annie skipped barefoot across the lawn whistling cheerfully. Robert watched her from the breakfast room window.

"Wilkes!" he roared.

"Yes, sir," came the prompt reply.

"Look! Look!" he muttered furiously, pointing to the impudent girl.

"At Miss Oriana, sir?" asked the valet innocently.

"At Miss Oriana, sir? At Miss Oriana, sir?" ranted Robert. "For five and a half days that brat has been missing and all you can say is 'At Miss Oriana, sir?' " And with that he threw open the window and bellowed out, "Oriana Gunn, come here! Immediately!" Annie looked up and waved cheerfully before skipping up the wide front steps.

"Hello, Uncle Robert," she sang out cheekily as she entered the room, ignoring her uncle's thunderous scowl. "Is breakfast ready? I could eat a whole cow!"

"I have a good mind to make you!" snapped her incensed guardian after a pause where he was shocked speechless by her brazen effrontery.

"Good morning, Wilkes," she said gaily. "Aren't you happy that awful woman has gone?"

"Oriana Rebecca Gunn, what am I going to do with you?" groaned Robert, shaking his blond head helplessly at her outrageousness. Annie shrugged with a sunny smile before dashing out of the house to find Mrs. Wilson. She leaped down the front steps and, singing merrily like a little lark, she skipped through the rose garden on her way to the kitchen. She stopped and frowned, though, at seeing her twin brothers busily digging, the rhythmic rasping sound of their spades causing panic to claw in her empty belly as the heavy perfume of the overblown roses filled her nostrils and smothered her breathing.

"No! No! What are you doing?" she screamed fearfully, forgetting in her panic that she had been missing for several days.

"Oriana Gunn! Where the hell have you been?" demanded Duncan angrily.

"What?" replied Annie, not understanding her brother's fury for a moment.

"Five days you've been gone!"

"I had to! I had to! That woman hated me," shouted Annie, remembering the governess and trying to still her new terror. "She hated me! I saw it in her eyes," she yelled.

"We had no idea where you were," scolded Duncan, grabbing her roughly by the shoulders and shaking her. "We've been worried near to the grave!"

"Grave!" The word burst from the child's mouth as she stared with horror up at her tall brother. "Father's grave! Father's grave! You've dug father's grave!" she cried hysterically.

Robert stood at the open library window privy to the exchange between the little girl and her brother.

"Hush up!" hissed Duncan, shaking her and looking truculently at his uncle.

"Oriana, go to Mrs. Wilson," said Will softly as Duncan put Annie roughly away from him.

"The roses are bleeding," sobbed Annie.

"Annie, Annie, that was just one of your bad dreams," groaned Will, spinning her about and holding her tightly.

"No! No! It wasna a dream!" screamed Annie, pushing him away and rushing headlong into her uncle, who strode up purposefully intent on knowing the whole. "The roses were bleeding!"

Michael crouched nearby under a bush, suddenly not caring that his elegant new clothes were getting wrinkled and soiled as his heart beat triple time. "The roses are bleeding," he mouthed silently as he backed away, not knowing what terrified him so but certain he wanted to get as far away from the rose garden as he could.

"Oriana, go with Wilkes and he'll see you have your breakfast," said Robert hoarsely, hoping the rebellious child would obey so he could question his white-faced nephews. There was a pause while the little girl looked up at him, as though waking from sleep. Infinite sadness was etched across her delicate features. She smiled wanly and nodded as she obediently reached for Wilkes's white-gloved hand.

"Come," said Robert tersely, leading the twins to the privacy of the small library, which had been stocked from floor to ceiling with books on every conceivable subject. "Michael, please read somewhere else, your brothers and I would appreciate some privacy," he demanded of the white-faced boy who was curled in a large chair immersed in a book. Michael nodded, his large amber eyes luminous in his pale face, his hands shaking as he held the heavy volume to his chest like a shield. Robert kept his eyes pinned to the sullen identical faces, unaware of the other boy's agitation as he backed out of the library and shut the door.

"I want to know everything," stated Robert, pouring himself a stiff drink as the memory of Annie's anguished words about bleeding roses and her father's grave stabbed into his mind. "I am aware it is still morning, but I am in need of sustenance. Would either of you care for a drop?" The twins nodded and accepted crystal glasses of amber whiskey that so matched their eyes. "Sit!" ordered their uncle, making himself comfortable, but the youths only looked at the delicate crystal in their grimy work-callused hands and down at their rough, stained work-clothes and the newly upholstered chairs. "Sit!" repeated Robert. Sheepishly the twins sat on the very edges of the fine furniture, feeling out of place and clumsy. "So, your father is dead!" stated their uncle baldly, deciding it was best to jump right into the thick of it instead of skirting tentatively about the edges. Looking at each other, the twins nodded silently. "Oh!" responded Robert after a shocked pause. "Well, did . . . er . . . Rebecca . . . er . . . kill him?" he probed awkwardly, unable to say either "your mother" or "my sister." The boys looked at each other again and then shrugged helplessly.

"We weren't there," whispered Will.

"Who was?"

"Our mother and another man," recounted Duncan harshly.

"And Annie," added Will softly, and his twin glared angrily at him. "'Tis best he know all."

"Oriana saw her father die?" gasped Robert.

"Aye, we think so . . . and the other man," answered Will. "But she doesna remember."

Robert stared out of the window at the innocent tangle of rosebushes. "How many are buried out there?" he asked hoarsely.

"Just two. Our father and the other man," sand Will.

"Is the other man the one Oriana calls Lochinvar?" asked Robert.

"One of them," laughed Duncan bitterly.

"What of the maid?"

"We paid her a lot of money and she promised to keep silent," confessed Will.

"How much money?"

"More than five thousand pounds!" snarled Duncan.

"About what I paid to unmortgage Kenlaren," remarked Robert. "And do you honestly think the wretched woman will keep her lips sealed?"

"It has been over six months and we've not heard from her and dinna expect to," replied Duncan defensively.

"Just wait until the money is spent," sighed Robert. "You must realize she'll return for more?" The twins stared silently at him. "And if you don't meet her demands what will she say?" He probed relentlessly and the boys shrugged. "What will she say?"

"That she saw us digging the graves," evaded Duncan.

"Farmers digging in the soil!" mocked Robert cynically. "You paid five thousand pounds for that? I demand to know everything . . . from the beginning!"

"Our mother wasna well . . . ever. She would lock herself up wie her books and sometimes she got confused between the books and . . . life," struggled Will sadly after a long silence.

"Our mother was a whore!" interrupted Duncan. "Men came here . . . for her favors!"

"She dinna ken what she was doing," defended Will.

"Doesna much matter. It is the same thing in the end. That is why Annie needs harnessing!" shouted Duncan bitterly.

"So it appears your father objected, which is quite understandable, and there was a fight which unfortunately resulted in the deaths?" suggested Robert.

"There were always fights. Ever since I first remember. But we'd just put our pillows over our heads and go back to sleep," recounted Duncan.

"Except that night we heard Annie screaming . . . and screaming, not from her room but from our mother's," added Will.

"When we got there our father and the other man were dead. There was blood everywhere and our mother sat in her chair as though there was nothing amiss, reading her poetry while Annie stood screaming and screaming. . . ."

Robert paced the room, appalled by what he was hearing. He poured himself another drink and took a burning swallow before turning back to the twins.

"Where was the maid?"

"We thought her asleep in her room. It was after we had burned them that she told us she knew all. She said—"

"No!" Will interrupted angrily. "Dinna repeat her ugly lies!"

"Lies? What lies?" insisted Robert as Will silently pleaded with his twin.

"Let's have it all out in the open!" Duncan shouted,

and Will turned furiously away from him and stared out of the window.

"What lies?" repeated Robert, somehow knowing he was about to hear something dreadful.

"That Annie killed the other man!" sneered Will, beating his twin to it. "Isna that ridiculous?"

"How?" asked Robert, the word wrenched painfully from his constricted throat.

"Dirk . . . he was stabbed over and over again wie a dirk!" informed Duncan harshly.

"Lies!" spat Will. "Who in their right mind would believe a wee eight-year-old-lass could kill a full grown man?"

"No one," determined Robert. "No one at all. It's too preposterous to even consider."

"We couldna take the chance of anyone hearing such lies. If it was not Annie than it was our own mother who killed," explained Will. "It wouldna have been right not to protect them from such talk."

"So your father is dead. Who is the elder of the two of you?" asked Robert after another lengthy pause.

"I am," replied Duncan.

"Sir Duncan Gunn," mused their uncle.

"How do you know?"

"Michael told Wilkes, who looked it up at the proper source," answered Robert wearily.

"We don't believe in titles or the like," retorted Duncan.

"Whether you do or not is unimportant. Unless you renounce the title and give it to a younger brother, you are still Sir Duncan Gunn, Lord Kenlaren."

"My father is meant to be very much alive in Africa," answered Duncan.

"That is easily dealt with. I can arrange for the news of your father's unfortunate demise in the Transvaal to be spread," stated Robert mildly.

"Then the title and land should go to Michael."

"Will is next in line."

"We are in accord," replied Will. "We had hoped with Michael and Annie in good hands we could start anew somewhere else. But now I can see why you'd prefer to wash your hands of us all." Robert frowned at the two morose faces, knowing if he had a shred of sanity he would indeed relinquish the responsibility and escape while he still could.

"And waste all that money I spent on your commissions?" he remarked dryly.

"You'll still take care of Michael and Annie?" exclaimed Duncan incredulously.

"You are meant to join your regiment next month," Robert informed them.

"But what of the rose garden? What if the maid comes back?" worried Will.

"Stop!" shouted Robert. "Unless you want to change my mind?"

"We just don't want you to regret your decision," replied Duncan.

"There's no help for it now. I'm already legal guardian to all four of you Gunn children, so there's no way I can wriggle out of it," their uncle confessed cheerfully, feeling relaxed and happy thanks to the generous amount of spirits he had consumed. "There is one thing you two can do for me before we all leave for London," he added thoughtfully.

"What's that?" they asked eagerly, their young faces open and shining for the first time since he had met them.

"Remove the evidence from the rose garden just in case the maid does return. By the way, what is the greedy woman's name?"

"Maude Potter."

The month passed quickly and pleasantly in a flurry of activity and soon it was time for the twins to depart for London with their Uncle Robert.

"Be warned, urchin," laughed Robert, hugging Annie and then standing back to assess her bare feet and boy's garb. "You'd best make the most of the next week because I shall be returning with a governess, and that means proper clothing, schooling, and residence in your new bedchamber as befits a well-bred young miss."

After tearfully hugging her twin brothers, Annie, perched on Dubh's high back, rode after the carriage, waving and shouting most inelegantly. She accompanied them to the busy thoroughfare that headed due south across the border to England before cantering across the moorland on her way home to Kenlaren.

It was a beautiful autumn day with the sun shining brightly on the collage of vibrant orange, yellow, and red leaves. Annie sighed, a tinge of sadness disturbing her golden excitement. She felt like the day, she mused, glowing with warm colors but with a hint of sharp frost. She slowed Dubh's fast pace to a walk as she brooded over her uncle's departing words. Soon nothing would be the same. Already there were such changes; the house and grounds were immaculate and well-staffed with maids, butlers, footmen, gardeners, and farm hands. Michael had changed so much it was hard to even like him, she thought sadly. His tutor had arrived two weeks before and Annie had felt a door firmly shut in her face as her brother and his teacher excitedly pored over musty books and lessons, ignoring her completely, as though she were beneath their notice. At the thought of Michael, Annie snorted with contempt and kicked the stallion back into his bruising gait. Michael in his well-tailored, expensive attire living in the formal part of the house and pompously ringing for his valet or a maid, unable to lift a finger to help himself—the picture made her seethe disgustedly.

Annie still hung on to her small room above the kitchen. Sometimes when no one was about she crept into her new bedchamber, curling her dusty bare toes into the plush carpet and staring about in awe at the lush, pretty furnishings. She would peer hesitantly into the forbidding-looking wardrobe in the adjacent dressing room and her heart would pound with fear at the long line of gowns and shoes. She'd quickly slam the door and lean back against it, convinced if she appeared in any of the beautiful clothes everyone would fall flat on their faces with hysterical laughter at the ridiculous sight of her.

As Annie neared Kenlaren she slowed Dubh's pace, loath to return home now that her twin brothers and uncle had gone. Except for Mrs. Wilson, she now lived in a house full of strangers—maids and manservants who called her "Miss Oriana" as if she were one hundred years old. She leaned forward and wrapped her thin brown arms about the stallion's muscular neck.

"It's just you, me, and Mrs. Wilson now," she whispered into the pricked ebony ears, and Dubh whinnied softly. There was such affinity between the young horse and the little girl, it was as if they had been companions for a lifetime instead of the brief few months since she had stolen him from Lochiel Montgomery. It *had* only been a few months, she realized, shaking her unruly head with disbelief. So very much had happened. So very much had changed and so very much was never going to be the same again, she mused mornfully.

She sat astride the enormous black horse, her lithe legs in ragged trews dangling as she stared down at the rolling lawns and formal gardens of Kenlaren.

"Will I ever learn to be a graceful, well-bred young lady?" she whispered doubtfully before giving a loud war cry and galloping wildly, scattering ducks, geese, and chickens as she went. Mrs. Wilson chuckled as she watched the rebellious imp charge into the stableyard.

"Och, none shall ever break my wee-an's braw spirit!" she resolved.

PART TWO

The clove-foot satyrs singing
Made music to the fauns a-dancing,
And both together with an emphasis
Sang Oriana's praises,
Whilst the adjoining woods with melody
Did entertain their sweet, sweet harmony.

—BEN JONSON

Chapter 8

The following years raced by, spinning Robert's head, as it seemed every three months or so some calamity occurred, making it necessary to advertise for a new governess and send Wilkes post haste to Kenlaren. By the time she had reached sixteen years, Oriana Rebecca Gunn had the doubtful distinction of possibly having disposed of more governesses than any other female in Scottish or English history.

"Twenty-three!" Robert exclaimed, clapping a hand to his aching head. He had just returned to London from Forsythe Castle, where his visit had exceeded the bounds of filial duty as his mother and sisters had pecked and carped, trying to bully him into marrying and producing a legitimate heir. At thirty-two Robert had not the slightest intention of marrying just to please his mother, especially considering the sort of pious lambs she paraded before him. He shuddered now at the thought of marrying any of those boring, vacuous women. "Wilkes? Wilkes?" he roared, and when the immaculate little man entered he could do nothing but impotently wave the letter and repeat inarticulately, "Twenty-three! By Jove, Wilkes can you believe it? Twenty-three!"

"Twenty-three what, sir?" asked the valet politely.

"Governesses! Governesses, Wilkes," groaned Robert, burying his aching head in his hands.

"Miss Oriana, sir?"

"Don't be a blithering idiot, Wilkes! Who else but?" he shouted. "Place another advertisement and ride north to see exactly what the brat has done now."

"May I be as bold as to suggest that *you* drop in on Miss Oriana, sir," blurted Wilkes bravely.

"I beg your pardon!" Robert was appalled at his usually very correct and deferential manservant.

"You haven't seen your ward for more than a year, sir."

"It may have escaped your notice, Wilkes, but I have been deuced busy since my father's unfortunate demise," returned Robert cuttingly. "I do not have time to gallop off to Scotland every few months for an undisciplined child!"

"She is not exactly a child anymore," informed Wilkes.

"How old is she?" He frowned, closing his eyes and picturing a small tousled minx astride an enormous black stallion.

"Sixteen, seventeen in May, sir."

"By Jove! Where on earth does the time go, Wilkes?"

"Might I suggest a companion for Miss Oriana instead of a governess, sir?"

"Where on earth am I to find a companion?" lamented Robert. "Especially one who'll not object to being buried alive in the wilds of Scotland with a small barbarian."

"There is Miss Montgomery, sir," suggested Wilkes, a hint of triumph softening his very precise tones although his face betrayed nothing but his usual deference.

"Miss Montgomery? Miss Montgomery?" puzzled Robert. "You can't mean Iona Montgomery, Falconhurst's sister?"

"The very one, sir!" chirped Wilkes.

"Lochiel Montgomery's sister?" postulated Robert, staring at his diminutive servant in disbelief. "Iona Montgomery," he mused with a grin, leaning back in his chair, placing his fingertips together and closing his eyes. "Iona Montgomery," he repeated with a tender smile as a tall, dark, dignified woman filled his thoughts. "What makes you think that Iona Montgomery would stoop to the lowly position of governess or paid companion?" he laughed, finding the picture incongruous.

"Because she has already," returned Wilkes smugly.

"Where on God's earth did you hear such poppycock?"

"Gossip, sir," replied Wilkes with alacrity.

"Gossip!" Robert raised his blond eyebrows. "Whose gossip?" he inquired, testing the reliability of the source.

"Your sisters, sir!" replied Wilkes a trifle gleefully.

"My sisters!" roared Robert.

"Your sisters were discussing Miss Montgomery's . . . er . . . circumstances."

"Which must be severely reduced or my pious sisters would not find them the least interesting," remarked the young lord dryly. "Wilkes, why is it females seem to thrive on each other's misfortunes?"

"It would seem it is not just females," returned Wilkes. "Ross Montgomery is thriving on the misfortune of his cousin, to hear your sisters tell it."

"Wilkes, were you listening at keyholes?" chastised Robert with a glint in his eye.

"There was no necessity for that, sir; your sisters' voices carry admirably."

"Terrible, isn't it? They can pierce the five-foot-thick stone walls of Forsythe Castle!" He winced at the thought. "Well, Wilkes, relate the malicious gossip to me. I am sure my dear sisters were tickled pink by Miss Iona Montgomery's desperate straits?"

"Quite so, sir," agreed Wilkes. "To hear you sisters talk, sir, it would seem that the young lady in question is now little more than a maid in her Cousin Ross Montgomery's household."

"I never could abide that pompous blowhard Ross Montgomery. It was downright indecent the haste with which he took over Lochiel's title and lands before news of the shipwreck had barely reached shore," snorted Robert. "What do you remember of Iona Montgomery?" he added with a grin, looking at his shrewd valet.

"She didn't waste words," recalled Wilkes approvingly, thinking of the tall, graceful beauty who stood out amongst the frilly, shallow, chattering brood of debutantes.

"Didn't mince them either," remarked Robert ruefully, thinking of the sharp set-down the dark young woman had dealt him when he had gotten too familiar in a rose garden. "So you think the haughty Iona Montgomery might be amendable to becoming Annie's governess or companion?"

"I could make discreet inquiries, sir."

"Please do so, Wilkes. I find I am quite looking forward to meeting the formidable Miss Montgomery again."

Iona Montgomery felt infinitely less than formidable as she galloped across the moorlands, the traces of angry tears still on her flushed cheeks. The morning had been particularly grueling, with the incessant demands and spiteful criticism of her Cousin Ross's wife, Mary, and their two spoiled and demanding daughters, Allison and Jeannette. Iona rode astride, breathing deeply of the fresh spring air, trying to dispel her bad mood and enjoy her brief freedom, but her rage intensified as she thought of her obese cousin strutting arrogantly about Falconhurst, abusing her brother's lands and title as he cheated and belittled the hardworking tenant farmers.

"Och, Lochiel, you canna be dead or I'd feel it in my heart!" she lamented aloud, thinking of her vibrant older brother. She rode, wishing there were some quiet place she could seek refuge instead of returning to the hated household where her relations tried to bow her head and break her spirit by relegating her to the most menial chores and insisting she wear a uniform and eat in the kitchen with the other scullery maids. Iona was delighted with the dining arrangements, much preferring the honest company of hardworking servants to the pompous spite of her posturing cousins.

It had been six months since the dreadful news of her brother's vessel foundering off the South American coast but nearly two years since she had seen him. On that terrible day six months before, she had returned to Falconhurst from an exhilarating ride to find numerous carriages and great confusion as her Cousin Ross Montgomery callously dismissed the entire staff of old trusted retainers, including Roderick MacDonald, her brother's personal friend and servant. She snorted cynically as she remembered striding into the central hall and imperiously demanding to know what the hell was going on, only to be coldly informed that her brother was dead, drowned at sea, and Ross, being the next male in line, was now Lord Falconhurst. As Iona recalled that bitter day, scalding tears of grief and fury spilled down her smooth cheeks. Poor Roderick MacDonald, where might he have gone? He had been with the Montgomery family since before Lochiel was born twenty-nine years before. In fact, the faithful man had served as a batman to their father on foreign battlefields. Then when Lochiel was a baby, their father had refused to follow convention, believing women were responsible for most of the weak men in the world, so he had appointed Roderick MacDonald to be his son's nurse and nanny until the boy was old enough to go to school, at which time the man stepped into the position of valet and close friend and confidant. Where could Roderick be, puzzled Iona, trying to remember if the man had ever taken a holiday or spoken of relatives. She shook her head with despair unable to recall a time when Mr. MacDonald had been anywhere except in the company of her brother. Since all the servants at Falconhurst had been replaced by Ross, asking any of them if they knew the whereabouts of Roderick MacDonald would be useless.

Poor Falconhurst, she sighed, thinking of the stately rooms that had been tastelessly redecorated with insipid pastel colors to better frame the anemic pink and white plump girls, Allison and Jeannette. Iona shook her ebony curls and dug in her heels as her fury surged. There wasn't one corner of the handsome family mansion that hadn't been defiled by her fat, greedy cousin, she seethed, thinking of the badly painted portrait that hung in the gallery next to her brother's. Each morning she arose expecting Lochiel's likeness to be destroyed or relegated to a dusty attic because Ross's unattractive corpulence next to her brother's dashing litheness was definitely unflattering.

"Miss Montgomery?" hailed a strange voice. Iona pulled on the reins, halting her horse as an immaculate little man with a monocle stepped down from the black carriage which bore an unfamiliar coat of arms.

Wilkes felt at a decided disadvantage craning his neck to address the tall woman, who was mounted improperly astride the large horse.

"Miss Iona Montgomery?"

"I am Iona Montgomery," she replied shortly, and Wilkes noted the husky timbre of her voice.

"Miss Montgomery, I am in the employ of Sir Robert Forsythe." Iona felt a shock sear through her at the mention of the young peer's name. She recalled their last encounter and sighed as she realized it seemed a lifetime ago in more ways than one. Then she had been little more than a child, carefree and infatuated with the blond aristocrat. Her hand tingled as she remembered the stinging slap she had delivered to his indolent face after he had the effrontery to capture her lips with his. It's been seven years, she mused sadly, feeling burdened by the loneliness of her spinster status and her nearly twenty-five years.

"I inquired for you at Falconhurst, but I am afraid I was not received very hospitably," Wilkes understated tactfully, as his reception had been decidedly rude. "So hearing from the gatekeeper that you were out for a breath of fresh air, I thought to intercept you."

"Why?" snapped Iona curtly.

"Sir Robert thinks he might be in a position to help you," responded Wilkes, choosing to be as blunt as she. "And you to aid him."

"With what?"

"His ward," replied Wilkes, admiring her directness.

"Och, I see news of my straightened circumstances has traveled like wildfire to the parlors and gaming clubs of London! Well, contrary to what my Cousin Ross Montgomery thinks, I do not empty chamber pots, nor do I play nursemaid or pincushion to spiteful spoiled girls," she stated, remembering the pious and judgmental Forsythe women and making no effort to politely suppress a shudder. "So I suggest you enlighten Sir Robert Forsythe and his brood of sisters with that pertinent fact," she added, preparing to resume her ride.

"Miss Montgomery, you have my heartfelt sympathy for the loss of your brother and for having to live off the charity of your uncharitable cousins," strove Wilkes. "But I may be in a position to be of assistance."

"Continue," she said brusquely after a long pause, staring down at the little man speculatively.

"If you are content with your present living arrangements, I shall take up no more of your time," informed Wilkes shrewdly. Iona looked at him sharply, expecting to see impishness, but he stared back blandly. She dismounted thoughtfully, unaware of Wilkes's assessment as he nodded approval of her long elegance and aristocratic bone structure. He estimated Iona Montgomery to be in her mid-twenties, an old maid by many standards but to his practiced eye a beautiful, well-bred woman in her prime. Just the mate he would select for his young master, Sir Robert Forsythe. Iona silently stared back at the tiny man, wondering what was going on behind the placidly polite countenance.

"If Sir Robert's ward is the offspring of one of his appallingly pious sisters, I think I am probably better off where I am," she stated forthrightly. Wilkes smothered a smile as he acknowledged to himself that she was probably right.

"Sir Robert's ward is a very spirited young Scottish lady," replied Wilkes, thinking it better not to apprise Iona of Oriana's parentage, but hoping to appeal to her patriotism.

"Allison and Jeannette Montgomery are also young Scottish ladies," remarked Iona dully, thinking of the plump girls with their acid tongues and insatiable desire for sweets.

"I should like you to meet Sir Robert's ward and make up your own mind," suggested the neat little man. "If you then consider your present position more to your taste I shall accompany you on your return."

"But I am expected back at Falconhurst within the hour," confessed Iona reluctantly, hating to admit to being so bound. "Nay!" she suddenly shouted. "What on earth have I got to lose?"

"I beg your pardon?"

"Take me there right now," Iona sang out, but at Wilkes's slight pause as he successfully hid his triumphant smile, her face lost its hopeful shine. "Is that possible?"

"Kenlaren is this side of Dumfries near the Solway

Firth—quite a long ride," replies Wilkes. "If I might be permitted to make a suggestion?"

"Of course."

"Tomorrow will be time enough, after you are well rested and have thought it through. You'll be able to pack a few needed items. . . ."

"Where is Sir Robert now?" Iona asked, scattering Wilkes's carefully chosen words.

"In London."

"He doesna live with his ward?"

"No, she lives in a charming old manor with an old cook and several servants."

"How old is she?" probed Iona relentlessly, hope beginning to gleam through the gray despondency of the previous six months.

"Sixteen." Wilkes felt extreme satisfaction at a job well done as he recognized Iona's intense interest.

"Sounds like a lonely life for a spirited sixteen-year-old girl."

"Miss Oriana is not a very conventional young lady."

"She isn't . . . er . . . um . . . you know?" asked Iona, twirling a finger near her temple to indicate mental instability.

"On the contrary," reassured the little man.

"Let's go now," resolved Iona, not wanting to set sights on or hear the demanding voices of the Ross Montgomerys ever again.

"Surely you need toiletries and a change of clothes," suggested the ever-practical valet.

"If I set foot in Falconhurst they'll not let me out. Today was my three hours off," she struggled to explain, suddenly feeling very close to the immaculate little man.

"Three hours off?" inquired Wilkes politely, not quite understanding.

"Each week I get only three hours to be by myself, to go to the village, to ride . . ." Iona's husky voice got huskier as she fought to control herself. It had been over six months since she had had a conversation with anybody who looked on her with a kindly eye. "I'm sorry," she sniffed, pulling herself together. "If I go back, I shan't be able to leave except in my uniform," she added after clearing her throat and striving to sound adult.

"Uniform?" echoed Wilkes, allowing his dismay to show in his tone but not on his face. Iona nodded. "Maid's uniform?" He gasped and again Iona nodded, her dark eyes standing out in her pale face, which was haloed by her black glossy hair. "My goodness, 'tis even worse than I heard tell," he thought aloud, forgetting his very correctness.

"I'm sure I'm the source of great amusement in the very best circles," sighed Iona bitterly. "Oh, well, it probably serves me right. Everyone said I should have married long ago, buttoned my lips, and stooped so I didn't appear so tall," she confessed candidly. "Oh! I hope you are not self-conscious about your size?" she asked, and whether she realized it or not she was rewarded with one of the very few expressions that ever crossed the little man's face, as he beamed at her.

"I am quite aware of and comfortable with my size," he reassured her with a decided twinkle in his eye. "So, you are positive you want to set forth immediately?" Iona nodded emphatically. "Then mount up, unless you would prefer a more decorous journey in this very prim carriage?"

The young woman put her head back and laughed, feeling free and joyous. "I like you and I don't know your name," she gurgled.

"Wilkes."

"Mr. Wilkes, I thank you, and I like you."

"Not Mr. Wilkes, just Wilkes."

"Do you have another name?" she asked.

"Just Wilkes," he replied. "Well, shall we be on our way?"

"Most assuredly, Just-Wilkes," she laughed, mounting her horse in a graceful fluid movement. "Lead on Macduff," she directed, and the little man whipped his tired-looking roan into a decent canter and they were off.

Annie looked at herself critically in the long mirror and sighed as she straightened her mask and wished fervently that she were taller. She shrugged resignedly, knowing there was no way to solve that particular problem other than with the high-heeled Spanish riding boots that she already was wearing. She nodded half-heartedly at her image that seemed to nod mockingly back. She looked like a slight boy dressed all in black with hat, mask, and handkerchief covering her mouth.

"Och, who'd ever take such a wee tobyman seriously?" chuckled a wheezy voice, and a small, bent figure stepped into the framed image beside her. Annie giggled as she looked at herself and Mrs. Wilson.

"Och, who'd ever take such an old witch seriously?" she chuckled in imitation of the old woman. "Dinna scold now," she chided when the old crone opened her toothless mouth to protest. "Just remember, Mrs. Wilson, if just one of your spells and potions had worked I'd not have to play highway man every few months or so!"

"Some worked! Some worked!" hissed Mrs. Wilson. "Remember your prune-faced governesses? Who rid you of them?" she challenged, thinking of the long line of women who had left Kenlaren bent double with agonizing stomach pains.

"I wasna talking of your purges," quipped Annie wickedly.

"I dinna like you going at it alone," fretted the old hag.

"I dinna have a choice unless you're willing to ride wie me," she laughed. "Dinna fash, wie Dubh I shall be fine," she reassured, softening as she saw the old woman wringing her gnarled hands with worry. "I'll nae stop anyone I canna handle, and I'll pick up some help at the roadhouse," she added, broadening her brogue to hide her own trepidations.

"Och, I wish I had had the strength eight years ago to wring that greedy bitch's neck," mourned Mrs. Wilson.

"I wish you had, too, but there's no crying over spilt milk as you've told me many times," teased Annie.

"Och, I love you, my wee witch-wife," croaked the old crone, pulling the slight figure into her stringy arms and kissing Annie's cheeks soundly. "Och, the Prince of Darkness and his redcaps'll watch over you, my dawtie," she sniffed, shuffling from the room and slamming the door behind her.

Annie sat at the open window watching the moonrise,

breathing deeply of the frosty spring night before she quietly tiptoed down the stairs. Without waking any of the staff she made her way out of the house and to the high meadow where Dubh grazed with his mares and colts.

Annie rode at a slow, even pace toward the main road that connected Glasgow to the north with all the thoroughfares that crossed the border to England. At the inn called The Feathered Bonnet she dismounted and swaggered into the noisy public room.

"Well, now, it is Wee Willie, and where have you been hiding yourself?" hailed several voices.

"Here and there and everywhere," responded Annie, ordering a pint of ale and swilling it back in imitation of the bawdy group.

"Still nae grown an inch nor deepened your voice!" sneered a foul-breathed, stout man who looked as though he could snap her in two with one brawny hand.

"Och, but you certainly have," jeered Annie, hiding the terror she felt by jabbing a finger into his rotund belly. A round of merriment greeted her sally and the large man snarled, drunk and boisterous enough to accept any excuse for a brawl. As he pulled back his thick fist to punch the slight black-garbed youth, a dirk whistled through the air and pinned his sleeve to the stained wall of the sleazy roadhouse.

"Who'll ride wie me?" Annie asked. She retrieved her knife at a languidly measured pace that belied the frantic pounding of her heart as the bully slunk away with muttered filthy curses. "I just need one or two men. Even share of the purse," she added when there were no volunteers.

"Aye, what aboot the larst time?" challenged an angry voice, and Annie's belly turned to liquid at the disgruntled mutters that echoed as they gossiped about a botched-up encounter several months prior.

"Aye, Mattie MacAlister was sent to Australia at the Assizes," recounted a tipsy but very accurate voice.

"Och, the futret panicked and couldna even keep his seat," answered Annie scornfully.

"Well, I'll nae ride wie you!"

"Nor me!"

"'Tis your scrawny young neck that'll be stretched on a gibbet, Wee Willie!"

"Och, you yellow-livered cowards! 'Tis no wonder the English rule Scotland!" And with that parting insult she swaggered out of the door and leaped astride her black stallion. "I dinna need any but you," she crooned to Dubh as they galloped toward the busy thoroughfare that bisected Scotland.

At a dark bend in the road where the woods were dense on either side, she waited, able to hear hoofbeats approach from either direction.

"We've done it alone before, Dubh," she said to reassure herself more than the large horse, who stood still and quiet in the darkness as bands of noisy travelers traversed the road. The night passed so slowly that even the patient Dubh stamped his great feet on the thick grass under the trees.

"Does no one travel alone?" despaired Annie, stretching her aching body, knowing it would be unwise to attempt to hold up several people. Then in that very dark time just before dawn, when she was about to return empty-handed to Kenlaren, as there had been no activity at all for nearly an hour, she heard the trundle of light wheels and the sharp staccato of no more than two horses echo down the empty road. She quietly edged the stallion through the trees, knowing that timing was of the essence. There she sat poised, her heart beating triple time, as a black carriage bowled along, followed by a single horseman. Annie hesitated for a split-second, unnerved by the unexpected. She had guessed from the sounds that there was one carriage drawn by two horses, which meant the travelers would be contained within one vehicle. A warning screamed silently in her brain but she brushed it aside and rashly galloped out on to the road, determined that the long, boring wait would not prove fruitless.

"Stand and deliver!" she ordered, her voice muffled by the handkerchief that covered her nose and mouth.

The carriage was halted and the single horseman pranced sideways, causing Annie to back away in order to keep both within firing range. A long silence broken only by her pounding heart ensued as neither traveler made any effort to deliver anything.

"I've no interest in jewelry, just money," she directed

as a small erect figure climbed out of the carriage. Annie frowned and squinted in the darkness; there seemed something very familiar about the stance and presence of the dim figure. "Wrap it in a handkerchief!" she added abruptly, edging Dubh backward and trying to keep both people at bay with her twin dueling pistols. "And hurry," she snapped, her ears straining for sounds of any other travelers as the tiny man very slowly did as he was told. Finally he held out a small white bundle. "Put it down and get back into your carriage!" she demanded. Dubh had picked up her tension and was prancing nervously. "Drive off!" she shouted, firing one of the pistols. The single rider's horse reared and whinnied with fear before galloping off, followed by the light carriage. Annie listened intently before dismounting, picking up the small bundle and returning to scramble back up onto Dubh's high back.

"What goes on there?" bellowed a voice, and Annie quickly directed her horse into the thick woods. She quietly wove her way in and out of the trees, cutting across the countryside back to Kenlaren, deciding not to examine her haul until she was safely in her own room.

Wilkes reined the carriage after half a mile and called out to Iona. "How are you, Miss Montgomery?"

"I am not sure," she returned frankly. "I've always supposed I would be terrified of a highwayman, but he seemed more afraid of us."

"Making him more dangerous," replied Wilkes dryly, frowning at the persistent thought that there had been something very familiar about the lawless youth.

"How much farther do we have to go?" asked Iona, her back aching from the hours in the saddle.

"About five miles, no more," reassured Wilkes. "Would you like to ride in the carriage, Miss Montgomery?"

"No, thank you. I can manage another five miles."

Annie stabled Dubh in the barn, and after pulling off her boots she tiptoed into the house and up to her room. She lit a candle in her window and watched for the sign that Mrs. Wilson had seen she was safely home. She smiled as she saw the old woman's shadow made enormous by the lantern she carried, and she was just about to blow out her candle when she heard the sound of horses and a carriage coming up the driveway crunching the gravel. Mrs. Wilson had obviously heard it also, for Annie saw the lantern slowly bobbing as the old crone made her way to see what was happening. Quickly Annie undressed, hiding her black clothes in the back of her wardrobe before pulling a night-dress over her head and brushing out her long auburn hair. She blew out her candle and opened the door, straining her ears to hear what was going on. She shook her head with irritation, unable to ascertain anything, then, coming to a sudden decision, she donned a wrapper and mussed her thick curls.

In the driveway Iona stared around at the rolling lawn and the graceful manor. The sun was just rising and the dawn chorus swelled. The air was fragrant with blossoms and newly cut grass.

"Who's there?" screeched a shrill voice, and one of the oldest crones she had ever seen hobbled toward them.

"Good morning, Mrs. Wilson," greeted Wilkes, stepping down from the carriage unwrinkled and immaculate despite the long hours of travel.

"Well, now, 'tis the wee mannikin, and what brings you here before cock's crow?" she demanded. "There's none stirring yet to take care of the horses, so ye'll have to do for yourself. Who's that?" she added, peering through the hazy gloom at Iona, who was still sitting wearily upon her horse.

"Miss Iona Montgomery, this is Mrs. Wilson," introduced Wilkes as the young woman stiffly swung herself down.

"Another of them governesses?" crackled the crone, hobbling close to Iona and lifting the lantern to examine her face.

"Well, well, well, she dinna look like a dried-up old virgin," she crackled irreverently.

Annie listened in the hall for a few moments before throwing the front door open and standing on the threshold, yawning and stretching as though she had just been awakened from a deep sleep.

"Mrs. Wilson? What is going on?" she asked sleepily.

"'Tis Wilkes wie another governess, Miss Annie," replied the old woman, hobbling back to the servants' quarters as though no longer interested in the proceedings. "I'll send a lad to take care of the puir animals," she added as she disappeared.

"I am sorry to have awakened you," apologized Wilkes, observing the mutinous set of Annie's mouth as she stared at Iona.

"Is she another governess?" she demanded rudely, looking daggers at the weary young woman.

"No," answered the little man, briskly bowing to Iona and leading the way up the front steps. Annie watched silently, her amber eyes narrowed as she realized whom she had held up scarcely an hour before. She hadn't even looked at how much money she had stolen, she remembered as Wilkes led the tall woman in riding clothes into the small study, where he rang for a maid. Annie followed, her eyes not leaving the elegant dark woman who reminded her of someone. Iona sat thankfully in a comfortable chair and returned Annie's unblinking gaze, assessing her from the top of her auburn head to her small bare feet just as openly.

"I am Oriana Gunn," she stated baldly.

"I am Iona Montgomery."

Annie sat curling her feet under her, waiting for Wilkes to tell her why this Iona Montgomery was at Kenlaren, but neither the little man nor the woman herself offered any explanation. A sleepy-looking maid knocked, entered, and bobbed a curtsy.

"You are Millie, are you not?" asked Wilkes.

"Yes, sir," yawned the freckled maid.

"Please see that a bedchamber is prepared for Miss Montgomery, and a bath drawn as soon as possible," ordered Wilkes efficiently. He was rewarded by a grateful smile from Iona who then closed her eyes and leaned back in her chair, unable to cope with the sharp amber eyes of the beautiful woman-child.

"I'm going back to bed," stated Annie, flouncing out of the room and running up the stairs to her bedchamber, realizing she wasn't going to receive any answers from those two taciturn people, and suddenly full of curiosity about exactly how much money she had stolen that night. Cautiously she slid the bolt to lock her door before entering her dressing room and rummaging through the black clothes she had flung into the back of her wardrobe. She carefully untied the knot and unfolded the snowy linen handkerchief.

"Six crowns," she sighed with great disappointment, knowing it meant she would have to spend another night dressed in the black garb in order to obtain enough money to give to Maude Potter. "Will it ever end?" she whispered aloud as her shoulders sagged with fatigue. For six years she had tried to meet the woman's increasingly greedy demands, first as a mere child of ten and now at nearly seventeen. "It should get easier," she mourned as she lifted a loose floorboard and placed the coins between the joists. "But it only gets harder." She replaced the flooring and covered the spot with a scatter rug before climbing into bed as bright sunlight flooded through the window and the roosters noisely welcomed the morning.

Iona relaxed in the warm scented water. She stretched like a cat and looked about with appreciation at the sunny, pleasant room. The large, comfortable-looking bed beckoned, so she quickly washed off the dust from the long journey and climbed naked under the covers. Several nagging thoughts probed her sleepy mind—what would she wear the following days, since everything she owned was back at Falconhurst? And what was she doing trusting a total stranger no matter how precise and immaculate? And what was she expected to do for the wild-haired, beautiful woman-child who glared at her so hostilely? And why did her heart still pound excitedly when she thought of Sir Robert Forsythe? There were too many thoughts, too many questions for her tired mind, so she thrust them from her and snuggled down in the cozy bed, feeling more relaxed and less lonely than she had since the news of her brother's death.

Chapter 9

The late afternoon sun bathed the room in a warm glow of red and orange when Iona finally opened her eyes. She blinked, wondering what had awakened her, when a sharp knocking cut through the lazy stillness. Before she had time to respond, the door was thrust rudely open and she quickly tugged the eiderdown about her shoulders to cover her nakedness. Annie, dressed in boy's clothing, entered the room and stood silently staring at her.

"Good day, Oriana," she greeted, her husky voice sounding deeper as she ignored the girl's very truculent expression. "Och, what a very good idea!" she exclaimed. "Do you think you could manage to find some of those very sensible clothes for me?" Annie's golden head cocked to one side warily.

"Why?" she demanded sharply, suspecting a trick. She had hoped to shock the tall dark governess and was not at all prepared for the reaction she was receiving.

"Well, I find myself in a devilishly awkward predicament," confessed Iona.

"How?"

"How? It is not how, but what. You see, I haven't a stitch to wear except that very unattractive, travel-stained habit I arrived in yesterday."

"Why?" barked Annie unsympathetically.

"I had to leave the place where I was in rather a

hurry," explained Iona, liking the girl despite her rebellious attitude and wanting her trust.

"Why?"

"It is a long story," replied Iona softly with such a sadness that Annie felt ashamed.

"I'll see what I can find," she said brusquely before quitting the room. She was back within a few minutes with a dressing gown. "At least you can get out of bed now," she said mischievously before disappearing again. Five minutes later Annie reentered, laden down with an odd assortment of male apparel. "You're very lucky that I have three brothers, all wie long legs. You are very tall for a female," she said in a forthright manner. "But not as tall as my brothers, so maybe the legs will be too long. I would like to be taller," she chattered, staring in the mirror at her barely five feet one inch with disgust. "'Tis near tea time," she said casually over her shoulder as she walked to the door. "You missed breakfast and luncheon." The door slammed behind her and Iona grinned, convinced she would get along with the unorthodox young lady, as she climbed into a pair of Michael's trews.

After a very filling high tea of hearty farm fare, including new laid eggs, fresh clotted cream with raspberries, and drop scones, Iona and Annie walked out into the crisp evening.

"Your horse is in the high meadow wie my Dubh," informed Annie.

"Dubh?" repeated Iona, feeling a flood of sadness. "That is what my brother called his horse."

"Just means black," shrugged Annie, puzzled at the sorrow that emanated from the older woman. "Why are you sad?" she asked directly as they came to the gate of the high meadow and she gazed at the horses silhouetted against the setting sun. Iona silently shook her head, unable to speak for a few moments. "Wait until you see my Dubh," said Annie proudly before giving a piercing whistle. Iona gasped when the enormous stallion galloped swiftly to his young mistress and stood before her, majestically pawing the ground and tossing his great handsome head.

"'Tis Dubh," she whispered hoarsely before turning to

Annie, her dark eyes standing out in the sudden pallor of her face.

"What is it?" asked Annie, as Iona stared accusingly.

"It was you!"

"What was me?" puzzled the girl.

"No, it couldna hae been," cried Iona, putting a hand to her whirling brain and her accent slipping into a brogue.

"Wha' couldna hae been?" imitated Annie, unnerved by the dark woman and feeling a clutch of fear, which she strove to hide.

"My brother had such a stallion with which he hoped to sire a mighty strain, but when the horse was about two years and a half, he was stolen by a wee child," related Iona. "Roderick was sure it was one of the fairy folk that stole Dubh, as the horse would not let any but Lochiel touch him, let alone mount and ride."

"Did the horse mean so much that still you cry?" asked Annie in a very small voice when she saw the tears well. Ion turned away to compose herself, and Annie watched her glossy black head shake vehemently. At last she realized why the woman looked so familiar.

"My brother's dead!" Iona said when she was sufficiently composed.

"No!" shouted Annie savagely. "He's not dead!" Iona looked at her in amazement.

"Why do you say that?" she whispered.

"I would know if he were! Dubh would know too!" stated Annie without thought.

"What are you saying?" exclaimed Iona. Annie looked at her and shook her auburn head with confusion.

"Nothing!" she shouted, leaping onto the stone wall and mounting the stallion.

Annie raced across the meadow and Dubh took the wall easily, rising gracefully into the air. Iona marveled at the fluid movements of both horse and rider, knowing that soon she would have some answers. She walked slowly back to the manor, hoping Wilkes was about and not busy.

Annie was only conscious of the wind in her ears and the pounding of her heart, not realizing where she was headed. She reined Dubh on the beach where she had first met Lochiel Montgomery more than seven years before.

When had he first filled her dreams, she wondered as great heaving sobs wracked her body. She lay with her thin arms embracing Dubh's muscular neck as her tears dampened his thick black mane so like the hair of the man she remembered. Lochiel Montgomery's memory had lain dormant in her child's mind, while it was not ready to receive romantic dreams, until her body had rounded to womanhood, and then she had remembered and hoped that one day she would race neck in neck with him again across the sand by the sea. Now she kicked her bare heels into Dubh's hard girth, thinking of the healthy black colts and fillies the proud stallion had sired. Would they give Iona consolation, she wondered, knowing they gave her none.

"Annie Gunn, you're a fool!" she screamed to the gulls before wiping her wet face and sniffly nose in very unladylike fashion on her sleeve. "How can you think yourself in love wie a man you met once when you were nine years old?" she wailed, her voice blending with the wheeling birds' cries and her tear-filled eyes straying to the sheer sharp cliff that had cut her so cruelly when she had tried to escape from the dark man. She looked to the palm of her right hand at the only scar that remained, and there joining her heart and life lines was another line making a very definite *M*. "*M* for Montgomery," she whispered. "Lochiel Montgomery." For so long his lean brown face under the glossy black hair had filled her romantic dreams. "You canna be dead. You canna!" she keened.

"When did Annie get the stallion Dubh?" asked Iona.

"The first time I laid eyes on Miss Oriana she was riding that enormous horse, and that was about seven years ago," answered Wilkes.

"Do you know where she got him?"

"No," replied the little man cautiously.

"Such an incredible coincidence. It canna be true, but it is," muttered Iona, pacing about the library looking very graceful and feminine despite the male clothing. She shook her dark head in disbelief, her nerves and thoughts jangled as though she had been whirled about and set down on another planet.

"Is anything amiss?" inquired Wilkes politely.

"I don't know." Continuing her long-legged pacing of the elegant room, she looked like a high-strung thoroughbred filly. "Wilkes?" she said suddenly after a long silence, while she had absently fingered the embossed spines of several books.

"Yes, Miss Montgomery?"

"Iona," she corrected him, the formality grating her nerves.

"Miss Iona," acquiesced the valet.

"The black stallion Dubh belonged to my brother Lochiel," she blurted. "And was stolen about seven years ago from my Cousin Ross's estate near Glenwillie, about twenty-five miles from here."

"I see," nodded Wilkes noncommittally. "Horse stealing is a very serious charge," he added after a brittle pause.

"Oh, no, you dinna understand. Please, I am not speaking of pressing charges or making accusations. It's just such an incredible coincidence . . . so painful . . . so eerie!" She stopped, unable to speak as tears welled and her throat was choked with emotion. "As you are aware . . . my brother is dead and . . . I miss him very much. We were very close . . . he was all I had in the way of family since our parents died. . . . Och, there're the Ross Montgomerys, but I'd sooner be kin to a rat!" she shouted brokenly.

"Handkerchief, Miss Iona?" proffered Wilkes, seeing the distraught young woman frantically search in the pockets of her borrowed raiment.

"Thank you," sniffed Iona before roughly blowing her nose trying to control herself. "It was just such a shock seeing Dubh again . . . it was as though there was suddenly a link and Loch would come striding across the field to mount him. He had such plans for that stallion. As you know, he had several stables. . . ." She chattered as the tears continued to pour.

"Your brother's stables were internationally known and admired," soothed Wilkes, pouring a small glass of sherry for the sobbing woman, who stared blearily out of the window trying desperately to collect herself.

"He was a fine horse breeder," sobbed Iona, unable to stem her grief. "He dinna have to make that voyage . . . he did it for the yearlings he was taking to America . . . he wanted to be sure they survived the trip. Thank you," she sniffed, accepting the delicate cut crystal glass. "I'm so sorry," she apologized as she broke into another storm of tears.

"I quite understand," comforted Wilkes. "It is a very strange coincidence indeed."

"Aye, so very, very strange and so very, very painful," whispered Iona. "Well, I feel better," she admitted after taking a deep breath and draining the glass. She turned to face him and gave a brave, watery grin.

"And what do you think of Miss Oriana Rebecca Gunn?" asked the tiny man after a tactful pause that he filled by pouring some more sherry into her empty glass.

"The littlest horse thief?" gurgled Iona damply. Wilkes inclined his head and refused to commit himself. "Och, I dinna ken what to make of her," she added soberly.

"I believe I apprised you of the unconventionality of her nature," returned the dapper little man. He had already decided he'd be wise not to inform her of his suspicions as to the identity of the previous night's highwayman.

"What would be my position in regard to Oriana?"

"A companion who will be able to guide her toward her debut next year," replied Wilkes, choosing his words very carefully.

"Definitely not a governess," laughed Iona, sensing the aversion Annie had for that noble profession. "Guide her toward her debut?" she repeated, shuddering at the remembrance of her own entry into society. She had felt like a lamb being led to the slaughter. Ogled, eyed, and occasionally pinched by prospective purchasers who were more interested in her dowry from her brother's lucrative stables and her pedigree than her taller-than-fashionable form and more-intelligent-than-fashionable mind. She shook her head now at the thought of the wild auburn-haired hellion behaving with the necessary decorum. "That is a very tall order," she stated finally.

"Maybe you should wait until you are better acquainted with Miss Oriana and Kenlaren before you make a commitment," suggested Wilkes, and Iona nodded in agreement, not wanting to return to Falconhurst and the Ross Montgomerys.

"Wilkes, would you by any chance know a gentleman's gentleman by the name of Roderick MacDonald?" asked Iona. "He was with my family for many many years."

"I can make discreet enquiries, if you wish?"

"Oh, I should be so grateful. He really is family and my cousin turned him out after my brother . . . died, and it was like losing another dear family member," she explained, trying not to burst into another torrent of tears.

"What family member?" asked Annie rudely as she abruptly entered the room, her face closed and angry. Iona looked sharply at her, noting that the amber eyes seemed slightly red and swollen, as though the girl had also been crying, but her exquisite little face glared mutinously, allowing no room for a kind word, so Iona purposefully refused to answer. She turned back to Wilkes.

"I am so very grateful to you," she said in her low, husky voice.

"If there is anything else you need, please inform me," he said softly and she gave him a warm smile as he bowed and left the room. Annie snorted and fumed, knowing that she had been deftly put in her place like a rude child.

"I stole your brother's horse!" she stated, hoping to shock.

"I know," answered Iona softly, striking fear in Annie's heart.

"You canna have him back!" shouted Annie vehemently, her eyes brimming with tears at the thought of losing her only true friend.

"He was never mine, so I canna take him back," returned Iona. "But maybe now you can feel the way my brother felt at losing him," she said firmly before walking out of the room.

For the next few days Annie watched Iona from a distance, puzzled that the woman didn't seek her out and try to curry friendship as the other governesses had done. She frowned with disapproval at Mrs. Wilson's obvious liking for the quiet dark woman, who had no objection to rolling up her sleeves and pitching in with whatever work had to be done. Wilkes nodded with satisfaction at Iona's tactics as he observed Annie's bewilderment. The child was used to controlling, and Iona Montgomery couldn't be controlled. Wilkes was eager to return to London and Sir Robert, but he bided his time, waiting for a commitment from Iona.

Iona was determined that the rebellious girl should approach her first, so she spent her days getting to know the people and the land. Kenlaren was a beautiful spot, she decided, feeling at ease as she had once at Falconhurst before her Cousin Ross took it over. The evenings she spent talking to Wilkes and Mrs. Wilson and sewing a gown for herself with some material the old cook had found in the attic. Annie brooded sulkily, feeling left out and ignored. She stared with disgust at Mrs. Wilson when the woman carefully pinned up the hem of the burgundy dress as Iona stood on the kitchen table.

"Those used to be curtains," she said disparagingly.

"I know," returned Iona cheerfully. Mrs. Wilson couldn't speak, as her mouth was full of pins, so she just gave the girl an angry shake of her old head. Annie curled in a chair and watched the domestic scene. None of the other governesses had ever set foot in the kitchen or any part of the service area of the manor. Mrs. Wilson hadn't been able to tolerate those women any more than Annie had. Why was Iona Montgomery so different, she wondered, wishing the woman would leave so she could talk to Mrs. Wilson. The end of May was fast approaching and she had to have more money. She had sold three of Dubh's colts and it had broken her heart; she was determined not to sell any more. Maybe she should kill the greedy woman, she mused.

"What's that long, mopey face?" croaked Mrs. Wilson, spitting out the last of the pins. Annie looked up with a start at the two worried faces. Iona was standing on the table with her hands on her hips, frowning down at her. Annie shrugged, got up, and slammed out of the kitchen.

"She's a strange child," observed Iona.

"Aye, but a charmed one. A wild, strange, *charmed* child," stressed Mrs. Wilson. "Aye, she better be charmed," she sighed.

"Why?" probed Iona, catching a quiver of fear in the old woman's voice.

"'Tain't my business to say," retorted Mrs. Wilson,

wanting to trust the tall, dark Miss Montgomery. "Just keep yer ears and eyes open."

"My ears and eyes open?" repeated Iona, mystified.

"Och, dinna listen to the ramblings of an old witch," clucked the crone. "Yer hem is nice and straight. Mind you, dinna prick yerself on the pins when you take it off . . . could be you'd sleep for a hundred years," she crackled, turning away and busying herself at the stove.

"Thank you, Mrs. Wilson," Iona said, but the old woman just nodded and waved her away with an impatient flap of her gnarled hand.

Iona sat in her room hemming the velvet gown and brooding over Mrs. Wilson's oblique references. On an impulse she put aside her sewing and made her way to Annie's room. She knocked lightly on the door and heard a furtive scrambling but no answer. Iona frowned and knocked again. The door was wrenched open and she stared into Annie's belligerent face, which still bore the traces of tears. Without a second thought Iona pulled the smaller, younger girl into her arms. She felt Annie stiffen, so she immediately released her. Annie stepped back and something dropped heavily to the floor. Iona froze as she stared down at the gun. She looked inquiringly back to the tear-stained face, which hardened.

"'Tis not loaded," stated Annie huskily, bending to pick up the weapon.

"May I see?" asked Iona, holding out her hand. There was a moment's pause and then grudgingly Annie complied.

"Nice. Well-balanced," remarked Iona, handing it back.

"Have you ever wanted to kill someone?" whispered Annie. Iona's face registered shock before she nodded silently.

"Who did you want to kill?" asked Annie.

"My Cousin Ross and his whole family."

"I think I met him. He's fat? Has a horrible daughter?"

"Two of them," laughed Iona. "When did you meet him?"

"When I took Dubh," replied Annie, sitting on the wide window seat. Iona sat beside her and they both stared out at the peaceful moonlit night. "Why do you have to work here and make gowns out of old curtains?" asked Annie directly.

"Because I choose to, sooner than live with the fat cousin with the two horrible daughters," returned Iona lightly.

"I think I would too. How did your brother die?"

"A shipwreck," said the dark woman quietly.

"I'm sorry about Dubh," whispered Annie, her voice breaking with emotion.

"In a way it was for the best," replied Iona, her dark eyes also filling with tears. "Ross would have had Dubh destroyed or sold when he took over Falconhurst. Anything that showed dislike of his boorish ways—that he couldn't whip into shape—was destroyed or dismissed," she stormed. Annie tentatively reached out to comfort Iona, who squeezed her hand reassuringly. "So you see, it was a good thing Dubh was with you," she said, smiling through her tears.

"Thank you," sniffed Annie, and both of them burst into tears and hugged each other.

"Now, Annie Gunn, who is it you'd like to shoot?" asked Iona after blowing her nose loudly.

"Just someone," avoided the girl. "Iona, do you need money?" she blurted out.

"Go on," encouraged the older woman, intrigued by the sudden change of topic.

"Well, it seems to me that Ross Montgomery needs a lesson taught to him and surely there is plenty of money for all of you and really it should belong to you as you're Lochiel's sister and . . . well? What do you think?"

"Whoa, I canna make head or tail when you string all of it together," laughed Iona.

"Let's rob him!" proposed Annie triumphantly.

"What?" exclaimed Iona.

"Och, I finally shocked you!"

"Rob him?"

"Why not?" probed Annie. "The mucker robbed you!"

"Not in the eyes of the law," protested Iona.

"Morally, he certainly did!" returned the fiesty girl and noting Iona's raised eyebrows she added cheekily, "Oh, you dinna think I knew anything of morals, did you?"

"You are so right," laughed Iona delightedly, enjoying Annie's quick intelligence. "How do you propose we go about this venture?"

"Highway robbery!" pronounced Annie with relish.

"That was you!" declared Iona. Annie froze, turning an alarming shade. "Oh, Annie Gunn, how can you steal from those who love you?"

"Wilkes? Love me?" laughed Annie awkwardly.

"You know he does, in his inscrutable way."

"I dinna know 'twas him until it was done. I put the crowns back in his drawer," confessed Annie.

"Annie, you take my breath away. 'Tis dangerous! You could get yourself killed! Why? For heaven's sake, why?"

"For the money. I need the money."

"Doesn't Sir Robert, your guardian, give you pin money?" asked Annie.

"Dinna tell Uncle Robert! He gives me money and takes care of Michael and me."

"Annie, why do you need more money?"

"Because I canna sell any more of Dubh's colts until they're older and even then I dinna want to. . . ."

"Dubh's colts!" exclaimed Iona.

"Aye, you've not seen them? I keep them in one of the far pastures. I had hoped to gie them to your brother one day in return for Dubh."

"But you've not told me why you need money."

"You maun promise never to tell. 'Tis a matter of life and death!" stated Annie urgently. "Promise!"

"I promise."

"'Tis to buy a silence."

"Buy a silence?" ejaculated Iona. Annie nodded. "What does that mean?"

"There is a woman who knows things that can harm my mother and brothers. If those things were known it would . . ." Annie found it impossible to continue.

"Can't you tell your guardian, Sir Robert?" asked Iona.

"No! If he knew, it would mean the end of everything—Michael's education, Duncan and Will's commissions. Och, I've heard about my Grandmother Forsythe and all my holy aunts. They wouldna even acknowledge me and my brothers. My mother Rebecca . . ."

"Rebecca! Your mother is the infamous Rebecca?" exclaimed Iona, familiar with the scandal that had rocked the English aristocracy. "Och, I am sorry, Annie, I dinna mean to malign your mother. I understand she lives in seclusion in one of the towers of Forsythe Castle."

"I dinna ken where she is. I never really knew her," replied Annie candidly. "She went away when I was barely nine."

"So there is a woman blackmailing you? Asking for money or she will spread some slanderous tales about your mother and brothers?"

"Aye."

"How do you know the tales are true?"

"Even if they're not, I canna take the chance, but I think there is some truth in them. . . . I feel it clawing in my belly almost as though somewhere inside of me I know," groaned Annie.

"What could be so terrible?" probed Iona, her curiosity peaked.

"I canna tell you, but you maun never say a word. You promised, remember," she pleaded urgently.

"I'll not say a word unless you say I can," reassured Iona, giving the tense, pale girl a loving hug. "Thank you for trusting me. I sorely needed a friend, and, Annie Gunn, I think we're going to be very good friends. You know, it has been so long since I had a close friend."

"I have Dubh and Mrs. Wilson."

"And Wilkes," added Iona.

"*And* Wilkes and Uncle Robert."

"Do Mrs. Wilson and Wilkes know about the secret?"

"Just Mrs. Wilson. She tried a few spells to strike down the greedy bitch, but none worked. Perhaps she's too old," sighed Annie. "You know, Iona, you are as alone as I am," she observed. "Maybe everyone is really alone."

"Maybe," replied Iona, thinking how lucky she was to have met this unpredictable, wild girl who was turning out to be not only a highwayman but a philosopher.

Many hours later Iona lay in her comfortable bed unable to sleep, as the encounter with Annie churned in her head. She smiled in the darkness, remembering how her brother had ranted and raved about the auburn-haired brat seven long years before. She had been barely eighteen and in London making the rounds of the balls and soirées as she was introduced to society, grudgingly presented by her Cousin Ross's wife. Now here she was all these years later feeling much love and affection for the golden rebel who had stolen one of her brother's prize possessions.

"Och, Lochiel, I wish you were here to help us both out of a de'il of a schlorich," she whispered into her pillow. Her anger flared and she imagined the wonderful satisfaction she would feel at having Ross Montgomery at her mercy, cowering and begging for leniency at the end of her rapier. "Och, aye," she crowded quietly with delight, knowing she would indeed help Annie rob her greedy fat cousin.

Wilkes bowed over Iona's offered hand before climbing into his prim black carriage, content that the capable, well-bred Miss Montgomery could successfully harness and school the recalcitrant Oriana Rebecca Gunn. The two young females in question waved dutifully before running off to practice their shooting against the dilapidated old outhouse in the orchard, scaring the chickens and causing Mrs. Wilson to cackle happily as she recognized kindred spirits in the tall dark woman and the petite golden girl.

"Aren't they bonny?" breathed Annie later as she leaned over the gate staring proudly at the glossy sons and daughters of Dubh. "These are the two- and three-year-olds," she informed as the spirited black horses rambunctiously played and raced around the verdant meadow.

"Where did you get the mares?"

"Dinna ask," laughed Annie ruefully.

"Why?"

"I dinna think you want to know!"

"Oh, no, they weren't stolen too?" exclaimed Iona.

"Only two of them and that wasna any of my doing. 'Twas done before Uncle Robert came. He gave me Victoria for my tenth birthday. Victoria was a beautiful black mare, a fit mate for Dubh, but she died last year. 'Twas a breached birth. I couldna save her," she said sadly. "Come, let me show you the twins she died giving life to."

Iona smiled softly at the two boisterous colts, who at seven months old had the promised look of their father. The sun glinted on their glossy jet-black coats as they gamboled and played without a care.

"You help wie the birthing?"

"Of course, they're my horses," returned Annie, and then she blushed, remembering who really owned the stallion responsible for siring her stable.

"My brother, Lochiel, would have been happy with Dubh's fruitful lot in life," reassured Iona. "Let's go for a ride," she suggested, wanting to be astride the beautiful black daughter of Dubh that Annie had insisted she accept.

"When do we ride after your wicked cousin?" asked Annie as they mounted the fresh, lively animals.

"Annie?" hailed a young voice.

"Michael!" rejoiced Annie, leaping off Dubh's high back and running toward the slim auburn-haired youth. "Why are you home?" she asked after giving him a hug.

"It is the end of the term." He stared beyond his young sister to the dignified dark woman astride the black mare.

"Och, I'm forgetting my manners. Iona, this is my brother, Michael. He's very toplofty and at the university," she shouted proudly. "Come for a ride wie us, Michael," she urged.

"Right now all I want is a long bath, a good meal, and a comfortable bed. I rode down from Edinburgh without rest. Your stable looks very impressive," he remarked, gazing at the healthy colts that gamboled.

"Aye, it is very impressive," agreed Annie, not believing in humility. "We will see you at supper," she yelled, remounting her stallion and galloping after Iona.

Michael handed his weary horse to an ostler and strode through the kitchen on his way to his suite of rooms.

"Send a maid and some hot water and food to me," he ordered curtly.

"Not so fast, Michael-mine!" admonished Mrs. Wilson, crowing with delight at seeing him. "Where's my kiss, you lummock?" Michael dutifully pecked her leathery old cheek.

"Here, get the dust from your mouth," she crackled,

pouring a mug of cool malt brew for him. Michael thirstily drained the tankard and thumped it down on the table.

"Send Millie to me," he ordered, wiping the foam from his hairless top lip.

"The woman was by again. Annie has to pay her soon," informed Mrs. Wilson cryptically, halting his exit.

"But we paid her at Hogmanay," he protested.

"And Annie has paid her twice since!"

"Where did she get the money?"

"Sold three of her colts and took to the road twice," recounted Mrs. Wilson.

"Will it never end?" cried Michael.

"Maybe not until the greedy bitch is dead!" muttered the old crone, chilling the youth's blood. "Och, said it is that the sins of the mothers be visited and revisited upon the innocent bairns."

Chapter 10

Robert whistled cheerfully as he strode down the front steps of Falconhurst toward the carriage piled high with trunks and hastily packed boxes. He sardonically doffed his hat to Mary Montgomery, who stood fuming at a parlor window, her rage shaking the lace curtain she wrung in her plumb, dimpled hands.

The sun was setting as Wilkes and Roderick MacDonald whipped the horses into a steady gait and the carriage bowled back down the formal driveway, followed by Sir Robert on horseback. Wilkes and Roderick chuckled to themselves as they passed through the tall wrought-iron gates.

"Miss Iona is going to be delighted to have something to wear other than curtains, farmer's smocks, and maid's uniforms," remarked Roderick, appalled by all he had heard of Iona's treatment at the hands of the Ross Montgomerys.

"She is going to be delighted at seeing you, Mr. MacDonald," returned Wilkes formally.

"Just MacDonald, Wilkes," corrected the equally correct gentleman's gentleman. A sharp rapping on the carriage door caused Wilkes to excuse himself and pop his head out of the window to see what his employer wanted.

"Yes, sir?"

"Pull up!" shouted Robert over the clatter of hooves and rumble of wheels. "I heard a shot! I say, look out!" he warned, giving the carriage horses a sharp smack on their rumps with his quirt as a runaway team thundered down the road toward them. Yet another sharp retort cracked the dusky evening.

"It is the Montgomery crest, sir!" informed Roderick as he adeptly guided the team and the runaway phaeton passed, narrowly missing them.

"Wait here!" ordered Robert, riding onto the grassy verge to muffle his hoofbeats and galloping toward the source of the disturbance. He whistled silently at the scene that met his eyes when he rounded the curve of the road. He reined his steed under cover of some thick bushes and stared with interest at the comical sight of Ross Montgomery fuming and cursing with his trousers about his ankles. In front of him stood a small masked youth with a smoking pistol in each hand. Another similarly garbed youth held three beautiful black horses, one of which was a decidedly familiar stallion. Robert's eyes narrowed speculatively as he watched a taller youth stow a pouch—presumably the booty—in a saddle bag.

"Someone's coming," hissed one of the youths as sharp hoofbeats echoed. Lithely the three mounted and were off. Robert followed, still keeping to the grassy verge to muffle his pursuit.

Ross Montgomery shook his fists and gave a howl of rage as he got tangled in his clothing and fell flat on his face at the moment that Wilkes and Roderick rounded the bend in their prim, overladen carriage.

"Good evening, sir," greeted both gentleman's gentlemen, lifting their hats politely to the obese, half-naked man who was sprawled gracelessly in the middle of the thoroughfare. Ross Montgomery's colorful stream of epithets was momentarily stopped with shock as the carriage bowled gaily past, leaving him in a cloud of dust.

Annie tore the mask from her face, threw back her head, and laughed triumphantly. Her hat blew off and her thick gold-streaked auburn hair cascaded. Iona's husky chuckle joined in and she stole a mischievous glance at Michael, whose serious, earnest face belied the twinkle in his eyes.

"Och, Michael-mine, that was a stroke of genius cutting through his belt and braces and dropping his drawers so he couldna run!" laughed Annie, tears of merriment pouring down her cheeks as she remembered the comical picture.

"How did you think to do such a thing?" chuckled Iona, feeling pure righteous joy at her cousin's humiliation.

"I read it in a book," confessed Michael very seriously, looking behind anxiously to see if they were followed.

"Aye, Iona, that's why he's at the university in Edinburgh," gurgled Annie, bent double over the horse's neck, her stomach aching from laughter as the tension eased from her.

Robert heard Annie's distinctive bubbling laughter drifting back with the staccato of the horse's hooves on the moonlit road. He bided his time, keeping a certain distance between them and hoping that they would have the good taste to stop for an evening repast at a remarkably good tavern five miles farther up the road. At the thought, his stomach growled hungrily.

He smiled with great satisfaction as he watched the three hand their mounts to waiting ostlers and saunter into the Craigie Arms Tavern. He frowned, though, wondering who the third figure was; he easily recognised Michael, whose auburn hair glowed under the warm lantern lights, and Annie, even though she wore an enormous hat.

Annie, Iona, and Michael sat at a large table in a dim corner, eagerly awaiting their meal. All three were ravenous. Their nervousness before their encounter with Ross Montgomery had robbed them of their afternoon appetites, but with the heady relief of their successful venture, their saliva flowed.

"May I recommend the pheasant under glass?" idly suggested a deep, cultured voice.

"Uncle Robert!" yelped Annie as Michael hastily scraped back his chair and stood respectfully.

"Michael," nodded Robert before turning his gaze to the third member of the lawless trio. Iona felt the blood rush to her cheeks under the tall blond man's scrutiny. He was as strikingly handsome as she remembered, his bright blue eyes gleaming in his tanned face. "May I join you?"

he asked rhetorically, seating himself but keeping his piercing gaze on Iona, who tried to keep her expression aloof despite her pounding heart.

"What are you doing here, Uncle Robert?" asked Annie after exchanging a worried look with her brother. It had been more than a year since she had seen him, and meeting him now in such an unexpected place disturbed her.

"I was about to ask you the same question, infant," returned Robert, still staring intently at Iona, who longed to drop her eyes but instead returned his gaze challengingly.

"Oh, well, we just got tired of Mrs. Wilson's cooking and needed a change," prevaricated Annie as she frowned at her uncle's unwavering scrutiny of her friend. "Oh, I'm sorry, this is Iona Montgomery," she introduced hastily.

"Well, 'tis refreshing to see that the vast expense of twenty-three governesses was not entirely wasted. You do have some knowledge of the bare rudiments of acceptable manners. I was beginning to wonder," he answered cuttingly, his eyes pinned to the dark beauty. "Miss Montgomery and I have met albeit several years ago when she was attired somewhat differently," he added, allowing his gaze to encompass her male garb.

"In a rose garden, if I recall correctly," returned Iona sharply, trying to set him down a notch.

"I am extremely flattered that you remember," replied Robert roguishly, and to her horror Iona felt herself blush hotly at the memory of a stolen kiss. Annie looked from her uncle to Iona, not understanding the current that ran between them. "The reason I am in this vicinity is entirely due to Miss Montgomery," stated Robert, grinning lazily as he noted the heightened color of Iona's cheeks. Stretching his long legs out before him, he idly nursed a snifter of brandy but kept his gaze steadily pinned. Iona sighed noticeably with relief as the arrival of their food provided a welcome diversion, and she dropped her eyes to the sumptuous repast that was being spread before them. Tender young roast chickens and squab, savory veal and ham pie, with generous jugs of dark ale and a large bowl overflowing with succulent cherries, strawberries, and raspberries.

Iona bent her head and ate hungrily, trying to ignore Robert's gaze as she pondered his reference to being in the vicinity on her account.

"I'm expecting an old friend of Miss Montgomery's. He should have been here sooner, but we ran into a small diversion on the road from Falconhurst," remarked Robert casually. Annie swallowed hard and looked at Iona, who seemed to have difficulty chewing. Michael, taking a long swig of ale, choked.

"Down from Edinburgh for the summer, Michael?" asked his uncle, ignoring Annie's and Iona's wide-eyed worry.

"Yes, sir," replied Michael dutifully.

"So none of you are even mildly interested in my presence in this unlikely place? Not even slightly curious about the diversion I encountered on the road from Falconhurst?" Robert was rather enjoying the discomfort of the black-garbed threesome. He raised a sardonic eyebrow as their forks clattered onto their plates. "Losing your appetites?" he added mercilessly, tearing off a chicken leg and taking a healthy bite.

"Are you playing with us, Uncle Robert?" challenged Annie angrily.

"Oh, Oriana, you still haven't learned when to keep a still tongue in your head, have you?" sighed Robert softly. Annie's amber eyes flashed rebelliously and she opened her mouth to hotly retort, when Michael kicked her shins sharply under the table. She let out a small, furious squeal and Robert nodded approvingly at his nephew just as Roderick MacDonald and Wilkes entered.

"It's Roderick!" exclaimed Iona, following Robert's gaze toward the door. "Oh, please excuse me," she said as she rose and quickly crossed the room. Annie and Michael exchanged puzzled glances as the woman happily greeted a weatherbeaten old man. Wilkes approached the table, and if he was surprised to see Annie and Michael at such an unlikely location dressed in sinister clothes in the middle of the night, he gave no sign.

"I have taken the liberty of reserving chambers for everyone, sir," Wilkes informed Robert.

"We hadn't planned to stay the night," replied Michael awkwardly. "There's a full moon, so there should be no difficulty returning home to Kenlaren."

"'T'as clouded over and there's a storm brewing, Master Michael," replied Wilkes as Iona and Roderick approached the table.

"Then we had best be on our way before it breaks," said Annie, bouncing to her feet and then sitting sharply as Robert placed a firm hand on her shoulder. Roderick MacDonald's eyes narrowed as he looked down at Annie's rebellious face. He nodded and then his wrinkled face beamed, breaking into a thousand radiating lines.

"Well, well, 'tis wee Rob Roy MacGregor!" he chuckled, clapping his hands together with delight. "Och, lassie, I nair thought to set these old eyes on you again. And how is that great stallion, Dubh?"

"He's a father many times over," laughed Iona when Annie didn't answer but stole a shamefaced look at her dumbfounded uncle. Iona followed her gaze and grinned cheekily at Robert, feeling triumphant that suddenly he didn't seem so composed and in control. "Sit with us, Roderick" she said gaily, pulling up two extra chairs. "Sit, Just-Wilkes. it would be a pity to waste all this good food. Our eyes were too big for our tummies."

"And I thought it was my presence that had dampened your young appetites," quipped Robert, regaining his equilibrium but determined to find out the relationship between Annie and Roderick. "I was just telling these children," he continued loftily, smiling brilliantly at the insult to Iona, "about the entertaining diversion we encountered on our way back from Falconhurst."

"Why were you at Falconhurst?" demanded Iona.

"Making certain that you would not have to continue dressing in that deplorable fashion," replied Robert witheringly. He nodded his appreciation to the waiters, who placed several more aromatic steaming platters before the group.

Annie sat seething as the three men and Michael resumed eating, leaving her and Iona to watch them chew. She wanted to scream at the tension. Outside, the storm gathered and finally broke, causing bright shuddering blue lights to fill the dim room before the thunder shook the rain-drenched windows. Unable to sit still and quiet, she stood, wanting only to be out in the battling elements, but she was stopped once more by her uncle's large hand.

"I need some fresh air," protested Annie.

"Then excuse yourself politely," he demanded. Annie swallowed hard, feeling shamed and embarrassed before excusing herself in a low voice that shook with rage. Robert released her and signaled to Michael to follow, knowing the headstrong girl would ride Dubh to Kenlaren, storm or no storm. With a sullen pout Michael obeyed his uncle.

"You may cancel two of those rooms, Wilkes," he said dryly.

"Why?" asked Iona, feeling abandoned as Michael disappeared after his sister and Roderick and Wilkes left the table.

"I am afraid your two companions will not be back," sighed Robert. "Or should I say, your two accomplices? Don't you know the propensities of my willful ward by now, Miss Montgomery?" he asked innocently as she looked daggers at him. "She likes nothing better than to defy authority—any authority, including the elements," he added as a loud clap of thunder shook the tavern. "What is it, Wilkes?" he asked sharply as the tiny man burst into the room decidedly out of breath, his usually passive face red with exertion.

"You're reserved in the large bedchamber on the second floor in the front, sir. I regret that Ross Montgomery is here with several constables looking for three highwaymen!"

"Oh, my God!" gasped Iona.

"Courage, infant," soothed Robert, taking Iona's hand. "Wilkes, I think 'tis time *my wife* and I retired to our bedchamber. Please see that her luggage is brought up." The small dapper man bowed as Iona's mouth dropped open and she made a small squawk of protest, not quite sure that she had heard correctly.

"What? What did you say?" she gasped as she was dragged to the back of the inn toward the servant's staircase.

"No time for maidenly protests, unless you want to explain your strange black garb to your irate cousin and the authorities," hissed Robert, taking the steps three at a time and nearly pulling Iona's arm out of its socket as she tripped and scrambled trying to keep up. "Get undressed!" he ordered tersely as he pushed her into a dark room and bolted the door. Once more Iona emitted a strange squawk, not sure if she understood. "Thank God, Annie took it into her head to go home," he muttered as he hurriedly stripped to the waist and sat on the bed to remove his boots.

"Ouch!" cried Iona as she walked into a hard piece of furniture and barked her shins. "This is preposterous, Sir Robert!"

"Hush!" hissed Robert as he heard hard-booted feet clattering up the stairs. "Get those incriminating clothes off!" he added when lightning illuminated the room with a shimmering blue, showing her fully-dressed state. "Off with them!" he forcefully insisted, tearing the black shirt from her unceremoniously so that she gasped with indignation. Ross Montgomery's bellowing voice echoed down the corridor outside, freezing her blood. She stood in a state of confusion as Sir Robert shimmied the trews down over her shapely hips. "Sit!" he hissed, sitting her on the bed and wrenching off her tight riding boots. "Back!" he ordered, shoving her onto her back and skinning off the black trews. "Into bed!" This command was unnecessary, as Iona had recollected her wits and dived under the bed covers to hide her nakedness in fear of another illuminating sheet of lightning. Robert swiftly bundled up the discarded clothing and crammed it between the mattress and the springs before following Iona into the large bed.

Angry voices and the sound of doors being opened and slammed proceeded down the long corridor, drawing closer and closer. Iona forgot her very compromising position as she remembered her cousin's ugly temperament. Robert felt her intense shudder of fear and loathing and put out a strong arm. He felt a very pleasurable shock when her warm, silky body leaned against him. Iona recoiled as her bare skin pressed against his cool hard muscles, but as she pulled back to protest there was a loud hammering at the room next door.

"Open up in the name of the law!" thundered Ross's

hated voice, and Iona's heart raced triple time against Robert's broad chest as she curled closer, seeking protection, holding desperately to his strength.

"Courage, love," whispered Robert hoarsely, bending his head and capturing her quivering lips. Iona felt the lightning that shattered the room for a brief second fuse with her blood, shocking her from the top of her head to the tips of her toes. For several moments she drowned in his kiss, which awoke delicious aching sensations deep in her body. A violent knocking nearly splintered the door and caused her to press even closer to the delighted young lord.

"Open in the name of the law!" bellowed the bully officiously, and the brutal crashing was repeated. Reluctantly Robert withdrew his mouth from the soft, pliant lips. He grinned roguishly in the darkness as he heard her regretful sigh.

"For God's sakes, what's that infernal racket?" he roared, getting out of bed and donning a handsome brocade dressing gown.

"There had better be a bloody good explanation for this ill-timed intrusion!" he stated as he wrenched open the door to Ross Montgomery and three sheepish constables who stood with lanterns in hand as other irate, night-gowned figures shook fists and muttered angrily before returning to their rooms.

"Sir Robert Forsythe!" exclaimed Ross, completely taken back. "What are you doing at the Craigie Arms?"

"Did not your good wife inform you I was in the vicinity?" answered Robert coldly. "I had to pick up a few oddments belonging to my wife, Lady Iona." He waved a distracted hand toward the bed and covered a grin as he heard a faint indignant squawk. "Look, old chap, I haven't the dickens of a notion what all this commotion is about but I would prefer to get back to the business at hand," he said airily, trying to close the door.

"Your wife? Lady Iona?" screamed Ross, pushing by and advancing, lantern in hand, toward the bed, intent on seeing his kinswoman.

"I say!" exclaimed Robert, catching Ross by the shoulder and swinging him about. "That isn't cricket, old chap!"

And with that he neatly punched the fat man in the nose so he collapsed in a heap on the carpet. "Take him away, dear chaps, if you don't mind," pleaded Robert to the stunned militia. "I am Sir Robert Forsythe," he pronounced pompously, drawing himself up to his full six feet one and a half inches and sneering down at the stunned country constables.

"Sir Robert, what is going on here?" came the familiar tones of Wilkes as he and Roderick smartly marched down the corridor carrying a large trunk.

"Haven't a bloody clue, my man!" responded Robert irreverently. "I' would seem my wife's cousin is a trifle bosky," he added, pushing the inert body with his bare foot.

"Shocking," clucked Wilkes, and he and Roderick shook their heads with disapproval. "Where do you want Lady Forsythe's pormanteau, sir?"

"Where do you want your portmanteau, my love?" asked Robert roguishly. He frowned comically at the muffled, strangled cry that issued from under the covers as Iona burrowed, trying to be invisible. "Set it right over there," added Robert, lighting a lantern and directing the two men. "And then please remove that unwanted presence!" He pointed at Ross Montgomery's prone corpulence, which Wilkes and Roderick were in the process of stepping over.

Iona thought she was going to suffocate. Her cheeks burned from the predicament she was in as well as from the weight of the thick covers. By the sounds of the many feet that reverberated through the bed frame, it would seem that half the population of Ayrshire was congregating in the bedchamber to witness her final disgrace.

Robert shut the door behind the last of the unwanted company and turned to survey the large bed with the provocative lump under the covers. He grinned with appreciation and leaned casually against the bolted door before slowly crossing to the bed and patting a rather rounded protuberance.

"Iona, you can come out now," he said, laughter warming his voice as he felt her start and then freeze. Once more he knocked against a pleasantly firm part of her anatomy.

"They have all gone," he reassured her. Iona emerged red-faced and tousled as well as gasping for breath.

"I find nothing humorous about this situation," she panted as she glared up at his beaming face.

"That is because while you were suffocating yourself under all those bed clothes, you missed one of the most delightfully funny scenes it has ever been my good fortune to witness. Never could care for Ross Montgomery. I've wanted to set him down a peg for years," informed Robert, sitting intimately on the bed and rubbing his hands together with relish. Iona shimmied away from him, keeping the covers pulled primly up to her chin. Her eyes widened as Ross's furious voice suddenly boomed along the corridor.

"The door is locked," comforted Robert, answering the panic in her expression. "So you are quite safe."

"I am in a man's bedchamber, in his bed without my clothes, and you say I am quite safe," Iona recited, trying to keep her tone well modulated and matter-of-fact. "If you were a gentleman, you would leave," she added, severely unnerved by the roguish grin on his handsome face.

"I'm not leaving," replied Robert airily.

"Then I am!"

"With that still going on?" he asked, putting a hand to his ear as Ross Montgomery's bellowing continued. "There's also the simple matter of your 'hightoby' apparel," he added, his light tones laced with steel. Iona flushed at the censure she felt emanate.

"I should like to get dressed," she stated coldly.

"Not until I've had some explanation," replied Robert. Iona looked away, not knowing what to say. "I am waiting, Miss Montgomery, to find out why a respectable young woman hired as a suitable companion-governess to my young ward, would gallop around the countryside dressed as a highwayman, robbing members of the peerage and dragging her young charges with her?"

"Young *charge,*" Iona corrected lamely but with as much dignity as she could muster. She had no other answer, so the silence lengthened as she avoided the piercing blue eyes but felt the searing gaze. How on earth had she gotten herself into such a tangle, she fumed.

Robert watched her, enjoying her heightened color

and the soft curves that were apparent as she pulled the covers tightly around herself, trying to conceal but actually molding the material to her lithe form. Outside, the storm still raged, the sheets of lightning shimmering and the thunder crashing directly overhead. Iona started, convinced the ceiling would shortly come tumbling down as the thunder shook the very rafters.

"You don't look like the sort of young woman who's afraid of a mere storm," remarked Robert, breaking the silence between them. Iona tossed her head, trying to hide her fear as her nostrils flared.

"I am not afraid of the storm but of the situation I find myself in," she replied acidly.

"I am still awaiting your explanation of it," returned Robert glibly, getting perverse pleasure at her discomfort.

"I have no explanation," she stated stiffly. "I am aware it was irresponsible, and under the circumstances I can understand why you would prefer me not to continue as companion to your ward. Now, I think that concludes our business, Sir Robert."

"Don't be ridiculous!" growled Robert, taken aback. "Where would you go? What would you do?"

"That is my business," she replied tartly.

"On the countrary," disagreed Robert. "You committed yourself to taking care of my ward and I hold you to it."

"What?" exclaimed Iona, not understanding Robert Forsythe's position at all. "Do you mean to say, my lord, that you have no objection to your ward being in the company of a common footpad?"

"Knowing my niece, the little minx, you probably need protection from her!" he laughed. "It was probably her idea anyway."

"I am quite well able to take care of myself and protect myself," bridled Iona, angry at the inference that a sixteen-year-old girl could lead her by the nose.

"So it was you who thought to hold up your detestable cousin?"

"Of course, and as you so aptly put it, I dragged your young wards with me," confessed Iona. "Why am I sitting in this uncomfortable position having this inane conversation?!" she shouted angrily.

"My sentiments exactly, especially when we could be using the time much more enjoyably," said Robert in a low, husky tone. Iona couldn't think. She was so unnerved by his close proximity and his attractive male assurance, she hit out at his handsome grinning face. The sound of her slap cracked the air like a gunshot, and his lazy, twinkling eyes hardened to a cold iciness.

"Sir Robert, my circumstances may be reduced because of the death of my brother, but that does not mean I—" Her impassioned speech was interrupted when she followed his scorching gaze to find herself sitting up and exposed to the waist.

"That is one habit I should like to cure you of," remarked Robert regretfully as she clutched the covers to her neck. "You hit often?" he asked.

"When the situation demands it," she retorted.

"Get dressed," he said suddenly, after walking to the window and peering out. "It seems your objectional relative is leaving, followed by the Ayrshire constabulary. You'll find several gowns with the accompanying accessories in that large portmanteau in the corner," he added, stamping into his riding boots and taking off his ornate dressing gown. Iona looked away hurriedly but not until she had seen that he wore his tight riding trousers. She had supposed him as naked as she. She heard the rustling sound of him donning his shirt and shrugging into his jacket, and then she was conscious of a feeling of dejection as he strode to the door. "Be ready to leave at first light," he ordered peremptorily.

Iona sat hugging her knees, not making an effort to examine the contents of the large trunk. Her emotions and brain swirled in a most confused manner. She shook her head, trying to be sensible as she told herself that she was just overtired, overexcited, and nothing more, but then her eyes went misty as she recalled the feel of her bare skin against his, the feel of his firm lips against hers, and the deep voice that could make delicious shivers race through her. Nearly seven years before she had felt the selfsame way when, in an English rose garden, she had shamelessly opened her lips under the insistent pressure of his. He had been the first man ever to kiss her as a woman, and she had drowned in the wonder of that first kiss until his easy assurance and her fear of losing control had caused her to strike out—more to rein her own raging emotions than to chastise him. There had been other kisses from other men since then, softening the memory of that first one, but none had ever come close until just now, she realized, touching her tingling lips. Tears dropped slowly down her soft cheeks as she thought of their very different stations in life. She was his employee, his servant, like Wilkes and Roderick. At the thought of Roderick she scrubbed her tears angrily, despising her vaporous weakness. There was an alternative, she decided. She didn't have to meekly return to the position as companion to Sir Robert's ward at Kenlaren. She and Roderick could go somewhere and make a new life for themselves, she planned, pushing away her sorrow at the possibility of never seeing Robert Forsythe again.

"Who'd want to see him again," she hissed. "With those abominable sisters and that even worse mother!" With that comforting thought, Robert Forsythe's family being a very sobering if not nightmarish consideration, Iona threw the covers back and stepped off the bed at the exact moment the door was thrown open, and Ross Montgomery staggered in. The obese man, his nose and mouth quite swollen out of shape to match his stomach as a result of Sir Robert's punch, drew an appreciative breath through his slack lips at the sight of her nakedness. Iona opened her mouth and screamed as the hateful man leered and approached, his pudgy hands flexing with anticipation as the thought of squeezing and caressing the firm young breasts. Iona screamed again and again as she fought the clutching, pinching fingers and tossed her head to avoid the fetid breath. Her hair was caught in a savagely painful grasp as her head was wrenched back and she was toppled backward onto the bed with the weight of her drunken cousin atop her. She kicked out blindly, fighting with every ounce of strength she possessed. Suddenly the nauseous weight was removed and a dead thump rocked the room, but still Iona kicked and screamed until very strong arms swaddled her in the eiderdown to confine her wildly kicking legs and punching arms.

"Hush, my love, hush. 'Tis all right, 'tis me, Robert. Hush now," he crooned very uncharacteristically as Wilkes and Roderick mopped Ross Montgomery off the floor once more and took him out. Robert cradled Iona like a mere babe despite her five foot seven inches and locked the door decisively. "'Tis all right now. Shush, 'tis me, everything's going to be all right," he crooned idiotically.

"But . . . but . . . but," hiccoughed Iona, unable to get a word in with all his crooning endearments.

"I'll not let him hurt you anymore. 'Tis all right Iona, my love," he continued.

"But . . . but . . . but," strove Iona.

"But what?" coached Robert gently.

"But . . ." Iona managed before bursting into a flood of tears as she remembered Ross's slack, fetid mouth, and once more the stream of repetitive endearments continued.

"Please, kiss me," sobbed Iona when she was able, wanting to eradicate Ross's assault and not caring how forward she sounded. Robert's firm, warm lips encompassed her mouth and she sighed deeply and reached up, wrapping her arms about his neck, not caring that the eiderdown fell to her waist and exposed her lithe, naked form.

Robert's loins were on fire and with a groan he wrenched his mouth from Iona's and laid her back, covering her nakedness very decisively. Iona stared up at him and even in the dim, warm glow of the lantern's light, he could see her dark eyes veiled with passion.

"Iona?" he said hoarsely, terrified of the answer he might receive. "Have you ever . . ."

"Ever what?" she said, straining toward him.

"This?" he croaked, unable to resist the erect nipple that enticed him so. Iona writhed as he caressed her. "Have you ever made love?" he managed to say.

"No," she breathed, thrusting up and trying to connect. "Wha!" she gasped, finding herself unceremoniously dumped back on to the bed and his strong, beloved arms removed. Robert groaned at the hurt and confusion he saw eloquently mirrored on her face. He groaned even louder when he saw the confusion turn to shame.

"Why aren't you dressed?" he asked for want of something better to say, as he opened the portmanteau and rummaged, not looking for anything in particular but simply needing something to do.

"I was thinking," replied Iona dully. "Would you send Roderick to me?"

"I rather think Roderick's hands are full of your bosky cousin," returned Robert. "Put this on." He held up what he thought was a nightgown but was in actual fact her only decent summer garden party dress, decorated with delicate appliqués of poppies and wisteria. Iona closed her eyes, not wanting to cope with anything more except sleep. She held the eiderdown tightly around herself and drifted off to sleep, her breathing still punctuated with shuddering sighs. Robert also sighed with frustration as he stared at her tempting, cocooned shape. He dropped the light, frothy frock into the portmanteau and leaned back against the headrest of the bed.

A light tapping at the door made his eyelids fly open.

"Yes?" he mumbled sleepily.

"Everything all right, sir?" asked Wilkes's dulcet tones.

"Top notch!" yawned Robert, wriggling his rangy body until he lay prone, with his long legs protruding off the end of the wide bed. With a sigh of satisfaction, he stretched, relaxing his tired muscles, and soon was fast asleep, albeit fully clothed with his boots on.

Chapter 11

Iona blinked and opened heavy lids to the assault of a sunny day. She rolled onto her back, trying to get her bearings, and frowned as she rested against a firm body. Cautiously she turned her head and surveyed Sir Robert Forsythe, who lay soundly sleeping, fully clothed, with a very satisfied smile across his handsome features. She frowned again, remembering the events of the previous night and apprehensively peeked under the eiderdown that was wrapped about her. Seeing the length of naked flesh, she blushed and bit her bottom lip as she tried to think of a strategy for clothing herself without waking the sleeping gentleman.

Robert lay perfectly relaxed, his breathing even and innocent as he watched Iona's dressing. Every so often she whirled about suspiciously in the midst of her toilette, but each time reassured he slept, she resumed. Robert ran his very alert eyes down the long, graceful line of spine to the flushed, firm buttocks that so matched her dusky-rose cheeks as she stepped into her undergarments and then into a very severe, spinsterish riding habit of questionable years.

"What a positively disgusting article of clothing!" he exclaimed with an audible shudder. "Remind me to burn it!" Iona spun about and glared at him but he looked so winsome and engaging, rather like a small mischievous boy, that a laugh burst involuntarily from her lips.

"That's better," he approved with an impudent grin. "Do I get a good morning kiss?" he asked hopefully. Iona snorted and resumed packing her trunk, successfully rejecting him and firmly ignoring his low sigh of agony at her cold cruelty. "Don't forget the incriminating evidence under the mattress," he added as soon as he saw her close the lid and lock it. Now she sighed with intense irritation, knowing he had purposefully timed his words. She turned and glared at him angrily, waiting for him to either remove his weight from the bed so she could collect her clothes, or do it himself, but he did neither. He just lay there idly watching her and enjoying her confusion, rather like a cat with the cream.

"Sir Robert," she said severely, "you have managed to totally destroy my reputation, so I have no recourse but to accept your employment if you still want me."

"I most certainly still want you," declared Robert wickedly, causing dangerous flutters to start writhing through Iona's traitorous body.

"Want me as a companion for your ward!" she amended hastily as she blushed at the gleam in his eyes and remembered her wanton behavior. Inside she squirmed but she kept her face stern and composed.

"I think, though . . . well, perhaps it would be better if Mr. MacDonald and I went . . . well, somewhere else and . . ."

"Roderick MacDonald is in my employ until your brother returns," stated Robert, swinging his long legs off the bed and standing.

"Until my brother returns!" exclaimed Iona.

"That is what I said," yawned Robert, stretching.

"My brother is dead! I think your sense of humor is slightly warped."

"My sense of humor is more than slightly warped, according to my mother," corrected Robert gallantly. "There has been news of your brother. It would seem that he is very much alive, but on the other side of the world."

"Alive? Loch is alive?" gasped Iona, her dark eyes shining with unspilt tears. Robert's cheeky expression softened as he stared into her upturned face.

"A man answering his description has been located on

a small island off South America, but maybe 'tis unfair to raise your hopes," he said gently.

"How do you know this?" asked Iona wonderingly, not aware she clasped Robert's hands tightly nor of how appealingly vulnerable she was with her large dark eyes pinned so trustingly to his face.

"I have several sugar concerns in South America, and when I heard of your desperate straits and the undue haste with which your cousin claimed title and land, I made it my business to make inquiry," he said huskily, staring into her luminous eyes and choosing not to inform her of Ross Montgomery's heinous treachery in the sabotaging of Lochiel's vessel.

"Why?" she whispered, lost in his blue eyes and anticipating a romantic, claiming answer.

"I don't know. It was a long, boring winter. It provided diversion from my pious sisters," he stated airily after clearing his throat and striding to the window. "We should be on our way." He shrugged into his many-caped greatcoat and picked up his riding crop.

"By all means," barked Iona, swallowing her disappointment and choking as she wrenched her riding boots from between the mattress and the springs.

"Allow me," Robert offered gallantly.

"I can manage," she snapped. Robert grinned cheekily at her apparent bad temper and whistled nonchalantly. "I sincerely hope my brother calls you out when he returns!" she hissed shrewishly as she stamped into her boots and marched to the door. She hesitated. "Maybe I should leave first and you should follow in a few moments?"

"Nonsense, that sounds like a very cowardly retreat," decided Robert, taking her arm in a firm grasp and opening the door with a flourish. "Chin up, old girl," he directed wickedly, marching her briskly down the corridor toward the central staircase. Iona knew that to object would cause even more attention, so she haughtily stuck her small nose in the air and pretended to be somebody else. They had just trod majestically down to the first landing and were poised to promenade to the hall when a loud strident voice caused them both to freeze in mid-stride.

"Boo-boo!"

"Robert?" whispered Iona, clutching his arm as he stared with undisguised horror at his sister Sarah, who had been married in Rebecca's stead to the baron with the appalling reputation.

"Boo-boo!"

"Sarah, what brings you to Scotland?" he asked after silently descending to her level with a white-faced Iona still clutching his arm. "I say, deuced surprised to see you, old thing. Do you know Lady Iona?"

"Delighted to meet you," gushed Iona, extending a hand to the plump, pink woman.

"I was on my visit to my dear school friend, Mary Montgomery, but there was this simply dreadful storm, so we were forced to put up for the night in this simply dreadful place," chattered Sarah, staring at her surroundings and then at Iona with absolute disgust. "Aren't you Iona Montgomery?" she accused sharply, remembering all her dear friend Mary had imparted about Iona being such a gawky imposition. Iona felt her cheeks stiffen and she pulled herself up to her full great height and stared witheringly down at the plump, pink woman.

"Iona is my wife," stated Robert, squeezing her arm reassuringly as his sister gasped and froze with her mouth agape. Iona giggled, not sure whether she was awake or asleep, as Robert politely nodded to his aghast sibling and strode casually out to the front courtyard. There Roderick and Wilkes sat patiently in the prim carriage, and two young ostlers held the fresh, spirited horses, who pranced sideways, eager to gallop. Iona allowed Sir Robert to help her into the saddle before she sedately trotted down the drive, conscious of the curious eyes that burned a hole in her proud back.

They rode in silence for several miles. Once or twice Iona stole a peek at Robert's face, but he rode happily, seeming to appreciate the sunshine, birds, and flowers as though he had not a care in the world. She shook her head with stupefaction, unable to grasp the events of the past hours and certain only that they had totally destroyed her reputation. She couldn't believe Robert's lack of concern for the predicament she was now embroiled in.

"How can you whistle!?" she snapped crossly, digging

in her heels and cantering ahead of him. Robert watched her go and he grinned, kicking his own mount into a canter. He drew abreast of her, still whistling merrily. She glared at him, but he smiled back engagingly. "How can you?" she repeated, trying to resist his charm and thinking of the fun the gossips would have in London sullying her name and tearing her reputation to shreds.

"How can I what?" asked Robert with a hurt innocence.

"Whistle!"

"Well, you pout your lips as though to kiss, and then you blow."

"How can you make fun! You have got me into about the worst predicament imaginable and all you can do is be flip," she raged.

"I got you into the worst predicament?" returned Robert mildly, lifting a blond eyebrow. "I was under the impression I was trying to extricate you from several fates worse than death, none of which, incidentally, were any of my doing."

"Saying that we were married!"

"Would you have preferred that I told your Cousin Ross otherwise when he saw you naked in my bed?" asked Robert lightly.

"Telling your own sister!" gasped Iona in outraged tones. "She will tell your mother!"

"Poor old Sarah, married to that dirty old baron with a penchant for small boys. She's known to hit the bottle . . . an incurable dipsomaniac and can you blame her?" returned Robert with infuriating glibness. "Mumsy won't believe a thing out of her mouth! She'll have her say a few hundred Hail Marys and have her wear out her poor old knees kneeling on those cold chapel stones," he added cheerfully.

"Ross Montgomery will back up her story," stated Iona quellingly. "For God's sake, stop whistling!" she snapped.

"No need to swear, my dear."

"My reputation is in tatters and you tell me not to swear! Well, bloody hell, I will swear!" she swore, wishing she were in possession of a more colorful and extensive vocabulary as she dug in her heels and galloped away from him.

"You are magnificent when you are in high dudgeon!" he called, digging in his own heels and easily catching up with her. "You are a delight to tease." He laughed merrily at her outraged face.

"And you, Boo-boo Forsythe, are impossible!" she gasped before turning her face to the front and refusing to look at or converse with him for the rest of the journey.

Wilkes and Roderick watched the exchange between Robert and Iona, and smug smiles of satisfaction flitted across their usually inscrutable features.

"I think they're ideally suited," approved Wilkes.

"Aye," agreed Roderick as they drove the prim carriage behind the young riders toward Kenlaren, where a very anxious Annie waited.

"Go out and spend that energy," begged Michael as his sister paced the library carpet.

"How can you sit reading? Iona should have been back hours ago," worried the girl, cracking a riding crop against her trousered thigh. Michael slammed his book shut with a sigh. "Do you think Uncle Robert turned her over to the constable?"

"We can but wait and see," answered Michael wearily. "Come in," he called as a timid knock sounded at the door. "Yes, Millie?" he said, greeting the freckle-faced little maid.

"Please, sir, Mrs. Wilson wanted to know if you are wanting luncheon?"

"We should wait for Uncle Robert," replied Annie as her brother opened his mouth to answer.

"You can wait. I am ravenous," stated Michael, eager to be away from his anxious sister. "Millie, tell Mrs. Wilson I'll eat in the small dining room . . . informally."

"Aye, sir," bobbed Millie.

"Uncle Robert wouldn't turn Iona over to the authorities," said Annie, trying to reassure herself as her brother stood. "Michael, did you notice Uncle Robert and Iona last night?"

"Aye," answered the young man with his hand on the door handle. He turned back to his sister with a puzzled frown on his face, not sure whether to share his suspicions with his young sister. He had noted a certain intimacy, an attraction that caused a tension between the two, and had wondered whether Robert and Iona were former lovers or destined to become such.

"What?" probed Annie, noticing her brother's hesitancy.

"Nothing." Michael quickly quit the room, and Annie snorted with frustration. She stared out of the window, willing Iona and Robert to appear on the formal driveway as a host of frightening suppositions filled her head. What if Iona had been captured? What if Ross Montgomery had retrieved his money? What if Iona were going to be transported or imprisoned at the Assizes? What if? What if? hammered in her brain so that she was deaf to the hoofbeats and carriage wheels on the graveled driveway outside. Robert's deep voice as he dismounted finally penetrated her musing, and she stared out of the window, her legs sagging with relief at Iona's stormy appearance.

Iona marched into the house and up the stairs, not heeding Annie, who whistled and beckoned. Annie fleetly raced up the stairs after her but reached Iona's room only to have the door slammed in her face.

"Iona? Iona?" she hissed, knocking furtively.

"What?" snapped Iona, wrenching the door open so violently that Annie nearly fell into the room. "Oh, it's you!" she breathed with such irritation that Annie took a step backward, frowning at the hostility in the dark, flashing eyes.

"Aye, 'tis me," whispered Annie, looking cautiously behind her. "Can I come in?" Iona looked as though she were about to refuse, but then she resignedly stood aside and bowed ironically, giving grudging permission. "Where did you get that awful riding habit?" gasped Annie.

"Out!" snapped Iona holding the door wide. "You Forsythes are as bad as each other," she added.

"I'm a Gunn, " protested Annie indignantly.

"This habit was so generously given to me by my cousin's wife," Iona said bitterly.

"And I repeat, it should be burnt!" answered Robert's deep tones as he made his way to his suite of rooms. Iona slammed her bedroom door and leaned against it, not knowing whether to give in to weeping hysterics or violent rage.

"Iona?" whispered Annie. "You are being very strange. Are you all right? I was terrified for you. I thought you were caught," she chattered, unnerved by the change in the dark woman, who paced in a furious manner muttering all sorts of unintelligible things. "Iona?" called Annie, trying to get her attention.

"What?" hissed the tall beauty, spinning abruptly on her heel.

"Do you have the money?"

"What?"

"The money?" repeated Annie, the words sticking in her throat. She felt very mercenary asking, when it was obvious that something was greatly disturbing her friend.

"The money?" repeated Iona in a daze and Annie nodded, unable to say the dreaded word again. "Oh, my God, where's the money?" gasped Iona, distractedly ruffling her ebony hair in a confused manner. "I put it in my saddle bag, which I left at the inn. Oh, my God! I entirely forgot! It's still at the Craigie Arms. I put it on the floor by my chair when we ordered our food, and then wie all the confusion! Och, I am so sorry, Annie!"

"What happened? I saw Ross Montgomery and the constables at the Craigie Arms. I was so afraid they'd catch you. How did you escape?"

"Thanks to your uncle, I am all of one piece but I canna say the same for my reputation," replied Iona bitterly. "Now, if you'll excuse me, I have a splitting headache." Annie nodded forlornly. "I am so sorry about the money," Iona added, seeing the girl's dejected manner.

"It doesna matter. I am just glad you are all of a piece," she said with a forced little smile. A sharp knock at the door caused them both to jump and then giggle at their nervousness.

"Yes?" called Iona.

"'Tis Roderick wie your portmanteau, and Mrs. Wilson says to inform you luncheon is served," came the reply. Iona gasped with surprise when she opened the door and saw her saddle bag casually draped across the large trunk that was carried by two liveried manservants. "Where would you like it?" asked Roderick, who was directing the operation.

"In the dressing room, please, Roderick, but don't have it unpacked. Please, tender my apologies to Mrs. Wilson, but I have a terrible headache. . . ."

"Caused, no doubt, by hunger!" interrupted Robert, striding into the room.

"Sir Robert, this is my bedchamber!" stated Iona in very quelling tones as the servants discreetly left, followed by Roderick MacDonald. "Roderick?" she protested desperately.

"Oriana, luncheon is served," dismissed Robert, holding the door open pointedly.

"But Uncle Robert . . ."

"Out!" he ordered in such steely tones her eyes widened with shock, and she opened her mouth to fight. The words caught in her throat, though, when she saw her uncle had eyes only for Iona, who glared at him with her color considerably heightened. There was something undefinable crackling between the two. Annie stood hesitantly by the door, not knowing what to do and fascinated by the silent but eloquent drama, when a strong firm hand reached into the room and forcibly removed her. Annie gasped and glowered at Roderick, who emphatically slammed the door, allowing Robert and Iona their privacy. He stared down at her with a benign expression, his leathery old hand still holding her arm in a firm grip.

"It is time for luncheon, Rob Roy MacGregor," he said softly. "Then I should like to be reacquainted wie the stallion Dubh." Annie looked into his weatherbeaten face and nodded, showing none of the inner turmoil she was feeling. "Ye've grown into a beautiful lass, Rob Roy," he added, his shrewd eyes noting her exquisite features and rare coloring. Everything about her was golden, he observed—hair, eyes, skin, and even the aura that emanated from her. He grinned widely, knowing the wild, vital spirit that she had displayed as a small bairn was still present.

Contrary to Michael's wishes, luncheon was formally served in the large dining room. He sat with his nose in a book, ignoring Annie's truculent expression as they waited for Iona and their uncle. After about ten tense minutes of silence, broken only by Michael turning pages and his sister's impatiently tapping foot, Iona stalked in followed by Robert, who seemed inordinately pleased with himself. Michael sighed with relief and closed his book as the delicious aromas wafted and his saliva ran. Annie tried to catch Iona's eye, but the tall dark beauty ignored everyone and concentrated on pushing the food round and round on her plate. Annie frowned at Michael, puzzled by Iona's very evident fury, but her brother also ignored her while he ate ravenously.

"What the hell is going on?" she demanded furiously, looking from Iona's simmering wrath to her uncle's blithe happiness. Robert grinned lovingly across the table and lifted a roguish eyebrow at the dark beauty, who looked daggers at him as she curled her graceful fingers about the edge of her plate, obviously longing to hurl the contents at his handsome, smiling face.

"Now, now, now, my pet," chided Robert. "That would be an appalling example to set for Oriana and Michael."

"I am not your pet!" hissed Iona, very confused and very infuriated as he continued to grin adoringly at her.

"Sheathe your claws, my love," he teased.

"Neither am I your love!"

Annie stared wide-eyed at this exchange, and even Michael forgot his haste and chewed slowly, enthralled by the drama across the luncheon table.

"What the hell is happening!" repeated Annie, crashing her water tumbler down so the liquid slopped and beaded on the damask cloth.

"It would appear that my wife is in high dudgeon," observed Robert mildly before concentrating on his entrecote with horseradish sauce. Iona emitted a very unladylike squawk, which most fortunately drowned Annie's utterance of a very choice epithet commonly heard in more basic surroundings; and Michael choked on his Burgundy, further dampening the damask tablecloth. Robert continued eating in a most unconcerned manner.

"Wife?" echoed Michael squeakily when he was able to speak.

"Quite so," confirmed Robert cheerfully. "I say, this steak is superb, don't you think so, Michael?"

"Aye," swallowed the youth, totally flabbergasted. "You are married?"

"Married!" exclaimed Annie with disgust and outrage.

"Infants, your education seems to be lacking. In order to have a wife one has to be married to the particular woman whom one calls wife," Robert explained sunnily before beaming into Iona's stunned, stony face.

"Iona Montgomery, how could you do something so . . . so . . . traitorous and not tell me? I think it's the shabbiest, most horrible . . . most disgustingly dishonest . . . rank . . ."

"Enough!" roared Robert, successfully silencing Annie's stream of adjectives. *"Sit down!"* he added as the girl leaped up to leave the room.

"No!" she shouted before slamming the door behind her. Robert shrugged sheepishly at having his authority dampened.

"Excuse me," whispered Michael as he saw Iona was about to give vent to her very obvious emotions. He slipped from the room as unobtrusively as he could.

"How can you sit there and tell such barefaced lies to your wards?" asked Iona, trying desperately to keep her self in control although she longed to throw everything within reach at the man who now lounged back comfortably in his chair. "You have something wrong in the brain, Sir Robert. You need a doctor from Bedlam, it would seem."

"Hornet!" returned the infuriating man. "I am married to a hornet, heaven help me!"

"We are *not* married!"

"We *are* married," he contradicted firmly, helping himself to more steak and mushrooms. Iona's dark eyes narrowed. She opened her mouth to reason with him but then, remembering that one should humor lunatics, she closed it quickly, smiled a bit brittly, and stared down at her plate as she tried to think what to do. "We are married," repeated Robert. Iona smiled and nodded. "In fact, Roderick and Wilkes should be moving all your oddments into my suite right now," he informed her. Iona's eyes widened above the rim of her wineglass as she tried to smother the squawk that rose. Oh, my God, she thought frantically, he *is* mad! Sir Robert Forsythe is mad. Why was she so surprised, she wondered, what with those appalling sisters and that fanatically religious mother Why, it ran in the family, she realized.

"Cherry?"

"I beg your pardon?" She jumped at the sound of his voice.

"Would you like some fruit?" he repeated, offering a full basket of delicate Queen Anne cherries. Iona looked at the pink and white plump fruits and shuddered as they reminded her of Allison and Jeannette Montgomery and Robert's sister Sarah. Silently she shook her head, wondering how she could escape from the room.

Iona stared at Robert, thinking what a terrible shame it was that so handsome and attractive a man was so sadly afflicted.

"Are you still thinking that lunatics have to be appeased?" he asked roguishly, and he laughed as he saw the answer in her startled gaze. "Let's adjourn to a more comfortable surrounding," he suggested softly. Again he laughed low in his throat when he saw her back stiffen as she assumed he meant his suite of rooms. "The rose garden or the library?" he added innocently.

"I am perfectly comfortable where I am," she answered, pushing her back against the chair and gripping the sturdy wood of the table.

"Nevertheless, I think the servants would like to clear the remains." Robert held her chair so she was forced to stand. She was about to wrench his proprietary hand from her arm when the doors opened and several servants entered. Docilely, but seething inside, she allowed herself to be propelled to a small salon. As soon as the heavy door swung shut, allowing them privacy, Iona angrily pulled herself free of his touch and stalked across the room to the window to stare blindly over the sloping lawn and the profusion of roses that bloomed in every conceivable shade of pink.

"How I abominate pink!" she spat as Robert poured two snifters of brandy.

"Brandy?" he said, offering her a glass. "It'll either douse the raging temper you are enjoying or add fuel to the fire," he quipped, placing it on a small table before making himself comfortable in a large leather chair.

Robert lounged, watching Iona and marveling how any female could look so graceful and desirable despite the abominable cut and fabric of the ugly habit she wore. He appeared at ease. He appeared infinitely confident of himself, complacently confident that she would be grateful and honored to be in the enviable position of being his wife. Iona seethed, watching him out of the corner of her eye and refusing to admit to herself that the prospect wasn't entirely repugnant.

Robert was content with his excellent brandy. He felt replete, full of good food and good feelings. He congratulated himself on finding such an intelligent wife as he planned her wardrobe. With her striking dark locks she could wear any color in the rainbow, he decided. There were excellent bloodlines in the Montgomery stock, albeit they were Scottish, he mused.

"Now, what is this absurdity, sir?" quoth Iona suddenly, when she felt she had summoned up the necessary strength.

"Absurdity? I would have thought, my pet, that you of all people could coin a more colorful noun," remarked Robert idly.

"I am exceedingly sorry to disappoint you," she replied acidly. "And I repeat, I am not your pet anything!" She picked up her brandy snifter and took a large swallow, trying to stifle a choke and keep her composure as the burning liquid shocked her system.

"Drinking French brandy like lemonade," reproved Robert as he banged her very unromantically on the back. "Better?" he asked solicitously. Angrily she pulled herself free of his administrations and nodded furiously, her eyes still streaming.

"I . . . I wish . . . to discuss," she squeaked, her voice still affected by the rash gulp of harsh spirits, "the delusion you are under."

" 'Delusion'? Better . . . slightly better than 'absurdity'," he approved.

"Would you please explain your ludicrous assertion, Sir Robert?" asked Iona sweetly, wanting to throw the contents of her snifter at his patronizing countenance as he pompously nodded his approval at her selection of words.

"Unfortunately my assertion is correct, whether ludicrous or not. Marriage by declaration in front of witnesses and undenied by either party is legally binding by Scottish law," he informed her. "I see by your stricken expression that you are aware of the law?" he added as her face lost all color and she sat carefully.

"I've read of it but never known anyone . . . Are you sure it is still binding?"

"Positive," he answered cheerfully.

"Then why in heaven's name did you tell virtually the whole world!" exploded Iona. "Not content to declare to all and sundry at the Craigie Arms but to the Ayrshire constabulary, my cousin, your wards, servants, and even your own sister! Why?"

"Roderick did not inform me of the law until after I had declared us man and wife to the Ayrshire constabulary and Ross Montgomery," returned Robert. "I was unaware of the statute. You, on the other hand, by your own admission were aware. Why then did you not deny the fact?"

"Because it didn't occur to me!" Iona retorted hotly.

"Wouldn't have been quite the thing either," replied Robert matter-of-factly with a roguish lift of one blond eyebrow. "You, stark naked in my bed, virtually telling all and sundry, to use your words, that you were without morals. No, that wouldn't have been at all the thing to do." Iona looked at him and shook her dark head, unable to formulate one good retaliatory rejoinder as a strange assortment of grunts and angry sounds issued from her frustrated mouth. She raised her eyes from his relaxed, smiling face to the ceiling. "Well, my love, it would seem we are married—and high time, too, according to my mother, although I was in no hurry to be so bound."

"Oh, my lord! Your mother!" exclaimed Iona with horror. "And your sisters!" she added in appalled tones, clutching her aching head.

"Awful, aren't they?" sympathized Robert. "I'm afraid the worst of it is that we shall have to do the whole thing properly at Forsythe Castle in the chapel. Tradition and all that, otherwise my mother will call our children the most shocking names!"

"Sir Robert Forsythe, I have no plans to bear your children!" she stated firmly, her color considerably heightened as the thought of the intimacy he implied sent excitement quivering through her.

"I agree it would be preferable to wait awhile before having children. We can travel, and entertain. Pregnancy does seem to put a damper on having a jolly good time," mused Robert.

"I am sure you are much more of an authority on that than I am," returned Iona with asperity, remembering how skillfully he had managed to remove her clothes the previous evening.

"Well, I should sincerely hope so. Not the thing at all for an innocent, well-bred young lady to be an authority on."

"Are you ever at a loss for a glib answer?" snapped Iona, irritated by his verbal facility. Robert nodded mutely. At last goaded beyond endurance, Iona stared around frantically for something to throw. "You are without doubt the most infuriating . . . the most provoking . . . exacerbating person!" she uttered, letting fly several cushions, which he skillfully caught before catching her and pulling her into his lap. He stared down lovingly into her flashing eyes, and before she could continue her list he captured her lips so her words were muffled.

Once again Iona felt exhilarating shock waves shoot through her, and unconsciously her arms crept about his neck until she held him tightly.

"Are you truly positive that you really want to be married to me?" she whispered huskily several long minutes later.

"I am becoming increasingly more excited about the prospect," returned Robert hoarsely, trailing a line of burning kisses down the slender column of her neck.

"What on earth is the matter wie me?" gasped Iona, trying to understand and free herself from the passion that threatened to completely submerge her, and from the demanding lips that kept her a willing captive on his lap and therefore very aware of his rising passion. Robert didn't answer but just stared deeply into her dark eyes, his handsome features intense and serious. He placed his large hands to each side of her beautiful face and gave her one more swift, hard kiss before setting her firmly aside and standing.

"Burn that abomination, my pet," he ordered, flicking a careless finger against the drab habit. Then he strode from the room imperiously, demanding Wilkes's immediate presence. Iona sat stunned, shaking her head blankly at the sudden curt rejection.

Less than an hour later she stood in a complete daze watching him, freshly shaven and dressed in clean clothes, mount a chestnut gelding.

"No more mischief-making, infants," he cheerfully called to his wide-eyed wards and a dumbfounded Iona before galloping away from Kenlaren, followed by the more sedate Wilkes in his prim black carriage.

Annie glared stonily at Iona's stricken expression as Robert disappeared from view.

"Och, if his past behavior as uncle or guardian is any indication, you'll be lucky if you see him again in a year or so," she pronounced cruelly. "Och, how could you be so deceitful?" she continued, hardening her tone when she felt herself softening at the desolation she saw in Iona's eyes. "To pretend to be my friend, while you were married to him the whole time?" she ranted.

"Hush yourself, lass," ordered a deep voice, and Annie glowered up into Roderick's lined face. "Things are not as they seem, Rob Roy," he added softly as Iona stood staring down the empty driveway with tears flowing down her dusky cheeks.

"Is anything as it seems?" retorted Annie. She stormed off to find her stallion and ride out her anger and confusion.

Chapter 12

The next weeks passed dismally, the weather mirroring the gray depression of all at Kenlaren. Iona kept to herself, and Michael, more than a little infatuated with her, found it impossible to study as he mooned over the tall dark beauty, who grew thinner and paler daily. Annie watched them both sullenly. She needed the money they had stolen from Ross Montgomery, yet she was loathe to approach Iona. Each night she tossed and turned, consumed with anxiety as Maude Potter's face disturbed her sleep and mingled with the terrifying smell of roses. Each day she stormed about, short-tempered and tired, glaring and snapping at anyone or thing in her way.

"Och, stop your disapproving looks!" she raged at Mrs. Wilson and Roderick MacDonald as they silently watched her, concern showing plainly on their old faces.

"What is it, me wee witch-wife?" clucked the old crone. "It canna be the greedy bitch due again so soon?"

"Leave me be!" hissed Annie rudely as she strode out into the drizzly weather.

"The greedy bitch?" echoed Roderick as the kitchen door slammed behind the girl.

"Aye, the greedy bitch gets greedier and greedier," sighed Mrs. Wilson, busily stitching a small rag doll. "Och, I wish I had some of the hair from her ratty head or some parings from her grasping hands to sew on this poppet," she muttered furiously, jabbing the needle in and out of the small limp body.

"And what greedy bitch would that be now, Mrs. Wilson?" Roderick asked casually, trying not to wince at the ferocity with which the old woman was piercing the doll.

"The one my wee-an has to pay, of course," returned the crone impatiently. "Och, for the past eight years I hae tried everything! Spells, brews, and now this!" she snapped, shaking the poppet roughly and stabbing it repeatedly in the heart. "But I maun be too old! I hae lost my touch, for I've nae killed that greedy Maude Potter yet!"

"Aaah! Of course, Maude Potter, *that* greedy bitch!" crowed Roderick with feigned enlightenment.

"Die!" screeched the old woman, throwing the stuffed effigy into the bubbling cauldron and prancing about gabbling dire-sounding, unintelligible incantations.

"And when do you think Maude Potter will be coming for her money?" asked Mr. MacDonald with a shudder as Mrs. Wilson stopped for breath.

"Only my wee-an knows that, you daffy feller!" replied the hag, shaking her snaky gray locks despondently. The bouyant effigy floating in the pot seemed to grin triumphantly at her. "But it will be soon, I feel it in my bones. Drown, Maude Potter! Drown!" she commanded, trying to submerge the poppet by poking it with her wooden spurtle.

"How often does Miss Oriana have to meet the greedy bitch?" probed Roderick, but the old woman was prancing and chanting about her black cauldron, oblivious to his presence.

Roderick quietly left the kitchen and breathed thankfully of the damp air, trying to clear his head of the spicy closeness of Mrs. Wilson's potion. Mindless of the steady drizzle that beaded thickly and then saturated his homespun tweeds, he strode through the rose garden, where the heavy blossoms bowed their fullness almost to the ground.

Iona sat at the open French window, staring bleakly across the misty, muted countryside. Roderick's already-furrowed brow frowned further at the intense sadness he saw etched on his young mistress's wan face. She looked so lost and forlorn. She caught his eye with a start and tried to smile.

"Is there anything I can do?" he asked softly, but she sadly shook her head.

"There's nothing to be done," she said dully before disappearing into the shadows within the house.

Annie rode Dubh through the constant fine rain as she tried to find the right words to approach Iona for the money. Several times she had nearly asked, but she had bitten her tongue, unable to be so insensitive and mercenary in the face of the woman's obvious misery. Annie sighed deeply and headed for home as Dubh plodded wearily around the boggy fields. She rode him into the large dry barn and methodically rubbed him down as her mind wrestled with her dilemma.

The sun had set and yet the rain continued as Annie sloshed across the yard and let herself into the kitchen. She stared thoughtfully into Mrs. Wilson's cauldron at the sodden doll that floated facedown in the noxious-smelling brew.

"Traipsing mud across my clean floor!" scolded the old crone, hiding the fear that filled her at the sight of the girl's set white face. "And soaked to the skin! Hasna the sense to get oot of the rain!" she gabbled, plucking at Annie's wet clothes.

"Leave me be, old woman!" snarled Annie, pushing the gnarled hands away and helping herself to bread and cheese.

"Your dinner is laid out in the dining room wie Master Michael and Miss Iona."

"I don't want company," retorted Annie. She slammed the door behind her and headed to the privacy of her room. Mrs. Wilson and Roderick MacDonald exchanged looks.

"It'll be tonight, mark my words," muttered the old witch, stabbing at the floating effigy of Maude Potter and imperiously ringing a handbell to summon a maid. "And that lass needs a guid hot soaking to get the rain from her bones. I'll nae hae my wee witch-wife ailing. Fair blue and pinched she looked," fussed the old woman.

"Witch-wife?" queried Roderick, the name suddenly sharp and forbidding to his ears. "Why do you call the lass that?"

"Mind your business!" snapped the old crone, glaring malevolently. "You heed me, auld mon! Mind your own business!"

Annie submitted absently to the long, hot bath and climbed numbly into bed, hoping to fall asleep the moment her head touched the pillow, but just like the previous nights she tossed and turned as anxiety and terror roiled and stabbed. She tried to think of happy things, such as Dubh with his mares and colts frolicking in the sun-drenched pasture, but the heavy perfume of the full-blown roses seeped into her senses, pounding her pulses as phantom screams tore through her memory and chilled her blood. She flung her pillow across the room, shattering a crystal vase, and sat up pressing her back against the carved headboard. She took a perverse pleasure in the torturous position that now made sleep and dreams impossible. She must not sleep or the nightmares would reach through her unaware layers and pull her into the suffocating panic of the past. The cloying redolence of roses in the damp night air filled her nostrils, causing her heart to race as though she were being stalked by an unseen evil.

"No!" she gasped aloud, leaping from the bed. She would not let her mind dwell on the half-formed shadowy impressions of that long-ago night that still haunted her, she resolved. She would go to Iona's room, claim the money, and buy Maude Potter's silence for another few months. She shrugged into a robe and tiptoed down the dark hall, not noticing Roderick dozing in the shadows.

The old man awoke to full alertness and watched Annie as she stood poised outside Iona's bedchamber with her small hand raised to knock. She sighed resignedly, dropped her hand, and half turned, as though to return to her own room, but changed her mind and put her ear to the wooden panel of the door, listening intently before rapping. She started as the sharp sounds echoed loudly through the still house. After a pause Iona opened the door and stood with candle in hand, staring sorrowfully at the smaller girl. Roderick was moved by the pathos as the flickering light accentuated the dark smudges beneath Iona's eyes and the hollows beneath her prominent cheekbones.

"I want the money!" demanded Annie without preamble, her young voice sounding vulnerable in its desperation. Iona nodded and stood to one side, allowing Annie to enter, and then the door was softly closed. Carefully Roderick eased his stiff old body to a standing position and crept down the corridor, hoping to listen through the thick oak door.

"I need the money now," repeated Annie awkwardly after a long silence while Iona just stood staring sorrowfully at her.

"Aye, the money," echoed the dark woman, staring with bewilderment about her room as though trying to remember where she had put it. "What money?" she cried, unable to understand what Annie requested.

"That we stole from Ross Montgomery," whispered the girl. "I am sorry but I really need it." Iona nodded her understanding of the urgency as she tried to pull herself together and think rationally. Annie was moved by the depths of suffering she felt emanating from Iona. "You really love my Uncle Robert, don't you?" she whispered wonderingly. "I'm sorry, I didn't know or I wouldn't have been so mean. But you shouldna be so sad, Iona, all men are like that. They come and go as they please. So you canna mourn and waste away, there's no point," she explained sagely, sharing her great experience of men, which included a father who had never shown any affection, twin brothers who raised her for nine years and then left for Africa without a backward glance, and an adored uncle who forgot her existence for months on end but would reappear with his engaging charm, knowing she would accept him the way he was. "My Uncle Robert, well, he doesna ken any other way to be. Och, he's a guid man but well . . . careless. It just doesna occur to him that he might be missed, unless Wilkes says something. If it wasna for Wilkes, I doubt he would remember that we existed at all," she said comfortingly. She felt very uncomfortable, though, when it seemed Iona was about to burst into tears. "Oh, please, Iona, dinna cry more, it is fair wearing me out," she begged as Iona's dark luminous eyes brimmed. "And I already feel very, very bad about asking you for the money when you are suffering fit to die . . . but if I do not get the money, terrible things will happen and I shall feel much worse!" Much to Annie's relief, Iona had the grace to look disgusted with herself for her copious tear-shedding. She sniffed ruefully and resolutely flicked away the teardrops that hung suspended on her dark lashes.

"Now, divert me from my self-pity," she said huskily with a brave grin. "Tell me, what terrible things will happen if I don't give you the money?"

"I cannot," whispered Annie, wishing that she could share her nightmarish burden. "Just give me the money, please?" Iona stared long and hard into Annie's stubborn little face before nodding resignedly and going into her dressing room. She returned with the worn saddle bag.

"There's nearly four hundred guineas," she informed dully. "And I was sorely tempted. The other night I was dressed and ready to flee Kenlaren with the money to some foreign clime where your detestable, arrogant, abominable guardian couldn't find me."

"That would have been robbery!" exclaimed Annie in shocked tones.

"Aye," replied Iona wearily, not having the energy to get into a discussion on morality with her young charge.

"Why didn't you?" asked Annie, her curiosity getting the better of her.

"Why didn't I what?"

"Flee to foreign climes?" asked Annie, her romantic imagination fired by the phrase and not wanting to return to her lonely chamber and her tortured dreams.

"I don't know," evaded Iona. She wasn't willing to admit she was waiting for Robert despite her better judgment. "When do you have to deliver the money?" she added, wanting her mind off her lover before she dissolved back into tears. Annie shrugged, loathed to involve Iona with the blackmailing Maude Potter. "Good night," she said politely, edging out of the room with the heavy saddle bag.

Roderick managed to scurry into the shadows before Annie ran down the corridor to her bedchamber. He cocked his grizzled head to one side as he heard two bolts being shot firmly into place. He made his old bones comfortable on the stair landing that led to his room on the third floor and watched Annie's door, certain that she would make the rendezvous with Maude Potter that night.

The night dragged slowly and Roderick dozed between each quarter of an hour, when the deep chimes of several clocks sounded, slightly out of syncopation, waking him. He was about to admit defeat and crawl achingly into his beckoning bed when he heard muffled cries and whimpers. He frowned and shook his head sadly in the darkness, recognizing the pitiful, heartrending sounds he had heard several times each week. He stretched and softly approached Annie's door and listened, wishing there were some way he could comfort. She was so strong and independent by day but at night he heard her suffer alone as no living thing should. What had happened to the beautiful golden child, he wondered.

Annie wrenched herself from the clawing nightmare and sat up soaked with perspiration and tears, trying to dispel the last ragged remnants of the dream as the sickly scent of roses seeped through the window, almost smothering her once more in terror. She forced herself to think of the pressing matters at hand; anything was preferable to the dream, even the blackmailer Maude Potter. Why had the greedy bitch suddenly changed the plan? All the other times there had been a badly spelled cryptic note on a filthy scrap of paper telling her where to meet the woman.

She had been ten years old when Maude Potter first contacted her. Ten years old and trying desperately to be the well-bred young lady her adored Uncle Robert wanted her to be. She had hobbled herself in pinching shoes, restricting undergarments, and skirts, and had even tried to ride sidesaddle. She had been proud and excited about showing off her new accomplishments to her uncle, who could pop up unexpectedly at any time or not turn up for months on end—but she didn't know that then, she remembered. That first time she had ridden sedately, perched on the sidesaddle, knowing Dubh looked his best stepping high and proud across the moors, hoping that any second her uncle would appear, clapping his hands and roaring out his approval, but it had been Maude Potter who had suddenly appeared by the Devil's Stepping Stones.

Annie hugged her knees, listening to the drizzling rain beat rhythmically, and she recalled it had started to rain that day. She had worn a new velvet riding habit, and the Spanish saddle was stiff and uncomfortable. She snorted sardonically now as she pictured herself at ten years old being so haughty in her ridiculous plumed hat, perched sideways on the enormous stallion. Och, she had felt so superior and sure of herself until she saw Maude Potter's shifty face, and then the bile had risen in her throat as the nightmare tore in, turning her back into a tiny grubby child. No! A tiny dirty child, she amended. No! A tiny bloodstained child! The smell of blood and the smell of roses joined together with phantom screams, and she slithered off Dubh's high back and vomited in the heather, soiling her elegant velvet habit and shining riding boots while Maude Potter laughed and laughed with glee. She had been still shaking with dry heaves when the woman had pulled her up by her hair, forcing her to listen to what she had to do.

In the beginning she had bribed the woman with jewelry tokens and pin money that her uncle carelessly showered on her, but when that didn't satisfy the woman's demands Annie resorted to stealing anything she could find, from silver bonbon dishes to tarnished candlesticks from the attic. She confided in Michael, hoping for help, but her brother had very romantic memories of his tragic mother and he became helpless with sorrow and rage at hearing she could be labeled an adultress and a whore. Annie sighed as she recalled the incredible loneliness and fear that had overcome her when she realized she was stronger and more capable of handling the situation than her older brother was. She firmly impressed upon him the necessity of protecting their family name and bullied him into sharing his very generous allowance.

For a while the worry about paying Maude Potter was assuaged, but then Michael went off to the university in Edinburgh and the nightmare resumed, forcing her to resort to highway robbery in order to satisfy the woman's demands.

Annie breathed deeply and forced her thoughts back to the present. Why had Maude Potter suddenly changed her mode of operating? Instead of the grubby misspelt scrap of paper, this time a neatly sealed envelope had been pushed under her bedroom door. When she had questioned Millie, the freckle-faced maid had shrugged, denying any knowledge, as had the rest of the house servants. Annie shivered as she thought of Maude Potter gliding through the corridors of Kenlaren, melting in and out of the shadows and watching her. The woman struck terror into her very heart, terror like the smell of roses and the phantom screams. Not only had Maude Potter's stationery changed, so had her handwriting and method of collecting the money. Instead of meeting under the cloak of darkness at the Devil's Stepping Stones on the moor, now Annie was expected to ride into the busy market town of Annan in bright daylight on a Wednesday when the road would be choked with farmers and peddlars. She had been instructed to leave the money in a flour sack at a certain spot, to speak to no one, and to return straightaway to Kenlaren Manor. Annie shook her head. She should be overjoyed at not having to witness the grasping woman's salivating mouth as she ran her greedy hands through the coins and cackled insanely. That chilling laugh grated down Annie's spine now, mingling with the screams and blood that spiraled her back to that awful night in the murky past.

Despite her intentions to stay awake, Annie fell into an exhausted but fortunately dreamless sleep and awoke several hours later to yet another dismal, drizzly day. She stretched her aching body and stared out of the window at the mopey sky, thinking of the long ride to Annan, before reluctantly clambering out of bed.

Roderick and Mrs. Wilson rose early at their advanced ages, loath to miss any more of their remaining days than was necessary. They frowned with concern this morning as Annie grabbed a burlap sack and silently rode out without breakfast, dressed as a ragged stableboy.

"Well, it canna be the greedy bitch; she's always at night," mused the old crone, turning back to her cauldron of porridge as sturdy fieldhands filed into the kitchen and sat expectantly at the table.

By the noon meal, Mrs. Wilson wasn't so sure, as there was no sign of Annie, and by evening both old people were sadly out of temper, uncharacteristically snapping at the hardworking servants, who just wanted a tranquil, filling meal. In the midst of high tea in the late afternoon of the following day several carriages bowled up the driveway, commanding attention and causing servants to run in every direction as Sir Robert arrived overflowing with incredible presents for his bride. Unfortunately for the impulsive, generous groom, his spouse had ridden off earlier, determined on finding solitude.

"Then where in Hades is Oriana?" Robert imperiously demanded, only to be answered with helpless shrugs. "Michael then?" This question had elicited some slight reward, as his nephew was located moping in the library.

"Annie has not been seen since this morning," tattled the youth sulkily.

"What is so unusual about that?" snapped Robert. "My gracious, old boy, you look like something the cat scratched up! Take your nose out of those wretched books and get into the sunshine! You look like a vaporous female!" he continued, irritated by his nephew's wan looks and whining tone and put out by the dreary pall that covered Kenlaren. Michael, grossly insulted, opened his mouth to hotly retort, but one look at his uncle's stern face changed his mind. Obediently he took himself outside to the dismal countryside, where there wasn't the slightest vestige of sunshine, only unrelenting rain.

Annie returned wet, bedraggled, and hungry just as the absent sun had presumably set behind the thick clouds that shrouded everything.

"Where's Iona?" thundered Robert as soon as she trotted up on the exhausted Dubh. Annie shook her head in exasperation. Her uncle never changed, she seethed; he just took off without warning and expected everyone to be waiting, doing nothing, when he took it into his head to return. With a sigh she dismounted and handed the reins to a cowering ostler, who gingerly skirted Sir Robert to escape the booming ire that had been vent on everything at Kenlaren from chickens to people.

"It is good to see you, too, Uncle Robert," returned Annie sweetly.

"Where is my wife?"

"I am not your wife's keeper," she returned pertly, trying to keep her temper, only to be swung about most violently. "I have no notion where Iona is!" She tried to shrug free of his hard hands so she might change out of her uncomfortable wet clothes and soak her aching muscles in a warm bath. "And where have you been, dear uncle?" she inquired when his firm grip showed no signs of relenting. "I do declare your new bride has fair wasted away pining for you." Robert frowned at Annie's cold censuring tones.

"She did?" he said in a most uncharacteristic voice. "Oh, there is a new gown in your bedchamber," he informed her as he released her at last and looked about in a very distracted way.

"A new gown? Why?"

"For the wedding," returned Robert, heedless of the heavy rain that was pitting the pile on his new coat.

"Whose wedding?" asked Annie, totally confused.

"Mine."

"Who are you marrying this week?" she returned, thinking the poor man touched in the head.

"Don't be ridiculous!" snapped Robert. He turned and strode up the muddy lane that led to the wild stretch of moorland. Annie watched him go, shaking her sopping head with exasperation before racing into the house. Roderick and Wilkes, dressed appropriately in voluminous mackintoshes, also shook their heads and exchanged knowing glances as they heard Robert splashing through the muddy dusk bellowing for Iona.

Iona heard Robert's booming voice and she reined her horse, her heart beating rapidly with the excitement that curled in the pit of her belly. She curbed her desire to dig in her heels and gallop toward him as her anger surged at the autocratic ring she heard in his demanding tones. Purposefully she rode in the opposite direction, circling Kenlaren so she arrived back at the house while he still strode over the dark, wet moors.

"Sir Robert is looking for you, Lady Iona," informed a tense ostler, holding her horse as she wearily dismounted.

She nodded, acknowledging the news, before splashing across the yard to the house.

Half an hour later Iona lay soaking in a relaxing bath. Drowsily she listened to the incessant rain beating against the windowpanes. On a small table by the tub was the untouched tray of supper she had requested, not having the energy or courage to deal with Sir Robert Forsythe and his two unpredictable wards in the formal dining room. She sighed deeply and idly sipped a glass of rich Burgundy, somehow sensing her tranquility would be short-lived. She closed her eyes and felt the warming liquid slip down her throat, and she wondered whether she would be furious if Robert thundered at her door or disappointed if he didn't. She drained her glass savagely, out of patience with herself and the hold he had over her. When she reached over the side of the bath for the wine bottle she avoided looking at the pile of boxes and bags that were piled higgledy-piggledy in the corner because her dressing room was already overflowing from Robert's shopping spree.

"I canna be bought!" she stated, squelching her desire to tear open the wrappings and, instead, poured herself another full glass of the earthy wine. She sipped, sinking lower into the rapidly cooling water. She found to her disgust that she was listening for his bootsteps.

Robert sat in the formal dining room, his wet hair slicked back close against his head. He toyed with his food and then impatiently pushed the full plate away and refilled his wineglass. Annie chewed slowly and watched him. She had changed from her stableboy rags into a soft, flowing gown, somehow hoping to incite a response from her uncle, but he was oblivious to everything. Michael ate nervously, looking from his uncle's set face to his speculative sister.

"Uncle Robert, why don't you go upstairs and see Iona, so Michael can read his books and I can eat with my fingers?" suggested Annie impishly.

"Did Wilkes explain everything to you?" asked Robert, ignoring her suggestion.

"I'm not going! Our grandmother has made it very clear that she doesn't acknowledge us! Thinks of us as bastards!" stated Michael stubbornly.

"And I'm not going either," informed Annie airily. "You got married without us before; I am sure you can do it again."

"I see," replied Robert heavily after a long pause as he looked from brother to sister wearily. He shrugged, refilled his wineglass again, and leaned back in his chair, contemplating the dark red liquid gloomily. "Ungrateful brats! Do you think I'm looking forward to it either?" he lamented, thinking of his mother and sisters and the cold sharp stones of the Forsythe chapel.

"The wedding or our grandmother?" asked Annie candidly.

"Your aunts and grandmother," he embellished with a wry smile at the way Annie never skirted the truth but dove right in.

"Och, I dinna understand all the fuss about ceremony and religion and tradition. None of it seems to make the least bit of sense except to cause unhappiness, inconvenience, wars, and rude names," she sighed. "Now, when I fall in love, none of those stupid conventions will inconvenience me!" Her statement caused Robert to raise his eyebrows in alarm as previously unthought-of dangers sprang into his mind. He gazed at her in horror, noting the soft, sensuous curves under her clinging gown.

"Some of the conventions are not quite as stupid as they might seem," he strove hoarsely. "Dash it all, Oriana, everything has a perfectly good reason."

"For instance?"

"I am going upstairs to see Iona," he said, standing very suddenly and draining his glass. He was unwilling and unable to discuss carnality with his curious young ward, who leaned over the table, her eyes alight with avid interest. He walked silently to the door, stopped, and looked back at Annie's vibrant face and hair, then shook his blond head dolefully and sighed. Thank God he'd had the foresight to get married to a sensible woman, he congratulated himself. Now he could place the whole sticky problem of the nubile female in his wife's capable hands.

Robert strode thoughtfully up the stairs. He stopped outside Iona's room and flexed his hands, not knowing whether to knock. Suddenly he hammered authoritively on the door. He heard a low gasp and the sound of water lapping against a hollow side.

"Iona?" he roared peremptorily, subconsciously wanting to cover his fear of possible rejection with a loud noise.

Iona stood in the tub shivering, trying to orient herself. She must have fallen asleep, she mused, staring at her wrinkled, sodden hands that were now an unattractive chalky color. When the thunderous knocking was repeated she stared about, looking for a towel.

"Who is it?" she asked unnecessarily, as Robert's imperious voice could probably be heard in every corner of the house and across Kenlaren's rolling lawns. She wrenched open the door and her knees felt weak at the sight of him. Robert frowned at her very wan face, which seemed much thinner than he remembered. She stared up at him mesmerized, her dark eyes seeming enormous and luminous. There was a very long silent moment . . . broken when Iona suddenly shivered violently.

Robert shook himself free of the inertia and took in her sopping state as she clutched a towel numbly about herself and stood with water puddling at her bare feet. Without thought he strode into the room slamming the door behind him. Picking up a dry towel, he draped it over Iona's dripping wet head and swung her into his arms. He sat on her bed, cradling her on his lap, drenching himself, and ruining the crease of his tailored trousers as he dried her hair and scolded like an English nanny.

"Oh, you silly Billy, look at those pruny hands! It is extremely dangerous to fall asleep in the bath. Dash it all, you could have hit your head! Drowned! Caught pneumonia or any other of a host of infernal diseases!" he ranted. "Look at those poor dear toes!" he added in outraged tones as he laid her back against the pillows and tenderly dried her feet. He ran out of words under her silent but direct gaze. "Did you miss me?" he asked hesitantly. Silently she nodded, her dark eyes brimming. With a groan Robert enfolded her in his arms and she burst into tears and clung to him, feeling like the most despicable type of weak female, but unable to stop herself.

"Robert," she sniffed after a while. She had determined that it was necessary to have a discussion before he vanished again, as seemed to be his wont.

"Handkerchief?" he asked, gallantly offering a neatly folded one. Iona nodded her thanks and availed herself of the proffered respite as she mopped her cheeks and sought the appropriate words.

"Robert," she started bravely. "We have to talk." She shook her head as she heard her triteness.

"Now?" he lamented, kissing the tip of her nose. She nodded sternly. "I say, you didn't open any of my presents!" he complained indignantly, catching sight of the enormous pile that spilled out of the dressing room, and eager to change the subject for fear she was going to say something he didn't want to hear.

"Robert?" she cried helplessly, but he had already crossed the room and was tearing open one of the gift boxes, hoping to woo her with the contents.

"Look," he commanded, holding up exquisite underthings of silk and lace. Normally she would have blushed at the intimate, frothy scraps in his large, tanned hands, but she just sighed with despair and lay back, swaddled like a naked baby in bath towels on the wide bed.

"Robert!" she snapped shrewishly, deciding to take the reins. He turned, losing his boyish excitement and forgetting the coquettish absurd little hat he held, its long plume tickling his nose. "Och, Robert," she repeated. He looked as vulnerable as she felt. His blue eyes looked at her anxiously, like a puppy expecting to be kicked. "Robert, I have to talk to you," she insisted softly. He nodded sheepishly and sat at the foot of the bed.

"Ready, aim, and fire," he joked, putting the silly little hat on his head.

"Robert, I love you," she stated simply, her overrehearsed speech deflating before it could be aired. "I haven't finished," she added hastily as he made a move to bound up the bed exuberantly. "Now, I know you declared us married to protect me, and I really do appreciate that, but I dinna think we should allow that to bind us to a situation . . . that . . . is repugnant to you. . . ."

"Repugnant!" exclaimed Robert, now bounding up the bed.

"I haven't finished," said Iona, trying to stave him off.

"You have! By Jove, Iona, I can't be humble and self-effacing any longer. It is totally against my nature!" he interrupted, taking her in his arms and wrenching off the towel, irritated by its cool dampness. He held her warm nakedness possessively to him.

"Robert, this is really quite unconventional . . . decidedly improper!" She struggled, at the same time snuggling nearer, loving his smell and the feel of his cheek against hers.

"Yes, isn't it!" agreed Robert happily. "Do you know I learn more and more from that totally unbridled, untamed, unpredictable brat of mine?"

"Who?" questioned Iona, utterly confused by his sudden change of subject.

"Oriana," returned Robert. "Do you know how I've spent the last week, my darling?"

"Och, say that again?" pleaded Iona.

"Oriana?"

"Not that! Say 'my darling' again?" she asked shyly.

"My darling. My love," he growled, kissing her each time. "My pet."

"Purr," murmured Iona, curling closer. "You were saying?" she prompted after a long passionate kiss that left them both breathless.

"What was I saying?"

"You spent the last week?" cued Iona.

"Making lavish arrangements for a most traditional, highly acceptable Catholic wedding in the chapel at Forsythe Castle," he recited, and then stopped when he felt her grow tense in his arms. "Under the covers with you," he ordered, seeing the goose bumps raised on her shivering flesh and preferring to believe it from the cold—despite the room's humid warmth—than from aversion to his family.

"What do you learn from Annie?" asked Iona when she was snugly tucked under the covers and he lay beside her on top of the eiderdown.

"That when one falls in love, tradition and formality have no place," announced Robert rashly. "There's a Catholic church in Dumfries, and allowing a few days for the banns to be read, we could be married by the end of the week," he said, frowning as he saw her elation fade. "Oh, my God! You *are* Catholic, aren't you?" he exclaimed with horror.

"Yes, but . . ."

"Thank heavens!" he interrupted with great relief.

"Robert, you are an only son. I canna ask such a sacrifice of you. Your family . . ."

"Is right here at Kenlaren Manor and has been for many years. Oriana, Michael, Wilkes—even Mrs. Wilson—they are my family," he stated with surprise. "And now there is Roderick MacDonald and you, my darling. And you, my love, hold my heart, my soul . . . and my manhood." With that husky admission he lost himself in her sweet, submissive mouth. Iona obeyed the pressure of his insistent tongue and opened to the firm thrusts that claimed her mouth. She struggled against the covers that he had tucked so firmly about her, for now they were frustrating her like a veritable chastity case.

"Robert?" she begged, her body writhing and on fire, but he breathed deeply and tucked the covers even more tightly.

"We have to talk, Iona," he insisted in a very good imitation of her earlier statement. "Now, from certain things that popped out of Oriana's mouth, I think it is imperative that a woman explain things to her that I have no business explaining and I'm having an even harder time controlling. Stop wiggling, woman," he protested as she pressed sensuously against him in an effort to stop his talking. "I have made arrangements to have Forsythe House in London totally refurbished and we shall take up residence there in September to prepare Oriana for the season."

Iona froze, remembering the long, painful months she had spent in London during the season she made her debut into society. Robert frowned with disappointment as her sensuous gyrations abruptly ceased. "Anything you don't like there you have full authority to change, provided we are in agreement . . . and I promise there is no pink anywhere in the house," he informed her. "You can resume your wiggles," he added hopefully.

"London?" whispered Iona, her raging passion thoroughly doused.

"London," Robert concurred. "That is where I live most of the time. It's time we dug Oriana out of the country and polished her into the brightest debutante. . . ."

"I could be a detriment to Oriana's success!" interrupted Iona harshly. "You must recall, Sir Robert, I wasn't quite up to snuff. The society matrons looked askance at my barbaric Scottish manner."

"They were jealous because you put their simpering daughters to shame," declared Robert. "But as my wife, you'll jolly well have nothing to fear from those old battle-axes."

Iona loved the security of the strong arms that cradled her, but nevertheless the elation and excitement of a scarce few minutes before had been squelched.

"You dinna need a wife, Sir Robert, you need a chaperone and governess for your ward," she teased, trying to lighten her mood.

"True," agreed Robert. "But I have to admit a wife can be bloody convenient, especially with respect to certain intimate needs of my own," he confessed suggestively, kissing the velvet warmth below her ear. Iona rubbed her nose against his bristly cheek, inhaling the male scent of him. With her eyes tightly closed she sought his mouth, wanting to submerge herself with him so she didn't have to think about the future.

"And what sort of needs would those be?" she asked mischievously, struggling to remove both arms from the restriction of the the cocooned bed clothes, but Robert's weight made it impossible.

"Needs that I shall thoroughly enjoy educating you about at the end of the week," he said infuriatingly, kissing her forehead like an aged grandfather.

"Robert?" she gasped with outrage as he strode to the door.

"Yes, pet?"

"Where are you going?"

"To bed, of course. I should sincerely regret doing anything to damage your reputation."

"But it's already in shreds!" she exclaimed. "And we're married . . . by declaration," she added hopefully.

"But not by the Holy Roman Church," chided Robert with a rueful wink before blowing her a kiss and opening the door. He looked surreptitiously up and down the corridor before popping his head back inside. "You are my wife, not some bit of fluff, old girl."

"What?" squawked Iona indignantly, sitting upright. "Bit of fluff?"

"Bit of fluff? Cyprian? Trollop? Strumpet?" explained Robert helpfully.

"Cyprian? Trollop? Strumpet?" repeated Iona. Annie, running barefoot up the carpeted stairs, stopped in amazement at hearing this extraordinary exchange.

"Hetaera? Odalisque? Paramour? Concubine?" recited Robert with great alacrity, thoroughly enjoying himself.

"Odalisque? Wife," pondered Iona aloud. "Paramour . . . wife," she continued, making the word *wife* sound drab and dreary and the synonym for "bit of fluff" like poetry. "Concubine? Wife."

"I think I prefer *concubine* and *paramour* to wife," stated Annie baldly, popping her head between her uncle and the doorjamb and staring with interest at Iona, who sat in bed naked from the waist up. "I have never heard the word *odalisque* before. Sounds like a rotten smell." She pushed past her uncle into the bedchamber and made herself most comfortable on the window seat. Iona and Robert looked at her with stunned amazement. "I think 'fille-de-joie' is preferable. Girl of joy . . . doesn't it sound better than 'wife'? Fille-de-joie," she whispered dreamily.

"There is a particularly fetching nightgown over there somewhere," informed Robert, pointing to the untidy pile of packages. Iona looked down to where his eyes pointedly stared even though one dictatorial finger indicated another direction. She curbed the instinct to cover herself defensively and stared back at him rebelliously.

"Good night, Sir Robert, I would hate to have you compromise yourself on my account. You can never tell when the cyprian in me might rise from the shreds of my reputation," she pronounced, covering her fury with a liberal dose of sarcasm. Annie's eyes rounded with admiration. Iona looked magnificent, her long black hair loose about her shoulders and her bare breasts high. All her anger at Iona melted and she grinned and looked expectantly at her uncle, waiting to see how he would react.

Robert looked from his barebreasted bride to his young ward, who sat in an extremely unconventional manner with one knee drawn up. The other lithe brown leg was dangling, the gracefully arched foot swinging rhythmically and brushing the deep pile of the carpet.

"London will not be boring, it seems," he sighed, looking from one to the other and not missing the crackling mischief present despite the open, innocent looks of both young women.

"London? When?" squealed Annie.

"Who said you were to go, infant?" teased Robert.

"Iona, we're going to London?" asked Annie, ignoring him. "Can we have faro parties and soirées? I've always wanted to gamble. I think I could make my fortune," she chattered excitedly.

"Gambling!" ejaculated Robert. "Definitely not! Iona will teach you a little bridge and whist, but positively no gambling and *absolutely no 'fille de joie-ing'!* Is that clear?" Annie looked at him as though he were mad before raising a questioning eyebrow at Iona, who meanwhile had discreetly edged the sheet so that it modestly covered her breasts.

"Fille de joie-ing?" giggled Iona.

"Good Lord, Oriana, why couldn't you have stayed nine years old? Then you were pretty much of a handful, but now you are bloody impossible!" snapped Robert once again appalled at how her soft gown molded sensuously to her curves. "Iona, it occurs to me that that riding habit your Cousin Mary gave you would be quite the thing for Oriana. Give it to her." He was thinking that a pair of spectacles might also help to hide his young niece's attributes.

"I can't. I burned it as you told me to," replied Iona sweetly, much to Annie's relief. "Fille de joie-ing?" she questioned wickedly, giving Robert a provocative look.

Chapter 13

The wedding day dawned sunny and clear, a perfect June day filled with birds and butterflies. Annie twirled and spun about in her free-flowing, virginal gown, barefoot as usual, with daisy chains entwined in her streaked auburn hair. Michael's solemn young face shone with pride and anxiety as he fingered the wedding band entrusted to his care, terrified that he would misplace it. He stood stiffly next to Robert, the two of them facing the wizen old priest and waiting for Iona to walk down the aisle, with Annie holding the long train of Belgian lace.

In the first pew to the right sat Wilkes, impeccable as usual, as the member of the groom's party, and to the left sat Roderick as relative to the bride. Mrs. Wilson sat in the middle of the central aisle, cross-legged in the center of a strange, chalked sign she had drawn, bedecked with every plant and root she knew of to protect her from the Christian spirits and to aid fertility.

Outside in the brilliant sunshine Dubh stood proudly, with mock orange blossoms and daisy chains woven in his mane and tail, next to Wilkes's prim black carriage and Robert's gaily decorated curricle. There had been a very happy floral procession after an early breakfast of strawberries and May wine.

In the dark recesses of the vast church Annie frowned at Roderick's straight back, wondering why he was sitting when he should have had Iona on his arm. Her piercing whistle to get the old man's attention was drowned out by the pumping of a wheezy organ that signaled the start of the ceremony. Iona motioned Annie to pick up her train.

"You'll have to carry it yourself. I canna be your bridesmaid, Iona."

"Why?"

"I maun be your father," sighed Annie, lapsing into a soft brogue.

"What on earth for?" laughed Iona.

"Well, someone has to give you away. Someone who loves you," she explained. Iona looked lovingly down at her and then over her golden head and nodded, tears of happiness filling and overspilling from her dark eyes. Annie frowned and then her heart turned somersaults in her breast as she saw reflected in a window a very tall, very dark man. Even though his aristocratically chiseled features were not clear from where she stood, she knew who he was. Her blood ran strangely and she wasn't sure if it felt boiling hot or icy cold, but it thundered, numbing her senses. In a daze she picked up the yards of fine Belgian lace and followed the tall dark couple down the long aisle, nearly falling over the rocking, chanting old woman in her bipartisan position.

Lochiel Montgomery stared about the dark cavernous interior of the church, not certain if he was awake or asleep. The close musty darkness was in direct contrast to the almost blinding colors of the tropics, where he'd spent the previous long months. He strode down the aisle with his sister on his arm, mentally trying to clear his head as everything around him seemed to have a nightmarish quality, and there was a deep ache between his eyes blurring and distorting his vision. Who was the tall, blond man who stood expectantly at the altar next to a slim, auburn-haired youth? He sucked in his breath, about to give voice to violent objections when he recognized Sir Robert Forsythe, whom he felt to be one of the most indolent, boring, and self-centered of the English peers of his acquaintance. He felt Iona tug slightly on his arm and he stared down into her expressive face, which glowed with love and silently implored him to understand. He frowned, showing his confusion.

"I love him," mouthed Iona silently. Loch bit his lip and held his peace, but the glower he gave Robert told all.

Robert stared languidly into Lochiel's ebony eyes and nodded, understanding the implicit warning but not intimidated in the slightest. His blue eyes deepened to a profound azure and he allowed a reassuring smile to curl the corners of his full, sensuous mouth but Loch's thin, sculpted lips just tightened as he reluctantly handed his radiant sister into the Englishman's keeping.

Lochiel stepped back and sat beside Roderick MacDonald. His seething thoughts swirled miles away from the simple ceremony being enacted before him. He closed his blurring eyes and rested his pounding head against the uncomfortable carved pew, afraid he was delirious and back in the oppressive humidity of the South American rain forest being attacked by swarms of biting insects. An irritating buzzing crackled in his ears, joining with the deep drone of the priest and the rhythmic incantations of the ancient crone who crouched in the central aisle. He sighed as he admitted that there had been times in the previous months when he would have welcomed death, as he had felt he was rotting alive in the steaming jungle, where the strident mocking cries of the vibrant birds joined with the memory of the anguished screams of his imprisoned horses as they panicked and splintered their delicate legs trying to escape from the burning ship. Mrs. Wilson's chanting crescendoed and the priest raised his voice to be heard, causing Loch to open his eyes and stare about with bewilderment. Feeling a reassuring touch on his arm, he gazed into Roderick MacDonald's concerned old face and recollected his surroundings. He was in Scotland. Back in his homeland after interminable months of a nightmarish existence. But what was he doing in the echoing, cavernous interior of this nearly empty church? He furrowed his brow, trying to piece together the previous few days, or even hours, as though to anchor himself to a concrete reality. He remembered the fleet vessel that had rescued him. He had stood at the prow watching the water divide and ripple symmetrically away from the craft as it cut cleanly through the vast ocean. He remembered the undulation of the ship and the rhythm of the waves, not daring to believe he was going home to Falconhurst. He remembered staring with distrust at the coasts of Ireland and Wales, and as the cutter sailed triumphantly up the Solway Firth of Scotland, he had smothered all his emotion for fear it was an illusion. He had disembarked at Glencapie, where he had been met by several solicitous men who arranged for a comfortable room and a bath. In a daze he had submitted without question to their administrations, allowing himself to be dressed in formal highland clothing he knew to be his own, but not having the energy or inclination to demand explanation. He had been deposited on the steps of a large church in Dumfries, where he now sat watching his sister marry an Englishman. He turned to Roderick and roughly grabbed his arm but the old man shook his head gently and raised one gnarled finger to his pleated lips, begging silence. Once again Loch closed his eyes.

Annie heard very little of the service as the priest droned on and on, so mesmerized was she by Loch's strong shoulders and ebony hair. Several times she found her eyes fastened on his chiseled profile, tracing the stern, prominent bones as a strange pulse beat achingly in the core of her. When the priest pronounced the couple man and wife, Annie dropped the bride's train, anxious to be free of the dark, disturbing stranger, and she dashed out of the church into the blinding sunlight.

At the altar Robert drowned in Iona's sweet mouth, uncaring of his very holy surroundings. All he could think of was her desirable body. His well-manicured hands roamed up her supple back, putting to memory each curve as he held her tightly to the center of him, which burned with need. A violent tug at his coattails by Michael, red with embarrassment, brought him to the reality of his surroundings and reluctantly he removed his mouth from Iona's sweet lips and grinned at her rueful little squawk. Robert turned like a happy sleepwalker and stared into Loch's obsidian eyes with their silent but potent warning. He looked back at Iona's equally dark eyes, which brimmed and overflowed with happiness as she linked arms with her long-lost brother and her husband.

"Where's Annie?" she sniffed as tears of joy ran unchecked down her smooth cheeks.

"We'll not worry about Oriana today, my love," said Robert as they broke out of the dark recesses of the church into the bright June sunshine. "She's still about," he added, observing the black stallion. He handed Iona up into the gaily decorated carriage and swung himself up beside her. "We shall meet back at Kenlaren for the wedding luncheon," he called out, whipping the matched grays into a brisk canter, eager to be alone with his radiant bride.

Roderick MacDonald stood silently, watching Lochiel appraise the dark stallion.

"Aye, 'tis your own Dubh," the old man said gruffly, his heart aching with happiness at seeing his young master safe. Loch turned to look at his oldest friend, and Roderick saw changes in the chiseled features. There was a hard ruthlessness in the sunburnt face that had not been present before. Loch turned back to the proud animal, who shook and butted his large head up and down, trying to shake free the daisy chains entwined in his glossy mane.

Annie watched the tall, hawk-faced man with her stallion and she was afraid—afraid of losing Dubh and of the dark stranger himself, this man who had filled so many of her dreams. She pursed her lips and gave a piercing whistle, summoning her untethered horse. Dubh pricked up his ears and whinnied softly but did not obey immediately the way he usually did. Annie's heart beat painfully and she whistled again. Obediently the great horse slowly walked toward her, swishing his long tail.

Loch stood silently, watching the majestic animal and the petite golden girl, her exquisite little face set on hard, challenging lines, one small brown hand laid claimingly against the ebony hide. There was a long pause before the elfin female leapt upon a low wall and onto Dubh's high back, her long white dress flying up to show lithe suntanned legs and bare feet.

Roderick knew the beauty of the golden girl astride the large dark horse was lost upon Loch as he saw the aquiline nose flare with anger. After a moment Loch untethered his horse and mounted.

"That young mon has a bee in his bonnet," clucked Mrs. Wilson, hobbling stiffly down the wide granite steps of the church, clutching her roots and herbs. Wilkes sat quietly in his prim carriage, his solemn face thoughtful. He had witnessed the silent encounter between Loch and Annie, and he knew a gauntlet had been flung down by the impulsive girl. Roderick helped Mrs. Wilson into the carriage, where she sat heavily, shaking her head from side to side.

"There's a storm a-brewing," she stated as Wilkes urged the horse into a sedate pace. Neither Roderick or Wilkes looked to the cloudless sky, but their eyes stared rheumily in the direction Annie had taken, followed by Lochiel.

"Do you think they're on their way back to Kenlaren?" asked Wilkes as they came to the crossroads at Castle Douglas and he stared pensively down the southern fork toward the Solway Firth.

"Och, my wee witch-wife'll gie him the slip, I'll be bound," cackled Mrs. Wilson. "Och, aye, she will."

"Och, you dinna ken Lochiel Montgomery," returned Roderick in defense of his own young master. "If he has a mind to catch her, he will." His leathery old face frowned as he thought of the new ruthlessness he had observed etched on the face of the young man.

"From the pucker on your brow, auld mon, 'twould seem you're nae so sure of your young-un," snapped Mrs. Wilson cunningly.

"My lad's had a hard time. Needs fattening up a wee bit after a lot of pagan food on those heathen shores," returned Roderick fiestily, trying to assuage his nagging doubts.

"There's nothing wrong wie pagans and heathens!" stated Mrs. Wilson cantankerously.

Annie grinned with satisfaction as she watched Lochiel Montgomery thunder past. She waited until Wilkes's prim carriage had followed before doubling back and riding across the open moorland, determined to hide Dubh where Lochiel couldn't possibly find him.

Wilkes reined his carriage in the courtyard. Roderick alit and turned to help Mrs. Wilson, who stood with her gnarled hands on her hips, cackling triumphantly at the furious expression on Lochiel Montgomery's face.

"Och, I told you my wee-an could gie yours the slip!" she crowed before heaving herself down the carriage steps and nearly flattening Roderick as she overbalanced, still jiggling merrily with mirth. "Keep away from my wee-an, she's nae for the likes of you even if you do hae the look of the de'il!" she warned, pointing a bony finger.

"Roderick," clipped Loch's imperious voice.

"Hold yer horses, laddie, your Roderick is gie-ing this auld witch a much-needed hand," scolded the old crone, leaning heavily on the man's arm and limping as though she were crippled. "Mr. MacDonald, tell your uppity young master there that if'n he harms one hair on my wild lassie's head I'll weave one of my most embarrassing spells and wilt his private parts," she hissed. At the kitchen door she turned to assess the dark young man. "Black Scot canna mix wie the Red Scot," she stated as a bleak ache of foreboding flooded through her. "'Tis like oil and water!" she ranted and slammed the door angrily behind her.

Roderick walked steadily back to Lochiel, searching the young face for gentleness and vulnerability, but the black eyes were as hard as coal. He smiled in an effort to coax the set features to soften.

"Och, 'tis so guid to have you back, Lochiel," he rejoiced. "You look a mite tired."

"Aye," snapped Loch shortly. "What the hell is going on, Mr. MacDonald?" he demanded as the pain in his head reached unbearable proportions.

"Going on?" repeated Roderick, not quite knowing where to start.

"I have spent the last seven months or more just managing to stay alive in an insect-infested, snake-infested jungle in the middle of nowhere. I step off a vessel this morning after a month at sea and am met and assisted by men I do not know. Then I find myself deposited on the steps of an empty church where a mad witch sits weaving spells and a changeling child appears riding a black stallion with flowers in his mane—*my* own Dubh, stolen so many years ago," raved the usually taciturn young man. "And as if all this incredible madness is not enough, I find my only sister dressed as a bride . . . and in the midst of it all is you, Mr. MacDonald, with a happy grin splitting your face as if everything is normal and . . . and . . ." He stopped, putting a hand to his tousled black hair as a wave of dizziness overcame him. Roderick reached out to steady him and a frown creased his wrinkled face when he felt heat emanate.

"You're not well, lad," he stated softly.

"Where's the girl?" demanded Loch, impatiently pushing away the old man's fussing hands.

"Loch?" called Iona. He turned to see her at the open French doors, looking radiant, with Robert's arm possessively about her slender waist.

"And . . . and I find her marrying that spoiled pompous sassanach Forsythe!" he muttered furiously out of the side of his mouth as he waved to his sister. Roderick wisely refrained from comment as he and his young master strode into the house.

Annie sat quietly, her wineglass in hand as Lochiel entered the small dining room where a small tasteful wedding buffet had been laid out. She watched as he was warmly embraced by Iona, who laughed and cried at the same time, not quite believing her brother was alive and present on her wedding day. Iona frowned as she brushed a wayward lock of hair from his forehead and felt the heat. Loch, seeing her concern, smiled boyishly and removed her hand, holding it in his.

"Are you happy?" he asked huskily, and she nodded, unable to voice the fullness she felt. He gave her a quick hug before turning to accept a proffered glass of wine and cast his eyes around the well-proportioned room.

Annie felt a shock surge through her as his dark eyes met hers. She kept her face stony and unemotional and raised her glass in a mocking toast. Iona looked from Annie to Loch and smiled, remembering the circumstances of their one previous meeting. She wondered how they would deal with the situation now, especially when her brother saw Dubh's handsome offspring. She was too happy, her eyes too full of joy and love to notice the subtle change in her brother. She touched his hair lovingly, not seeing the ruthless set of his jaw or the way his smile didn't quite reach his eyes as he looked at the petite golden girl.

"You and Annie should get formally acquainted. Lochiel, Oriana—Oriana, Lochiel," she said mischievously before turning back to her adoring husband, who fed her little tidbits with a cheery expression. It was evident Robert wished to have her all to himself but was too cognizant of propriety to make such a vulgar display.

"Can I get you anything, your lairdship?" gushed a bobbing maid who thought Lochiel Montgomery was quite the handsomest man she had ever seen in kilts and had apprised the whole staff of Kenlaren of the fact.

"A large brandy, lass," replied Loch, his deep voice sending thrills through the girl. Annie snorted with disgust and walked over to Michael, who was balancing a full plate of food, two books, and a glass of wine. She flopped down beside him, jogging his elbow so his lap and books were thoroughly drenched with Burgundy.

"Annie Gunn, what the bloody hell do you think you're doing?" he screeched, standing quickly so that books, food, and wine showered onto the carpet. "Why can't you grow up and act with decorum?" he raved, desperately trying to salvage his precious books and roughly shoving Annie away as she tried to help. Annie blushed scarlet, conscious of Loch Montgomery's gaze as he drank deeply of the generous portion of spirits, trying to dull the sharp pain between his eyes.

"Dinna talk to me like that, Michael Gunn!" she spat angrily. "Who the bloody hell do you think you are anyway!"

"Children, children," groaned Robert. "It is my wedding day."

"Then take your bride and be gone," advised Lochiel wearily. "Surely you would prefer to be alone wie her?" he added, amazed at the English, who put etiquette before their basic needs.

"Well, actually, old man, I can think of nothing I would like better, but I didn't want to appear too hasty," returned Robert, caressing Iona with his eyes. "Not quite the thing to seem too eager, you know," he quipped huskily.

Annie watched Iona and Robert leave the room before turning to the open French windows, determined to make her own escape, but she was stopped by a firm hand that sent shock waves darting through her. She glared up into

Lochiel's dark eyes and swallowed hard at his impenetrable gaze.

"I will talk to you later," he stated, turning away. Annie smoldered at his curt dismissal.

"Like hell, you will!" she hissed.

"Your brother is right. 'Tis time you grew up. There's little change from the brat of seven years ago!" answered Loch witheringly before striding out of the room in search of Roderick. Annie was so furious, she stamped her bare foot as the door closed after him. Michael laughed softly.

"I think you've met your match, Oriannie Gunn," he teased, and he left hurriedly to change his wine-drenched clothes as she picked up a cut-crystal decanter. His laughter increased as he agilely escaped and there was a loud, shattering crash against the closed dining room door.

"Has no one sought to discipline her?" asked Loch with amazement.

"Over twenty governesses," shrugged Michael before mounting the stairs to his room. Roderick watched his young master eye the dining room door thoughtfully.

"Well, at least she's not riding about the countryside dressed as a boy and taking off all her clothes, so I suppose there's been some slight improvement," Loch stated loudly. An outraged gasp was very audible but neither Loch nor Roderick made a sign that they had heard. They entered the library, closing the door firmly behind them. "Now, Roderick, pour me a stiff brandy and tell me what we are doing here," sighed the young man wearily, staring out of the window at the rolling lawn.

"You look exhausted and not at all well, could it nae wait?" worried Roderick, handing a snifter to Lochiel.

"I'm grown, Roderick, I dinna need a nursemaid! Why are we here and not at Falconhurst?" he demanded.

Upstairs Annie virtually ripped off the delicate flowing bridesmaid's dress, tugged on a pair of tight trews, and buttoned up a full-sleeved shirt and a leather jerkin. She tied her unruly thick hair back from her face and fleetly ran barefoot down the backstairs.

Mrs. Wilson looked up from her cooking and smiled toothlessly as the lithe girl raced into the sunlit courtyard.

Annie rode Dubh across the sandy beach to the ebbing

tide, remembering the first time she had seen Lochiel Montgomery. She dug her small heels into the stallion's firm girth so they galloped through the surf as she recalled the exhilarating race years before. She reined the horse and stared up at the steep, cruel escarpment and she wondered when she had first entertained romantic dreams about Lochiel Montgomery. She had thought his face diabolic and merciless—then why had her mind softened and enhanced it in the intervening years? He was sardonic and autocratic—so why did his very presence cause her heart to beat faster and her skin to prickle? Annie wheeled Dubh about and raced him back into the sea so the water sprayed as she tried to erase Lochiel Montgomery's forbidding features from her mind.

Loch sighed deeply and whirled the amber liquid in his glass. He thought of Annie Gunn's flashing eyes that caught and held the gold of the sun very much like the brandy, as he struggled to understand all that Roderick had to tell him.

"How dare Ross Montgomery treat Iona in such a fashion," he barked, not knowing what to do with the pulsating anger that coursed through his aching body. "He's taken over Falconhurst and my stables?" he asked rhetorically.

"Sir Robert has sent news of your rescue to the London and Edinburgh newspapers . . . also notice to Ross Montgomery to vacate. . . ."

"I can take care of my own affairs!" roared Loch, who then subsided back in his chair with a groan. "Tell me of the girl," he demanded, determined not to give in to the weakness he felt.

"Of Oriana?" replied Roderick softly.

"Are there others?" returned Loch sardonically. "I sincerely hope there is only one unprincipled, undisciplined brat."

"She has her principles."

"Och, do I hear an affection for Rob Roy MacGregor?" jeered Loch sarcastically, remembering nearly eight years before when the old man had been more concerned with the child's torn feet than with his stolen horse.

"It has been a strange, lonely life for a motherless, fatherless child," defended Roderick, remembering the cries he often heard from Annie's room at night.

"Dinna try to break my heart, old friend," said Loch wearily. "Just show me to my room and turn the bed down."

Half an hour later Roderick entered the kitchen, his wrinkled face set on very worried lines.

"What is it, Roderick MacDonald?" asked Mrs. Wilson.

"Sir Lochiel is burning up wie a fever."

"And?" probed the old woman.

"And," sighed Roderick, "and . . . I dinna ken. He's dark and brooding. There seems no charity in him," he mused aloud sadly.

"Dose him wie this," ordered the old crone, taking down a very dusty bottle. Roderick looked at her with great suspicion.

"I have heard of your uncomfortable and oft times embarrassing potions, Mrs. Wilson," he said carefully, not wanting to insult the woman so that she doctored any of his vituals.

"You have?" exclaimed the old witch. "Aye, I have the knack," she added proudly.

"What is this for?" asked Roderick, uncorking and sniffing the contents.

"For sleep. The dark lad looks worn out wie worry and need for rest," replied Mrs. Wilson innocently.

"I'll take it in case," decided Roderick, feeling the bottle would be safer in his hands. "Thank you," he added doubtfully as the old woman roared with laughter and rubbed her bony hands together with glee.

Annie returned at nightfall after hiding Dubh. She entered the kitchen and raised her eyes at Michael, who sat eating his supper.

"Didn't expect to see you until Iona's brother had left," laughed Michael.

"He's still here?" she groaned, hoping desperately that he was.

"Aye, and would seem he's here for a while." added Mrs. Wilson bitterly.

"He's sick," explained Michael.

* * *

Annie carefully opened the door of Lochiel's room and peered in. Not able to see anything in the dark room, she tiptoed to the bed, curious to see how he looked while relaxed in sleep. Even in repose his features seemed ruthless and unyielding, she noted. How long she stood gazing down at him, she didn't know. She lost track of time and place as her eyes traced the magnetic lines of his sun-bronzed face. He was covered only by a light sheet to the waist, and her eyes dropped lower, caressing his strong brown chest and delighting in the way the bedlinen was molded to his muscular legs, accenting his manhood. She felt the blood rush hotly to her cheeks and she was about to tiptoe away when her slender wrist was caught in a vise-like grip and she stared into Loch's coal-black eyes.

There was a long crackling moment where neither of them moved. Then slowly and inexorably Loch pulled her down until she felt his hot breath on her face. She was imprisoned not only by his hand but by the gaze he kept pinned to her amber eyes. His lips drew closer and closer until they fused with hers and lightning flashed through her. She closed her eyes and submerged herself in the heat of him, not believing a kiss could awaken so many feelings.

Feverishly Loch rubbed his palms along her lithe, pliant coolness, probing her soft mouth with his firm tongue and eager to connect to bare flesh instead of the frustrating fabric and leather. Annie writhed as his large hands cupped her bared breasts and he lifted her so she was pressed to his aroused maleness. She had no thoughts, no reasoning, just the most incredible sensations and an overwhelming hunger to be completely one with him, as she had been so many times in her dreams. She had seen Dubh claim and cover a mare many times and she had watched, thinking of Loch's ebony hair as an unbearable empty ache had spread throughout her body. Now that ache was magnified a hundred times.

Lochiel opened his eyes and stared at Annie's aroused, misty expression. He groaned as realization crashed into his bursting skull. He had been dreaming like an adolescent, only to awaken to the reality of the brat pressing wantonly against his nakedness. Why was he so surprised to find the wild child in his bed, mused his cynical mind. Obviously she was totally amoral and unprincipled.

"Take your clothes off," he growled, not having the energy to fight the obstructing material. His dictatorial tone acted like a splash of cold water. Annie froze, still lying intimately on top of him. She tried to wriggle off, only to be caught at each side of her narrow waist and turfed rudely on to her back. Loch loomed above her, his eyes fixed hungrily on her naked breasts, which rose and fell at a frantic rate.

"Let me go," she hissed, but he shook his head and roughly unbuttoned her tight trews. She summoned all her energy and fought him, but even weakened by his illness his strength was no match for her, and soon she lay naked beneath him.

Loch ground his mouth to hers and kneed her slim legs apart to position himself. Once again Annie felt desire throb through her and she gave up fighting and surged to meet him. When sharp pain caused her to gasp, Loch stopped his thrusting and lay still, buried deep inside her as realization of her just-lost virginity penetrated his fevered brain. As the pain receded, Annie bucked impatiently against him.

"Rob Roy MacGregor," sighed Lochiel, not knowing whether to laugh or roar with rage. He looked down at her small, lithe body as his own desire surged and he thrust into her, delighting in the way she rose to meet him, matching him stroke for stroke, eager to give and eager to learn. She tried to hurry him but he silently tempered his rhythm. "Maybe this is how you need to be tamed, Annie Gunn," he murmured as she obediently followed the tempo of his body.

Annie clung to Loch as the sensations culminated and exploded within her. As Loch felt her climax, he let himself go, racing toward his own fulfillment. Infinitely tired but feeling more relaxed and at peace than he had for a long time, he held her tightly in his arms and rolled onto his side, still deeply nestled in her warmth. Annie snuggled closer and gave a purr of contentment. She buried her small nose in the fragrance of his neck and, feeling as though she was complete for the first time in her life, she drifted to sleep.

Roderick MacDonald crept in with a lantern in hand to check on his young master, and the sight that met his old eyes nearly stopped his heart. He stared down at the petite naked golden girl who lay entwined with the dark naked man. One shapely leg was thrust intimately between Loch's muscular thighs and a small graceful hand curled against his lean cheek, softening the chiseled lines. Even though he was deeply surprised and no less shocked, Roderick felt there was something right about the two being entangled on the bed. He tiptoed out, remembering Annie standing naked and proud in front of Loch all those years ago. Then she was an unformed child but now she was a desirable young woman.

As the door closed quietly behind Roderick MacDonald, Loch stirred and muttered in his sleep. Annie's eyes flew open and she lay still, trying to orient herself. Feeling burning heat throb through her wherever her skin touched his, she frowned and tried to sit up, but his strong arms held her possessively. She placed her hands on his broad chest, worried at his apparent sickness but aroused by his proximity. Finding there was no way to escape from his firm hold, she relaxed, allowing him to enfold her closely while her mind remembered the intimacies they had shared. A smile curled her lips and caused her eyes to dance as she conceded that the experience had been more than she had ever dreamed of. She wondered if Iona and her uncle were so engaged.

Iona and Robert were aboard his yacht sailing down the coast of Cumberland toward the south of England. After a delicious dinner of course upon course of delicacies, each with a complementary wine, they now walked arm and arm around the dark deck, staring up at the enormous bowl of the sky. Iona shivered, feeling tiny and insignificant instead of a mature married woman. Robert held her close, her back pressed against him as he filled his nostrils with the fragrance of her sea-swept hair.

"Are you cold?" he asked, somehow loathe to go below to their cabin even though he longed to consummate their union. Iona didn't answer, as she felt very shy and unsure. She wished that some magic would transport her into her nightgown and into bed with her emotions already as roused as they had been at the Craigie Arms and that rainy night at Kenlaren. If Robert had been honest with himself he, too, would have admitted to being nervous. He rather prided himself on his sexual prowess but he had never made love with so much at stake. His bedpartners had never been gently reared or highly regarded. They had been actresses, dancers, worldly, well-rehearsed bedmates whose interests in him had been solely for money and lust of the moment.

Iona shivered again as she watched the white-tipped waves splash against the side of the yacht, spraying a salty mist that beaded finely on her face and in her hair. A brisk wind filled the sails and slapped the ropes against the mast. Summer lightning shimmered on the horizon and the full moon sailed across the vast sky, which sparkled with stars.

"You *are* cold," murmured Robert, folding his coat about them both.

"No, I'm afraid," admitted Iona softly. "There's so much sea and sky and so little of us," she added hastily, unable to state what she really had apprehensions about. Robert turned her about and looked down at her face, which she quickly averted. He caught a plaintive vulnerability before she turned away.

"'Tis time for bed, my pet," he stated firmly suddenly feeling strong and virile, his own apprehensions blowing away with the brisk breeze and her plaintive expression.

"But . . ." started Iona, wanting just a little while longer to summon up her courage.

"Now, my love," insisted Robert dictatorially, lifting her chin and staring into her fathomless dark eyes. Iona's parted lips quivered. Robert lowered his head and captured her trembling mouth before lifting her into his strong arms and holding her against his rapidly beating heart.

Iona closed her eyes and hid her face against his coat as he agilely descended the narrow companionway to their cabin. Wilkes silently sighed with relief at his master's appearance. He had supervised the turning down of the large bed and the preparation of the honeymoon cabin hours before. Several times he had replaced the ice in the champagne bucket and paced the galley in an effort to keep awake. His jaw ached from yawning, as he had valiantly waited after sending the cook, butler, and two maids to bed, and had attempted to keep Lady Iona's personal maid awake so she would be alert enough to prepare her mistress for her marriage bed.

Iona felt a shock of cold fear streak through her as Robert left the cabin, leaving her to the administrations of a strange, uniformed maid, who bobbed up and down like a cork in the sea. She stood in shock, staring at the firmly closed door, irritated by the maid's hands that fumbled sleepily with the fastenings of her gown.

"What's your name?" she asked, tempering her tone although she longed to slap at the clumsy fingers.

"Dunnock, ma'am," yawned the woman.

"That'll be all, Dunnock," dismissed Iona.

"Thank you, ma'am," answered Dunnock gratefully, virtually running from the cabin. Iona stood staring out the porthole at the endless expanse of dark sea, feeling very sad and lonely. As the waves slapped rhythmically against the sides of the vessel she felt her panic grow. What was she doing on a yacht off to heaven knew where with a man she barely knew but to whom she now belonged? She paced back and forth as her overtired mind took nightmarish twists and turns.

Robert entered quietly and frowned at his young bride, who stood, still fully dressed except for several buttons undone, crying silently and wringing her slender hands. He had taken great pains with his appearance, including having Wilkes shave him twice to insure that Iona's petal-soft cheeks would not be marred. He was garbed in a majestic royal purple robe, which set off his tanned skin and blond hair to great advantage. Iona turned away, trying to stop her flood of tears.

"Iona?" exclaimed Robert softly. "What is it?"

"I'm tired, that's all," returned Iona huskily, trying to control herself.

"Where's your maid? Why hasn't she—"

"I sent her away," interrupted Iona, remembering the

time Robert had quite efficiently undressed her. At the remembrance her eyes filled with tears again. "I didn't want anyone else," she added, and then closed her mouth quickly lest she make herself too vulnerable.

"I don't want to share you with anyone else," said Robert, instinctively understanding and finishing her thought. Iona looked up at him, her brimming eyes sparkling with hopefulness at his intuitiveness. "Come here, my pet," he ordered softly, opening his arms to her. Iona shyly walked to him, expecting to be enfolded to his strong chest, only to be turned about like a child as he played lady's maid and finished unbuttoning her gown.

Robert started undressing Iona in a very practical, parental way, but as she stepped dutifully out of the gown and he gazed at her tempting decolletage, his eyes lit up and he sat, pulling her to him. Iona shivered as Robert buried his face into her cleavage and she felt his lips gently nipping and kissing, sending her worries and fears far away. Slowly Robert loosened the straps of her chemise until it floated to her feet and she stood just in her laced corset and pantalets. He spanned her tiny waist with his broad hands as he took one of the ends of the laces with his teeth and pulled, nuzzling the soft warmth of the creamy orbs that were thrust up by the tightness of the foundation garment.

"I think this article of clothing was invented to drive men insane with passion," he stated huskily as he teasingly unlaced so her breasts spilled out to be captured by his lips. Iona's legs felt weak as delicious sensations streaked through her and she stood obediently between his parted thighs. At last he had taken off every article of her clothing, and he assessed her glorious nakedness. "You are my wife," he stated with wonder, finding her more exciting than any other woman he had ever known. "You are my wife!" he repeated joyfully, as though unable to believe his incredible good fortune. "My wife," he repeated, losing his excitement and looking anxiously to her face, where he expected to see disgust and repulsion. Iona's glorious happiness clouded as she saw Robert's sudden change.

"Have I done something wrong?" she asked anxiously, feeling infinitely vulnerable in her nakedness.

"I have never been with a wife before," he said awkwardly. "Well, not mine, at any rate," he added, and then wanted to bite through his runaway tongue as he saw her blanch.

"I have never been with a man before," Iona answered, for want of something to say.

"I should sincerely hope not," he retorted indignantly, picking up a diaphanous nightgown and tugging it angrily over Iona's dark head. "Get into bed," he ordered sternly. He blew out the lantern, unwilling to remove his dressing gown until the cabin was dark.

Iona lay in the wide bed at its extreme edge, miserably staring out at the starlit sky through the porthole as Robert slid under the covers, keeping as far from her as possible. Too late he remembered the champagne, which might have made the whole situation a little easier. They lay wide awake for a long time, listening for a sign that either of them was asleep and very conscious that neither was.

"Iona?"

"Yes," she whispered.

"I love you very much and would hate to disgust you," he admitted, trying to curb the desire he felt while she lay so near and yet so far from him.

"You could never disgust me," sobbed Iona. "I love you too." Robert reached across the bed and touched her wet cheeks and then with a groan enfolded her in his arms so their naked skin pressed together. "Love me, Robert," begged Iona, uncaring that he might think her common or of reprehensible character. With a groan Robert gave in to his baser urges and hungrily kissed her. Iona returned his kiss with fervor, opening her soft lips to allow his thrusting tongue admittance. Thrill upon thrill raced through her as she felt his arousal press against the smoothness of her slim thigh and she instinctively opened her legs. Robert entered the heat of her and she gasped as pain knifed through. He felt exhilarated, masterful, and he slowed his urgency and captured her lips, giving her time to adjust. Iona felt the sharp, rending pain recede and give way to an aching pulse that caused her to writhe impatiently against him, urging him to move. Robert grinned in the darkness and allowed her to set a pace until they were both caught up in a swirling, unthinking vortex of sensation that accelerated until they strained against each other. With a great sigh of contentment Iona cuddled against Robert, the echo of that incredible sensation still ticking deep inside her. She lay still, hearing his rapidly beating heart slow to an even pace that matched his steady breathing. She propped herself on one elbow and gazed down on his sleeping face lit eerily by the moonlight that flooded through the porthole. How could he sleep so quickly after such an incredible experience, she wondered, and she suppressed a mournful sound as she felt him slip from her, destroying the precious bond that had made them one for such a brief time.

Chapter 14

Annie lay beside Loch, staring with adoration at the handsome face softened by the moonlight that streamed through the window and over the pillow. He slept fitfully, his skin hot and dry, with one muscular leg flung claimingly across her slender hips. She wished she could get up to fetch cooling cloths and a drink to bring down the fever that wracked his long, lean body, but each time she moved he muttered angrily and grasped her roughly.

As dawn touched the eastern horizon and the rich night sky weakened to a dismal gray, Loch suddenly started thrashing about. Annie was brutally awakened by a sharp blow to the cheek, and she sprang up with a scream. She crouched at the end of the bed, avoiding his flailing arms and legs as he battled unseen demons in his delirium. Forcing herself to full awakeness, she raced across the room to the washstand and poured a basin of cold water. Then she totally saturated a thick towel and draped it over Loch, squeezing it so a flood of cooling water washed over his face, causing him to choke as it poured into his nostrils.

"What the bloody hell!" he roared, sitting up and staring about with bloodshot eyes.

"Lie back!" ordered Annie as he started to shiver uncontrollably. To her great surprise he obeyed, clutching his aching head in his hands and closing his eyes with an anguished groan. Despite her worry about his health, Annie couldn't help grinning broadly at his passive obedience. She wrung out the towel and gently sponged his body, delighting in the hard strength of his long, well-shaped muscles. Curious, she examined every inch of him, smiling tenderly at his relaxed manroot, which now seemed so deceptively vulnerable in its thick nest of jet black curls. She stroked him wonderingly as she remembered the size and hardness of several hours before.

Roderick stood at the door, watching the naked girl gently nurse the unconscious man. He noted the bloodstains on her lithe golden legs, evidence of her entry into womanhood, as he wondered how to make his presence known without embarrassing her.

"Miss Oriana?" he called quietly. She turned and smiled wearily at him, as unselfconscious in her nudity as she had been at nine years old. "What happened to your face?" he exclaimed as he saw one eye was nearly swollen shut.

"He has powerful big hands," she explained ruefully. "The fever is still high but I think it is down a wee bit. Could you bring some more cold water, Roderick?" she asked, turning back to her muttering charge. The old man nodded and took the empty water pitcher, leaving her to tend his young master.

"Why the long face, auld mon?" clucked Mrs. Wilson as she bustled about cooking breakfast. Roderick grunted, unsure of how to explain Oriana's unconventional behavior as he stalked by her on his way to the pump in the yard. The old crone watched him suspiciously, and she hobbled after him to the door. "Is your lad still burning up?" she shouted.

"Aye," answered Roderick shortly.

"And?" probed the crone.

"And Miss Oriana is wie him," replied the old man reluctantly.

"And you dinna dose him wie the potion, I'll be bound!" hissed Mrs. Wilson malevolently. Roderick MacDonald looked at her sharply, wondering why she was suddenly so hostile. "You think I dinna ken the goings-on at Kenlaren? I knew it would happen as soon as I set my eyes on that Black Scot! Could smell it! That's why you should have physicked him with my wilting concoction! 'Tis your fault the wee witch-wife has lost her maidenhood, so you'll hae to pay the de'il his due!" she screeched, stabbing her bent bony fingers at him and liberally spraying spit.

" 'Witch-wife'?" exclaimed Roderick, his leathery skin prickling with foreboding. "You constantly call the lass that, and you hae no liking for the Black . . ."

"Aye, witch-wife, and she's promised to another, so you keep your nose out, old mon!" interrupted Mrs. Wilson, scurrying back into the dark recesses of the kitchen.

Annie and Roderick bathed Lochiel until his temperature lowered to a more comfortable level and he slept peacefully. Only then did Annie return to her own room and relax in a hot bath before crawling into her own bed to sleep soundly. She awoke at noon and stretched lazily like a cat, feeling sated and complete. She smiled dreamily as she felt the tenderness between her thighs and remembered the previous night's ecstasy. She got out of bed and padded to the window, delighting in the warm sunshine. It seemed the whole of nature rejoiced with her as the bees droned busily amongst the multicolored profusion of flowers, and birds competed by swelling their breasts and raising their voices from the treetops. Gone was the gray pall that had seemed to shroud everything for so long. Annie laughed aloud, feeling happier and freer than she had in her whole life. She surveyed herself in the long mirror and was surprised that she didn't appear different. Facing her in the glass was the golden, tousled girl of the day before. She made a mischievous face at herself and then dashed into her dressing room, reappearing almost at once with a very fashionable riding habit and a lace jabot. She giggled as she quickly dressed, refusing to look at herself again until she had pulled on the exquisite high-heeled hand-tooled Spanish boots that Robert had brought her from one of his trips.

"Tra-la!" she sang as she spun about and opened her eyes to her image in the glass. She didn't see the sophisticated, tall, worldly woman she had envisioned, so she scowled for a second and then winked resignedly at herself before cramming an elegant hat on her wild golden head.

"If it wasn't for the black eye . . ." she decided after critically examining her appearance. She flung the pert feathered hat out of the window so it caught the wind and sailed across the lawn, dispersing several indignant birds before landing gracefully in a stand of budlea, where the butterflies fluttered about it as though it were an added blossom.

Annie turned back to the mirror and grinned roguishly at herself as she decided that at least she looked fairly passable from her neck down. Her golden sunburned face with its black eye and wild mop of hair would have to be improved upon another time, she concluded. For now she was eager to be on Dubh's muscular back racing across the heathered moorland to the sea. On her way out she popped an inquisitive head around Lochiel's door and smiled mistily at the innocent picture he made, sleeping peacefully with his glossy black hair curled like a halo, giving him a boyish appearance. Roderick noted her gloriously happy expression and bit down on his curiosity. He longed to ask her about Mrs. Wilson's veiled and not-so-veiled references. "Witch-wife," to him, conjured up visions of Satanism and yet there was something so childlike and innocent about the silly old woman it had to be just colorful words, he mused.

"Take care of him, Roderick," whispered Annie huskily, gently running her fingers through the wayward curls on Loch's brow.

"Aye, that I will, lass," the old man reassured her. "Och, you look bonny," he added, admiring her elegant habit. Annie grinned ruefully, not knowing how to accept the compliment.

"Annie Gunn, get your tail in here!" screeched Mrs. Wilson, catching sight of the girl making her way merrily through the orchard.

"I'm not hungry," she sang out happily.

"I said to get your hind quarters in here this minute!" screamed the old crone shrilly, waving a large spurtle. Annie shrugged and obeyed, not wanting anything to mar the beauty of the sunny day and her sunny feelings. "Drink this down!" ordered the old woman as she thrust an evil-smelling concoction at her.

"Why?" questioned Annie. The rancid mixture caused her eyes to water and her stomach to churn.

"Dinna play the innocent wie me, my girl," snapped Mrs. Wilson. "Och, I know what you've been aboot!"

"You think I'll catch the sickness from Lochiel Montgomery?" puzzled Annie, unable to suppress a delicious shiver that thrilled her at the thought of him.

"That's the least you'll catch from that Black Scot!" snarled the crone. "You let him mount you! Plant his seed!" She nodded as Annie's expression confirmed her suspicions. The girl smiled wistfully, thinking of Lochiel's children, dark and glossy-haired like Dubh's colts, running free across the verdant rolling hills. "Drink the brew!" screeched the hag, but Annie had left the dark, cool kitchen and was eagerly running through the fragrant orchard toward the hidden green meadow where Dubh ran with his mares and foals.

Annie rode the black stallion across the heathered moorland, enjoying the contented buzz of the bees and the sudden whirr as partridge and grouse flew up from the purple and pink brush. High in the infinite blue sky larks soared, singing their arias to divert predators from their nests of young, and powerful hawks circled higher and higher with seeming nonchalance.

Annie rode Dubh down the steep cliff path to a secluded beach, where she pulled off her elegant but restricting attire and lay baking in the hot sun, dreaming and reliving the ecstasy of Lochiel's hard strong body joining with her own. She closed her eyes, the sun behind her lids making her feel golden inside and out as she tried to hold on to and remember all the wonderful emotions in addition to the incredible sensuality. There had been more. There had been a feeling of safety about the strong arms that had tucked her so naturally to him in sleep. She had fitted so neatly into the curve of his belly, as though she belonged. Annie sat up and hugged her knees as she stared across the sand to the sea. She had felt safe, she realized. She had never, ever really felt safe at night before. When she was a tiny girl she had tiptoed to the forbidden part of the house, drawn like a magnet to the vague, beautiful woman who was called "mother." She wrinkled her brow, trying to remember exactly when the frightening night pilgrimages began, as it seemed something she had always done. Always regretfully but dutifully she had slipped out of her warm bed and crept through the forbidding shadows of the night to listen to her mother weave her fantasies. Always crouched outside her mother's room, wanting to enter but afraid. Always crouched shaking with cold or fear as the poetry and romances were narrated or enacted behind the closed door. As Annie remembered, her flesh goose-bumped with a sudden chill despite the hot sunshine.

Annie tried to free herself from the dark fears of the past, wanting to be back with the more recent, more sensuous and safer memories of Lochiel Montgomery's strong, claiming arms. She leaped to her feet and raced down the hot sand, plunging into the bracing salt water of the Solway. She floated on her back, gazing at the gulls that soared above, and she wished she wasn't so land bound. She smiled, imagining that she was freely flying with Lochiel over the mountains and valleys, their wingtips touching as they circled gracefully in the swirling air currents. Suddenly she turned on her stomach and swam swiftly back to shore, eager to be back at Kenlaren, needing to feel and smell the maleness of him.

For four days and four nights Annie kept the same pattern. Each night she insisted that Roderick retire to his own quarters, and she lay beside the dark man, breathing his fragrance and hoping he would claim her again, but he slept fitfully, unaware of her presence even though she took care of his most intimate needs and was familiar with every inch of his virile body.

Mrs. Wilson fretted and fumed, ranted and raved, and wove her spells, but Annie firmly closed her ears and the door, ignoring the shrill incantations in the corridor. The maids, however, grew more and more uneasy and took to carrying hastily made crosses.

Each night before entering his room, Annie took great pains with her attire, hoping his dark eyes would open and he would see her as a sophisticated woman instead of the hoydenish child.

On the fifth day, as the sun touched the eastern horizon and the dawn chorus was at its peak, Lochiel opened his eyes and gazed at the streaked golden head that lay beside his on the pillow. Carefully he sat up and stared down thoughtfully at Annie, who slept like a small child with her knees drawn up, one small hand curled by her cheek and the other cupping a pert breast. Her nightgown had ridden up, exposing her suntanned thighs and tiny, high-arched feet. He climbed out of the bed, frowning down at his nakedness as he felt a wave of dizziness, and he clutched at the headboard to regain his balance.

"What are you doing?" cried Annie, jerked awake as he lurched heavily against the bed. Loch sat quickly with his back to her as he looked desperately for something to cover his loins. "Get back in bed," she ordered, trying to smooth her riotous mane of hair and seductive gown in the hopes of appearing imperious and adult.

"What the hell are you doing here?" asked Loch roughly as the girl walked around the bed to face him. He quickly draped the sheet about himself.

Annie wanted to crow with delight and wrap her arms about him when she saw he was well on the way to recovery, but there was something in his manner that made her afraid. Not trusting her voice to be steady, she refused to answer. She put out her hand to feel his forehead, only to have her wrist caught in a viselike grip.

"I asked you what you were doing here," he repeated, his deep voice hoarse with barely suppressed fury.

"Nursing you," she replied huskily, thankful that her voice didn't tremble. Lochiel's dark eyes narrowed to slits as he glared at her face, noting the blackened eye and the soft mouth that quivered as a misty, sensuous dream floated into his mind.

"Get out!" he ordered savagely, flinging her arm from him as an image of entering her virgin body thrust into his head. Annie pressed her trembling lips together and nodded, willing her burning tears to remain hidden until she could be alone. With her bright head held high and her back straight and proud, she quit the room, slamming the door behind her.

Roderick frowned as she blindly stalked past him, scalding tears pouring down her flushed cheeks.

"Lass?" he whispered, reaching out to comfort, but she avoided his arms, shaking her head vehemently, and dashed to her room. Fear shot through the old man and he ran down the corridor to his young master's room expecting to find Lochiel still and cold. He wrenched open the door and to his surprised relief was greeted by red-hot fury from the young man, who was in the process of dressing himself.

"What the hell is going on?"

"Och, lad, 'tis guid to see you up on your own two feet," exclaimed Roderick gruffly, ignoring the anger that crackled.

"What was that undisciplined brat doing here?" demanded Loch.

"She's been nursing you each night since you took sick," replied the old man softly.

"And how long is that?"

"This is the fifth day."

"And are there no other servants here at Kenlaren that you allow that horse thief . . . that undisciplined brat . . . that wild, unprincipled child barely out of the schoolroom, if she was ever in it, in my bedchamber where I lay naked and dependent?" raved Lochiel. "Good God, man! 'Tis a wonder I still have my manhood!" he ranted. Roderick shrugged and splayed his hands in a gesture of helplessness. "Well?" Loch roared when the old man didn't answer.

"Forgie that we are master and servant for a wee while," suggested Roderick, softly but firmly taking the wind out of Loch's sails as the young man recognized Mr. MacDonald was disturbed and unhappy.

"All right," agreed Loch. He felt a wave of dizziness, so he sat wearily on the bed and looked up at the old man. "Well?" he prompted as Roderick noted his pallor and hesitated to speak his mind.

"Lochiel Montgomery, I have known you since birth. In fact, I raised you," pronounced the old man carefully and Loch grinned ruefully, feeling he was back in the schoolroom, guilty of some misdemeanor.

"And?"

"And . . . glad I am that you are mended," said the old

man after a long pause while he decided that voicing his concern for Annie should wait until his young master had recouped his strength and temper.

"And?" Loch pushed impatiently.

"And I shall excuse myself and get your breakfast," Roderick lamely concluded. He left the room swiftly once again aware of the ruthless glint in Lochiel's dark eyes.

Loch stared at the closed door, curious but relieved that Roderick hadn't spoken his mind. A great weariness overtook him and he lay back against the soft pillows on the broad bed, where he caught a disturbing scent of Annie. It wasn't exactly a perfume, but more like the smell of the windswept heather by the sea, he decided as his eyelids drooped, and once again a sensuous, haunting scene played in his mind. He ran his fingertips gently across his lips, remembering the soft, tremulous mouth that had opened so obediently to his pressure. He shook himself awake, swung his long limbs off the bed, and strode angrily to the open window.

"Obedient!" he snorted. "She's never been obedient except to her own willful desires!" He dismissed the erotic memories as purely remnants of a delirium caused by his illness. He gazed across the peaceful green countryside, breathing appreciatively of the flowers that bloomed in profusion throughout the formal gardens below. A sudden movement caught his eye and he frowned as he recognized Annie running wildly. Gone was the feminine flowing gown. Now she was dressed in tight trews and a white smock, her arms and legs bare. Once again the disturbing sensuous memory tore into his mind as her lithe, sun-kissed limbs summoned to his thoughts her soft, perfect body. He frowned as he recalled each inch uniformly tanned from her pert little nose to the tips of her graceful feet. He relived the moment that he plunged into her warm goldenness and felt the tearing of her maidenhead against his thrusting manhood. A smile softened his harsh features as he remembered her impatience, her slim hips urging him despite the pain that must have ripped through her. Why had the child given herself so freely, he mused. He shook his ebony head angrily to drive the thoughts from him. His illness had caused him to revert back to adolescent dreams, he decided as his head started to pound and the room spun.

Roderick entered with a loaded breakfast tray to find Loch stretched out sound asleep on his bed. Quietly he covered the young man with an eiderdown and left the window wide, reasoning that the fresh summer air was better than a stuffy sickroom. He sat in a chair by the window, brooding about what was to happen when his young master recovered his strength.

"Who hit her?" asked a sleepy voice, and Roderick turned to see Loch's eyes open.

"Who?" replied the old man, looking at his watch and seeing to his surprise that several hours had passed.

"Rob Roy," answered Loch. "Who hit her?"

"You did," sighed Roderick, standing stiffly.

"She probably deserved it."

"You took her maidenhead too," pronounced the old man bluntly. Lochiel silently digested the information for some time.

"For God's sake, why did you not lock her out?" he asked. "Why did you allow her access?"

"It was out of my hands," replied Roderick.

"First my horse and now my honor," ranted Lochiel. "Is nothing sacred to that minx! I suppose I have no alternative, but to offer for her," he sighed, realizing the idea wasn't entirely repugnant to him. Roderick nodded noncommittally, allowing none of his exultant joy to show on his weatherbeaten face.

Annie spent the day in seclusion high on the barren moorland at the Devil's Stepping Stones, unable to look at the sea and the cliffs without thinking of Lochiel Montgomery. At sunset she returned to Kenlaren and, quietly avoiding the kitchen and Mrs. Wilson, made her way to her room. She sat on the wide window seat, watching the sun sink below the trees and bleed between the darkening leaves and branches until night fell and the dew beaded on the grass.

A soft tapping at the door didn't penetrate Annie's brooding silence until it was repeated. Numbly she turned and watched the door handle slowly move, and then Roderick's kindly old face peered into the room. He saw her silhouetted against the night sky.

"I've brought you some supper, lass," he said softly.

"How is he?"

"Weak but better," he replied, setting down a loaded tray.

"Guid," whispered Annie. She turned away to stare out of the window at the night.

"'Tis best to leave him alone until he's quite mended," suggested Roderick, not wanting the girl further hurt by Lochiel's temper.

"I have no intention of going anywhere near him," replied Annie, shivering as she remembered his sneering expression and the way he'd flung her away from him that morning.

"Good night, Rob Roy," said Roderick sadly after lighting several lamps so the room was warm and cozy.

"Good night, Roderick," answered Annie, looking so forlorn that the old man reached out his arms and held her tightly to him.

"Very touching scene, Mr. MacDonald," drawled a sardonic voice, chilling Annie's blood. Roderick kissed the top of her bright head before looking at Lochiel in the doorway. He frowned at the hard lines of the young man's face. Annie stood proudly mirroring Loch's disdainful, ruthless expression, with Roderick's veined hand still holding her shoulder comfortingly.

"Is there something you want?" she asked, unable to say his name.

"'Tis not what I want but what must be said," replied Loch coldly, and Roderick sighed and shook his head soulfully. "Is something the matter, Mr. MacDonald?" added the dark young man, raising a cynical eyebrow.

"There are things better said in the light of a new day when the words have been thought through and tempers and emotions are cooled," struggled the old man.

"Thank you, Roderick," dismissed Loch, holding the door wide.

"'Tis all right, Roderick," smiled Annie as the old man looked at her with worry etched across his face. Lochiel Montgomery's blood pounded furiously at what his still-weakened state saw as outright treason from his oldest friend. He slammed the door behind the old man and turned back to Annie, who stood with her feet apart and her legs pushed back against the window seat for support.

"I understand that your unbridled behavior has now put both of us in a damned compromising position," stated Loch. "Which forces me to offer you marriage not because of any affection or desire I have for you or for that fettered state, but because of the love and high regard I have for my sister, who happens to be married to your guardian."

"I don't wish to be married to you!" returned Annie.

"You should have thought of that before you crawled into my bed like some common slut!" Annie's blood boiled at his high-handed arrogance. Her amber eyes flashed and she dug her nails into the palms of her hands, wanting to fly at him and rake his ruthless face which in the flickering lantern light appeared almost satanical.

"If I had to marry every man who had mounted me, I would have a veritable stable of studs," sneered Annie, turning away from him. She gasped as he grasped her chin and forced her to face him.

"You add dishonesty to your list?"

"List of what?" she challenged.

"Most maidens have a list of virtues. You, unfortunately, have a list of transgressions which include theft, undisciplined behavior, highway robbery, and, now, dishonesty," replied Loch cuttingly. Annie felt panic start to pound in her breast and she swallowed hard, trying to control herself. "Roderick MacDonald is without doubt the most honest man I have ever had the good fortune to know. He swears you lost your maidenhead to me. The sheets were stained with your blood," he said ruthlessly.

"Roderick MacDonald was mistaken. There is other reason for blood on the sheets beside proof of your virility," she returned witheringly.

"I felt your maidenhood tear," he stated harshly. Annie felt heat flood her face and she had to force herself not to look away. "Well, it is a surprise to see that you can blush."

"You bastard!" swore Annie, so frightened that she fought any way she knew to keep from being submerged by the flood of panic that threatened to sweep her away. She almost welcomed the hard hands that gripped her shoulders and shook her roughly.

"You'll not speak to me like that!" he roared, and then, seeing her eyes were wide with terror, he relaxed his grasp. "'Tis good to see you afraid of something," he added gruffly, feeling rather like a bully.

"Dinna flatter yourself that 'tis you I'm afeared of!" she spat, wrenching his hands off her as the smell of roses drifted in through the open window and her overwrought mind heard the nightmarish screams from the blood-splattered room of long ago.

"What is the matter?" he asked after a long silence while he watched her usually healthy complexion drain to a sickly pallor, perspiration beading on her forehead and top lip. Annie stared at him as though coming out of a deep sleep. Her amber eyes narrowed and she pulled at her full lower lip thoughtfully. Loch reached out to feel her forehead, expecting she might have caught his illness, but Annie ducked as though she were about to be hit. He caught her chin and felt her forehead, relieved to find it cool. She tried to pull free, but he held her in an effortless grip and examined her bruised cheek and eye. "'Tis no wonder you duck. Seems you didn't move fast enough," he said softly, running a gentle finger around her flashing eye.

"Let go of me," demanded Annie as his proximity and soft tones set her blood racing with a different kind of passion. Loch shook his dark head silently, staring at her quivering lips, which she licked nervously as an aching heat spread from the center of her.

"Take your clothes off," ordered Loch huskily. Annie silently shook her head, trying to break the magnetic hold of his hard, dark eyes. Slowly he lowered his head and barely touched his lips to hers. His nostrils flared as he felt a shiver ripple through her, and his eyes fell and encompassed her thin smock, which revealed the erect state of her nipples as they strained against the light fabric.

"You don't have to marry me. My mother was a whore, too . . . she even slept with a Loch, but his name was Lochinvar," she said with a mischievous grin even though her eyes brimmed with tears. Loch gazed down thoughtfully at her, and idly he caught a tear on the end of his index finger, where it quivered like a dewdrop, seeming to have a pulse. Slowly Annie took her clothes off until she stood before him in all her golden nakedness. Loch sat on her bed and watched her as though in a dream. He had to admit to himself that he had never seen any woman so exquisitely perfect as little Annie Gunn.

"Come here," he said softly, and he smiled as she walked unselfconsciously and gracefully toward him, her eyes wide and luminous as they looked anxiously into his. Tentatively she reached out and traced the prominent lines of his chiseled face and grinned impishly as she saw them soften. She stood between his muscular thighs and strained against him, delighting in the feel of his hardness.

"Roderick tells me that you became very familiar with my body when I was ill and unable to defend myself," he said huskily, determined to avail himself of the same benefits as he firmly put her away from him before he lost control.

Annie fought and tried to surge back against the heat of him but he held her at arm's length, running his eyes and large hands down the length of her.

"I'll teach you obedience, Miss Oriana Gunn," he laughed, knowing she was so aroused that all he had to do was press his lips to her central sweetness and she would climax. He picked her up, delighting in her firm litheness, and laying her back, he parted the rich auburn curls and gently touched his lips to hers.

Annie's breath hissed and she thrust as ecstasy streaked through her. Loch's gentle kiss ignited as he felt the spasms shudder and he ground his mouth to the central core of her, drinking deeply. Annie fought to control her breathing as wave upon wave of pleasure lapped through her.

"Now your impatience is taken care of, 'tis time to teach you the savoring," said Loch as he laid her against the pillows and started diverting himself of his clothing. Annie stretched like a cat as she watched him, grinning mischievously as his aroused member was released from his tight britches.

Loch laughed aloud at Annie's earnest ingenuity as she

eagerly copied his lovemaking and kissed his rearing manhood until he forgot all plans to teach her patience and the savoring of certain acts. Finally he turfed her onto her back and positioned himself between her lithe golden thighs. Annie stared down curiously at the throbbing member poised at the small, aching entrance to her body. She looked up to his dark face, offering her lips as he placed himself teasingly without entering. She poked a saucy tongue between his firm lips and bucked, trying to drive him into the yearning depths of her, but he made it clear who was master. She tempered her impatient movements and grinned pleadingly at him.

"Do I have to say please?" she asked cheekily. Loch pinned his fathomless black eyes to her amber ones and slowly drove himself in to the hilt. Annie gasped and arched against him, pressing her firm breasts against his chest and grinding her pelvis to his. The vague worry in Loch's mind, that Annie was too petite and small to accommodate him, was soon dispelled as she matched him strongly, following his lead faster and faster until they were swept up into the whirling vortex that spun them into exploding excitement. As heartbeats and breathing slowed back to a normal pace, Loch turned onto his back, swinging Annie so she lay atop him, his manroot still deep inside her.

"'Tis naptime, and then I shall teach you how to savor," he yawned, pushing her curious head down so it was pillowed on his broad chest. "Now sleep for a while," he ordered. Annie lay silently, hearing his steady heartbeat beneath her ear. "Och, Annie Gunn, you'd make the very devil of a whore," he muttered, tightening his arms about her silky nakedness. Annie felt panic pound through her, fanned by his words and the delicate perfume of roses that wafted in through the open window.

"Rebecca Gunn's whoring's done! Rebecca Gunn's whoring's done," she mouthed as she held him tightly, burying her nose into his chest to try to smother the terrifying smell of death.

Loch was awakened by Annie thrashing about in the throes of a nightmare. He tried to wake her gently, but she fought him fiercely as he became part of her dream. It took most of his energy to contain her wildly flailing arms and avoid her butting head. His blood ran cold as he heard her eerie rhythmic screams.

"Let go of me!" she sobbed and Loch released her, curious to see what she would do. Annie leaped off the bed and ran into her dressing room. After rummaging about she returned slowly with a dagger in her hand. She stopped in the middle of the room and stared about with confusion, as though not knowing where she was. A wild cry burst from her mouth as she saw the knife in her hand and she dropped it, gazing at her palms with horror. She rubbed them together frantically as heartrending sobs shook her naked body.

"Rob Roy?" whispered Loch as Annie spun on her heels, her eyes wide and terror-filled. She hid her hands guiltily behind her back.

"I've done nothing. I dinna go in Mother's room! I dinna!" she protested, her voice shrill like a small child's.

"Oriana?" he said, trying to wake her by shaking her gently but firmly.

"Dinna hit me, Duncan!" she cried, protecting her small buttocks with her hands and looking fearfully behind her at a large armoire.

"Och, I'll not hit you, Rob Roy," promised Loch huskily, unable to bear the hollow pain he saw in her beautiful eyes.

"'Tis just paint on my hands, Will! No, it is the dye from the horses, Duncan," she gabbled wildly as Loch held her hands in his large ones. "Honest, it isna blood, it is dye!"

"There's nothing on your hands," he reassured her. Annie frowned up at him, trying to focus but still caught in the nightmare.

"You're not Will or Duncan," she accused as his dark, chiseled features penetrated her confused mind.

"Nay, I'm Loch," he answered gently, smoothing her wild mane of hair back from her poignant face.

"Young Lochinvar has come out of the West," she chanted in a spine-chilling, unemotional voice.

"Lochiel, not Lochinvar," he corrected her. He swung her up into his strong arms and softly kissed her tremulous lips.

"What did I say? What did I tell you?" she worried as

she awoke to awareness. "Tell me what I said," she screamed, beating her small fists against his broad chest.

"Hush, it was just a dream . . . just a dream," he crooned, trying to still the panic that raced her pulse.

"Aye, it was just a dream . . . a silly dream, nothing more." She longed to submerge herself in his protective strength and drown the last vestiges of the terrifying nightmare, but she was afraid of what she might reveal. "Let me go! Go away!" she ordered, trying to fight free.

"Not until you're calm," returned Loch firmly, depositing her into the bed and tucking her in as though she were a small child.

"I am calm!" shouted Annie, struggling against the restricting bed clothes. Loch looked down at her stormy face and sighed. "I am very calm," repeated Annie, quieting her tone and trying to hide the tremor in her voice. Loch didn't answer but stood staring out of the open window into the moonlit night. Annie watched his dark silhouette as she tried to compose herself, knowing he wouldn't leave until he thought she was asleep. What had she said in the throes of her nightmare, she worried as she kept her eyes pinned to Loch's forbidding profile. How she wished she was back in the strong safety of his arms!

Lochiel turned and saw her motionless and for a moment debated climbing back into her bed to avail himself of her silky seductiveness. Instead, regretfully, he picked up his clothes and quietly left the room. He grinned wryly as he heard Annie's bare feet scurry across the floor and heard her slide the two dead bolts into place, locking him out. He stood in the corridor imagining her golden nakedness flattened against the door as she listened for his movements.

"All right, Mr. MacDonald, what do you know of it?" sighed Lochiel, sitting wearily on his bed and indicating that Roderick should also sit.

"Just teasing bits and pieces," replied Roderick. "Miss Oriana has terrible nightmares, two sometimes three nights a week, and there are some dark secrets here at Kenlaren."

"Her mother was Rebecca Forsythe, Sir Robert's sister. I don't give much credence to English society gossip, but I do recall some vague scandal attached to her name," pondered Loch aloud.

"Aye, she eloped wie Sir David Gunn the day before she was supposed to marry Lord Drakenberry of Lumbleigh," supplied the old man. "I'm not one for gossip either, but Lord Drakenberry was linked to some quite unsavory debauchery," he added confidentially.

"*Was?* Still is!" Loch barked sardonically. "Whips, chains, and choirboys."

"Lady Rebecca's younger sister, Sarah, is now Lady Drakenberry," informed Roderick.

"Poor woman," sympathized Loch, staring out the window at the tranquil moonlit countryside. "Tell me of the dark secrets of Kenlaren," he sighed wearily after a long pause filled with just the comforting chirping of crickets.

"Well, there are two other Gunn offspring besides Master Michael and Miss Oriana. Twin boys . . ."

"Duncan and Will," interrupted Loch, remembering Annie's half-awake words.

"Aye," answered Roderick.

"Where's the father?"

"Dead," returned the old man. "And 'tis unco. Supposedly the mon died in Africa *after* the two young-uns had been adopted by Sir Robert. Why would Sir Robert adopt Master Michael and Miss Oriana if their father was still alive?"

"I have no idea, Roderick, but you seem to have; so please continue."

"And why did the twin lads have to take their poor demented mother to Forsythe Castle *alone*?" crowed Roderick excitedly, striding backward and forward as he tried to fathom out the reasons.

"What are you getting at?"

"Why didna David Gunn take his wife back?"

"Had too much sense!" laughed Loch. "I'd not face that religious fanatic for all the money in China!"

"And who's the greedy bitch, Maude Potter, who Miss Oriana has to pay? And why does the puir wee lass dress up like a hightoby and commit highway robbery?" rattled off Roderick, insulted by Loch's apparent levity. "And what happened to the puir wee-an to make her scream and cry so in her sleep?"

"Tell me, old man, as I'm sure you have many theories," laughed Loch, much to Mr. MacDonald's indignation.

"I dinna think Sir David Gunn died in Africa. I think the puir mon was murdered right here at Kenlaren . . . and Miss Oriana witnessed it," pronounced Roderick triumphantly, unable to suppress a small glimmer of satisfaction when his statement wiped all trace of amusement from Lochiel's face.

"Go on," prompted the young man harshly, remembering Annie's anguished screams and the way she tried to hide her small hands from his sight.

"That's about it." Roderick splayed his hands in a gesture of defeat.

"What about the woman referred to by that unfortunate appelation?" probed Loch.

"Och, aye, the *'greedy bitch'*!" exclaimed the old man. "Maude Potter, Lady Rebecca's maid, but I have not been able to locate her. There is a very unfortunate rhyme bandied about the village . . . quite frankly, there are a number of very cruel rhymes to do wie the Gunns of Kenlaren."

"Don't wander from the subject, Roderick," hissed Loch. "We were talking of a maid?"

" 'Rebecca Gunn had a maid and now the maid is daid,' " chanted Mr. MacDonald. "But it would seem Maude Potter is very much alive and blackmailing Miss Oriana, if I'm not mistaken."

"You've missed your calling, Roderick," quipped Loch, trying to hide his concern.

"And what would that greedy bitch use to blackmail the lass?" continued Roderick, his voice cracking with suppressed rage. "But that her father, Sir David Gunn, was murdered here at Kenlaren?"

"By whom?" asked Loch softly after a long silence as an image of Annie with a dagger in her hand flashed through his mind. "Oh, my God, by whom?" he repeated almost under his breath. Roderick shook his head mutely and both men stood at the open window staring over the moonlit lawns of Kenlaren as the heady perfume of the roses hung in the dewy night air.

Annie also stared over the rolling lawns as Lochiel's words played over and over in her head.

"I'll never be your wife," she hissed, trying to convince herself as the thought of being in his arms tempted her. "I'll not marry someone who does not want me," she added, remembering his stony expression and cold, measured tone. " 'Rebecca Gunn's whoring's done. Rebecca Gunn's whoring's done'," she chanted as the cruel rhyme spiraled into her mind. "Oriana Gunn has just begun," she added with a bitter twist as she recalled Loch's words about her crawling into his bed like a common slut. "Rebecca Gunn's whoring's done but Oriana Gunn has just begun," she sang repetitively as she dressed quickly, determined to leave Kenlaren and Lochiel Montgomery as soon as possible. She surveyed herself in the mirror as the thought of never seeing Loch again caused pain and tears to well. Furious with herself, she dashed the tears away and sneered at her defiant reflection.

"Och, Annie Gunn, you'd make the very devil of a whore," she spat. "Or a whore for the very devil," she added, and frowned at the familiarity of the words.

Quickly she packed extra clothes and a blanket into a saddle bag and descended the servants' stairs to the kitchen to get some food just as the gray fingers of dawn softened the horizon.

"About time you come to your senses," cackled Mrs. Wilson, appearing from the pantry shadows as Annie wrapped bread and cheese up in a napkin. "Stay away until Lochiel Montgomery has gone," she ordered instinctively, knowing the girl was running from the man as well as her heart. "And if you miss your monthly flow, leave me signs at the Stepping Stones and I'll weave a spell of herbs," fussed the old woman, brushing the vibrant hair aside and looking into the sorrowful depths of the amber eyes. Annie nodded, gave the old woman a quick hug, and dashed out of the house.

Roderick stood by the door frowning as the girl disappeared into the orchard with a bulging saddle bag. He didn't look at the crone as she hobbled up and stood beside him, staring after the girl with misty eyes.

"The de'il takes care of his ain," she sighed, and then blew her nose loudly.

"Then she'll need no abortifacients from you, auld woman!" he snapped harshly.

"What do ye ken of my spells?" she croaked. "Shouldna listen to that which dinna concern you, auld mon!"

"Where is she off to?" questioned Roderick, but the old woman snorted angrily and shuffled back into the dark kitchen. "Is it the greedy bitch again?" he persisted, following her.

"I dinna ken what you're prattling aboot!" answered Mrs. Wilson, her ancient face closed. Roderick nodded slowly, understanding he would get no information. He sighed deeply and wondered whether he should wake his young master or not. Lochiel needed all the sleep he could get if he was going to regain his strength, and yet, what if the lass didn't return, he worried.

Annie rode Dubh across the high moorland toward the sea. She needed solitude to think through the emotional upheaval that churned within her.

Lochiel awoke at noon and after a leisurely bath and breakfast he dressed for riding and strode downstairs, expecting to see Annie. Michael looked up from his studying as the dark man entered the library.

"It's good to see you up and about, sir," greeted the younger man formally.

"For heaven's sake, Michael, dinna call me sir; you make me feel quite ancient," laughed Loch. "Where's your sister?"

"I haven't seen her all day but that's not unusual. She's very independent, goes where she wants when she wants," returned Michael.

"And for as long as she wants, it would seem," remarked Loch that evening as he and Michael faced each other across the dining table.

"Aye," answered Michael cheerfully, eating with gusto. "Once she was away more than two weeks," he added with a full mouth. He nearly choked as laughter overtook him at the memory. "That's how long it took to get rid of that particular governness!" he howled, slapping his thigh as mirth overcame him and he recounted the story of one of Mrs. Wilson's more potent potions. "If you could have heard that puir woman's stomach! I vow it could be heard all the way to Glenwillie!" he chortled.

"So she stays away until unwelcome visitors leave?" remarked Loch dryly. Michael's laughter died away as he saw his dinner companion's lack of amusement.

"I did not mean to infer you were unwelcome, sir," said Michael, blushing to the roots of his auburn hair.

"Am I then to regard this meal as suspect?" asked Loch, thoughtfully pushing his laden plate aside.

"I really have no way of knowing, sir," replied Michael as he resumed eating heartily. "But I cannot think why the old woman would take exception to you, Lord Falconhurst."

"Do you mean it is not all visitors who are treated to Mrs. Wilson's unfortunate concoctions?"

"Nay, only those who have the sheer effrontery to criticise my sister, heaven forbid," returned the youth sarcastically. Loch frowned at the bitterness that laced the boy's tones.

"Well, I can certainly see much I could criticize in your young sister," he stated slowly.

"I wouldn't, if I were you. The old hag thinks my sister is perfect, and any statement to the contrary is regarded as a slight upon her," chattered the youth, basking in the attention he was receiving.

"It would seem the sooner that alliance is terminated the better. I'll not have my wife consorting with such an incorrigible influence!" snapped Lochiel, extremely hungry but not trusting the appetizing dish that steamed in front of him.

"Wife!" choked Michael as the irritated young man strode angrily to the door.

"Have me informed as soon as your sister puts in an appearance!" ordered Loch without turning. Michael sat with his mouth gaping open in amazement as the door slammed rudely behind Lochiel Montgomery.

"Hah!" screeched Mrs. Wilson, popping her grizzled

head through the serving hatch and causing Michael to start with a scream. "Och, I heard him! He thinks to get my wee witch-wife, but I'll get him! Tie him in knots!" she vowed, stabbing a bony finger. Michael shuddered and opened his book, preferring to ignore the seething old crone as she wrung her gnarled hands in her apron and planned a long list of dire spells and potions to twist and wither Lochiel Montgomery's virile body. "He'll never hae her! Never!" she promised.

PART THREE

Then sang the shepherds and nymphs of Diana:
Long live fair Oriana.

—BEN JOHNSON

Chapter 15

The following week crept by at an agonizingly slow pace as Annie slept out on the open moorland, determined not to return to the comforts of Kenlaren until Lochiel Montgomery had gone. The nights seemed interminable as she lay in the scratchy heather dwarfed by the enormous bowl of the sky and conscious of the stark coldness of each star. She was aware of loneliness for the first time in her life. She cursed the arms she longed for, wishing she had never experienced their strong safety. She cursed the tall, dark man who had claimed her so thoroughly and disdained her so utterly; and her pain melded with a pulsating rage, making sleep impossible.

Each morning at first light she rode fearfully to the Devil's Stepping Stones to collect the food and messages Mrs. Wilson had left. What if Lochiel Montgomery was still at Kenlaren? What if he wasn't?

Listlessly she tended her horses and then spent hour upon hour perched high atop the sharp cliff overlooking the secluded beach where she had first encountered the dark man. Over and over again she relived the moment when they had raced their horses neck in neck across the sand. Below her fell the jagged teeth of the escarpment that had painfully scraped her child body when she had tried to escape from him eight years before. Annie wept, wishing she were still the innocent child whose unformed body hadn't yet been awakened to a lover's touch.

"Why didn't I escape? Why did I let him catch me?" she screamed to the wheeling gulls who circled with the gathering thunderclouds.

Dubh nudged her as though sensing her deep pain, and she rubbed her hot face against his velvety nuzzle before dashing away her angry tears and leaping on to his high back with the aid of a large boulder. She dug her small bare feet into his muscular girth and urged him into a prancing gait along the rocky coast road, eager to race out the tempest within.

"I hate him! I hate him! I hate him!" she chanted aloud, trying to convince herself as the horse's hooves pounded rhythmically, the dry earth powdering and puffing up like smoke.

Lochiel reined his steed and smiled without humor upon recognizing the small vibrant-haired rider perched atop the giant black stallion, streaking across the purple moor. The preceding week had crawled by at an irritating snail's pace. He was impatient with his body, still weak from illness, and impatient with Roderick's hovering presence as the loyal man sought to protect him from Mrs. Wilson's suspicious brews. Mrs. Wilson, he snorted, feeling only disgust toward the fanatical woman who pranced out of the shadows to draw strange symbols and chant unintelligible incantations. How Robert Forsythe justified the madwoman's presence at Kenlaren was beyond him. Especially with the terrible example that she set to the already undisciplined Oriana, he seethed. He was short-tempered and humorless and wouldn't admit to himself that one of the reasons the week had crept by so slowly was because he missed a certain golden, vivacious presence. He was just savagely thankful that the wild girl was not crawling into his bed to sap the energy he was determined to conserve in order to heal himself. He needed his full strength to come to terms with the two pressing irritants in his life: namely, his treacherous cousin, Ross, who had usurped his title and lands, and Oriana Rebecca Gunn, who threatened to usurp his very freedom. Watching her wild ride, he felt a tightening in his groin. A devilish grin crossed his dark features as he envisioned other wild rides with himself firmly in the saddle.

"Maybe marriage doesn't have to be without some compensations," he murmured, kneeing his mount so he followed Annie at a more sedate pace. He surmised that she was on her way to the hidden meadow where Dubh's harem of mares and colts grazed peacefully. He snorted cynically when he recalled Michael's callow exuberance as he showed off the glossy herd and boasted of his little sister's many accomplishments. Besides the debatable virtues that Loch could add to the list, such as unabashed wantonness and highway robbery, apparently his future bride could hunt, shoot, throw knives, swim, dive, climb, and ride, and do all manner of things more suited to a country urchin than to the wife of a Scottish peer. He had probed the auburn-haired youth, trying to discover some of the secrets of Kenlaren, but to no avail. Loch frowned, remembering Michael's young, earnest face, which seemed devoid of deceit when he recounted his father's sudden desertion eight years before and his death in Africa the following year. Either it was the truth as the boy knew it or Michael Gunn was an accomplished liar, which he seriously doubted. When Loch had broached the subject of Maude Potter, however, there had been a much different reaction. The youth had turned alarmingly pale and become very taciturn. Maude Potter had been his mother's personal maid and that was all, and no matter how Loch approached the subject, Michael stubbornly refused to divulge anything else. It was his very agitation that made Loch feel Roderick's suspicions could very well be correct.

Lochiel reined his horse and watched Annie's proud stance on top of the stone wall that skirted the horse pasture, where Dubh was greeting his mares and firmly disciplining his rambunctious colts. Quietly he dismounted and approached her, nodding his approval of the girl's unerring eye for excellent horseflesh.

"Dubh certainly keeps order in his family," Loch remarked softly, spanning her tiny waist with his broad hands. Annie froze at his touch, and the sound of his deep voice reverberated through her. She ached to turn and bury herself in the fragrant safety of his strong body, but she stood stiffly, her pulse thundering in her ears.

Lochiel felt her tension and dropped his hands, surprised by the change in her usually graceful movements. He stepped back and eyed her awkward stance as she stood with her hands clenched at her sides, staring across the meadow.

"I need to talk to you," he said softly, but she made no motion she had heard. "I am not in the habit of talking to backs," he added. When she didn't turn to face him, he sighed with impatience and reached to make her comply.

At the feel of his hands, Annie unfroze and fought him, but she was no match for his strength.

"Look at me, Oriana," he ordered autocratically as she tossed her head to avoid his searing gaze. Loch's anger rose as she closed her eyes rebelliously and gave an ear-splitting whistle. "Another of your many accomplishments," he laughed mockingly as the stallion tossed his head up and down and whickered as though asking for more time with his adoring mares. Loch scooped Annie off her feet and, ignoring her kicks and colorful stream of obscenities, strode away from the pasture. Out of Dubh's sight he set her on her feet facing him. Annie stared at her dusty bare toes, feeling dwarfed by his imposing height as she waited for him to speak. The taut silence between them lengthened as overhead the thunder rumbled, gathering momentum. Unable to bear the tension, she threw back her head and glared up at him, trying to cover her vulnerability with a mutinous expression. Lochiel caught his breath as the glorious mane of golden hair flew back and her exquisite little face snarled up at him rather like the spitting kit of a wildcat.

"And what would you be wanting of a common slut, Lord Falconhurst?" she challenged, unnerved by the lights that flickered in his black eyes.

"Och, dinna tempt me, Rob Roy," he said huskily, sending delicious shivers down her spine, igniting her passion and her fury. "There is nothing I'd like more than to tumble you here and now, to mount you as it would seem Dubh is mounting one of his mares." He saw the flush deepen under the gold of her cheeks as they heard the unmistakable sounds of the stallion mating. "But, unfortunately, I have neither the time nor the inclination right now, as I am intent on leaving your dubious hospitality," he added sardonically and was surprised and not a little ashamed to note a fleeting expression of pain cross the small mutinous face. "I should have thought you very relieved at news of my departure," he remarked, feeling strangely elated.

"I am," returned Annie, her voice sounding husky as though she were near tears. She tore her eyes away from his as, to her horror, the unmistakable sounds of Dubh's lusty rutting caused her own body to tingle. Lochiel grinned and leaned nonchalantly against a tree, very aware of her discomfort and of the reason.

"I am pleasantly surprised to observe you are capable of being embarrassed," he noted roguishly. "Am I to hope that you might have some maidenly modesty?" He wanted to goad her, as he rather enjoyed the battle of wills between them, but Annie only clenched her teeth, knowing there were no words to respond without losing even more face. She seethed at hearing her horse's lusty antics and very aware of Lochiel's lounging virile body. Not knowing what to do, she gave another ear-splitting whistle to summon the stallion.

"For shame," chided the dark man. "I would have thought you had more sensitivity and would allow the puir horse his pleasure." Annie shook her head. She longed to throw herself on Dubh's high back and put as much distance as she could between herself and Lochiel Montgomery. She turned away from him, intent on going back to the horse pasture, but then realized she couldn't witness the mating with Loch's dark eyes on her. He would know what she felt as she watched the black horse claim the mare. He would know she ached deep inside, longing to couple and be claimed. Loch laughed softly, quite aware of her dilemma as she suddenly stopped on her way back to the pasture and stood hesitatingly, unable to face him.

"I'll geld him!" yelled Annie, goaded by his obvious delight in her discomfort. "I thought you in a hurry to leave!" she spat, needing to vent her rage as the air was charged and the sky darkened, seeming like night.

"Dinna worry. I shall be back as soon as I've set my house to order," teased Loch.

"I shall not be here."

"You *will* be here," insisted Loch, challenging her to disobey him.

"I shall be in London making my debut," stated Annie, wishing she were taller and trying to be imperious.

"You, a debutante!" exclaimed Loch derisively before roaring with laughter, unable to picture her a simpering, virginal, obedient young lady. Annie wished she had something to throw. She was so full of rage there were no words, just furious noises bursting from her mouth. To her relief she heard and felt Dubh's hooves reverberate through the ground as he leaped the stone wall from the pasture and made his way to her.

The stallion walked slowly between Loch and Annie, sensing the tautness and tossing his handsome head up and down in greeting. He blew through dry lips and pawed the ground, uneasy with the tension. As though to break the fury, lightning flashed and large heavy drops of rain started to pit the earth.

"Come, Dubh," ordered Annie as the horse playfully butted Loch, firing her jealousy. When the stallion turned reluctantly to obey, Lochiel grasped the bridle and swung himself easily onto the high glossy back.

"No!" screamed Annie. "Up, Dubh, up!" she cried, frantically trying to make the animal rear and dislodge the man, but Loch controlled the horse and galloped away, looking as though he were part of the stallion. "No! You can't!" howled Annie, unable to move, unable to comprehend that Loch had actually taken her horse. "No," she muttered, shaking her head in disbelief. "He just wants a ride," she convinced herself, trying to still the icy clutch of fear that kept her rooted to the spot as the rain increased. "He'll be back. He'll be back," she promised herself as her thick hair was plastered down and the thunder rolled and the lightning cracked the dark sky.

Lochiel Montgomery galloped across the high moorland through the raging storm, delighting in the sensitivity of the enormous animal. With the gentlest command of his knee or hand the horse obeyed. He threw back his head and laughed aloud, exhilarated by the stallion and the battling elements, feeling more virile and alive than he had for a long time. He nodded his appreciation of Annie's diligent training, which had disciplined the giant stallion without breaking his spirit. His mind turning to Annie, Loch became thoughtful. It had not been his plan to retrieve Dubh, but now that it was done it ensured his reunion with Oriana Rebecca Gunn. He knew she would not give up the black horse without a battle. First, however, he needed to put his life in order before he could concentrate on the wild, undisciplined girl whose life seemed fated to be entangled with his own. He laughed out loud remembering her flushed cheeks when she had tried to hide her obvious embarrassment at the sounds of Dubh's lusty appetite. It was going to be very interesting and exciting trying to tame the rebel without breaking her fiery spirit, he concluded. He frowned as the rumbling thunder and dark clouds increased and he remembered the strange, oppressive secrets of Kenlaren. His scowl deepened as he thought of Roderick's suspicions, of Mrs. Wilson's abortifacients and purges, and the terror-filled cries of Annie's nightmares. He decided to ride out to Falconhurst alone and leave Roderick to watch out for the capricious girl until he returned to claim her as his wife.

Numbly Annie moved one heavy leg after the other. She was bowed down by the torrential rain and the overwhelming loss of her stallion. She had stood awaiting Lochiel's return for over an hour before the awful realization had penetrated. He was not returning. He had claimed his stallion. Dubh was gone and she was now more alone than she had ever been in her life. She was unaware of the mewing cries that rhythmically burst through her lips with each slogging step through the mud.

"Och, you puir wee-an," clucked Mrs. Wilson, catching sight of the drenched muddy girl at the kitchen door. Roderick looked up and frowned at the sight of Annie's blank, vacant stare. The farmhands looked up curiously before turning back to devour their high tea. "Get yourself out of them wet clothes," fussed the old crone, pulling at the girl so she came into the dry kitchen and slamming the heavy door to block out the raging storm. Annie just stood with the rain running off her and puddling on the tiled floor.

"That fancy Lord Falconhurst rid off on your horse," volunteered a youth with his mouth full.

"Hush up!" screeched Mrs. Wilson as she saw pain flood across Annie's face and saw the amber eyes widen and fill with panic.

"He's gone?" whispered Annie, and Roderick groaned at the agony he witnessed, knowing there were no words to console. "He took my Dubh!" she said wildly, pushing away Mrs. Wilson's stringy arms that sought to comfort. "I will kill him! Kill him!" she screamed, and rushed back out into the stormy evening.

"Tha's right, lass, hate him. Hate him wie every bit of you. Hate him wie every ounce of fiber you hae," cackled the old crone, her voice high and strident, setting Roderick's nerves on edge. "My wee witch-wife isna fer the likes of him!" she crowed, rubbing her bony hands together with satisfaction.

"The bairn's in need of comfort, not celebration," snapped Roderick angrily.

"Och, she'll hae her revenge! She's no stranger to death!" rejoiced the old woman. Roderick looked startled and very conscious of the curious stares from the field-hands. He pushed Mrs. Wilson out into the rain and slammed the door shut.

"No stranger to death? What do you mean by that?" he probed, propelling the old woman through the teeming rain toward the front door of Kenlaren Manor.

"Curiosity killed the cat!" chortled Mrs. Wilson, prancing through the rose garden where the flowers bent their heavy heads under the force of the drumming rain. She picked up a few frail petals and crushed them, sniffing their perfume noisily before letting them drop, bruised and graceless. "Och, these roses could talk of death!" she sang out. "Couldn't they, my wee witch-wife?"

Roderick stared with compassion at the small figure huddled in the rose garden. Sensing another person, he looked to the open library window where Michael watched, his face gaunt and pale.

"Aye, curiosity killed the cat," chanted Mrs. Wilson,

prancing about the petals and puddles and delighting in the rain, which streamed her stringy gray hair, and in the sharp cracking lightning that ripped the dark sky.

"And satisfaction brought it back," challenged Roderick, his hands itching to throttle the cackling old hag.

"Tha's because a cat has nine lives and a mere mortal just one," she returned gleefully.

"What death has occurred here at Kenlaren?" persisted the old man, trying to be heard above the rumbling thunder.

"Kenlaren's more'n four centuries auld. There's a body moldering 'neath the cornerstone to keep the glaistigs and revenanters awa . . . och, and many a Gunn hae died here by some means or other," she chortled.

"Miss Oriana is but seventeen years old," probed the old man. "What death has she been privy to?" He was unable to keep from grabbing the triumphant old woman, who seemed to delight in the huddled misery of the girl.

"Och, take your hands off me or the Prince of Darkness will strike you dead!" rasped Mrs. Wilson, her eyeballs rolling back wildly.

"A Satanist, are you?" shouted Roderick, fear freezing his blood. "And I thought you none but a harmless auld crone!"

"Mrs. Wilson is no Satanist!" exclaimed Michael.

"Well, 'tis too late even if she were!" declared Roderick.

"Too late for what?" asked Michael.

"Miss Oriana is no longer a maiden!" stated Roderick, ignoring the youth and glaring into Mrs. Wilson's furious face.

"How dare you!" shouted Michael, anger and embarrassment staining his cheeks.

"What do you know of the black rites?" snarled Mrs. Wilson, her clawlike hands trying to loosen Roderick's grasp around her scrawny neck.

"Enough to know 'tis only virgins sacrificed at the black sabbat," replied the old man tersely.

"Stop it!" screamed Michael through the open French windows as he covered his ears, terrified of what he was hearing. The thunder rolled and the lightning cracked and the two old people were oblivious as they stood locked in combat.

"You canna stop it! 'Tis her fate! From the very womb Oriana Rebecca Gunn was a wee witch-wife!" screeched the hag.

Annie heard the words as the perfume of the bruised roses filled her nostrils with the nightmarish smell of death.

"From the very womb I was a witch-wife," she repeated.

"Aye," agreed the crone victoriously. "Soft and silky, stealthy of approach, treading oh, so lightly . . . and loving above all things to be caressed, stroked, and pleasured."

"No!" screamed Michael.

"Och, e'en from the cradle my wee-an burst wie every naughty, wicked lust. Her very existence is for that supreme dark midnight moment when her cleft will be filled by the awesome tool of the Great Horned One," rejoiced the woman, now writhing wantonly against Roderick.

"Stop her mouth!" screamed Michael as the old man threw the crone from him in disgust. Mrs. Wilson continued to cackle triumphantly and she squirmed sensuously in the mud.

"Och, his seed is so burning hot it feels like ice," she rejoiced, slowly sifting the slime through her taloned fingers and drooling it over her drooping breasts.

"Hush up! Dinna fill the puir bairns' heads wie such filthy muck!" roared Roderick, looking from Annie's pale, detached expression to Michael's terrified face and wanting to grind the old woman under his heel.

"I dinna hae to fill her head. She knows it all. The lass is the daughter of the de'il and maun lie wie him," cackled the crone, writhing obscenely in the slime. "She kens, don't you, my dawtie? Och, my wee-an knows she's evil. She knows there's something powerful that sets her apart, don't you, my wee sorceress?" Annie nodded mutely and the old woman chortled with glee and splashed in the mud.

"Aye, I always knew I was bad—that is why my own mother never held me. She couldna even look at me," stated Annie in a voice devoid of emotion.

"She never touched Michael either. Tell her, lad," begged Roderick, but the youth stood mute and terrified.

"Save yer breath, auld mon!" giggled the crone. "She's mine and she knows there's a dark secret locked within. She's bad, lusty, and evil and 'tis a wondrous thing. She doesna belong to ordinary mortals. She's wild and free and as randy as all of nature. I have raised her for the Prince of Darkness and his legions!"

Annie walked slowly away from the grotesque crone who still dribbled muck between her long, bony fingers as she writhed and laughed hysterically. Annie felt as though she were sleepwalking as the old woman's laughter joined with the howling wind and raging storm. The woman's words echoed in her mind, so frighteningly familiar that she couldn't remember when she had first heard them. She stopped by the pump in the yard and stared into a large puddle that despite the violent ruffling of the water seemed fathomless as the true understanding of the words settled in her brain, churning her gut. Lochiel's face, dark and satanic, appeared superimposed upon the roiling muddy water.

Roderick, with one arm about Michael's quaking shoulders, watched the girl, wondering what was going through her mind. Mrs. Wilson scrambled to her feet, intent on scurrying after her.

"You're mine! Remember, you're mine!" she screeched, sensing a wavering resolve in the small figure, who stared as though mesmerized by the large puddle. Roderick reached out and grabbed the old woman, recoiling as his hands slipped on the thick slime that liberally coated her gnarled arms. "There can be no changing, Annie Gunn! We canna undo the past! Remember, you've already killed!" she shrieked desperately.

Annie froze and then slowly raised her hands, staring at her splayed palms as the sickly scent of overblown roses choked her breathing and shrill screams filled her ears. Her eyes widened as visions of flower-sprigged wallpaper splashed with blood flashed into her head and the smell of death quivered her nose. She opened her mouth to howl, but there was no sound. Panic flared and she took one lurching step, needing desperately to fling herself on Dubh's high back to race out the nightmarish cobwebs of memory—but then she remembered and the pain of her loss meshed with the pounding terror.

Roderick saw Annie's arms open wide and then gasped as she spiraled to the ground, splintering the mud puddles.

"Dinna touch her. She's mine!" screeched Mrs. Wilson. "She can stand alone. She doesna need any of you. She's strong!"

Roderick shook off his stunned inertia and raced toward the unconscious girl. He bellowed with rage as the clawed hands clutched at his clothing, and he raised a clenched fist. The old woman fell back whimpering, shielding her face from the threatened violence as Roderick's fury erupted. He laid cruel hands on the crone's bony shoulders, shaking her and shaking her as though she were a filthy bit of vermin, before flinging her aside and picking up the limp girl.

"Gie her to me, she's mine," whined the old woman, her slack lips sucked into her toothless mouth. "You dinna ken the rules. You dinna ken," she mewled. Roderick resisted the urge to kick the groveling woman out of his way and instead walked deliberately around her as he called for maids to prepare their young mistress a bath. He strode up the front steps of the house and the door was shut behind him. Michael, cowering in the bushes, breathed deeply to still his racing heart and then fled through the rose garden and into the library, shutting the French doors and drawing the heavy drapes.

Mrs. Wilson sat in the mud, staring at the firmly closed doors as the storm continued. She didn't feel victorious. She didn't feel defeated. She felt empty. As the wind howled, sending a mournful, hollow ache through her bones, she knew a circle had ended. She lumbered to her feet and, slipping and sliding, she blindly made her way to the kitchen. She didn't hear the raucous laughter that greeted her muddy appearance as the fieldhands, well fortified with ale and her hearty cooking, reluctantly pulled on their oilskins and went about their chores in the inhospitable storm.

Roderick was impervious to the pathos of the bent old woman who sat rocking and wringing her gnarled hands, tears pouring down her mud-encrusted face. He directed a bevy of servants to carry buckets of water and a hip bath up to Annie's room. Mrs. Wilson was blind and deaf to the hive of activity. She felt old and confused. The rhythm of her life seemed disjointed and purposeless, and she was lonely. All she had left in the world was her wee witch-wife and her memories, moments from the past that she had hoped to experience again. Once, for one brief night, she had belonged to a coven. A happy, carefree group who unashamedly partied on the moors and drank of the ecstasy of forbidden pleasures. She had stumbled upon them quite by accident and had never found them since. Throughout the years she had heard of occasional sabbats and had chased across Scotland searching for the lost moment of happiness. All she found were dark and furtive meetings, and she had watched from the shadows feeling afraid and ridiculed. On certain full moons she still hitched up her cuddy to the pony cart and rode up to the high moors to summon the devil among the caves and giant boulders, but he never came. He never came because she had grown old and undesirable and now he would never come because Lochiel Montgomery had destroyed her supreme sacrifice by claiming her wee witch-wife for his own. Mrs. Wilson raised her head and howled out her rage and sadness.

The old woman's loud, eerie keening moaned with the lamenting wind, shivering the spines of the fieldhands as they bedded down the animals for the night and of the young maids who ran about the house obeying Mr. MacDonald's curt orders.

Annie stood at her bedroom window watching the storm, oblivious to the hissing cluster of frightened maids who huddled in the dark corridor outside her door, all of them unnerved by the wild keening from the kitchen that howled with the wind and rattled the windows and shook the rafters. She stared at her reflection on the mullioned glass that made her seem like she was at the bottom of a whirlpool, sucked to the depths below ring upon ring of swirling currents. The lightning flashed and for a brief second her image disappeared. She shivered as though it were a premonition of her own death.

"Death," she whispered aloud. "You've already killed,

Annie Gunn," she intoned, remembering Mrs. Wilson's words. She stared at her reflection captured at the center of the swirls of thick glass as the gale buffetted the panes. "Who did you kill, Annie Gunn?" she asked herself softly, looking down at the palms of her small hands as her nostrils filled with the sickly scent of roses. Suddenly she tore herself from the window and rushed to her door, frantically sliding back the bolts she had locked so firmly a short time before when she had desperately wanted her solitude.

"Michael! Michael!" she screamed, and then stopped short at seeing the frightened maids with white faces and wide eyes. "What's wrong?" she gasped. Dazed and not quite comprehending their gestures toward the stairs or their obvious fear of her as they backed away, Annie turned to the stairs and listened Mrs. Wilson's haunting laments.

"Annie?" called Michael as he ran toward her tying his robe, his hair wet and tousled from the toweling he had been giving it when he heard her call to him.

"She's cast a spell on Miss Annie too," whispered Millie as the gaggle of maids shifted uneasily. "Dinna look her straight in the eyes." The sibilant words sifted back to Annie and she slowly turned and surveyed the group with disdain before giving a strange, eerie scream so they ran howling up the backstairs to the attic rooms.

"Aye, run, for I am evil and can turn you into any manner of slimy creature!" she shouted, crossing her eyes and making extravagant gestures.

Roderick shook his head at the bitter malice that hardened Annie's beautiful features.

"Did you want something, Mr. MacDonald?" she asked coldly, and the old man silently shook his head again as the brother and sister entered her room and the door was firmly closed. Hearing the bolts being shot back into place, he wondered what Oriana Rebecca Gunn planned with her brother. He sighed and raised a grisled eyebrow as he thought on her resilience. An hour before she had seemed a bedraggled, defeated little waif, half-conscious and soaked to the skin, her eyes pain-filled and haunted. Now she seemed anything but defeated, he acknowledged as he made himself comfortable in the shadows within sight of her room, wishing he was privy to the conversation within.

"Michael, did I kill someone?" Annie was asking.

"Annie, I think Mrs. Wilson is addled . . . probably senile. I wish Uncle Robert were here."

"Hush up!" interrupted Annie rudely. "Michael, what do you know of that night?"

"What night?"

"The night . . . Father went away?"

"Nothing," shrugged Michael.

"He dinna go away, you know. He's dead. Duncan and Will buried him in the rose garden."

"Father died in Africa!" stated Michael firmly.

"Och, Michael, if you'd take your head out of your books long enough," sighed Annie with exasperation. "Why do you think we've been paying Maude Potter all these years?"

"I'll not discuss it!" snapped Michael. He refused to speak or even think about the indelicate details of their mother's conduct.

"Och, Michael, has the university turned you into a prude?" jeered Annie impatiently. "Do you think I'd pay the greedy bitch just because our mother was a whore?"

"Stop it!" gasped Michael.

"Like mother, like daughter," chanted Annie, her amber eyes glowing strangely in her pale face. "I am a common slut just like our mother, did you know that Michael?"

"You are overwrought; you don't know what you are saying!"

"I know what I am saying, Michael. Open your eyes and your ears," hissed Annie. "What do you know of the night Father died?"

"Nothing! Nothing!" spat the youth as he tried to block out the gentle swish of carriage wheels and the unearthly screams that her words conjured in his head.

"You do!" accused Annie, seeing his face blanch, and sweat bead his upper lip.

"Just the sound of fairy wheels and Mother and Father fighting and screaming . . . but it was a dream . . . just a dream."

"It wasn't a dream!"

"It *was!*"

"Do you want to hear what I remember?" asked Annie after a long pause.

"No!" he croaked hoarsely.

"I remember splotches and blots of redness, either blood or roses, I can never tell which . . . splotches and blots of redness all over the pretty walls . . . all over the pretty mother . . . and all over me."

"It was a dream!"

"I remember Duncan and Will digging graves in the rose garden in the moonlight," continued Annie.

"It was a dream!"

"Aye, one of your dreams of fairy coaches swishing down the drive, bringing Lancelot and Lochinvar to worship at the altar between our mother's thighs!" spat Annie savagely, and Michael gasped and recoiled.

"Don't speak of Mother like that," he whispered.

"Och, Michael, you great fool! You stupid innocent!" She laughed wildly. "Did you really think we paid the greedy bitch to protect our mother's honor?"

"Aye! We couldn't have Maude Potter spreading those lies!"

"Lies? Our mother didn't have any honor! She was just like me!" she howled with tears of cynical mirth pouring down her cheeks. "Rebecca Gunn's whoring's done! Rebecca Gunn's whoring's done! Remember that one, Michael? And you thought to protect her good name! What good name? She didn't have one! They probably have ballads about Randy Rebecca from John O'Groats to Land's End!"

"Stop it!" screamed Michael, slapping his sister smartly across the face. "Don't you ever talk about Mother like that," he sobbed. Annie stared at him silently and then turned away and walked pensively across the room to stare out at the dark, wet night.

"Everyone knew about our mother except you and me," she said softly. "I only realized the truth when I lost my own innocence." She turned to face him, appearing very small and vulnerable.

"To Lochiel Montgomery?" questioned Michael tentatively.

"Aye," she replied wistfully.

"God damn him! How dare he take advantage of our hospitality and seduce you!" roared the outraged young man, pacing furiously about.

"I seduced him," confessed Annie ruefully, taking the wind out of Michael's sails. He was about to declare he would avenge her virtue with dueling pistols or rapiers if need be.

"What?" he choked.

"Mrs. Wilson is right, you know. I am not as a gentlewoman is supposed to be. I am a witch-wife." Annie thought of the many frustrated governesses who had tried in vain to mold her into a proper young lady of society.

"No!" protested her brother. "You may be wild . . . er . . . undisciplined . . . imprudent," he stammered, choosing his words very carefully. "But you are definitely not a Satanist!" he postulated. "Are you?" he added fearfully when she didn't answer.

"I don't know what I am, Michael," replied Annie. "But whatever I am is not acceptable! It's no wonder Lochiel Montgomery found it amusing when I told him I was going to London for my debut. Can you imagine the scandal? Ladies and gentlemen, I should like to present to society Lady Oriana Gunn, the sluttish daughter of the infamous harlot Lady Rebecca! It is no wonder Uncle Robert kept me hidden here at Kenlaren all these years . . . and now it'll get worse when he finds out the rest," she wailed.

"What rest?" floundered Michael, wishing he could escape to his library and lose himself in a book about ancient Greece or Rome. "Do you mean about losing your . . . maiden . . . hood? Well, I am very shocked and disgusted by your lack of . . . er . . . restraint, but I think it only right that Falconhurst offer for you. If he doesn't I shall force him to make an honest woman out of you!" stated the youth pompously.

"Och, Michael, dinna be so silly," giggled Annie with a watery waver in her husky voice. "How on earth can anyone make an honest woman out of me? I've been stealing horses since I was eight! Anyway, I wasna talking of Uncle

Robert finding out about my lack of virtue and honesty but about Mother's. It is one thing to be known as the daughter of a whore and quite another to be known as the daughter of a murderess," confessed Annie with a shudder. "It would be even more humiliating to find out Mother wasn't the killer after all," she whispered, going alarmingly pale.

"What nonsense are you rambling about?" hissed Michael.

"I would feel like a complete idiot paying off that greedy bitch all these years," snarled Annie, trying to cover her sudden overwhelming feeling of terror with a rebellious attitude. "Well, I was too young before to know what a whore was, let alone know I had inherited the lusty trait!" she added in an effort to excuse herself as she thought of all the money she had stolen to silence Maude Potter.

"Stop talking of our mother like that and stop talking about yourself like that!" ranted Michael angrily. "It is not your fault that Montgomery took advantage of your youth and innocence!"

"I never had innocence!" yelled Annie. "I am just like our mother, born from between those thighs where many knelt!"

"Stop it!" whimpered Michael, covering his ears.

"Didn't you listen to Mrs. Wilson tell how I loved to be caressed and stroked, Michael? Do you hear me? Pleasured? Mounted? Covered? It was wonderful!" she shouted. "I loved it!"

"Stop talking like that!"

"Have you ever rutted? Mated, Michael?" she challenged.

"Stop it! This is not a fit subject for a young lady!" he cried desperately.

"Who is it a fit subject for, Michael?"

"For whom is it a fit subject?" corrected the youth.

"For whom? Go on, say it, brother," insisted Annie. *"Say it!"*

"No!"

"Say it!" demanded Annie. "Say *whore!"* She stared at her brother for a long, still moment, feeling very lonely and afraid. He was her older brother but she felt older and wiser than he. "We've never really been very close to each other, have we?"

"I am your brother," protested Michael. "I love you."

"Aye, and I love you too," sighed Annie. "Och, puir wee Mikey-lad, dinna fash, go and wrap yourself in your books." Michael's face hardened. He opened his mouth to respond, but instead he nodded curtly and walked to the door. He listened a moment.

"All's quiet now," he whispered, hearing nothing but the steady drumming of the rain.

"I preferred it before," replied Annie dully, wishing the wind still howled, bending the trees, and the thunder still deafened her ears to the frightening questions that swirled in her mind. "Sweet dreams," she quipped lightly, knowing her own would be filled with terrors from the past.

"Go to bed, Annie," begged Michael as she swung a cape about her slight shoulders and hooked it at her throat.

"I have to know what happened that night. I am going to ask Mrs. Wilson," she informed him airily, trying to hide the apprehension she felt.

"Let the past lie," pleaded Michael as terror pounded his pulses. "Mrs. Wilson is old. Her brain is addled. She had no right saying what she did."

"She had every right, if it was the truth," retorted the determined girl.

"As much as I hate to admit it, I think Lochiel Montgomery's right to wonder why Uncle Robert left Mrs. Wilson here to fill your head with . . ." He trailed off as Annie walked out of the room and fleetly ran along the corridor and down the stairs.

Roderick watched the youth standing in the doorway of his sister's room. He noted the scowl and the dejected slump of the boy's shoulders. Michael sensed his presence and turned. He nodded shortly before heading for his own room.

"What the hell!" he roared as he tripped over a full bucket of water and drenched himself. "What is this mess?" As he yelled he overbalanced and sat in a tepid bathtub. Roderick held up a lantern to illuminate the row of full buckets in the hallway. He helped the youth to his feet.

"It was for Miss Oriana's bath. I'm afraid the maids were spooked by the storm and Mrs. Wilson's wild ravings. They've locked themselves in the attic and will nae come out until daybreak for fear of the kelpies and ghoulies she may have summoned," explained Roderick, shaking his head at the sopping condition of Michael's brocade dressing gown. "If I were you, young sir, I would get myself oot of those wet clothes," he suggested, eager to follow Annie.

"Mr. MacDonald?" said Michael urgently, not wanting to be left alone. "I sorely need to talk." He squelched along the corridor to his room. "I am in charge here, you know. I am the laird . . . and Oriana is my little sister, but I don't know what to do. I know all this talk of witchcraft is just comical country nonsense," he struggled as he sat on his bed, pulling off his saturated slippers and hose. "And Satanism! Well, I mean the black arts died out centuries ago, didn't they? I know Mrs. Wilson was called a witch, but that was just a word, nothing more. We used it affectionately. The villagers called her witch out of ignorance because of her brews and medicines. Puir folks from the crofts on the moor who can't afford the doctor used her as a midwife. She was always helping the less fortunate, so there was no reason to think of her as a Satanist. A witch with her brews is one thing, but a Satanist is something very different," cried the youth with great agitation. "I mean, having people call Mrs. Wilson a witch was very convenient. It insured our privacy, kept curious, malicious people away, especially after our parents . . . left. But a real practicing black magic . . . Satanist . . . raising me and my sister?" he gasped, his brain scrambled by the utter incredibleness of the idea. "Roderick, I'm talking about Satanism with all its sexual ceremonies! And to think my own wee sister was a part of it is inconceivable!"

"Aye, it is inconceivable," comforted Roderick. "It was just the wild ravings of a senile auld crone who's afraid and jealous of the love Miss Oriana has for Lord Falconhurst."

"Love for Lord Falconhurst!" sneered Michael, slapping his thigh, furious at his stupidity for trying to confide in Lochiel Montgomery's servant. "Love for Lord Falconhurst! Love for that rake! That seducer! That defiler of innocent young girls!"

"Aye, that's the mon," replied Roderick with a grin. "If Miss Oriana is a Satanist, that's her de'il, my lad Lochiel."

"How could he take advantage of Annie like that?" hissed Michael lamely, not knowing what to make of the gleeful old man.

"Come now, lad. When has any taken advantage of your wee sister—except maybe Mrs. Wilson," asked Roderick quietly, and Michael nodded ruefully.

"Annie admitted to me that she seduced him," confessed the youth. "Mr. MacDonald, I do not understand my sister. I am not very experienced with women, but even so, I know her behavior is not . . . well, not . . . what it should be. Do you think there is any truth in what Mrs. Wilson says?"

"Of course not," stated Roderick firmly.

"Then maybe she's fed spells and brews to Annie," said the boy. "Maybe aphrodisiacs!" he added with great excitement.

"Aphrodisiacs?"

"That's why she is so . . . wanton!" declared Michael victoriously. Roderick nodded seriously, knowing there was no way he could even try to explain the golden girl's naturally sensuous nature to her studious brother.

"Aphrodisiacs," muttered Roderick for want of something better to say. He stood and stretched, determined to take his leave and find the girl in question.

"Aphrodisiacs," echoed Michael pompously. "And despite their use and despite what our mother . . . did . . . or did not do, I think it only fitting that Lord Falconhurst offer for my sister!"

Roderick stopped with his gnarled hand on the ornate door handle and turned to face the youth, who stood imperiously by the hearth with one foot on the fender, trying to look in control.

"I believe Lord Falconhurst has every intention of doing so," he remarked mildly, suppressing a wicked twinkle.

"He has?" gasped Michael, deflating and sitting heavily with his mouth gaping with astonishment.

"Aye, that's why he left me here to keep an eye on things until his return. So unless there is anything else, young sir, I shall bid you a good night and try to locate Miss Oriana," he said formally with a slight bow.

"She went to the kitchens to talk to Mrs. Wilson," said Michael, sounding very dazed. "I'll go with you, as I feel rather peckish. I don't think we had dinner tonight, did we?"

"I dinna believe you did," replied Roderick, holding the door open for the stunned youth and following him with the lantern. "Watch yourself! Dinna trip over the buckets!" warned the old man belatedly as with a loud crash and a muffled curse Michael barked his shin and sloshed tepid water over his newly changed hose and slippers.

Annie stood in the dark kitchen listening to the steady drumming of the rain and smelling the fresh sweetness that the earth put out after a cleansing storm. She frowned when her eyes became accustomed to the dim light and she saw the farmhands' soiled plates and mugs were still strewn along the length of the usually immaculate table. She shook her head at the mess of congealed food that crusted the serving platters and tureens. The cooking hearth, which had always been alive with a welcoming, warm, red glow, was now a dark, hollow hole. She shivered and walked toward the cold gray ashes, unable to believe what she saw, and she was filled with an ominous dread. She lit a candle and her shadow loomed and wavered and rose to the ceiling, where it bent so she appeared to be a grotesque old woman. She watched her shadow and waved her hands, making them crooked and talonlike as a sorrowful grin cracked across her face and she gave a witchlike cackle. She twisted about wildly in the neglected, deserted kitchen, sensing that something was different, something was missing, something would never be the same. She sniffed the air and shook her head from side to side as small snorts of frustration burst from her mouth. Something indefinable but vital was missing, something that she had always taken for granted. A certain intangible, sparkling energy, a certain musky warm aura was gone.

"Mrs. Wilson," she mouthed. A deep ache dug into the very center of her and a low, mournful howl sobbed from her throat. "Mrs. Wilson?" she whispered, wrenching open the heavy door to the farmyard.

Roderick laid a warning old hand on Michael's arm as he saw Annie silhouetted against the shining wet darkness at the open door. Sensing their presence, she turned and looked at them with dull eyes before waving her hands to indicate the cluttered table and cold cooking hearth.

"Look," she muttered.

"Mr. MacDonald said the maids were afraid of the storm so they took to their beds in the attic," explained Michael. "Maybe we should rouse them now that the worst of the storm is over?" he suggested when neither Roderick nor Annie responded to him.

"Everyone's gone, Michael," grieved Annie. "Everyone and my Dubh and now Mrs. Wilson, but none of them were really mine anyway, were they?"

"Who's everyone, lass?" asked Roderick gruffly. Annie looked at him sharply, losing her dull lassitude as Lochiel's dark handsomeness flashed into her mind. Roderick stifled a groan and the impulse to pull the unhappy girl into his arms for comfort. "Aye, I ken," he stated, stiffly kneeling in front of the hearth to light the fire and put some warm cheer into the gloomy room. He worked quickly and intently, kindling a small blaze. At the sound of a sharp clatter he looked up to see Annie rhythmically stacking the dirty plates.

"Leave that to the servants," protested Michael.

"Remember before Uncle Robert came? Before we tried to be different? When we were just . . . just . . . well, when we just were? Remember Michael?" she asked softly as she cleared the table.

"Aye," replied Michael, sitting heavily in a chair as waves of nostalgia washed over him. Roderick sat back on his heels listening to them. Sensing another presence, he looked to the open doorway and there loomed the tall figure of Lochiel Montgomery, who motioned him to be silent.

"I cleared the table each night. Remember? And Will and Duncan took care of us? And I slept in the wee room over the backstairs? Do you remember then, Michael? Do you remember before everything changed?" she continued, and Michael nodded. "Were you happy then?"

"I don't know," he answered huskily.

"I was very happy then," stated Annie firmly, as though challenging them to contradict her. "I was very happy because I just . . . was very happy. I didn't think about it, I just was. Why can't people leave things alone so they stay the same?"

"Unfortunately, we all have to grow up," murmured Michael, feeling very melancholy.

"I am not talking about growing up! I am talking of interfering people who should leave things alone. If Uncle Robert hadn't come here, everything would be all right. Everything would have stayed the same. Duncan and Will would still be here," retorted Annie angrily.

"Mother and Father wouldn't be here!" argued Michael.

"Everything would have stayed the same!" yelled Annie, sweeping a precarious pile of crockery off the table so it crashed on the hard tiled floor. She stared down at the scattered shards about her bare feet. "Everything would have stayed the same! I'd still sit on my little stool outside Mother's room listening to her poems and stories and she would have remained a beautiful, romantic woman and not a filthy, stinking whore! Everything would have stayed the same . . . without pain! Mrs. Wilson would be here too," she shouted. Then she yelped as she trod down heavily on a sharp fragment of crockery. "Let me be!" she ordered as both Roderick and Michael moved to help her when the blood welled and dripped thickly. "I am not a child!" she shouted, hopping on one foot and getting a perverse pleasure from the stinging pain.

"I am relieved that you are aware of that fact," agreed a deep, sardonic voice that caused her pulses to race and a warmth to spread achingly in the core of her. She gasped as Lochiel Montgomery stepped from the wet darkness with the rain running down the chiseled planes of his face. "I should stand very still on one spot if I were you," he added with a note of amusement that belied his concern when it appeared she was about to lacerate herself further by backing away from him through the splintered china.

"I am not a child!" repeated Annie lamely as she was firmly picked up and seated unceremoniously on the kitchen table.

"No, you're certainly not," murmured Loch, his eyes impudently caressing her soft curves. Annie glared at him rebelliously, trying to ignore the quicksilver sensations that quivered through her as she smelled the sensuous musk steam from his rain-drenched clothes and felt the seductive strength of his hands encircling her slim arms. Her heart pounded painfully and her breathing was fast and furious. She glowered into his craggy face, determined he should be the first to look away. But his hard ebony eyes seemed to know her thoughts and mock the tumultuous emotions he aroused in her. Long moments ticked by and she was unaware of Roderick and Michael, who observed the silent battle of wills, very conscious of the sparking undercurrents. Michael open his mouth to protest but the old man quietly led him from the kitchen.

"Damn you!" cursed Annie, wrenching her gaze from his searing stare to look down at the vulnerable sight of her dangling legs and the blood that slowly dripped and splattered on the light shards of crockery and the dark floor. "Damn you!" She fought to free herself from his strong hands. "Och, damn you," she whispered as he pulled her to him and cradled her against his broad chest so she heard the steady beating of his heart joining with her frantic pulses. "Och, damn," she sighed, breathing deeply of his safe fragrance.

Chapter 16

Annie opened heavy lids at first light. She lay back in the hay, staring bemusedly at the dusty rafters of the barn before sitting up and gazing at the beloved sight of Dubh, who stamped his hooves, impatient to be out of the stuffy enclosure and in the crystal freshness of the new day. She leaned her back against the rough wood of the stall as her hands unconsciously fiddled with the soft pile of a dark cape that partially covered her. Drawing the woolen garment up to her face, she rubbed her cheek against it, smelling the masculine scent of Lochiel Montgomery. They had sat side by side watching the proud, beautiful horse in the warm lantern light as the rain drummed softly on the roof. They had not kissed. They had not coupled. They had barely touched, and yet there had been an intimacy not present before—even when they had lain naked together. For the first time in her life she had felt shy, unable to meet his gaze, as it somehow made her feel defenseless. She had sat so still, so very aware of the heat of him less than an inch away from her, scorching and searing each pore. She had welcomed the lassitude that had crept inexorably, closing her eyes and stopping the many questions, fears, and emotions that addled her senses. Now she was awake and alert and alone. She blinked, trying to cool her hot eyes, close to tears. She wanted him so much, she admitted, so very, very much it hurt. She thought then of her mother, who had also wanted someone very, very much, and she steeled herself, remembering Mrs. Wilson and all she had said.

"Mrs. Wilson!" she cried aloud, pulling herself to her feet and dusting the straw and chaff from her clothing. "We maun find the old lady," she crooned to Dubh as she leaned against his firm, warm girth. She would have to ride to the labyrinth of dark caves amongst the Devil's Stepping Stones on the high moorland, where the woman went often when the moon was full.

Hearing a furtive whispering and scrambling outside in the yard, Annie peered through the dusty window and saw the huddle of hissing maids, who clustered like geese outside the kitchen door, holding hastily tied bundles.

"What's going on?" she asked, stepping out into the bluish half-light of the early dawn. The maids backed away, frantically crossing themselves.

"Dinna meet her eyes," squealed Millie, her freckles standing out on her pale face as she held a crucifix before her and backed away. "Run!" she screamed. The girls ran in all directions, tripping and dropping various items.

Annie watched them go as the cruel rhymes from her childhood spiraled into her memory. Roderick stood nearby in the open doorway of the kitchen, noting the emotions that crossed Annie's expressive face.

"It's very quiet this morning," said Annie with a frown, and Roderick nodded thoughtfully.

"There's no gillies in the fields either. It seems Mrs. Wilson has put the fear of the devil in just about everyone at Kenlaren, even the roosters," he said softly.

"Except you, Mr. MacDonald," she answered with a wistful little grin.

"Aye, except me," he responded huskily. "Where are you off to?" He spoke casually, trying to hide his concern as the girl led her stallion out of the stable and into the yard, where he stood snorting and pawing the cobblestones, eager to gallop.

"To find Mrs. Wilson," she answered shortly after giving him a long searching look. "Up on the moors," she added, waving a vague hand. "She took her cuddy and cart." She found herself chattering nervously and realized she was somehow loath to go alone. But why she was babbling about the old woman's donkey, and why did she think Roderick MacDonald would be interested?

"Are you afeared the auld crone has done harm to herself?" ventured the intuitive man, who, despite his abhorrence of the crazed woman, accepted the knowledge that the girl loved her.

"Aye," confessed Annie, feeling a great wave of affection toward him.

"Then I'll go wie you," decided Roderick, entering the stable and selecting a docile mare.

"Thank you." Annie realized that for one of the first times in her life she was welcoming the comfort and assistance of another person.

"How's the foot?" conversed Roderick as he saddled the mare. Annie laughed and rocked a small hand back and forth to indicate not good or bad before limping to a bale of hay and mounting the impatient stallion.

"Let me race the cobwebs out of him and then we'll meet up on the highlands," she called, leading the prancing animal through the orchard and giving him his head as they broke free into a wide, sloping pasture. Roderick, following at a more sedate pace, breathed appreciatively of the freshness and vibrancy of the rain-washed countryside.

At noon Michael awoke and rang a bell summoning a servant to bring hot water for shaving and his morning meal. After half an hour or more of furious janglings of the bell, he pulled on his clothes and stormed downstairs, bellowing as he went. He gasped with astonishment at the sight that met his eyes in the breakfast room. Cutlery drawers gaped open and empty and the mantelpiece, sideboard and table were devoid of their usual array of silver cruets, vases, candlesticks, and assorted knickknacks. He rushed into the large dining room and there, too, it was obvious that looting had taken place as drawers and doors were wrenched off tracks and hinges, and forks and spoons, and odds and ends were strewn higgledy-piggledy across the carpet, attesting to the greedy haste of the thieves. Michael followed the trail of spilled articles through all the formal rooms, spinning about with stupefaction at the violation of each cabinet and cupboard. In horror he peeked about the door of the library, terrified that he would find his own special treasures either vandalized or stolen, but to his overwhelming relief each volume stood intact in the usual straight, conforming rows.

"Rape and pillage!" he cried dramatically, and his face drained of all color as he thought of his sister. "Annie!" he shouted, and raced back upstairs to her chamber, remembering just in time to avoid the row of full buckets that still lined the corridor. At the open bedchamber door he fearfully peered inside, but the room had been undisturbed by the looters or by his sister. The bed had not been slept in, and her discarded clothes were in the same position as the previous evening. She obviously had not returned to her own bed, he concluded bitterly, his anger inflaming as he thought of the tall, dark man in whose arms Annie was probably writhing.

Muttering furiously to himself, Michael climbed the narrow stairway to the maids' rooms on the attic floor. He stared with contempt at the messy rooms, which had obviously been vacated hastily, as clothes drawers and wardrobes gaped open and empty. Slowly he made his way to the kitchens. He stared dispassionately at the drops of dark blood that had dried on the floor tiles and at the bits of broken crockery. The table was still littered with the remains of the gillies' meal from the day before, and once again the cooking range was out. Michael fought back furious tears, feeling completely abandoned. He stepped into the yard, glaring about blearily for a sign of life, but even the usually clamoring chickens and geese seemed muted and listless.

Lochiel awakened late in the afternoon as the sunset limned the rolling curves of the moors and the clouds with a blood red. Keeping his eyes closed, he lay in rosy suspension as the events of the previous day seeped into his relaxed mind. He smiled sleepily as Annie's golden vivacity radiated through him and he shrugged, still feeling the lithe arms that had hugged him so ecstatically when he had carried her to the barn to show her Dubh was there peacefully munching dry oats. He had placed her on the stallion's glossy back and stepped away to better appreciate the joyful reunion. Ruefully he admitted to a pang of jealousy as her long slender fingers reverently caressed and she stretched her pliant body along the length of the animal's back, her lean brown arms embracing the proud, arched neck, and her nose pressed into the ebony mane. Loch sighed and flexed his hand, feeling a delicious tingling as he remembered holding the graceful, slender foot that fit so snugly in the palm of his wide hand as he examined the jagged gash. The bloody wound reminded him of another time and place, the naked, defiant child whose fragile body had been so cruelly scraped in the frantic attempt to escape from him.

"Och, Rob Roy, there's no escape for either of us now," he sighed, admitting he was as firmly captured as she. The day before he had galloped away from her through the violent storm, delighting in his freedom, the feeling of the powerful Dubh between his thighs, so sensitive to his slightest command. He hadn't expected to return to Kenlaren for several weeks, if not several months, for his shipwreck and consequent exile had caused neglect to his home, farms, and stables; but Annie's anguished cry had rung in his ears, drowning out the thunder that rolled and roared overhead. That one moment, when he had swung himself onto Dubh's high back, was suspended in time, crystalized in his mind. The sharp scream of shock and the wild torment in Annie's amber eyes dug beneath his hard, cynical layers and cut him to the quick. He had raced the stallion across the storm-lashed moors to the jagged cliff overlooking the turbulent sea that dashed its foaming fury against the very sand where he and the wild-haired witch had first encountered each other eight years before. He had angrily shaken his dark, drenched head, trying to dislodge the guilt and remorse he felt as Annie's grief seemed to howl with the lamenting wind.

"You are mine!" he roared to the stallion as the golden, animated face haunted his mind and he sensed that she still stood where he had left her so small and valiant, buffeted by the brutal storm. "Mine!" he shouted as the lightning severed the dark sky and he felt her pain shoot through him. Fighting the unease that churned his guts and the desire to return to Kenlaren and Annie, he rode into the town of Dumfries, where he took a private parlor at a small inn, fortified himself with several glasses of well-aged whiskey, and tried to reason through his dilemma, but all he could see and feel and want was a certain golden-haired, wild waif. After writing letters to various people, including his solicitor, a prominent magistrate, the Ayrshire constabulary, and his Cousin Ross—informing him of the legal action he was taking and advising him to leave the country or face prosecution—Lochiel resignedly remounted the weary stallion and rode back to Kenlaren through the still-raging storm.

Lochiel now opened his eyes reluctantly, as it seemed a dark cloud eclipsed the setting sun, and his warm flesh tensed and goose-bumped as he remembered all Roderick had told him. The vibrant joy and hope he had felt since awaking now vanished, and he was aware of a brooding unease. The shadow of Kenlaren with all its mysteries and pain seemed poised, as though holding its breath, ready to pounce. Loch sat up, chilled by the eerie silence, and he swung his long legs out of the bed. He sat listening, but heard not the slightest creak within the old house or the quietest cheep outside. He strode to the open window and stared across the deserted landscape. Nothing moved. Not a person, not an animal, not a bird, not even the gentlest breeze so much as quivered a blade of grass. Even the blood-red sky with its violently angry striations seemed frozen. He quickly pulled on his clothes and stamped into his riding boots as anxiety clawed at him. When he opened the door to the corridor he listened again, but nothing disturbed the uncanny stillness.

"Roderick!" he bellowed, and his voice seemed to reverberate hollowly throughout the house and return faintly to mock him. He marched down the hall, his booted feet ringing authoritatively as he banged at each chamber door before rudely thrusting it open. He searched the entire house, from the attic rooms to the cavernous wine cellars beneath the sprawling kitchens but there was no one to be found. He lifted a black eyebrow as he noted the apparent looting. The barn was empty of animals and people, as were the fields that surrounded the graceful manor. Loch frowned thoughtfully at the havoc the violent storm had wreaked upon the ripened grain, the golden stalks battened down into the mire, making harvesting useless except for silage. Helping himself to a generous hunk of cheese from the pantry, he set out for the hidden high meadow where Annie kept her stable of ebony horses. He strode through the orchard noting the strange, muted behavior of the chickens, and he gazed about searching for the roosters that usually strutted noisily with their harems, but except for a few scattered bright plumes there was no sign of the crowing males. Pensively, he pulled an apple from a low-hanging, laden branch and bit into the crisp flesh with a satisfying crunch just as the sounds of wheels swished up the driveway, breaking the unearthly silence. Robert's cheerful, cultured voice sang out, demanding assistance. Loch debated continuing on his way, but upon hearing his sister's low, musical laughter, he turned back, not wanting to cause added concern when he remembered the state of the formal rooms and the blood and broken crockery on the kitchen floor, he flung his half-eaten apple at a brooding fat chicken and was encouraged by the indignant squawk as he strode through the rose garden, his boots stamping the strewn petals into the mud. He couldn't wait to give Sir Robert Forsythe a piece of his mind, he realized, wanting to release some of the anxiety that had been building.

"Oriana? Michael? Roderick?" called Robert, his handsome face looking very perplexed when no line of docile, uniformed servants appeared to welcome him back to Kenlaren. "What the hell is going on here?" he barked irreverently as Wilkes ushered him up the front steps and Iona spun on her heels, looking about uneasily as she sensed a certain eeriness.

"Loch!" she cried thankfully as she espied him silently watching her. She ran into his outstretched arms. "What is the matter here?" she asked after kissing his lean cheek and hugging him ecstatically, trying to dispel the nagging premonition of doom.

"Many things, it would seem," he returned enigmatically. He looked intently into her upturned face and satisfied himself that she was happy. She glowed, and joy and well-being seemed to exude from each pore. "It would be redundant to ask if you were content," he said ruefully, not wanting to mar her sunny disposition. "Don't go in," he warned then as she was about to run up the front steps. Robert's voice could be heard swearing, shouting at all he saw and didn't see.

"What is the matter?" repeated Iona. "Where is Annie?"

"Oriana is fine," snapped Loch shortly as Robert appeared at the open front door.

"Montgomery," hailed Robert guardedly.

"Forsythe," nodded Loch tensely.

"What the hell has been happening here?"

"You leave a senile old crone to fill impressionable young heads with superstition and Satanism, you're bound to have a few difficulties, Forsythe," replied Lochiel, his anger low and coldly controlled. "How on earth can you justify leaving that insane witch with Oriana?"

"Loch?" chided Iona, shocked at the suppressed fury in her brother's voice. She looked up at his handsome face, noting the hardness of his dark eyes, which glinted dangerously. "You cannot be talking of Mrs. Wilson?"

"I certainly am," he snorted.

"Excuse me, sir, but the small drawing room seems relatively undisturbed," offered Wilkes formally. He held the ornate front door wide as an indication that the gathered gentry should air their differences in private as befitted their stations in life, not like common peasants on the front doorstep, even though the environs seemed strangely deserted. "I have taken it upon myself to serve a small tiffin," he added to insure a degree of gentility to what promised to be a most unpleasant scene, judging from the barbaric glint in the dark Scot's eyes.

"What do you know of the goings-on here at Kenlaren?" asked Loch shortly when they were esconced in the small drawing room and Wilkes had tactfully withdrawn after serving a light report of assorted biscuits, hothouse fruit, cheeses, and white wine.

"My dear boy, I have not been here. You have! I have been on my honeymoon," replied Robert, languidly popping a grape into his mouth.

"I am not your 'dear boy'!" retorted Loch, rolling his *r*'s in a very Scottish manner, deliberately making a distinction between his deep brogue and Robert's effete English tones. As he spoke, his controlled fury grew to a roar. "I am not speaking about the past fortnight but the past history of Kenlaren. Your ward, Oriana Rebecca Gunn, takes to the road as a hightoby, robbing travelers at gunpoint. . . .

"Once, just once, a youthful prank. A game—and you should be jolly well thankful. It was that cad of a cousin of yours, Ross Montgomery who . . ." interrupted Robert cheerfully.

"It was no game! And it was not just once!" argued Loch. "She's been stealing for years and it's a wonder she's not been killed!" He was making every effort to point out Robert's very evident shortcomings as a guardian.

"She is kept very well in pin money. I have been more than generous, so why would she steal?" puzzled Robert, at a loss. "Maybe excitement?"

"Blackmail," answered Loch.

"Blackmail!" echoed Robert wearily. He shook his blond head, wishing he were back aboard his yacht with Iona, putting a great distance between himself and his willful ward.

"The greedy bitch," murmured Iona thoughtfully. Loch looked at her sharply, his thick, dark eyebrows raised. Robert shook his blond head and tutted reprovingly.

"Very indelicately put, my pet," he chided mildly.

"Aye, a certain Maude Potter," supplied Loch. "What do you know of her?"

"Nothing very much," confessed Iona, splaying her well-shaped hands in defeat. "Except that she was Lady Rebecca's personal maid."

"What happened here at Kenlaren?" demanded Lochiel roughly, intensely irritated by Robert's apparent nonchalance.

"Maude Potter? Impossible," replied the Englishman casually, pouring himself a glass of wine and holding the crystal up to the candlelight. "I dealt with that unappealing female years ago."

"Not very effectively, it would seem!" snapped Loch.

"Dealt with her how?" asked Iona.

"Besides—she's dead! I heard that she met with a very unfortunate accident several months ago," informed Robert. He seemed to ignore the dark brother and sister as he gazed through the stem of his wineglass watching the interesting distortions for several tense minutes. "It appeared that she had witnessed the twins burying their father in the rose garden," he explained finally, losing his congenial expression. "Maude Potter had a stranglehold on the Gunns. Before I came they had mortgaged Kenlaren to buy her silence for five thousand crowns."

"How did you deal with her, Robert?" repeated Iona fearfully.

"Threatened her with all sorts of dire things. Garroting, poison, the plague . . . also, I settled a comfortable little annuity on her and set her up in a rose-covered cottage across the border in Westmoreland," he confessed, unable to remain relaxed under the smoldering eyes of the two dark Scots.

"She cannot be dead. Annie gave her over four hundred crowns less than a month ago," protested Iona.

"Four hundred crowns!"

"Ross Montgomery's money."

"But there was no need. The bodies were removed from the rose garden," objected Robert, striding to the window and glaring at the pretty spot in question. "She could not prove anything!"

"Bodies!" exclaimed Iona. "Robert, you said 'bodies' . . . that means more than one," she added unnecessarily.

"Slip of the tongue, my dear?" he said hopefully, and then shook his head as he saw neither Iona nor Loch were gullible enough to accept that lame explanation. "You are both putting me in the dickens of a spot," he sighed. "Anyway, what has any of that ancient history to do with the present state of this house? Where are the servants? Where are my wards?" he ranted. "Where are the men? I am aware it is late, but there's not a sign of life out there!" Iona stood next to him, looking out across the lawns and fields before turning back and looking questioningly at her brother.

"There was a storm last evening . . . lasted most of the night," answered Loch slowly.

"I am more than a little aware of that fact!" snapped Robert, remembering the violent buffeting as the sea had whipped its fury against the yacht. "'Tis a wonder we're not at the bottom of the Sōlway Firth!" He poured himself another drink as his stomach churned at the memory.

"Your cook and housekeeper, Mrs. Wilson, who has filled Oriana's head with all sorts of . . . er . . . folklore of satanistic persuasion," began Loch, carefully choosing his words so as not to assault Iona's sensibilities.

"Why are you stepping so carefully, Loch?" demanded Iona angrily.

"What do you know of Mrs. Wilson?" he asked roughly.

"Well, she's a good woman. A little strange, but devoted to Annie. Would give her life for her," Iona defended.

"According to Roderick, Mrs. Wilson—the good woman—had the notion to sacrifice Oriana's virginity to the devil at a black mass!" informed Lochiel. He gave a fleeting smirk of satisfaction as Robert choked violently on his wine and had to be thumped inelegantly upon the back by his wife.

"I say, old boy, watch it!" coughed Robert. "Not quite the thing to talk of virginity in the company of the gentler sex!"

"Gentler sex?" laughed Loch sardonically, thinking of Annie's wildness and Mrs. Wilson's cunning toughness. "The long and the short of it is the old woman used the violence of the storm to frighten the servants and gillies away. And it would seem that several helped themselves to the household silver in lieu of back wages. As for the whereabouts of Oriana, Michael, and Roderick MacDonald . . . I am at a loss. The house and stables were deserted when I wakened, which was shortly before you arrived."

"What bodies?" shouted Iona, determined to understand the fragments of information so casually thrown about. "Who killed them?" she probed, trying to get the attention of the two tall men.

"This is extremely difficult for me," admitted Robert. "I was raised to ignore, more precisely, to be pointedly blind to, the transgressions of well-bred females, particularly members of one's own family. Grandmothers, sisters, and mothers are supposed to be regarded with the utmost reverence. I imagine that's why I found Oriana Gunn so very refreshing," he meandered dreamily, not wanting to pursue his first thought.

"Please keep to the subject, darling," pleaded Iona.

"Beg pardon?" questioned Robert vaguely.

"You were discoursing on the transgressions of well-bred females," cued Loch impatiently.

"So I was," sighed Robert. "It is hard to discuss my sister Rebecca."

"The bodies, Robert," groaned Iona.

"One was Sir David Gunn, Rebecca's husband, and the other was apparently one of her . . . lovers," he replied dully and then he frowned when he didn't receive the expected shocked reaction.

"What was his name?" probed Loch tersely and Robert shrugged.

"Who killed them?" asked Iona in a shaky little voice.

"I assume they killed each other . . . simultaneously," answered Robert airily, not wanting to divulge any more information. "Now, what's all this about Mrs. Wilson?"

"If Maude Potter is dead, who is blackmailing Annie? And why?" puzzled Iona.

"I suggest we find that particular young lady and ask her," decided Robert.

"Darling, isn't it quite a stretch to assume that the two men killed each other simultaneously? Who else was there to witness?" pursued Iona, desperately trying to fit the bits and pieces of information together and create some sense. Lochiel's and Robert's eyes met and a message passed between them as both young men sought to protect Annie. Loch's dark eyes narrowed as he saw Robert's usually lazy blue eyes sharpen to a steely gray as though to warn, and he remembered Annie's tormented nightmare and the way she had tried to hide her hands, convinced that they were covered with something incriminating. The two men stood with their eyes locked, communicating a chilling fear.

"What is it?" cried Iona with distress, feeling a hollow dread shroud the room.

"Some of Mrs. Wilson's ghosts and ghoulies are sparking your fervent imagination, my pet," replied Robert cheerfully, wrenching his gaze from his dark brother-in-law and tenderly embracing his new bride. Softly he kissed her mutinous mouth.

"Dinna treat me like some simpering lap dog!" she shouted, trying to wriggle out of his arms. "Don't leave me out. Tell me all you know," she begged, looking from her brother to her husband.

"Oriana was there that night," informed Loch soberly, his usually enigmatic face full of pain as he recalled the small, vulnerable girl who had screamed and cried, trying to free herself from the panic of the nightmare, grasping for the safety of reality only to discover reality more to be feared.

"Annie was present when her father was killed?" repeated Iona with horror.

"How did you find out?" sighed Robert resignedly.

"That is unimportant," parried Loch, unwilling to divulge the intimacies he had shared with the man's young ward, since it was indeed those intimacies that had made him privy to her nighttime terrors. "What is important is to find the chit and her brother," he stated harshly, staring out of the window at the impenetrable darkness that ringed the nearby lawns and fields.

"Unless the moon rises, there's nothing we can do until morning," remarked Robert morosely, and a gloomy silence fell as the three young people tried to rein their separate feelings of foreboding. A polite rapping at the door caused them to turn and stare at Wilkes, who popped his head into the room.

"Master Michael and Roderick MacDonald have just ridden into the stable yard," he stated. Nimbly he stepped aside as Robert and Loch strode swiftly to the door. "Is there anything you would like, Lady Iona?" he added gently as she sat with a blank stare, not noticing the ludicrous floral apron that covered the little man from neck to knees.

"Isna Annie wie them?" she asked fearfully.

"Miss Oriana was not accompanying them. Master Michael and Roderick MacDonald are settling their horses, as it appears that the fieldhands and ostlers—as well as the entire house staff—have departed." He was struggling to fill in the brooding silence as he and Iona made their way through the empty house, their shadows elongated and eerie in the bouncing lantern light.

Iona shivered when they entered the vast kitchen, remembering its usual cozy, welcoming atmosphere. She curled herself in one of the wide farm chairs, tucking her legs beneath her as she gazed about trying to understand the source of her unease. The room was clean and tidy, the cooking hearth glowing warm and red, and yet there was a ghostly chill.

"What is different here?" puzzled Iona, looking around. It wasn't just the absence of the delicious smells that usually issued from the cauldrons and from the clusters of dried herbs that dangled above the mantel, but something undefinable was missing, a certain essence, she reasoned. "What is missing, Wilkes?"

"I did my best," sighed the usually immaculate man, staring regretfully at his well-manicured hands. "But I am not accustomed to menial work," he added, rolling down his sleeves. He had been appalled by the sight of the unwashed crockery and pots, the unscrubbed table, and the filthy floor strewn with blood and broken china, so he had resignedly donned one of Mrs. Wilson's aprons and tackled the distasteful chore, detesting disorder above all things.

"Menial work?" echoed Iona, turning to stare at the usually unflustered, precise little man. "What are you wearing?" she exclaimed, noticing for the first time the garish pinafore that enveloped him from his neck to below his knees, wrapping about his tiny waist at least twice.

The entrance of the four men saved Wilkes an answer as Iona cried out in alarm at the sight of Michael's battered face when he limped into the room and sat heavily at the table.

"Michael, what happened?" she cried, leaping to her feet and rushing to examine his cuts and bruises.

"I rode into the village to get help and was stoned," he answered dully. "Annie will be pleased to know that everything is back as it was. Nothing is changed. 'Gunn, Gunn, your day is done! Gunn, Gunn, you day is done!" he chanted. " 'Rebecca Gunn's whoring's done! Rebecca Gunn's whoring's done!' " His voice was low and bitter.

"Where's Annie?" demanded Iona.

" 'Wild Annie, dressed in britches. She is one of Satan's witches!' " intoned Michael.

"She rode up to the moors to a place called the De'il's Stepping Stones to look for Mrs. Wilson. I went wie her but she rode on ahead and I couldna keep up. When I reached that godforsaken place there was na hide nor hair of either the lass or that wicked auld crone. I'm sorry, lad. I swore to myself I'd not let the lass out of my sight, but none can keep up wie the stallion Dubh," apologized the sorrowful old man. Lochiel silently nodded his understanding and, unable to sit or to appear serene and composed like Robert, he paced the floor, his boots ringing sharply on the hard tiles.

"Aye, but there's certainly hide and hair of your Cousin Ross Montgomery!" proclaimed Michael, who stared with bitter satisfaction into Iona's stunned face as she stood before him with clean swabs in hand, intent on tending to his cuts and bruises.

"What?" barked Loch, skidding to a standstill before the lounging youth. Michael sneered up at him and then deliberately reached for the brandy that was to be used as an antiseptic. Loch wrenched the bottle from his grasp.

"Cousin Ross—here?" gasped Iona, turning alarmingly pale as she remembered the lecherous assault at the Craigie Arms. Robert dropped his nonchalance and reached for his stricken wife, pulling her onto his lap.

"Elaborate, or receive several more bruises," warned Loch.

"Ross Montgomery is in the village. Kenlaren village," stated Michael as though he were talking to the hard of hearing. "Och, you should have been there! It was a welcoming sight reminiscent of the old days. There was the most reverent Vicar Nevins and his wife, the aforementioned Ross Montgomery, our own freckle-faced Millie, and every one of our servants from the house, fields, and stables . . . all armed wie rocks, crosses, rifles, and pitchforks! When they saw me it was as though I had grown horns and cloven feet . . . och, I've never had such a reception!" recounted the boy with wry humor.

"And what was said?" prompted Roderick. "Tell them what you told me, lad," he urged as the youth pursed his lips mutinously.

"They're on a witch hunt!" he stated, covering his terror with a sardonic bravado.

"Witch hunt?" echoed Iona.

"They talk of burning Annie and Mrs. Wilson," giggled Michael, a hint of hysteria cracking his voice. "They called them 'the witches of Kenlaren' and it seemed to me, Lord Falconhurst, that your cousin was inciting them to violence . . . trying to convince them to burn the manor to the ground."

"Stay here, Roderick," ordered Loch tersely, thumping the brandy bottle onto the table.

"Loch, where are you going?" cried Iona as her brother strode purposefully across the room.

"To find that troublesome brat before the witch-hunting mob does," he retorted savagely, slamming the kitchen door behind him.

"Well, Uncle Robert, home wie your bonny bride to find Kenlaren Manor back as it was before your generous and benevolent hand cleared the goats off the lawns and the chickens off the stairs," mocked Michael cruelly.

"Michael?" protested Iona, shocked by such maliciousness from the usually gentle and studious youth.

"Och, Annie was so right!" continued Michael, after drinking liberally of the brandy. "We were happy before you came along, Uncle Robert, because we dinna expect anything more than the sunrise and the sunset. We got up in the morning and went to our beds at night just living each day, not expecting anything more. Is there anything to eat, Wilkes, I've not eaten since yesterday morning," he finished petulantly.

"Sit down, Wilkes, and take off that ridiculous garment," ordered Robert. "Michael is quite capable of seeing to his own needs. Get yourself food, young man!" he added with a steely ring in his usually drawling tones. "Your Uncle Robert might have removed the chickens from the stairs, but I am sure Mrs. Wilson has some cooked in the larder."

"Robert?" chided Iona softly as the youth limped sulkily across the room.

"Yes, my pet?" replied Robert affectionately, sending delicious shivers down Iona's spine despite all the dark mysteries that lurked in the shadows of Kenlaren.

"Aren't you being rather hard on the puir boy?" she whispered. "He's probably worried sick about his sister and that's why he's being so rude."

"I don't want to be accused of being too generous and benevolent again. Chickens and goats are all I shall take responsibility for," he returned roguishly, kissing the warm softness of the nape of her neck and trying to hide the hurt he felt at Michael's attack on his largesse.

"I expect you wish chickens and goats were all you *had* responsibility for," replied Iona seriously, echoing his thoughts precisely.

"Michael, I rather think Wilkes and Mr. MacDonald might also be somewhat peckish," remarked Robert as the youth entered with a laden platter and sat down at the table with his mouth wide, prepared to take his first bite.

"I beg your pardon?" said Michael stiffly.

"And so you should," replied Robert, deliberately misunderstanding. There was a still tense moment as Michael debated defying his uncle and picked up the well-ladened fork as though to fill his mouth. Robert regarded him with a slight smile on his face but a wicked glint in his eyes. Michael dropped the fork onto the plate with a clatter and noisily pushed his chair back from the table so the legs scraped painfully across the tiles. He stood with a sigh and, exaggerating his limp, slowly walked to the pantry, hoping to spark guilt and compassion from the watching people.

"I'll help you, Michael," offered Iona, uncomfortable in the tension. She was especially aware of Roderick's unease as the old man peered out of the kitchen window, keeping a vigil.

"You'll not," contradicted Robert, holding her firmly on his lap and nuzzling her neck.

Iona opened her mouth to protest but closed it, sensing that despite his behavior Robert was really as worried as she. She sat in silence as Michael made numerous trips from the pantry until the table nearly groaned under the weight of the food.

"Is that enough for you, Wilkes?" asked Michael sarcastically.

"That is quite enough out of you!" snarled Robert, leaping to his feet and nearly dumping Iona to the floor. Michael backed away from the sudden violence and stared at his uncle in awe. In over eight years he had never seen the seemingly benign man display anything as uncivilized as anger. He almost remarked on the phenomena but thought better of it, so he lapsed into silence and stared dismally at the abundance of food, feeling rather sick. He was angry, wanting to hit out at any and everyone. He thought of the past years and the satisfaction and joy he had received from his studies—but it was all a lie. His well-stocked, elegant library, his tastefully furnished rooms in Edinburgh, his studies at the university—all were pointless, an empty facade. Even his dreams for the future had no substance. He would never be Sir Michael Gunn of Kenlaren, a suave, well-bred, well-read lord, admired and revered by all. He would always be the same timid, ignorant boy who had no idea of what was happening around him until it was too late. He trembled as he remembered waking up one morning in a cold, wet, stinking bed after dreaming of violent screams to find his father gone forever.

"I woke up this morning and everyone was gone," he muttered aloud with his eyes fixed to the familiar grain of the wooden table. He traced the whorls and lines as he had as a small child.

"What did you say, Michael?" asked Iona gently, sensing an incredible vulnerability about the youth. He looked at her sharply and frowned as though not recognizing who she was.

"It's all going to happen again," he said haltingly as he grounded himself to the present by remembering who each person about the kitchen table was. "Will sat there.

Duncan there and Annie there. Father used to be there at the head and after he left the twins took his chair away."

"All *what* is going to happen again?" probed Iona.

"I don't know. I didn't know then, either, but it happened. I woke up and it had happened. All along it had been happening, and Annie knew but I didn't. I should have known as I am the older, but she knew and I didn't," he struggled.

"Knew what?" asked Robert, unable to make any sense of it.

"I don't know!" shouted Michael with great frustration. "I woke up and Father was gone and there was a terrible feeling of horrible, frightful things looming in the shadows and in the screaming fragments of dreams—and there were secrets—hissing, whispering secrets and I wanted to know and I didn't want to know, but Annie knew. She told me Father was killed and buried in the rose garden . . . how did she know?" He looked to each person at the table as though expecting an answer. Tears poured down his face. "Why am I bothering to ask any of you? You don't belong here!"

Lochiel cursed the impatience that had made him reach for the first available bit of horseflesh in the dim stable. He rode the ancient nag up the steep, muddy lane to the high moorland as he prayed that she was sure-footed. He tried to calm the anxiety that clawed him by breathing deeply of the dewy night air and concentrating on the steady rhythm of his docile mount. The going was slow and irritatingly laborious, but he curbed his desire to kick the over-rounded heaving sides of the poor dispirited animal. Willing himself to have patience, he fixed his smoldering eyes on the clearing night sky as the moon rose above the scrubby tree line. It was nearly full and of a strange, luminous green, causing each natural shape to appear distorted and grotesque. He swore aloud as he thought of the frightened, ignorant villagers who were so ready to blame their ruined crops on withcraft. They were probably staring at the eerie moon-shadows now, and weaving even more horrendous fantasies about Oriana Gunn and her foster mother, Mrs. Wilson. Why had his Cousin Ross come to Kenlaren, he worried, and why wasn't the vicar calming his parishioners instead of joining them in an outdated but nonetheless dangerous witch hunt. Deeply engrossed in his brooding thoughts, Loch broke free of the narrow confines of the rutted land onto the rolling barren moorland where the moon sailed high and victorious. The old nag blew uneasily through her loose lips and laid her ears flat along the sides of her head as her eyes flickered white with panic.

"Hush, lass," he crooned, trying to calm the spooked animal as he scanned the giant rocks that stood like menacing monuments to a bygone time. The moon caused ghostly silver ripples to weave and waver through the grass and heather and then disappear like vapor into the shadowy crevasses of the looming granite blocks. Loch narrowed his eyes, imagining the eerie moonlit mist to be the druids in flowing gossamer gowns floating through the darkness. He urged the old horse forward to the towering starkness of the Devil's Stepping Stones, but she shrilly protested, her sharp whinny snapping the still silence and echoing off the cold gray rocks. Loch keenly scanned about, seeking the slightest movement, but nothing stirred except the swirling mist that seemed to steam from the ground in ever-thickening tendrils, stinging his nose with a sulphurous stench. With a reluctant sigh he dismounted and tied the frightened nag to a stunted dead tree with gnarled, knotted limbs that appeared grotesquely human and witchlike against the strange night sky. The horse bucked against the restraint, wanting to take to her heels and return to the docile surroundings of her enclosed barn. She snorted and stamped the ground in a frenzy, clearly terrified by something. Loch frowned and painstakingly scrutinized the moor and the looming rocks, but nothing stirred other than the wisps of mist that seemed to tease and tantalize, beckoning him toward the natural monuments.

Lochiel carefully walked toward the giant slabs of rock, determined to examine every inch in his search for Annie.

Above, Annie watched Lochiel's tall, dark figure loom in and out of the swirling tendrils of mist. She sat hugging her knees tightly, excruciatingly aware of the keen eyes of the old crone, who had stopped her incessant rocking at the first screech of the frightened horse.

"It's him, ain't it?" hissed Mrs. Wilson, and Annie nodded, her eyes not leaving the shining black head far below her. "He'll nae find us unless you gie him a sign . . . and if'n you gie him a sign, he'll take you far far awae and I'll nae see you more," she whispered brokenly, her voice cracking with sorrow. Annie didn't answer or move a muscle; she just stared out over the desolate moor waiting for Lochiel Montgomery to loom again out of the swirling patches of mist. She and Mrs. Wilson were esconced in a cave high within the tallest of the stepping stones, which gave them an unencumbered view of their surroundings but kept them undetectable from the ground. For more than an hour Annie sat hunched with her back to the crone, her smooth cheek limned by the unearthly moonlight, hearing Loch's boots scrape and slide on the hard granite.

"He's gone," sighed Mrs. Wilson, stretching her cramped body and resuming her monotonous rocking. "And good riddance," she added, hoping to elicit some response from the motionless girl. Annie stared across the barren starkness, feeling as cold and desolate as the vista. Once she had thrilled to the freedom of the unfettered, rugged wildness, but now it only weighed her down with hollow loneliness. She strained her ears until her head ached, trying to hold on to the fading hoofbeats as Lochiel rode out of her life and all that remained was her own dull pulse. She sat remembering each line of his dark face and strong, lean body.

"You ken he were not for you, my wee witch-wife, dinna you?" strove the old woman, unable to numb her senses and soothe herself any longer. "Aye, you ken all right or you'd have choosen him but you dinna, you choose me, my dawtie. You choose yer auld Mother Wilson, dinna you, me lassie?" fretted the crone, unnerved by the girl's brooding silence.

"Aye, I chose you," replied Annie as the old woman's words penetrated, and she turned to look at Mrs. Wilson. She caught her breath with terror as in the greenish moonlight the crone's face appeared spectral. She froze, staring, trying to find the beloved familiarity in the shimmering glow that accentuated each wrinkle and line, collapsing the flesh as though there were no supporting bones beneath.

"What is it? What do you see?" whimpered Mrs. Wilson fearfully. Annie shook her head, trying to clear her vision, but the ancient flesh kept shrinking and the eyes flowed a macabre shade of green. Annie gaped in speechless terror as it seemed the fervent, gleaming eyes bulged, protruding as though they were about to be ejected. She backed away with her hands outstretched to ward off the approaching specter.

"Dinna leave me or I'll hae naught to live for," sobbed the toothless old woman, reaching out to the girl for comfort. Annie's back was pressed painfully against the hard, cold rock as the gnarled talon fingers stabbed toward her.

"No!" she howled, and then froze as she was wrapped in hard, pinching arms and shaken with the tremors that shook the grieving old crone.

"You're all I hae—all I hae lived for these past long years," cried the woman. Her terror dispelled, Annie stared bemusedly down at the tangled gray head that rested heavily on her breast. Slowly she raised her hands and stroked Mrs. Wilson's head, crooning comfortingly as she would to an unhappy child, much as the old woman had often done for her.

"I'll nae leave you. Shush now, dry your tears," she chanted softly, holding Mrs. Wilson close and remembering all the loving care the woman had given to her for as long as she could recall.

"Do you choose me?" whined the crone. Annie sighed deeply and nodded.

"Do you?" persisted the hag, clinging desperately.

"Aye, I do," whispered Annie sadly.

"You'll never leave me?"

"I'll never leave you."

"Promise?"

"I promise," vowed Annie.

Chapter 17

Iona, her long legs curled beneath her like a small child, sat in one of the wide farm chairs beside the glowing kitchen hearth, painfully conscious of the irritating ticking of the clock as it measured each tense, waiting second. Wilkes had suggested that she retire to the more proper surroundings of the formal rooms but she had declined, preferring the rustic coziness of the kitchen. She shivered and hugged herself close as she glanced at the shadowy corners that were untouched by either the warmth of the fire or the flickering candlelight. It seemed that something evil lurked in the chill darkness, but it was nothing to compare to the imagined terrors in the long, hollow corridors and vacant chambers in the main wing.

A long, mournful sigh caused her to look sharply at Michael, who slept restlessly, his tousled auburn head slumped on his forearms beside a nearly empty brandy bottle. Faintly she heard the low murmuring voices of Wilkes and Roderick, and an occasional clink and clatter as they busied themselves in the scullery.

Unable to sit still, she stretched her cramped limbs and stood, suppressing a desire to scream and shatter the brittle, tense waiting. She paced the tiled floor, wishing she had been able to dissuade Robert from riding alone to the village of Kenlaren. For a moment she peered out of the window, trying to convince herself there was no cause for alarm. It was the nineteenth century, not the Dark Ages, she reasoned, staring out at the ghostly moonlit countryside and the eerie spectral shapes that were grotesquely silhouetted against the weirdly colored sky. With a quick motion she tugged the homespun curtains across the glass as panic clawed in her belly.

"Och, Robert, Robert be safe," she whispered as she glanced at Michael's battered face, his bruised, swollen eye lids twitching as though he were in the throes of a bad dream. She resumed her pacing as she tried to still her raging imagination.

"Is there anything you would like, Lady Iona?" asked a respectful voice. She spun around and stared with confusion into Wilkes's noncommittal face.

"No, nothing, thank you," she replied, smiling tearily down at his unlined, ageless features. "What's that?" she cried, listening intently and raising her hand for silence. Wilkes frowned and shook his head, hearing nothing. Silently Roderick strode in, wiping his hands on a tea towel that he had tied about his waist.

"What is it?" he asked.

"Hush! There it is again," breathed Iona, and there was a faint rhythm of hoofbeats plodding closer and closer until they became a sharp, staccato clatter on the cobblestones in the yard. Iona threw off her stunned inertia and, with a small cry of relief, made a move toward the kitchen door, but Roderick quickly restrained her.

"Nay, lass. I shall see who it is." He took down a lantern and turned up the wick. Then they heard the squeak of saddle leather as someone heavily dismounted, and bootsteps joined the clopping of the shod hooves.

"But it must be Robert or Loch," protested Iona, wanting to be free of the kitchen and to follow the horse and rider to the barn.

"Your husband told you to stay put," chided the gaunt old man. Iona watched the door close quietly after Roderick as fear clutched, cramping her muscles and restricting her breathing.

"Are you quite certain there is nothing I can get you, Lady Iona? A nice civilized cup of tea?" suggested Wilkes, trying his hand at humor when he saw the way her graceful tapering fingers were brutally mutilating a fine lace hankerchief.

"No, no, nothing," replied Iona, shaking her head from side to side in a very agitated manner. "But thank you." She resumed her nervous pacing. The seconds ticked by at an excruciatingly slow pace until she thought she would go insane. "How long does it take to unsaddle a horse, dammit!" she shouted inelegantly. "Och, Loch, thank God!" she cried as the door opened and her brother entered, followed by Roderick. She flung herself into the comfort of his arms, clinging to his safety for dear life.

"I hear your headstrong husband rode off to tackle the witch hunters singlehandedly," he remarked cuttingly, and then groaned at her stricken expression as she stared up at him, her dark eyes brimming with tears. He held her close, needing comfort as much as she.

"He wants you to meet him there behind a tavern called The Kenlaren Arms," informed Iona, trying to control her wavery voice. "Where's Annie?" she remembered, pushing herself back so she could see his face. "You dinna find her?"

"Nay," murmured Loch, gently disengaging himself and sitting Iona in a chair by the fire. He would pour himself a sustaining drink before finding a rideable horse and setting out for the village tavern to meet his brother-in-law. Roderick, always alert to his young master's needs, stood ready with a whiskey jug and a glass. "There maun be a multitude of hiding places amongst those great boulders," Loch sighed after a long, punishing, burning swallow of the hard liquor.

"Aye, it is a godforsaken place, is it not?" shivered Roderick. "Even in broad daylight it is a cold, unwelcoming spot. It maun be fair bloodcurdling wie this unco moon," he answered, gratefully accepting a full glass of whiskey to warm his own fear-chilled old bones.

"No sign of Mrs. Wilson either?" asked Iona, knowing the answer but uncomfortable in the brooding silence. She was tempted to push her brother back out into the eerie night so he would find Robert. Lochiel, not responding to her question, stared contemplatively at Michael's battered sleeping face. Thoughtfully he picked up the brandy bottle and held it up to the lantern.

"How much of this did the lad drink?" he inquired of Roderick.

"The bottle wasna full and Sir Robert had a few pulls, but the lad doesna seem too accustomed to spirits," informed the old man as Loch put his strong hands on Michael's slumped shoulders and hoisted him out of his seat. The relaxed youth hung limply and mumbled incoherently. Loch shook him.

"I'm asleep," declared the boy, opening his blackened eyes and blearily peering into Loch's scowling features.

"I am certain you are aware of all your sister's hiding places," he stated firmly.

"I am going back to sleep," said Michael thickly, after futilely trying to free himself.

"Your sister's life may depend on it!" barked Loch. Michael's tawny eyes flew open, showing fear and alarm for several seconds, before a crafty leer crossed his battered young face.

"Annie Gunn leads a charmed life. Nothing can hurt her except you! She does not want you to find her, so go away and about your own business," he laughed, waving one finger insultingly in front of Loch's nose. "The de'il takes care of his ain!"

"Michael!" chided Iona, seeing her brother's jaw tighten as he fought to control his rising temper. "Michael, we all love Annie and we're trying to help her. We dinna want the villagers to hurt her as they did you," she added gently, wanting to soften the youth's mutinous expression as well as her brother's silent fury.

"They'll never catch Annie; she's too fleet and cunning for them. It is just dumb gomerils like me who get battered and bashed," he spat challengingly, staring into Lochiel's dark eyes. Loch sighed and relaxed his hold, allowing the youth to slump back into his chair. "So the great Lord Falconhurst, the defiler of innocent young maidens, the braw abuser of our hospitality, wants to find my wee sister?" jeered Michael. His sneering expression caused Iona to gasp and look questioningly to her brother, who fought to keep his fury under tight rein so he wouldn't mark the youth's face even more. But Michael wasn't finished. "Why, Lochiel Montgomery? Why? Do you need to ravish her more? Och, it is a great pity that our Millie and the rest of the upstairs maids absconded wie the silver, for I'm sure they would have been honored to crawl between your sheets. . . ."

"Stop it!" Iona screamed hysterically, interrupting and silencing the youth, who had the grace to look embarrassed before covering with belligerence and reaching for the brandy bottle. "Loch, what is this all about?" she whispered huskily.

"Your brother used my sister like a common whore!"

"That is enough!" stated Lochiel, his voice low and dangerously controlled.

"Aye, it is more than enough, you mucker!" returned Michael, slurring and swaying. "So why don't you get out of my house and go back to where you belong! You don't belong here! Go and leave Kenlaren in peace!" he continued as he clutched at a lantern, nearly knocking it over before getting a firm hold. "Just get out of our lives, you hear?" Finally Michael staggered out of the door leading to the main wing of the house. Iona made a slight move, as though to detain him, but she dropped her hand defeatedly and stood, sadly watching the door pendulate back and forth in smaller and smaller swings until it was still.

"I'll tend to young Master Michael," soothed Wilkes as they heard the youth crashing into furniture and swearing violently.

"Aye, before he starts a fire," murmured Loch tersely.

"Was there truth in what he said, or was it just the brandy talking?" asked Iona, staring up at her brother's hard, merciless expression and trying not to be deterred. "Tell me?" she insisted.

"Take care of her, Roderick," ordered Lochiel curtly as he fastened his cape about his broad shoulders.

"Take me with you. Don't leave me here wie all this unbearable waiting," she pleaded, catching his arm as he strode to the door leading to the stable yard.

"You'll stay here wie Roderick." He covered her hand

with his for a moment before trying to remove it gently, but she hung on.

"No!" she shouted rebelliously, and his hard expression softened for a second as it brought to mind Annie's wild manner.

"Aye!" he returned firmly. "You'll stay here in case Annie comes back."

"Tell me, do you love her, Loch?" she asked simply, her eyes sparkling with unshed tears in the lantern light.

Loch stared down into the vulnerableness of his sister's upturned face, his own dark features showing none of the fear and turmoil that roiled within him. Desperately Iona searched his chiseled face for an answer to her question, but all she recognized there was an almost fanatical determination and a grim rage.

"Keep her safe, Roderick," Loch repeated, prying her clutching hand from his sleeve.

"But do you love her?" Iona insisted, pursuing him across the kitchen. He stalked out into the eerie night and the door slammed shut with a ringing finality, and Iona was left trying to control the flood of tears that threatened. She felt helpless and desolate and wished she were back aboard the gently rocking yacht, safely tucked in Robert's arms. She sniffed loudly and squared her shoulders as she became aware of Roderick's presence behind her. Slowly she turned around and gestured distractedly with her hands, unable to speak.

"He loves the wild lass," stated the old man. "Truly loves her and doesna ken how to handle it. He's so used to holding the reins and now he has an emotion that he has no control over." Roderick sighed as he slid two large bolts into place, locking the kitchen door.

"I'm not sure it is a prudent match, as they are as stubborn and uncompromising as each other," gurgled Iona, her laughter and tears mixing.

"It'll not be boring, I wager," chuckled Roderick gruffly.

"Oh, God keep them all safe," Iona prayed, reaching out to the old man and burying her face in his chest as she gave in to the aching tears. Roderick held her tightly with a proud, grandfatherly expression on his lined, weatherbeaten face. He had held her close since she was a tiny child and now, a full-grown beautiful woman, she still turned to him for comfort, and it gave credence to his existence.

"I was always jealous that Lochiel had you," confessed Iona as she pulled herself together and dabbed at her wet cheeks with her torn hankerchief. "I had a long line of boring nurses and governesses, while he had you from birth. When Robert and I have children, I shall raise them myself and choose for them a special friend like you. I'll not give them over to prune-faced servants." She chattered, and then stopped. "I'm sorry—I dinna mean . . . but I dinna think of you as a servant, Roderick."

"I'm proud to choose to serve," reassured Roderick, trying to put her at ease.

"Robert told me that Rebecca Gunn never touched her children. I cannot imagine that. I think I shall love my sons and daughters so much, kissing and cuddling them . . . a child needs that," whispered Iona wonderingly. "What was my mother like, Roderick?"

"Like you. Strong and spirited and yet gentle and compassionate. She would have been proud of you," replied the old man softly, remembering the vibrant woman who had died giving birth to Iona twenty-four years before.

Outside, Lochiel had saddled Michael's horse, preferring it to the ancient nag he had ridden earlier, and was about to set out for the village of Kenlaren, hoping he would arrive before the tavern closed for the night. He mounted and walked the horse around the house to the winding driveway lined with stately oak and elm.

"Hey, Montgomery?" bellowed Michael's drunk voice, and Loch reined and turned in the saddle toward the house. The youth was sprawled out of an upstairs window, gesturing with a bottle. "I'm up here, Montgomery. Do you see me?"

"Aye," returned Lochiel wearily after a long pause while he debated whether he should answer at all.

"She'll not return to Kenlaren until you are gone, you know! She does not want you! Do you hear me, dammit?" he screeched as Lochiel turned his back and cantered down the driveway. "Annie'll not return until you are gone!"

Michael's slurred but ringing tones echoed through the strangely still night and repeated in Lochiel's brain with the sharp jolts of the horse's hooves. Annie's warm, sparkling vibrancy was imprinted in his head, and there was a cold, clutching dread in his gut. Angrily he kicked the horse's muscular sides, pushing the animal into a punishing pace as he attributed the provocative words to drunkenness. He leaned forward in the saddle over the straining beast's arched neck as waves of impending danger rushed through him.

Lochiel squinted his eyes to better focus in the distorting, eerie moonlight as another horseman appeared at the end of the long, silvery ribbon of road. He pulled sharply on the reins, veering his mount onto the shadowy verge by the dense hedgerow.

Riding through the still countryside, Robert frowned when he caught a sudden movement ahead on the road. He shook his blond head, trying to dispel the ghostly tremors that shot through him, and he eased the bruising pace of his high-strung horse.

"By Jove, you're imagining things, old man," he chided himself. "Soon you'll be seeing hobgoblins and pixies prancing out of the delphiniums, waving magic wands and rattling bones."

"Forsythe?" hailed Loch, kneeing his mount out of the shadows upon recognizing the flaxen hair in the moonlight. Robert reined his steed so sharply the horse reared in alarm.

"You got me at a decided disadvantage, popping out of the bushes like that!" snapped Robert after getting his skittish animal under his control.

"I'm pleased to see you all of one piece," answered Loch, raising his thick dark eyebrows as he saw that Robert's usually immaculate raiment was now muddy and covered with sticks and grass. "What happened to you?"

"Unfortunately one can't ride calmly through the center of the village asking 'Which of you God fearing people has the rather barbarous notion of burning my young ward, Oriana Gunn, at the stake for witchcraft?' can one?" sighed

Robert mildly, regaining his well-bred, bored manner and casually flicking a burr off his sleeve. Loch suppressed an ironic laugh, as that was precisely what he had expected the effete English peer to do. Robert gave him a long, searching look and then an impudent grin, as though reading his brother-in-law's mind. The two men rode side by side toward Kenlaren Manor.

"I didn't find Annie," stated Loch bluntly.

"Didn't think you would, old boy. No one has ever been able to find her if she doesn't want to be found. I always thought it a devil of a nuisance, but right now it is dashed convenient."

"Meaning?" probed Loch shortly, irritated by Robert's careless manner.

"Meaning that those infernal witch hunters, led, incidentally by your boorish Cousin Ross, won't be able to locate her either. The question is, old chap, how do we insure her staying well-hidden, since we obviously can't find her to warn her?"

"I have been assured by Michael that all I have to do is remain at Kenlaren to insure Annie's absence," laughed Loch cynically.

"Like that, is it, old chum?" returned Robert shrewdly. "She cost me over twenty governesses with her confounded disappearing."

"Is there any danger of them marching on the manor?" asked Loch tersely, insulted by the obvious comparison of himself to the abhorred governesses.

"Not tonight, but give your dastardly cousin a day or so and I am confident he'll have stirred those ignorant people to such fanaticism that they'll be too crazed to feel fear," warned Robert, his face tensing and his tone sharpening.

"Ross obviously knows Iona's and my whereabouts and is using Annie and the villagers' ignorance to destroy us," brooded Loch.

"I wish it were as simple, but there appears to be more to it than that," mused Robert thoughtfully. "Vicar Nevins and his detestable simpering spouse seem to have as great if not greater investment in inciting the villagers to do violence. Now, I know my mother paid handsomely to have records of my sister's marriage struck from the church register, but that would not be reason enough," reasoned Robert aloud.

"Struck from the register?" echoed Loch, at a loss.

"Yes, so it would appear that Oriana and her brothers were born on the wrong side of the blanket," explained Robert.

"And your sister would thereby retain her honor?" questioned Loch wryly.

"Exactly," nodded Robert. "Dashed ridiculous, isn't it? Poor Mother is quite unrealistic. The silly old bird doesn't know that Rebecca's reputation has been in shreds for years."

"I should have thought the destruction of her marriage records so it appears that she birthed four bastards could not have done much to enhance it."

"You don't understand Mumsy, old chum. To her, poor, besmirched Rebecca is dead and buried and has been since the day she eloped with David Gunn, so therefore the old girl is unable to conceive or bear any offspring. Remind me to show you the stained glass window in Kenlaren Church that is dedicated to my sister's memory. Purgatory in gory detail. Fire and brimstone and all that," he chattered as they wheeled their horses through the wrought iron gates that guarded the driveway to Kenlaren Manor.

"Destroying church records for a price could be reason enough for the vicar and his wife to join with Ross," offered Loch.

"Who could prove it? Mumsy would never admit to paying for a window in a Protestant church, even if it does depict the fires of Hell. No, Vicar Nevins is safe on that score and he knows it. Besides, that pious old toad Nevins is well aware that I know what he did—he's known that for years—so he must have another reason for his sudden animosity," declared Robert.

"I am willing to wager that my kinsman Ross Montgomery is that other reason," mused Loch grimly, staring ahead at the hollow-eyed Elizabethan manor perched starkly on the rounded knoll. The moonlight reflected on the windows and the surrounding tall trees, causing forbidding shadows that snaked across the silvered lawns. There was a ghostly splendor about the old house, and Loch shivered, feeling a muted scream emanate from deep within the stones and timbers that seemed to warn of impending violence. "Is my cousin putting up at the local inn?" he asked harshly.

"Unfortunately, he's firmly ensconced in the vicarage with the Nevinses," related Robert glumly. The two men lapsed into a gloomy silence, which was broken only by the steady rhythm of their horses' hooves on the rasping gravel.

Annie dozed fitfully, unable to sleep for more than minutes at a time, as her dreams were filled with warning cries. She would start awake and sit straining in the darkness, trying to decipher the ghostly whispers that prophesied doom.

"You hear it too?" hissed Mrs. Wilson and Annie turned to her, frowning and trying to hold on to the elusive sounds that welded with the faint sibilance of her breathing and the soft rustle of her clothing. Annie shook her head and stared up at the beam of moonlight that pierced the thick darkness through a jagged gash in the cold gray granite of the cave.

"I cannot hear a thing. Not a thing. Not an owl or even the faintest whisper of a breeze," she said with a shiver. "'Tis unco," she added, accustomed to hearing the wind moan and whistle across the barren moor and amongst the stark rocks on even the mildest days.

"'Tis Lammas," chortled the old crone, rubbing her bony hands together with glee. "Lammas. Tomorrow night when the moon is at her fullest and the Lammas Sabbat is here, there's them shall pay. Already the de'il has shown his displeasure by destroying the harvest, but tomorrow he shall come. There will be a great shadow in the sky and the earth shall tremble as his cloven feet alight. Och, he'll not be displeased wie you, my wee witch-wife," soothed Mrs. Wilson, seeing the tremors that shook Annie's small frame.

"Lammas, Samain, Imbolc, and Beltane," intoned Annie as though reciting catechism.

"Imbolc, Beltane, Lammas, and Samain," corrected

the old woman gently with a satisfied smile on her wrinkled face.

"Imbolc is the start of the new year, when the lambing begins," remembered Annie as the names of the four main sabbats spiraled into her mind. "I was born on Beltane Eve."

"Beltane for fertility," stated Mrs. Wilson with pride.

"As the trees swell their buds," mouthed Annie. "Lammas for the harvest as the corn turns golden in the sun."

"And Samain?"

"And Samain for death . . . of the year," stated the girl, feeling a chill seep through her.

"Tomorrow is Lammas," rejoiced the crone.

"It doesn't feel like it. It feels like Samain—cold and gray like November."

"It has been a long time, my dawtie," crooned Mrs. Wilson, stroking Annie's riotous mane of hair. "And they thought to take you from me wie their prune-faced, dried-up virgins and fancy manners."

"Did I kill my father?" Annie asked suddenly, and she felt the old woman shudder with shock, her long fingernails catching in the red-gold hair and pulling painfully.

"Now what sort of question is that?" she clucked.

"You said I had killed."

"I'm an old slummock; I say a lot of things," evaded Mrs. Wilson, shimmying away from Annie toward a dark, shadowy corner. "I rattle on and on. Age does that, you know."

"You said I killed," pursued Annie.

"And so you have, and you'll also be the death of me if you dinna stop your scraiching. I'm old and need my rest for the Lammas Sabbat tomorrow."

"Who did I kill?"

"What does it matter? 'Twas long ago and far away and that is that wie no more to be said. It canna be undone wie the knowing," snapped Mrs. Wilson testily, making herself comfortable in the corner. Annie stared thoughtfully at the rounded, hunched shape of the old woman before standing and stretching.

"What are you up to now?" complained the crone fretfully as the shaft of moonlight was blocked by the girl, who stared over the still moorland.

"I need to ride."

"You promised you wouldna leave me," screeched the woman hysterically, scrambling on her hands and knees toward the girl.

"I chose you, remember?" soothed Annie, appalled by the hideous abasement of the woman, who was now whining and groveling. "I just need to ride Dudh awhile and clear my head."

"Promise me you'll not try to see him," whimpered the woman, clutching at Annie's legs.

"I promise," whispered Annie as Loch's dark features flashed into her mind, causing an ache to yawn within her.

"You canna trust him. He'll use you . . . he wouldna think of taking the daughter of the de'il and a whore as a bride . . . let alone a murderess to gie birth and suckle to his heirs," she wheedled. "Och, I should've had my wits aboot me and protected you from the mucker. I should have dosed him wie my cramping potions and wilted him wie my knotting spells so he couldna take what wasna his and hurt you," she snuffled, rubbing her slobbering face on Annie's britches. Her wiry arms imprisoned Annie's thighs, making any movement impossible unless she was willing to harm the kneeling woman.

Annie looked away from the tangled, stringy hair that burrowed into her hip, and she gazed across the stark moorland. The moon seemed embedded in dark flatness, the sky having no dimension, no stars, and the lunar craters taking on the leering features of some demonic being.

"Annie, my wee witch-wife, dinna leave me," pleaded the hag, straining her scrawny neck, trying to see the girl's face.

"I'll nae leave you," soothed Annie, slowly sliding down the cold stone wall until she sat on the floor of the cave and held the shaking, blubbering old woman in her arms. "I'll nae leave you," she repeated. She decided to wait until Mrs. Wilson slept before stealing away to seek Dubh's strong comfort.

"You ken I love you, my wee-an?" hiccoughed the distraught beldam. "I know what is guid for you and I'll nae let any harm you more. You're mine. Couldna be more so if I had birthed you from my ain womb. I taught you, and nursed you, and loved you . . . and you are for him. For the Great Horned One. For the de'il himself, and tomorrow at the Lammas Sabbat he'll claim you for his own," she rambled, her voice eventually becoming unintelligible and punctuated with snores.

Annie sat, not daring to move for fear of waking the tense old crone, whose weight leaned heavily. Every so often Mrs. Wilson thrashed about, twitching and snorting, until she finally slumped into an untidy heap on the floor. Carefully Annie eased herself away and covered the old woman tenderly with her cape. She stood staring down at the woman who had always been there to comfort, before turning her gaze over the moonlit moor. Satisfied that the coast was clear, she agilely climbed onto a high ledge and squeezed through a narrow crack in the rock. She edged along a thin sill, blindly feeling her way as below her fell the sheer, precipitous face of the largest of the Devil's Stepping Stones.

Loch, too, was unable to sleep. He had nodded a cynical good night to Robert and Iona and, loath to lie alone in a wide bed knowing how his sister and her groom were probably occupied, had elected to remain in the large kitchen. He had firmly dismissed Roderick so he could be alone with his tangled thoughts. Now he leaned back in the comfortable chair beside the glowing hearth with his long legs stretched out, staring blindly at the muddy tips of his riding boots as he thought of the golden elfin figure of Annie perched atop the giant black stallion.

"Och, Rob Roy," he sighed, the thought of her causing his pulses to race and an unbearable ache to gather and spread to each part of him until it was impossible to remain sitting. Quietly he let himself out into the still night and strode through the moonlit orchard, which was redolent with the smell of apples. He walked without any thought to what direction he was taking and finally stopped short, surprised to find he had reached the hidden meadow where Annie kept her prize horses. Sensing another presence, Loch kept to the shadows of the trees that encompassed the suspended glen, his eyes moving from side to side, watching for the slightest movement. He was rewarded by the sight of a fleet shape that flittered through a shaft of moonlight and then melted into the darkness. A familiar low whistle and an answering whinny caused Loch to grin broadly and shake his own ebony head as the stallion Dubh disengaged himself from the dark mass of the herd and galloped across the silvery grass. The most obvious place to look, he realized. He had stupidly assumed that the girl and the horse were hidden in some network of catacombs beneath the hulking pile of rocks called the Devil's Stepping Stones. He had also assumed that the stallion was somehow magically enchanted, able to keep absolutely quiet on command so as not to divulge his young mistress's hiding place. All the ridiculous talk of witchcraft and Satanism was affecting him adversely, he decided as he watched Annie lithely mount the powerful animal and lie along his high back to clasp the proudly arched neck with slim arms.

Lochiel's broad grin faded as he heard the unmistakable sounds of grief. She was crying. His brave, mutinous, indomitable, rebellious Rob Roy was sobbing as though her heart were breaking. His own pain welled and he wanted to take her in his arms and comfort her, but he surmised if he showed himself she would dig in her heels and vanish into the eerie half-light of the near dawn.

The moon was sinking, the sky imperceptibly lightening to a lugubrious gray and the dawn chorus strangely muted as though mourning a death instead of celebrating the new day, when at last Annie sniffed and pulled herself into a sitting position on Dubh's glossy back. She swallowed a scream as her bare foot was firmly grasped in a strong, warm hand, and she stared down at the stern dark face of Lochiel Montgomery, who had moved quickly and quietly under the noise of her anguished sobs. Annie's chest still heaved with the shuddering echoes of her violent emotions but she tried to clear her blurred vision and remove the signs of weakness from her cheeks, unable to meet the dark eyes that made her feel like bursting into another torrent of tears like some despicable, vaporous female.

Loch felt a very uncharacteristic wrenching in his

chest as he recognized each of the raw emotions that crossed Annie's tear-stained face. He smiled ruefully when her tawny eyes hardened and sparked and her soft vulnerability was fired into bitter defiance as she kicked out wildly, determined to free herself from his strong grasp.

"Nay, Rob Roy, you'll not escape me again," he promised firmly as he pulled her from the high back of the stallion and into his arms. Annie's breathing was restricted by the iron grasp and his close proximity as she was held tightly to his broad chest. She felt the steady beat of his heart join with her own frantic pounding. For only a little while she would give in to the safe seduction of his arms, she told herself, knowing she was exhausted and no match for his superior strength. When she was fresh and well-rested, she would easily escape from him, she decided, sensing his surprise at her sudden docility as he strode quickly toward the manor. She kept her eyes tightly closed as the rhythm of his long paces jolted through her joining with the medley of warring emotions that jarred her aching head. A great part of her just wanted to relax into his warm masculinity and sleep so that nothing else existed but being with him. No past, no future, just now. No past, no future, just now, the refrain beat in her brain with the even tempo of his steady tread. As his boot soles left the muffling earth and rang sharply on the hard cobblestones of the stable yard, she tensed in his arms and started to fight, remembering her solemn promise to Mrs. Wilson, but Lochiel easily contained her as he approached the kitchen door.

"I thought I told you to go to bed," he snapped harshly when Roderick opened the door and stood beaming affectionately as though his young master held a meekly curled kitten instead of the spitting, raging wildcat.

"Let me go!" hissed Annie, feeling at a decided disadvantage in the presence of both tall men and trying to recover some dignity despite her demeaning position cradled in Lochiel Montgomery's arms.

"Will you need me for anything else?" asked Roderick formally with a twinkle in his eyes.

"Don't leave me wie him!" begged Annie, hoping she could wheedle around the old man. "I don't know what he wants wie me," she pleaded.

"Just your safety, lass," reassured Roderick, smiling his approval into the gleaming, ebony eyes of the young man. Annie wanted to turn her head and look into Lochiel's face, but she was afraid of what she would see. If his expression was hard and censoring, it would cut her to the quick, and if it was softly tender, it would destroy her even more thoroughly. "Look to your mon, lass," coaxed the old timer.

"Roderick MacDonald, I'm quite able to do my own courting," chided Loch. The old man chortled with glee as he saw Annie's eyes widen in shock.

"Then I shall leave you both and find my bed," chuckled Roderick.

"No," protested Annie, still unable to look up at the dark man who held her so possessively and whose claiming words echoed so painfully. "Don't leave me with him!" she shouted, but the door swung closed, leaving her alone with Lochiel, who set her gently on her feet.

"What are you afraid of, Rob Roy? Surely not of me," he murmured, and Annie shivered as his deep voice caused an aching void to tremble within her.

"Nay, I'm not afraid of you," she lied, throwing her head back and staring up at him with every ounce of bravado that she could muster. She had hoped to see his hard, chiseled face sneering down at her, but to her great consternation his harsh features were softened by the tenderest of looks. She felt as though the ground were shifting. She stepped backward and leaned against the table as her pulses roared and she found breathing difficult. "I have to go back. I promised," she said stiffly, wanting to believe the naked love that exuded from his dark, magnetic eyes but forcing herself to remember his hurtful words from another time when he had called her a whore. She had to protect herself, she determined.

"Whom did you promise?" he asked gently.

"I must go."

"Mrs. Wilson?" he probed.

"Nay, I promised my lover!" she spat challengingly, arming herself with the memory of his insulting proposal. He'd marry her because of an obligation to his sister, not for love. But what else could she expect, she thought wearily, allowing a bitter smile to touch her mutinous mouth. Like her mother, she was a whore.

"Your lover?" replied Loch mildly, looking as benignedly amused as her Uncle Robert.

"Aye, my lover!" she repeated savagely, furious at his apparent disbelief. "Leonard, demon of the first order!" She felt a spiteful glow of satisfaction at the black fury that blazed across Lochiel's face and she tried to remember other tidbits that Mrs. Wilson had rambled about during the years. "Och, you ken Leonard? Master of the sabbats? He has three horns and the ears of the fox . . . and his great tool puts yours to shame!" she declared with relish. To her utter surprise Lochiel lost his angry look and threw back his head, roaring with laughter.

"Dinna forget to light your green candles and bare your wee bottom," he advised teasingly, laughter warming his deep voice as he smiled down into her dumbfounded face.

Annie couldn't think of a cutting retort, so she clamped her lips tightly together and gave him what she hoped was a withering look, but it only served to increase his amusement. Despite her fatigue her blood boiled with fury, and she longed to scream and yell but knew it would just weaken her position. She folded her arms resolutely across her chest and stood silently, waiting for his laughter to cease. Lochiel's brimming eyes caressed her small, valiant body, marking the weariness that sagged her warlike stance.

"Och, Rob Roy, we both need our sleep," he said, reaching out and tenderly running his fingertips down her smooth cheek, which still bore the stains of her grief. Annie held herself stiffly in check, wanting to jerk away and yet longing to surrender to his soft touch. Loch put a finger under her chin and firmly lifted her heart-shaped face. He stared silently into the haunted amber eyes, recognizing the mute appeal for compassion before lowering his dark head and covering her tremulous mouth with his own. He had meant only to touch his lips softly to hers in comfort, but feeling the warm quivering, he groaned and masterfully enfolded her in his strong arms and crushed her to him.

Annie drowned in the wild possessiveness of his embrace. She reached up and wrapped her arms about his neck, glorying in the nonthinking passion that exploded as Lochiel carried her from the kitchen and up the servants' stairs to the maid's room where she had slept as a child before Sir Robert had tried to mold her into a fine lady. Gently Loch disentangled her lean arms from his neck and firmly placed her on the narrow cot as he fought to rein his surging desire. Annie whimpered and strained toward him, trying to reconnect to his heat, her eyes still tightly shut and her mouth slightly parted.

"It is not the time to make love, Rob Roy," he murmured hoarsely, although the whole of him was fired to do just that. Annie's eyes flew open and she stared up at him, bewilderment and pain flooding her face before she masked her vulnerability with disdainful rage at his rejection. Loch reached out to comfort but she leaped away from him, putting the narrow bed between them as she looked about the nightmarishly familiar room, her nostrils flaring and her eyes flashing.

"The great Lord Falconhurst does not rut wie sluts, just puts them in their rightful place!" she sneered.

"Rightful place?" questioned Loch, his thick brows nearly meeting as he frowned, remembering the cruel words he had been guilty of using. He watched her quizzically when she refused to answer, noting how her movements were tense and jerky, as though she recoiled from all her darting eyes encountered. "What is this room?" he asked. He had carried her into the small chamber not by design but because it was nearby and more convenient than the rooms down the long, dark corridors and up the winding staircase of the main wing.

"For shame, Lord Falconhurst, you mean to infer you dinna ken a mere servant's bedchamber? A scullery maid's garret? I would have thought from the very obvious contempt you have for my Uncle Robert's indulgent way of life, you would be most familiar wie even the lowliest members of a household . . . especially their bedrooms!" she spat insultingly.

"There is nothing I would like more than to lie wie you and lay claim to each and every inch of your perfect and infinitely desirable body," stated Loch almost casually, although his black eyes burned with an intensity that belied his measured tone.

"Hypocrite!" hissed Annie. Her limbs turned to liquid and she had to brace herself against the wall.

"Sit down," he ordered softly, disturbed by her pallor. He chose for himself a straightbacked chair as far away from her as possible in the small room. Annie edged toward the austere washstand, for even the sight of the bed caused her cheeks to burn with humiliation as she remembered her wantonness. "It is imperative that we talk," Loch said unemotionally.

"There is nothing I would like more than to sit and chat with you, but I have other, more pressing engagements," returned Annie primly, her voice dripping with sarcasm. "So if you'll excuse me?" she said, indicating his long legs that barred the door and waiting for him to remove them.

"There's a crowd of angry, frightened villagers who want to hurt you."

"There has always been a crowd of angry villagers wanting to hurt me," replied Annie coldly. "I didn't need you to inform me of that."

"What do you mean that there has always been?" he probed.

"Just that," she retorted. "Now, if you'll excuse me?" she said pointedly. Loch reached out and grasped her thin wrist, roughly turning her to face him.

"Rob Roy, they are armed. They have already hurt Michael." Annie froze, stilling her frantic movements to escape.

"They've hurt Michael?" she whispered.

"Just a few scrapes and bruises," reassured Loch feeling guilty at her panic.

"What's a few bruises? So what else is news? They throw a few stones, sometimes manure, and that's the end of it," she sneered, resuming her struggles to get free.

"This time they mean business."

"They always mean business. Whenever the crops fail or the fishing nets are empty, they rant and rave and carry on. Mrs. Wilson'll just chant a few incantations and brew a pungent potion and they'll run away like frightened sheep."

"This time there's talk of burning, and my Cousin Ross Montgomery is leading them," stated Loch harshly, determined to make her realize the danger that threatened.

"Burning?" repeated Annie dazedly.

"Aye, at the stake," he added brutally, and Annie shook her bright head at him in disgust.

"Dinna talk such stite. There's been no burning of witches since the seventeen hundreds!" Then she laughed as she remembered Ross Montgomery sprawled gracelessly in the road with his trews about his ankles. "So, your fat cousin is so angry because I robbed him of your money that by some strange happenstance he found me?" she added derisively. "Och, dinna gie me that, Lochiel Montgomery, I wasna born yesterday!"

"Ross Montgomery found you very easily through Iona. He is a very dangerous and desperate man and it seems he has found an ally in a certain man of the cloth named Nevins, who has an investment in having you and Mrs. Wilson burned at the stake for witchcraft!" Loch punctuated his sharp words with a few firm shakes. By Annie's stunned expression he knew he had finally broken through her mocking disbelief. "Now, why would this Vicar Nevins want to see you harmed?" he asked, tempering his tone, but Annie slowly shook her head, her amber eyes wide and terror-filled as the minister's face zoomed in and out of her mind, filling her with a nameless dread, and the pungent smell of roses teased her senses.

"I maun go back to Mrs. Wilson," whispered Annie.

"I'll go with you," stated Loch firmly, but the girl shook her head vehemently. "Then you'll not go."

"I promised," Annie cried, her eyes filling with tears as she thought of the poor frightened old woman who had groveled and crawled on her hands and knees. "I promised."

"You'll go nowhere without me."

"You don't understand."

"Then help me to," returned Loch, quietly pulling her on to his lap.

"It has nothing to do with you. I had to choose, do you

ken? I had to choose!" sobbed Annie, exhaustion and fear making her usually husky voice strident. Again she tried to free herself. "I didn't choose you! Let me go! I didn't choose you!" she screamed.

"Whom did you choose?" crooned Loch, cradling her and rocking as her voice rose with hysteria.

"Not you! She's alone! So alone! And she's frightened! You dinna ken how frightened and alone she is, even though she's suppose to be a witch. She isn't really . . . she's just a puir old woman who's so scared and I promised to be with her. She's my friend . . . my mother . . . and she's always loved me and nursed me and taken care of me . . . and I am all she has. So let me go!"

"Then we'll go together and take care of her," soothed Loch.

"She'll wake up alone and think I lied to her, so let me go!" screamed Annie, not hearing his words as she struggled against the strong arms that held her so easily.

"*No!*" roared Loch, shocking her to silence, so she lay stiffly across his muscular thighs. "Now, hush yourself and listen so we can go and take care of Mrs. Wilson. Here," he said, sitting her up and handing her a handkerchief. Annie sniffed and accepted the proffered cloth, trying desperately to control the terror and dread that filled her. She stood up, unable to find her pride, sitting like a child on the tall man's lap.

Loch silently watched the wild-haired girl as she walked away from him and stared out of the window at the dismal gray dawn. She straightened her shoulders and breathed deeply before turning to face him. He was filled with an aching tenderness as he saw her resolute little face still furrowed with salty tracks. She swallowed hard, unable to say a word as she met his gaze, and when he opened his mouth to speak, she raised her small hand mutely as though pleading for a few more moments of silence.

Annie tried to still her racing heart as she looked at the brooding features of Lochiel Montgomery. She wanted to be with him more than anything she had ever wanted in the world, even more than possessing her stallion Dubh, but she knew it wasn't destined to be. There was too much shame and too many shadows in her past for her to be the wife of a Scottish peer. She looked about the small, bare room that had been her haven from birth until Sir Robert Forsythe had instilled false dreams of grandeur, and she gave a long shuddering sigh and a little shrug. She looked back at the handsome man, as though committing each line of his aristocratic features to her memory. Behind her she heard the steady pitting of rain against the windowpanes.

"Tonight is the Lammas Sabbat," she stated slowly, holding up her hand again so he would not interrupt her. "Tonight at the full harvest moon the villagers will know where to find Mrs. Wilson, just as they do on each of the four great sabbats. Mrs. Wilson will . . . be waiting . . . for the . . . for . . ." Her voice trailed off; she could not say the words.

"For the devil? For Satan? For Black Leonard?" offered Lochiel harshly, his hatred for the manipulating old woman surfacing despite his vow for tolerance.

"No! She'll be waiting . . . for the lover who never comes," she said simply, making no move to hide or wipe away the tears that now streamed as she truly understood both Mrs. Wilson's and her own mother's hollow pain for the first time.

"The lover who never comes," repeated Loch with wonder as Annie fell silent, lost in thoughts of her mother's nightly vigils for her phantom lovers.

"I must warn Mrs. Wilson. Somehow get her away from there so the villagers don't hurt her," intoned Annie, a feeling of hopelessness tingeing her words as she realized that it would be nigh impossible to change the old crone's sabbat rituals.

"Is there a coven?" probed Loch, thinking of the usual thirteen people who congregated at purported black masses. Annie snorted with wry mirth and shook her head. "Any other . . . witches?" he asked.

"Aye, me," she sighed, and covered up her sudden feeling of sadness with a mischievous grin. "So I had best be off on my broomstick and hope the puir auld hag hasna awakened to this dreary Lammas," she joked.

"You are not going alone!"

"Then I'll go wie Dubh!" she returned feistily.

"You'll go wie me!"

"I canna," whispered Annie with a little smile. "I promised."

"Then you'll not go!"

"She hates you."

"I know, and the feeling is mutual!" he replied matter-of-factly. "She's jealous!" he added roguishly, grinning at her confusion.

"Jealous?"

"Aye, there she waits for the lover who never comes, but your lover has arrived," he murmured. Annie stood still, trying to control the aching feelings that welled at the seductive sound of his resonant voice. "You are mine, Rob Roy, and she knows it!" Annie thrilled to his possessive words and at the same time an enormous sadness welled within her as she accepted the hopelessness of her love.

"I have to go to her," she hissed, wrenching her gaze from his face and reaching for the door handle. Loch stood and followed her out and they walked in silence down the stairs, through the kitchen and out into the dismal drizzling day, their feet squelching in the sodden earth.

Not a word passed between them as they tramped through the apple orchard heedless of the rain that streamed down their heads, saturating their clothing. At the bottom of the long, steep lane to the moor, Annie gave a piercing whistle, summoning Dubh from his high pasture. Loch tensed and stared thoughtfully at her, wondering if she planned to gallop away from him on the back of the dark stallion. They kept walking up the rutted muddy path until, over the constant drumming of the rain, they heard and felt the reverberation of hooves. Dubh appeared before them, tossing his head and prancing in welcome.

Loch caught hold of Annie and threw her up on the stallion's back before mounting behind her and clasping her slim waist possessively with one strong arm, giving her no chance to escape him.

Annie was very conscious of Loch's hard, lean thighs pressing each side of her buttocks. She lifted her flushed face up to the cooling rain and felt his broad chest at her back as the horse broke free of the narrow lane and streaked across the wild, fenceless moorland. She sighed deeply as the wind roared in her ears, and for a few fleeting moments she forgot all heartbreak and thrilled to the exhilaration of the ride. There was something so natural and perfect about the two of them mounted upon Dubh's high back, something she had dreamed about many times through the years. She laughed aloud feeling a great bond, an exciting unity with the dark man and the dark horse. It was as though all three of them flowed together, three free spirits soaring in the sunshine above the brooding shadows, Annie mused, before suddenly reining her imagination as the Devil's Stepping Stones loomed starkly out of the dismal cloud cover and dampened her brief moment of joy.

Mrs. Wilson stared out at the giant black stallion carrying the two very different riders. Like sun and shade, she noted as Annie's gold-streaked hair flowed and wound about the dark young man. She tried to smother the scream that rose painfully from the core of her as she bitterly acknowledged the complimenting perfection of the young couple and knew she had finally lost Annie. She had awakened at the first imperceptible lightening of the mournful sky, her old eyes trying to pierce the thick shadows, and she had crawled about the small cave, sweeping her gnarled hands in front of her as she whimpered Annie's name. Finding herself alone, she had huddled like a pathetic bundle of rags in the corner, rocking and whining, as nightmarish terrors clawed into her.

"How did I get so old?" she had sobbed. "Where did all the time go?" She tried to knead away the panic that yawned in her belly. "Och, ye auld beldame, where is your pride?" she had screamed, pinching her sagging flesh cruelly and staggering to her feet to stand straight and true with her back braced against the cold, sweating granite. "It is Lammas and the wee witch-wife is just riding her great beastie across the heather to clear the cobwebs from her head," she muttered to herself reassuringly as she slowly walked to the jagged crack that rent the cave wall. She frowned and sucked in the air through her loose lips when she saw a long line of people silhouetted against the dreary curve where the bleak moor blended with the morose sky. Rubbing her eyes, she peered out again and saw flaming torches that broke the gray monotony with sporadic bursts of orange.

Mrs. Wilson had summoned her long departed youth into her stiff old bones and muscles, and clawed herself up to the narrow ledge to squeeze through the crack in the rock.

"Och, there's life in this auld goat yet," she cackled as she edged along the sheer cliff face, keeping her eyes pinned to the approaching line of people and away from the precipice below. Higher and higher she climbed until she reached a flat plane, where she crouched on her skinny haunches and caught her breath.

Now she roosted like a large black buzzard, her ragged cape fluttering about her as the rain drizzled and dripped off her stringy hair, and she watched her beloved child, Annie, with Lochiel Montgomery.

"Get awa' wie you, Oriana Rebecca Gunn! Go awa' wie your dark stranger and leave me in peace! I dinna choose you!" she screeched as the lithe golden girl leaped off the stallion and raced toward the rock face, her eyes pinned to her foster mother perched high above her. "Get awa' wie you! I dinna want you, you ken!"

Loch shaded his eyes from the rain and stared up at the old crone silhouetted against the gray sky, gesticulating wildly as the nimble girl shinnied up the steep granite.

"Awa' wie you!" screamed the old woman, prancing about excitedly and stabbing a bony finger toward the village where a long line of smoky torches slowly wended their way through the misty rain.

Annie stared from Mrs. Wilson to the approaching villagers.

"Come with us quickly. Dubh can carry us all," she begged, continuing her perilous climb up the sheer cliff face toward the old crone.

"Awa' wie you! I dinna choose you!" screeched the old woman, afraid for Annie's safety. She scrambled away from the nimble girl. "Lochiel Montgomery, take your lass and run!" she shrieked as the dark young man climbed fleetly despite his cumbersome riding boots.

"Come with us," implored Annie offering her hands.

"I dinna need you! I hae my fat cuddy in the cave below and that auld ass is all I need! I dinna choose you, so you maun go wie him!" spat the hag, backing away from Annie and Loch so that she roosted on the very edge of the topmost peak. "If either of you come any closer I shall leap off this satanic rock to fly straight to the moon, or I shall drop like a stone to splatter my messy mortal remains over these oversized gravestones!" she threatened, teetering on the highest point of the tallest slab.

"The villagers are coming to hurt you," yelled Annie, trying to make the old woman aware of the danger.

"Aye, I've been watching them since daybreak, tippytoeing along the horizon like cowardly snails. Too afraid of their own shadows to come at night. Too pathetic to come alone to harm a wee child and a doddering auld crone," she stated bitterly as the long line steadily approached and ringed the looming gray granite blocks.

"Come wie us now. We can escape on Dubh!" begged Annie, pulling at the woman's ragged sleeve.

"And run wie my tail between my legs like a cowardly one of them?" shouted Mrs. Wilson, shaking off Annie's hand and pushing her away. "Never! Now be off wie you!" she hissed as the line of people moved closer, tightening the circle. "Och, will you look at all those wretched gomerils and slummocks! Weak, pathetic cowards here to bully a puir, wee, motherless bairn and a crippled auld beldame," she taunted, her strident voice cracking the tense stillness as the fearful villagers silently ringed the rocks, holding up their torches and rude crucifixes. "How do you expect to burn a witch when you canna even keep your torches lit?" she chortled as the fine rain dampened the firebrands and thick black smoke spiraled upward. "Well, now, who do we have here?" she pondered loudly. "Well, good morning, Aggie MacLaine! How are you, Minerva Barrett? Hester? Lily? Are you all here to hae a last look at the auld witch who pulled you into this life when your parents couldna afford Doctor Murdock Murdock's murderous fees? Och, Duncan Muir, are you here to pay me for the abortifacient powders that I brewed for your puir wife when you knew the fifteenth child would mean her death and the starvation of your other bairns?"

Loch held Annie close as the old woman scanned the faces below and called out, reminding them of various medicines and midwife duties she had supplied. Sensing a furtive movement to his right, Lochiel glanced to a group of horsemen who had silently approached from the direction of Kenlaren Manor. Robert caught his eye and gave an almost imperceptible nod, indicating Wilkes, Roderick, and Iona.

"Och, I count at least thirty of you I birthed . . . pulled squawling from your mother's wombs!" proclaimed Mrs. Wilson. "Who are you going to use as midwife, chemist, and doctor when you've done awa' wie me?" she challenged, prancing about on her sticklike legs, delighting in her captive audience. "Now, where's that little toad of a vicar? Where's the rutting wee runt? Och, is he too timorous to venture out in the rain to burn a witch? Is he so cowardly that he sent you puir ignorant muckers to do his dirty work?" she derided him. "Well, it would be a terrible shame if you all had come out here on this drear day for nothing, so I'll make sure your precious time isna wasted. Next time you're all in the kirk and the wee toad is making you squirm in the pews wie all the guilty thoughts Godfearing people shouldna have . . . ask that pious worm Nevins what he was doing wie his pitiful rod between the legs of puir demented Rebecca Gunn the night Sir David disappeared!" There was a deathly hush as her raucous voice screeched triumphantly to a halt and the circle of villagers backed away. A sharp retort split the still air. As it reverberated between the cold gray stones, Mrs. Wilson slowly sagged to her knees, clutching her chest.

Loch roughly pushed Annie aside, protecting her with his body as he scanned the direction the shot had come from, but nothing moved. The villagers stood stunned, not comprehending what had happened as the old woman knelt atop the huge stone crag. Annie walked slowly toward her foster mother, certain she was mortally wounded.

"Help me up, me dawtie," ordered the crone, grasping Annie's arm painfully and hauling herself to her feet. She leaned heavily, her bony fingers pinching in an effort to stand firm and proudly face the country people who now mumbled angrily amongst themselves. "I'll nae die on my knees; they'll think me a Christian!" she hissed with a wicked giggle. "Stop your crying, lassie. Be happy for me dying on Lammas at the height of the year's golden glory—except to look at this miserable weather one wouldna ken it," she whispered as Loch stood the other side of her. "Dinna let me down, my braw laddie," she begged, coquettishly grasping his arm as her legs buckled and waves of faintness threatened to topple her. "I maun stand straight and tall and send them puir bastards aboot their business. And I canna die until I've set things straight," she confessed, beads of perspiration mingling with the rain on her face.

Annie and Lochiel stood on each side of the old woman as the villagers dropped their torches in the sopping heather and mutely made their way back to the village, their shoulders bent and defeated, their spirits bowed and gray like the morose clouds that hung low, nearly touching the bleak moorland. As the last smocked man disappeared over the rounded horizon, Mrs. Wilson sagged heavily and Loch caught her and swung her into his strong arms. He stared down at her lined old face, and wearily she winked up at him.

"Aye, feels good to be held by a braw, virile mon," she muttered before losing consciousness.

"She's not dead, is she?" gasped Annie as Loch carefully inched his way to the edge of the precipitous rock and handed the limp body to Robert, who was reaching up from below.

"Nay," returned Loch shortly. The two young men worked in concert to lower the suffering old woman to ground level. "She canna die until I have had a few answers," Loch said under his breath, and his thoughts were echoed by Robert, whose eyes met his grimly.

It was a gloomy procession that returned to Kenlaren Manor. Lochiel drove the donkey cart, where Mrs. Wilson lay with her grisled head cradled in Annie's small lap, followed by the riderless Dubh and the bent figures of Iona, Robert, Wilkes, and Roderick as they rode against the rain that increased, beating its fury against the earth so the mud splattered, coating and shrouding any summer color.

Michael watched dispassionately from the library window. He made no movement to help, and when Mrs. Wilson's small, limp body was lifted, he turned away from the sight and wrenched the draperies together blocking them all out.

Chapter 18

Mrs. Wilson, dressed in one of Iona's ruffled white nighties, looked like a tiny, shriveled child in the large four-poster. The only movement was her wildly shifting eyes and the gnarled hands that frantically opened and closed as she tried to push away the plump eiderdown that cocooned her.

"You mean to smother me wie all this fussy frippery," she whispered hoarsely, her voice weak but still feisty. "Where's my wee-an?"

"I'm here," reassured Annie, softly stroking the old worrying fingers that plucked at the bed covers. "Be still and save your strength. Uncle Robert and Roderick have gone to fetch Dr. Murdock."

"Och, I'll nae let that randy auld quack Murdock Murdock touch my wee body! He's been after it for years!" she hissed, trying to focus her eyes but there seemed to be a murky haze covering everything. When she tried to shake her head to clear her vision she found she couldn't move. "Hae you tied me down?" she cried. "I canna move anything save my eyeballs and fingers. Light a taper! Draw back the drapes!" she ordered piteously.

"Be still," sobbed Annie. "Be still, you silly auld witch."

"Who else is here spying on me?" spat the crone, fear coloring her words despite her brave attempt at cantankerousness as the thick haze darkened, shrouding everything so she couldn't even distinguish between light and shadow. "I feel eyes," she whimpered, helpless and vulnerable. Loch and Iona stepped nearer to the bed and gazed down at the old woman. Loch frowned and waved a hand directly in front of Mrs. Wilson's face, but the terrified eyes stared ahead fixedly.

"Can you see?" he asked gently, noticing that the gnarled hand clutched Annie's so tightly the knuckles were whitened.

"I dinna need sight. I'm to the end of the road," sighed the crone, trying to calm herself. "There's only one place that'll take the likes of me. . . ." And her voice trailed away as she fought the waves of panic. "Och, I dinna know why I am so afeared of dying except I have been a naughty auld lass . . . holding on to what wasna mine. Och, I never meant to hurt you, my dawtie. I never meant to cause you pain, my darling wee-an," she sobbed, blindly feeling for Annie's face but unable to raise her arm high enough. She clutched at the girl's clothes, pulling her down so she lay on the pillow beside her.

"You dinna hurt me," sniffed Annie, struggling to control her grief as the old hand touched her wet cheeks.

"Och, dinna cry, my wee-an," crooned the old woman, tears spurting from her sightless eyes. "I hae not much time to set things to right. I maun set everything to right."

"Aye," agreed Lochiel fervently, afraid the cantankerous old crone would expire before revealing all she knew. "You stated that Vicar Nevins was . . . closeted with Rebecca Gunn?" he probed, choosing his words carefully.

"Closeted?" whooped the old woman loudly. "Closeted?" she repeated, and Iona opened her mouth to protest her brother's lack of delicacy but realized that the crone was choking with laughter, not indignation. "Closeted?" gurgled the delighted old hag. "Och, that's a rare way of putting it! Och, you hae a droll turn of phrase, Lochiel Montgomery. Maybe there is some hope for you after all," she wheezed before a violent paroxysm of coughing seized her.

Loch continued after the coughing fit had abated and the woman lay exhausted, sunken in the overstuffed pillows, Iona gently bathing her wrinkled face with cool water. "On the night David Gunn died, was . . ."

"*Sir* David Gunn! My wee-an is as well-born as you, *Lord* Falconhurst!" she interrupted vehemently, miraculously regaining her fighting spirit.

"*Mrs.* Wilson, I couldna care who spawned Oriana—" retorted Loch impatiently.

"I am the daughter of a whore, spawned by the very devil himself!" intruded Annie.

"Hush up, wie your rude names," reproached the old lady crossly, feeling Annie's face and tweaking her tiny nose.

"He might as well hear it from me," said Annie cynically, laughing in an attempt to dispel her fear for Mrs. Wilson's condition as she saw blood seeping through the bandages and sopping the front of the borrowed nightdress.

"Sir David Gunn was your sire, not the de'il—that was just my fancy talking, trying to put the fear of the supernatural in those spiteful muckers who teased you when you were such a wee, puir, motherless bairn," struggled the old woman. "Do you ken?"

"Aye, I ken, but that doesna change the fact of my mother being a whore," replied Annie.

"Nay, she wasna a whore!" cried the old crone distressfully. "She was a puir . . . hurting female, her pretty head all addled and twisted wie shame and guilty feelings. She was taught to suffer, and so when she felt pleasure she felt dirty and soiled. Puir, puir Rebecca, shamed by her own beautiful body and natural desires. Puir, puir lass all bound up and strangled by that Christian stite. Och, my wee-an, she was no more a whore than you, my pretty," she concluded, stroking the wild mane of hair.

"Hah!" snorted Annie, staring up challengingly at Loch, who glowered back, stung by the eloquent innuendo he read in the sparking amber eyes and impatient to return to the subject of Vicar Nevins.

"What happened the night Sir David Gunn was *killed* ?" he demanded harshly, dropping all attempts at diplomacy.

"Och, it was a night like any other except the moon was at her fullest and so were the roses—voluptuous and dripping wie lust. Och, it was such a ripe, lusty night I should hae known something had to happen! The day was done and the bairns and animals fed and set snug for the night. My kitchen was as neat as a pin and I was rocking in my chair by the hearth," remembered the old woman. "Aye, a night like all the others. Like the one before and the one before . . . patterns never ending but always a wee variance here and there. Sir David Gunn took his full jug of whiskey and plodded up the stairs . . . bomp . . . bomp . . . bomp." She imitated the heavy tread. "His bedroom door slammed and after a bit his boots hit the floor. First one and then the other, same as every other night. I can almost hear the squeak and creak of his bedsprings as he lay back to drink himself to sleep as he did every other night. Everything aboot that puir man was sad and measured . . . labored . . . dull. A sad, sad lad, auld afore his time. No play, no joy . . . just plodding work. No humor, just dour brooding. Be careful, Lochiel Montgomery, it could happen to you! I'll not hae you dark and dour, dousing my golden girl's shining spirit!" she warned.

Loch breathed deeply to curb his impatience as the old woman's voice droned and her gnarled hand rhythmically stroked Annie's red-gold hair. Iona moved nearer, fascinated by the narrative and the bright animation of the tiny, wrinkled figure.

"Och, if Sir David was all dour, dull thuds, his Lady Rebecca was sharp, stinging chirps . . . jerky and shrill. I could hear the tinkles and giggles as Maude Potter, the greedy bitch, painted and patched and primped and prettied the puir, demented mistress. I dinna ken then it was like fattening the silly goose for the slaughter . . . dressing the lunatic bird for that vulture, Niall Potter. The clock ticked on and I heard Sir David's jug hit the floor and roll . . . back and forth . . . back and forth . . . smaller and smaller rolls . . . and then all was still. The house slept. I could hear the snores. Och, lusty snorers were the Gunns. Never in time. Never in harmony . . . always at sixes and sevens like several clocks all a wee bit out of tick. Aye, the house slept and it was Rebecca's time to weave her stories. I maun hae dropped off myself, for I dinna hear Maude Potter go to her bed. I did hear the muffled sound of carriage wheels."

"Aye, the ever-present fairy wheels swishing up and down the drive on a moonlit night. Och, but 'dinna fret, Michael-mine, 'tis but a dream,' " mocked a bitter voice. Annie tried to sit up to better see her brother lounging in the open doorway, but the old crone kept her fingers tightly wound in the girl's hair, forcing her to lie close.

"Stop your wiggling, Annie Gunn," she chided, her blind eyes shifting to the direction of the youth's voice. "Come closer, Michael-mine. Come closer to your auld nanny so she can touch you in her last earthly moments."

"I don't want your touch, you old witch!" spat Michael, and there was an audible gasp of horror from the others in the room.

"Och laddie, gie some respect for a dying auld beldame or she'll reach from the grave and make the rest of your life one big misery!" wickedly threatened the old woman, and the youth walked slowly to the bed and gazed down at the shriveled crone. "Where are you, Michael?" she fussed, keeping one hand firmly entwined in Annie's hair and waving the other feebly to locate the boy.

Iona sniffed and blew her nose noisily, trying to hold back her tears when she saw Michael's truculent expression melt as he gazed down at the weak blind woman.

"You're too wicked to die," cried Michael hoarsely, taking the crooked old hand and sitting beside her on the bed. Iona moved closer to Loch for comfort and support, overwhelmed by the loving bond between the frail, wounded woman and her two young charges.

"What happened that night?" demanded Loch sharply, shattering the awesome silence.

"Loch?" scolded Iona, frowning up at his stern features, not understanding how he could remain unmoved by the touching deathbed scene.

"The dark lad is right," agreed Mrs. Wilson, keeping tight hold on her two children. "Now, where was I?"

"Fairy wheels swishing up and down the driveway," stated Michael dryly. "Yes, just a night like any other," he added with bitterness.

"Aye, and I dozed by the hearth, hearing the snores and creaks of the sleeping house until the screams started," recounted the crone.

"There were screams here other nights. There were nights full of screams and I would wake up and be told 'You're dreaming, Michael. Go back to sleep. There are no fairy wheels! There are no screams! Just dreams! Just dreams!' " interrupted the boy angrily.

"These screams were different. It wasna you waking from a nightmare or Lady Rebecca screaming as she fought with her husband," struggled Mrs. Wilson.

"It was you, Annie!" shouted Michael. "Screaming and screaming and it froze my blood. I remember sitting in the thick blackness and your horrible screams ripped my ears. Not the screams of a little child, but screams of an animal . . . a vengeful animal!"

Annie felt the blood pound through her and still Mrs. Wilson stroked her head. Michael's words were sharp and they stabbed painfully, causing panic and terror to well. Loch stepped forward to comfort the girl who lay as though paralyzed, her amber eyes wide and staring, her mouth open in a silent howl of agony.

"When I got there the deed was done," stated the old hag, desperately trying to soothe the racing pulse of the girl who lay tense under her hand. "Hush, my dawtie. Hush, my pretty, it isna blood, 'tis just the dye used to change the color of the horses. Mrs. Wilson'll put you under the pump and soon her wee witch-wife'll be free of the sticky mess and smelling as sweet and fresh as roses," she crooned. "Dinna fight me, my dawtie. Dinna fight your auld nanny, my wee-an. 'Tis a dream, just a dream, and tomorrow wie the sunrise all the shadows will blow away and leave us in peace," she wheedled as Annie struggled and shrank away from the blindly clutching hands. "'Tis just a dream," she repeated tearfully, but Annie tore herself free and leapt off the high bed.

"It was not a dream!" shouted Michael. "It was not a dream!"

"Nay, it wasna a dream," whispered Mrs. Wilson, patting the empty pillow and feeling the warmth where Annie's head had lain. "Where are you, my wee-an? Come to me, my bonny," she wept.

Despite his dislike for the manipulating old crone, Loch's heart went out to the pitiful blind woman. He was torn, too, by the sight of Annie backed against the wall, staring with horror at her small, splayed hands.

"Did I kill my own father?" asked Annie, each word catching painfully in her dry throat. "Did I?" she screamed desperately.

"I dinna ken," answered the old woman. "Och, come to me, my wee bairn?"

"I am not a wee bairn! I am a woman. A full-grown woman, and I need to know. You have said many times that I have killed," stated Annie, her voice trembling despite her firm tone. "Now you must tell me. Did I kill my father?"

"I am a wicked, selfish auld witch. I only said you had killed so people would be afraid of you . . . would respect you . . . so you would be strong," confessed the crone.

"Don't lie to me!" yelled Annie.

"I am on my deathbed. I wouldna lie to you," returned the woman softly.

"And what's to stop you, old hag? The fires of hell?" spat Michael.

"Michael?" gasped Iona, appalled at the youth's callousness, but Loch quickly put out a strong hand to silence his sister.

"She's a Satanist! An evil, disgusting, perverted whore who doesn't believe in good, just evil. So why should she tell the truth?" retorted the boy as panic started to pound through him.

"It was talk, just talk. I was a homely, lonely girl afraid of my own shadow so I played my games to make others more scared of me than I of them. Annie was the bairn I always wanted to be. Braw and fearless, free and natural . . . a bold, brave, beautiful lass. I raised her unfettered. She wasna going to be crippled and bound like her puir demented mother . . . or ugly and cowering inside like me," she struggled to explain, panting painfully from the exertion but still unable to move anything but her clawed hands and sightless eyes.

"Over and over again you told me I killed," stated Annie, her voice low and controlled as she steeled herself against weakening at the pathetic sight of the dying woman.

Lochiel marveled at Annie's courage as she valiantly strove to learn the truth. He knew how she was torn between her love for the old woman and the need to put the past to rest. He ached to hold her, support her, lend her his strength, but he sensed that despite her fatigue she was absolutely determined to stand alone, and she would probably strike out at him if he dared approach.

"I lied. Over and over again I lied. I thought to protect you wie the lie so none could cower you. I thought to make you fearless wie the lie," sobbed the hag.

"No one could cower me . . . but me. You've made me afraid of myself," muttered Annie sardonically. "Dinna lie to me anymore?" she begged.

"Trust her with the truth. You have raised a strong, proud woman, Mrs. Wilson. You can trust her with the truth no matter how painful it is," stated Loch. Annie stared with wonder at the back of Loch's dark head, hearing his softly spoken words. She took a hesitant step toward him, wanting to bury herself in his hard, sheltering body as Mrs. Wilson raised a trembling hand toward the tall Scot's voice.

"Aye, I've raised a wondrous free spirit and she'll lead you a merry, lusty dance through life, Lochiel Montgomery," she chuckled hoarsely.

"Did I kill my father?" whispered Annie. "I know I was there with death. Every night in my dreams I know. I can smell the blood. . . . It is a hot, sickening stench . . . clinging and cloying . . . sticking my fingers together and stiffening on my skin," she continued, staring at her hands as she opened and closed her fingers. Loch turned to watch her, wishing there were some way he could spare her the pain she had to relive but knowing only the pain would liberate her so she could choose a future. "Pricking and pulling my skin . . . drying and stiffening so my flesh is stretched and torn . . . and I hear a creaking behind me . . . and someone is hiding in the wardrobe."

Iona shuddered and reached for Loch as they watched the girl holding her clawed hands in front of her. In her reenactment Annie was staring with terror over her shoulder.

"Aye, my wee-an, you were there wie death but I

dinna ken if you killed or not. When I got there Sir David and Niall Potter were already dead, and there you stood clutching a dirk wie blood splattered all over your wee nightie and . . . your pretty toes . . . your wee face . . . all covered wie blood," sobbed the old woman, reaching out blindly to enfold the girl in her arms. "Come to me, my wee-an?" she begged.

Annie stared down at her hands and then closed one as though she grasped a dagger. Slowly she moved her arm up and down in a stabbing motion as she frowned pensively, trying to recall such a moment.

"Mother said that the roses were bleeding and then she laughed delicately. Yes, delicately . . . a fine ladylike laugh. Such a proper, polite sound, like a well-bred lady is supposed to make to show amusement. 'The roses are bleeding,'" Annie pronounced primly, in very cultured English tones, and then she laughed artificially, a brittle, grating laugh that shivered the spines of the listeners. "Maude? Maude?" she called as she mimed ringing a small hand bell.

"Maude? Maude?" mouthed Michael. "Maude? Maude? The roses are bleeding," he intoned as the words caused a nightmarish panic to pound through him. "Stop it! Stop it! Stop that screaming!" he begged, covering his ears with his hands. Annie's terror was ripping through him smothering him in a thick blackness.

"I couldn't stop the ugly noise. It just screeched out of my mouth. I tried to stop it . . . I stuffed my hands in my mouth, but they were sticky with blood . . . salty and sticky to make my bile rise . . . and Father and Niall Potter dead on the floor and the door of the wardrobe creaking open . . . and I canna stop the screams!"

"Stop it! Stop it!" whined Michael, wrapping his arms about his head as he rocked and tried to block the phantom cries.

"Mother does not hear the ugly sound I am making. Mother doesn't see the wardrobe door slowly opening. She doesn't know Father and Niall Potter are lying on the floor. She just sits in her dainty chair with her beautiful ball gown billowing about her like a cloud. She is reading her poetry and she does not see the roses are bleeding and dribbling over the gold-edged pages and dripping and dribbling down her beautiful skirts. The roses are bleeding . . . spurting from her fingertips and through her pretty lace gloves."

"Maude? Maude?" called Michael. "The roses are bleeding all over the carpet and the pretty walls. Maude!"

"But Maude didn't come," said Annie, staring with horror at Michael.

"Mrs. Wilson came and Annie stopped her horrible screaming. Mother was going to cuddle me . . . hold me on her lap and wrap her beautiful silken gown about me, but Will and Duncan came in. They cried . . . an ugly noise . . . not as ugly as Annie but ugly with their hoarse voices. Mother laughed but it wasn't a proper ladylike sound. It was a sharp hurting titter. She wouldn't hold me but she embraced them . . . she put blood all over their bare chests. The twins slapped her. They slapped my beautiful mother . . . but she still laughed and she kissed Will . . . put her delicate gloved hands each side of Will's face and kissed him on the mouth. He screamed and hit her. It was a terrible . . . terrible nightmare," sobbed Michael.

"Maude didn't come until Will and Duncan were digging in the rose garden," stated Annie, remembering the tear stains and blood stains that mixed with the sweat and dirt on her older brother's bodies as they rhythmically spaded the earth. "At first I thought it was Mother . . . but it was Maude . . . wearing mother's clothes . . . standing in the shadows by the rhododendrons."

"It wasn't Maude. She watched from the house," choked Mrs. Wilson. "I saw her ratface watching from a window."

"It was Maude in the rhododendrons wearing Mother's clothes!" yelled Michael vehemently as tears poured unchecked down his cheeks and he entwined his legs like a nervous little boy despite his tall gawky frame.

"Where were you, Michael-mine?" probed Mrs. Wilson, her voice trembling.

"Sleeping. I was in my bed sleeping. I promise I was," sobbed Michael desperately.

"Come here, my wee manny," coaxed the old woman, swiveling her sightless eyes in the direction of the youth's snuffles. "Come near to your auld nanny and tell her all aboot the wicked bad dreams," she cajoled.

"I was in Mother's pretty room. In the dark wardrobe where the bogles hide," cried Michael, trying to rein the terror as he remembered the suffocating blackness and the smell of camphor. He shivered as he felt the cold shiny materials of his mother's gowns brush against him like ghosts.

"Tell your auld nanny what you heard and saw," she whispered.

"I don't know if it's the truth or a dream. Maybe I just dreamed I hid in the wardrobe," he sniffed. Annie silently shook her head, remembering the icy panic that had clutched her as she had watched the wardrobe door slowly creak open. The sight had sparked the screams that had frozen in her throat when she saw the bloody bodies of her father and Niall Potter.

"Michael, tell what you remember. It doesna matter if it was a dream or not," urged Iona as Loch stared with concern at Annie's pale, mesmerized face.

"I cannot!" sobbed Michael, burying his face in his hands and surrendering to the enormous wave of pain that welled up in him. "If it's the truth it is too horrible . . . too terrible," he cried. "It has to have been a dream. I have lots of bad dreams, don't I, Mrs. Wilson?"

"Aye, that you do, my wee manny," she soothed.

"I couldn't have killed anyone, could I?" he asked piteously. "I wanted to, but I am too weak . . . too cowardly. I was just a child . . . a lad of twelve, or barely thirteen. I didna hae the strength to kill a full-grown man, did I? Annie could kill . . . she's big and braw and free and fearless . . . but I am a weak . . . frightened . . . puny virgin."

"You wanted to kill?" questioned the old woman softly.

"Aye."

"Who did you want to kill?" the old crone asked gently. "Tell your auld nanny, my bonny lad," she coaxed.

"All of them! Every last one of them! Them in their fancy fairy carriages. She loved them . . . touched them . . . cuddled them . . . kissed them . . . but she never even looked at me. She was so beautiful . . . like a tragic princess, and Father was just a dirty farmer with his drink and his muddy boots. I would wait until everyone was asleep and hide in mother's pretty flowery room. I wasn't bad. I just wanted to smell her perfume . . . hear her voice . . . have her touch me . . . but she never touched me," he sobbed.

"In your dreams, did you kill?" probed Loch.

"In my dreams I have killed many times," replied Michael sweetly before spinning about and glaring malevolently at Loch. "Just last week I killed you, Lochiel Montgomery, for defiling my sister!"

"Och, Michael-mine," chided the old woman sorrowfully.

"And you, Mrs. Wilson, I have killed you a hundred thousand times for loving Annie more. You loved her best and made her strong . . . but what about me?"

"Och, Michael," mourned Mrs. Wilson, cut deeply by his festering agony.

"Look at her! Look at 'Wild Annie Gunn, dressed in britches, she is one of Satan's witches!' " screamed the boy, pulling away from Mrs. Wilson's clutching hands and pointing viciously at his sister, who had stepped backward, shocked by her brother's sudden maliciousness. "I have killed you over and over again, Annie Gunn! I am the son! I am the male! I am the laird! You are a whoring female and yet you do everything better than me!" he screeched, his voice squeaking and cracking with the violence of his rage. Loch reached out and wrapped a steadying arm about Annie's slim waist as she swayed, and she leaned thankfully against him but kept her horrified eyes pinned to her brother's blazing face.

"Och, Michael," she whispered, appalled by the hatred she felt crackling in the space between them. "You are much cleverer than I am. I cannot understand the books you are always reading. Greek, Latin, French, German . . ."

"Oh, yes, poor Michael Gunn wrapped up in his books like his poor, demented mother Rebecca. Lunacy runs in families, you know. Poor, cowardly Michael Gunn too afraid to live life . . . just a parasite feeding off the dreams of others," scoffed the boy.

"Och, Michael," groaned Annie, not able to find any words to comfort.

"Don't pity me!" screamed the youth, lashing out at her, and Loch felt a violent tremor shudder through Annie's weary body. He pulled her close and rejoiced when she didn't resist him but seemed to mold herself naturally against him, joining her strength to his. "I hate you. Do you hear me? I hate you! Filthy whore! Disgusting, loathsome whore . . . giving yourself to Falconhurst like some tart! Well, you'll pay. Nevins and Ross Montgomery will see you pay and it serves you both right," he sobbed, throwing himself down on the bed.

"Puir wee lost laddie," crooned Mrs. Wilson, stroking his head. "Pay no heed, he doesna ken what he's blathering aboot. 'Tis just a dream, my manny, just a nasty dream."

Loch stared speculatively at the grieving youth and then down at the top of Annie's bright head, where she stood in the sheltering circle of his arms. He sensed that no matter how Michael Gunn showed his jealousy and hatred, his younger sister would remain fiercely loyal and would protect him as though she were the older sibling.

"So we're back to Vicar Nevins," he murmured, imperceptibly shaking his head in warning at Iona, who had opened her mouth in alarm at the mention of Ross Montgomery's name. Annie gasped and stiffened, trying to push his arms away. "Annie, did you see Nevins that night?" he asked, turning her about to face him and looking into her wide, haunted eyes. Annie nodded and then shook her head, her face full of confusion as the gargoylelike face of the little minister zoomed into her mind, causing panic to pound through her.

"He wasna the only futret that slithered. Half the county had crawled beneath puir demented Rebecca's skirts to be called Romeo and Lancelot and Galahad and Lochinvar—and me wie all my love potions and charms never got so much as a wink. None ever wanted me unless I threatened them wie spells, but then they were so terrified they wilted and were not good for anything. Och, Michael-mine, I know your pain . . . it's like my own, but you have your whole life and I'm going to the grave wie nothing but a bunch of lies. I am not even a *Mrs.* No one wanted me. I'm just a *miss* . . . a miss . . . a nothing . . . I called myself Mrs. Wilson hoping for some respect but got none.

So I called myself '*witch*' and got plenty of fear, which was a puir substitute but better than nothing. Och, dinna get me wrong, I'm nae going to the grave a virgin. I lost my maidenhood one sultry Lammas Sabbat when I was sixteen. I never did see his face . . . he wore the mask of a goat. I never did see his tool either," she cackled. "He wore this great thing strapped to the front of him!"

Loch sighed deeply. Further questions would be futile with the old woman's mind rambling about. It seemed she knew very little of what had happened on that night so long ago. The knowledge was locked in Annie's and Michael's minds.

"Let go your anger, Michael-mine," wheedled Mrs. Wilson now as her busy fingers caressed the hair on the back of his neck. "I chose you, my laddie. I chose you, not Annie, but you," she crooned.

"It's too late," sobbed Michael.

"Hush up!" hissed the old woman suddenly, her eyes flickering uneasily as she heard a shuffling and a muffled muttering in the corridor outside. "Who's there?" she called, sniffing the air, her nostrils flaring with distaste. "'Tis the futret! The vermin! I can smell the stench of his fear!"

Loch watched Annie's body tense with terror as Vicar Nevins was unceremoniously propelled into the room by Robert. Iona's sunny smile of welcome faded abruptly as she saw her husband's usual mild expression was afire with barely suppressed fury, and he had one well-manicured hand clenched about the minister's scrawny neck.

"Oh, do be careful, darling," she urged. She didn't at all like the look of the vicar's mottled bluish, complexion or his bulging eyes and was fearful that another murder was about to be committed—but this time with no mystery attached. "I don't think he can breathe," she added, patting her husband's hand so he would relax his grip.

"Who else is here?" hissed the old crone.

"Dr. Murdock and Vicar Nevins have come to pay their respects," stated Robert as Roderick entered with a gray nondescript man who nervously clutched a medical bag.

"Well, I've no use for either of the muckers," snarled

Mrs. Wilson with such venom that Robert raised a blond eyebrow at Iona, who gave a small squawk of amusement.

"It seems I was laboring under a misconception," remarked Sir Robert languidly. "I supposed you to be on your deathbed, Mrs. Wilson?"

"I am, so dinna be impertinent!" returned the old woman feistily. "Well, where is he? Where is the slimy futret? Help me up!" she ordered imperiously and Loch laughed despite himself before picking up the frail woman in his arms while Iona hastily plumped and stacked the pillows to prop her. Dr. Murdock gasped at the sight of the bloodstained nightgown and moved forward to attend the old woman, but Annie grasped his arm and silently shook her head. "Well, say something, you miserable slug!" hissed Mrs. Wilson, and Nevins nervously cleared his throat and took a pompous stance with his hands behind his back and his portly belly thrust forward as though he were about to berate his congregation. "Hah!" crowed the old crone triumphantly, locating his voice and stabbing a bony, bent finger in his direction. "So you dare to show your ugly face at Kenlaren Manor agin, you murdering lecher!" she accused, and chuckled with gleeful satisfaction at his shrill squeal of fear.

"I am not here of my own volition," babbled the terrified man as his chest deflated with a snakelike hiss and he cowered against the wall to avoid the accusing finger and the eerie eyes that seemed to spark and flame from the tiny, shriveled body propped in the enormous bed.

"Stirring up the ignorant country folk again, my wee-an?"

"I assure you it was not my idea. It was Ross Montgomery's and Michael Gunn's," informed the little man, pointing his own accusing finger at the youth sprawled to one side of the old woman. Loch and Iona exchanged looks and then stared at Michael, who didn't seem the least disconcerted.

"Where were you the night Sir David Gunn was killed?" probed Loch.

"Sir David Gunn died in Africa," replied Nevins smugly.

"You were here that night! I couldna see you but I

smelled you . . . sweating like a cornered rat . . . wie my wee-an screaming and screaming . . . her father's blood splattered from her bonny face to her wee toes," snarled the old woman. "So stop your lies!"

"Michael Gunn stirred up the villagers it wasn't me. I tried to reason with him but he wouldn't listen. It was he, not me! He wanted them to burn his own sister at the stake. He even brought Ross Montgomery to Kenlaren. They plotted murder together. I heard them. Your murder, Lord Falconhurst," Nevins babbled, turning to the dark Scot for support. "It's true, I swear it," he whimpered as he heard Iona's sharp intake of breath. "Michael Gunn promised to help your cousin kill you, in return for a great deal of money. I told them I most certainly disapproved, but they were determined. Ross Montgomery covets your title and lands. . . ."

"Tell everyone why you didn't inform the proper authorities if you so certainly disapproved," giggled Michael, seeming unperturbed by the vicar's accusations. "All Ross Montgomery's gold was in our most moral clergyman's desk. All these years we thought Maude Potter was blackmailing us—but in actual fact it was Vicar Nevins," he laughed.

"No, I saw Maude Potter. I paid Maude Potter," protested Annie.

"Who in turn paid Vicar Nevins. Poor, poor Maude Potter, she's dead! Tripped and broke her neck, isn't that right, Vicar Nevins?" declared Michael. "Vicar Nevins, that most religious man, who worshiped at the altar between my mother's thighs!"

"I must protest!" squealed Nevins. "I find this decidedly distasteful!"

"I quite agree," noted Loch sardonically. "I gather you were a frequent visitor at Kenlaren?"

"As a minister I came to counsel Lady Rebecca. . . ."

"Counsel?" hooted the old crone. "Counsel? Och, that's even funnier then closeted!" she choked.

"Lady Rebecca was unbalanced . . . ailing. She did not attend services at the kirk. And being a devoted servant of the Lord, I felt it my duty to attend to the needs of my flock," explained the frazzled man, unnerved by Mrs. Wilson's snorts of laughter and Annie's intense stare as she moved closer and closer to him, searching his face and her memory.

"Hah!" chortled Mrs. Wilson. "The randy auld ram servicing his flock. Why you auld goat! What a disappointment to find that devil is nothing but a wee, limp runt wie chicken legs!"

"Help me?" whispered Annie as her memory was suddenly sparked and she was eight years old again, standing under the pump as Mrs. Wilson scrubbed the sticky blood from her shivering body, while her twin brothers rhythmically spaded the earth. She squinted her eyes, trying to pierce the darkness and clearly see the face under the drooping brim of her mother's hat.

"You were there that night," she stated. "Whenever I smell blood and roses I see your face and I'm caught back in the terror of that time. Did you wear my mother's clothes and hide in the rhododendron bush?"

"Certainly not!" said the vicar, trembling indignantly.

"You were there!" insisted Mrs. Wilson.

"I know you were there," repeated Annie, staring at the putty features of the cowering little man. "Your face is just like my ferret MacTavish's," she said, referring to his tiny beady eyes that shifted nervously and the specks of foam on the thin, snarling lips. "I thought you were going to bite me," she whispered as once again she was back in her mother's pretty parlor. "Help me! Please help me?" she whimpered. Nevins's distorted face zoomed in and out of her circle of screams and she saw her own bloody hands reaching out through the swirling eddies of terror, but the vicar recoiled, his lips flattened against his bared teeth.

"I admit I was there that night. I came to see Lady Rebecca on . . . spiritual matters, but she was otherwise engaged, so I left," recounted Nevins.

"How did you know she was otherwise engaged?" probed Robert. "Well, did you knock on her door? Speak to her? What?" he added when the man seemed at a loss for words.

"A child was screaming in there and I felt it was not an opportune time," snapped Nevins primly.

"And you didn't find that unco?" pressed Loch.

"Why should I find it strange for a mother to be disciplining her daughter?" answered the vicar glibly.

"For Rebecca Gunn it would be very unco!" cried Dr. Murdock and then fell silent as all eyes stared at him with astonishment.

"Aye," agreed Mrs. Wilson, sliding down the plumped-up pillows until it appeared she was about to be suffocated by the fluffy eiderdown. "Help me up," she hissed, desperately clutching at Michael, who lay beside her looking bored by the events.

"Everyone for miles aboot knew Lady Rebecca never touched or spoke to her bairns," explained the doctor after Mrs. Wilson had been propped up again.

"So, Vicar Nevins, it appears you entered Lady Rebecca's room where Sir David and Niall Potter were murdered," stated Loch harshly.

"I most certainly did not!" denied Nevins vehemently.

"Then how did you know it was a daughter screaming?" asked Loch casually.

"By Jove! Dashed astute reasoning, Falconhurst!" applauded Robert.

"He wouldna help me," whispered Annie, backing away from the little man.

"Maybe because he's the one who murdered Sir David and Niall Potter!" suggested Mrs. Wilson.

"They were already dead! It was done! That girl held the bloodied murder weapon . . . waved it at me as though she were as demented as her mother!" screeched Nevins. "She killed her own father and Maude Potter's brother!" he accused, pointing a finger at Annie, who backed away until she rested against Loch's strong body, and he held her to him, feeling the terror pound through.

"Roderick, take this whining cur and lock him away before I commit murder!" he ordered in a low, dangerous tone. His hands itched to throttle the cowering, spiteful man of the cloth.

"Kill him! He's vermin!" hissed Mrs. Wilson as Roderick took the minister by the scruff of the neck and propelled him unceremoniously out of the room. "Murdering mucker comes here to do mischief wie the puir mistress

. . . kills Sir David and Niall Potter and then dresses in woman's clothing and steals away, leaving a wee bairn to deal wie the horror of it," she panted as blood dribbled from her pleated mouth. Annie shook her head in confusion as she tried to remember.

"He didn't kill anyone. He was too clean . . . all black and white and gray and clean," she recounted, turning and burying her face in Loch's strong chest and breathing deeply of his safe masculine scent. "Och, I am so tired," she sighed.

Loch held Annie close, feeling her fatigue but knowing there would be no real rest until all the shadows of the past were illuminated.

"Face the darkness, my wee-an," urged Mrs. Wilson as though reading Loch's mind. "Put the ghosts awa' so you can hae a rosy future," she begged.

"The full moon woke me up . . . it shone across my bed. In the night I heard the fairy wheels and I thought I went back to sleep, but I didn't because I found myself on my little stool outside Mother's room. The door was not shut fast as it was supposed to be. It was open a little crack. Mother was reading her favorite poem. 'Young Lochinvar has come out of the west. Through all the wide border his steed was the best.' I just opened the door a wee bit more. I just wanted to see her. She was so beautiful. The most beautiful mother in the world. My mother," remembered Annie, and then she shuddered violently and shook her head wildly from side to side, unable to speak.

"What did you see?" croaked the old woman. Annie clung tightly to Loch's encircling arm.

"Father was lying on the pretty rose-patterned carpet with a dirk stuck in his back. It must have been hurting him horribly but he dinna cry out. Fathers are meant to be braw, I thought, as I pulled it out. He's strong and brave like Lochinvar—that is why he's not making a sound. He was dead but I did not want to know it. There was so much blood pouring out of his back and down my arms. I tried to make him get up but he wouldn't move. And then I saw Niall Potter wie his trews about his feet and blood coming out of his mouth. I wanted to scream but I couldn't. And the smell of the blood was thick and sickening mixing wie the roses . . . and I heard the sound of a carriage outside, and the door of the wardrobe started to open and the screams came out of my mouth and I couldna stop them. Even when Vicar Nevins came I couldna stop screaming. He wouldna let me touch him. He wouldna hold me. I couldna talk. I reached for him but he backed away, snarling, and I thought he was going to bite me. I couldna stop screaming and he ran away. I heard his carriage go away and then Mrs. Wilson came." Annie sighed, feeling drained and longing to curl into Loch's secure strength, and sleep.

"You heard Nevins leave?" questioned Iona, and Annie nodded.

"Go on, my love," urged Loch gently, determined that she should remember the whole. "Mrs. Wilson came?" he prompted.

"Aye, she took me out of there . . . through the kitchen. She tore my nightdress off and threw it in the fire," recalled Annie, and her body jerked and froze with terror as again she was eight years old and standing naked under the pump in the moonlit yard, hearing Mrs. Wilson panting with exertion as she scrubbed at the sticky blood while Will and Duncan rhythmically spaded the earth in the rose garden. "My brothers cried as they dug into the dirt. They had blood and tears running down their faces and bare chests. Mrs. Wilson sang a lullaby as she washed me."

"Soon, och, soon my bairn will be as sweet-smelling as the dewy roses," crooned the old woman, transported back to that tragic moonlit night, "Soon, aye, soon, my wee-an."

"I can still hear Will and Duncan's shovels digging . . . digging and I'm standing in a puddle and Mrs. Wilson is singing and washing the blood from me, and someone is standing in the shadow of the rhododendron bush," she intoned, squinting her eyes as though to see into the past. "No!" she screamed, trying to erase the face that loomed out of the stark moonlight. Loch felt Annie's body stiffen before she wrenched his arms from her and staggered to the window. Below her she saw the rhododendron bush, its enormous showy blossoms bent under the weight of the rain.

"Who do you see in the bushes?" queried the crone,

her voice trembling as though she were terrified of the answer.

"I dinna ken!" lied Annie frantically. "Just a maid . . . a servant . . . someone."

"We had no such thing back then," hissed Mrs. Wilson.

"It must have been a trick of the moonlight. It had to be that and Maude Potter," insisted Annie desperately.

"I told you Maude Potter was watching from her bedroom window," choked the old woman. "As I pumped I looked up and saw her greedy face."

"Then there was no one there. It was my fancy. The shock of everything," cried Annie brokenly, unable to look at her lounging brother. Michael started to laugh.

"Tell the truth, Annie Gunn," he jeered spitefully. "Tell the truth, you little harlot! Tell them whom you saw dressed in our mother's straw hat, the one wie the pretty pink ribbons that floated down the back. Tell them who wore the pastel gown with the little lacy shawl! Tell them!" he roared, losing his fiendish smile and snarling as his sister backed away from his malevolence.

"No . . . no," she whimpered, tossing her head and trying to dispel the hideous image of her brother dressed in their mother's clothes.

"Tell them!" he screeched.

"I canna," she sobbed, tears pouring down her cheeks as the memory stabbed into her mind.

"You tell us, Michael," suggested Loch softly, reaching out and pulling Annie into his arms.

"Let go of her, Falconhurst! She's not your whore. She doesn't need your protection! She's charmed! The devil takes care of his own, right, Mrs. Wilson? She's wild Annie Gunn . . . braw, strong, able to outrun, outride, outshoot, outswim . . . *me*!" he howled. "You don't think I'm a man, do you, Annie?" he asked quietly after a long silence broken just by the old woman's labored breathing. *"Do you?"* he screamed when she stared at him mutely.

"Of course I do," she managed.

"Still lying! Well, I don't need your lies! I don't need your protection! I'll be damned if I'll hide behind your harlot skirts," he snarled. "Tell them whom you saw in the shadow of the rhododendrons!"

"I saw you," sobbed Annie clutching Loch as waves of faintness swirled about her.

"Come close to me, Michael-mine," hissed Mrs. Wilson, too weak to fuss at Dr. Murdock, who carefully wiped the blood from her lips. "Come close, Michael-mine, and tell your auld nanny what a fine braw lad you are," she wheedled.

"I watched our father kill Niall Potter. I saw Niall Potter hurting our mother . . . squashing her . . . crumpling and bruising her beautiful gown . . . tearing her poetry books—and she just laughed. He was brutal and base and ugly and she was delicate like a flower and she just laughed. Father stood there watching for a while and then he pulled him off her. I thought he was saving her but he was no different from Niall Potter. They fought and Potter fell down with blood pouring from his mouth. Then Father threw himself on mother . . . he was hurting her and she was crying . . . so I pulled the dagger from Niall's chest and tried to get Father to stop but he wouldn't. He didn't even care that I was there. He wouldn't notice me no matter how hard I hit him . . . he just kept on hurting Mother like he was a bull and she nothing but a cow. I hit him and hit him, forgetting I was holding the dirk . . . and soon he stopped."

"Och, Michael," mourned Annie, wanting to comfort her brother. At her words his soft, sad expression changed and he spat venomously at her.

"Don't pity me, you maggot! Don't look down on me, you whore!" he shouted, while tears drenched his cheeks. "I am not as weak and ineffectual as you think. I am strong! I can kill! I killed my own father!" he stated. "I killed my own father," he repeated wonderingly.

"Och, my wee manny, you dinna ken what you were aboot," soothed the old woman hoarsely.

"I did! I did!" lied Michael. "I knew what I was doing. I am not just a timorous, bedwetting coward hiding in wardrobes. I am powerful. I can kill. I may not be able to give life but I can take it away!"

Iona shivered and clasped Robert's broad hand as she watched the crazed youth, who paced and searched each face, looking desperately for some sort of confirmation.

Lochiel and Robert seemed very relaxed and unimpressed as they successfully hid their concern.

"Ha! I'm scaring you, aren't I, Annie Gunn?" crowed Michael, peering into his sister's tear-stained face. She nodded silently. "Good, good, that's how it should be!" he rejoiced triumphantly. "Och, you're going to be even more afraid of me when Ross Montgomery kills your lover! Hah, you thought you were so clever . . . the only one who could make money with your fancy stable of horses . . . looking down your nose at poor, piteous Michael who cannot satisfy a woman or support himself. Well, when my plan is played I shall be rich and beholden to no one. Not you, little sister, or you, Uncle Robert. I shall be a man!"

"Hush your prattle, laddie," scolded Dr. Murdock, not paying attention to the youth's anguished words but only conscious of the rattle of death that shook the old women. "The end is near," he pronounced somberly, and if the scene had not been so macabre, Loch might have laughed at Michael Gunn's dumbfounded expression when everyone ignored him and circled the bed.

Annie reached out and took the gnarled hand in hers before bending and kissing the wrinkled brow.

"Thank you, Mother," she said simply as tears welled.

"She'll not die! She cannot die! She's not mortal!" shouted Michael, fear cracking his voice. "She's not human! She's a witch! She cannot die!" He rushed out of the room and slammed the door so hard it reverberated through the whole house. Annie felt the force of the crash shudder the shriveled body, and the sightless eyes widened with shock.

"Mmm . . . Mmm . . ." struggled the crone, trying desperately to call to the distressed youth.

"Michael will be all right," soothed Annie, wanting the old woman to die peacefully.

"Nooooo," mourned Mrs. Wilson before giving a small cry and slowly slumping deeper into the pillows, her very last breath hissing out like an anguished sigh.

Lochiel silently stared down at Annie's bright, bowed head and the entwined hands, one gnarled and old and the other smooth and young. His arms ached to embrace but he sensed Annie needed to be alone to grieve for the passing of her oldest and dearest friend. Quietly he followed the others from the room, stopping for a moment at the open door to look back as the cloud cover thinned and brilliant sunshine flooded through the leaded latticed windows to illuminate the still tableau of the vital golden girl and the still, gray old woman.

Chapter 19

Annie dug her bare feet into the stallion's firm warmth and flung back her head. She closed her eyes and saw the deep red of the glorious sunset filter through her lids and felt the sensuous touch of the rushing wind as it streamed through her luxuriant hair. The giant horse thundered across the rolling moorland to the towering cliffs that overlooked the sea. The earth smelled sweet and fresh after the long days of drenching rain and Annie sighed, wishing she could feel so purged and throw off the grim shroud of mourning to embrace a joyous future with Lochiel.

Annie reined Dubh and stared over the shimmering water as she thought of Mrs. Wilson. The old woman was dead, leaving a void that would never be filled by another person, and Annie accepted that fact as the natural order of things like night and day.

She had sat holding the gnarled blue-veined hand and remembering the golden days and shadowy days, spiraling back to her first beginnings, and Mrs. Wilson had been a part of them all. Teaching, nurturing, scolding, hugging, and spinning her spells. The sun had streamed through the leaded latticed window, bathing her in a patterned warmth as the old woman had got colder and harder, reminding Annie of a doll she once had. No matter how many layers of clothes, no matter how affectionate the hugs, the doll had remained frigid and unyielding, so she had thrown it away in disgust, preferring warm, living appreciative toys like ferrets and mice. She thought of the doll's fixed china hand as Mrs. Wilson's hand had frozen in her grasp, stiffening and losing color until she had to pry the bent fingers apart to release the old woman's hold on her.

"Good-bye," she had whispered again and gently kissed the cold, lined face before covering up the corpse that bore no resemblance to the sprightly, mischievous old crone who had lovingly raised her. She had left the room intent on finding her brother. Quietly and methodically she had searched Kenlaren Manor, purposefully avoiding the formal rooms where she heard the deep drone of voices. She had blanched, her heart thudding with fear upon recognizing two forbidding black carriages belonging to the County Constabulary and, frightened that her uncle meant to have Michael arrested, she had hidden in the shrubbery.

Annie watched dispassionately as Ross Montgomery was dragged out of the house blustering and bellowing, his thick hairy wrists manacled behind his back, followed by Vicar Nevins, who positively crawled, whining and blubbering.

Annie giggled and grinned over her shoulder as she sensed Mrs. Wilson's presence and heard a wicked cackle on the breeze. Satisfied that the constables had not arrested her brother, she had watched the cumbersome carriages lumber down the driveway and disappear through the wrought iron gates before making her way to the high meadow, where Dubh frolicked with his mares and colts. She had thrown herself onto his high glossy back to race out her sorrows before resuming her search for her brother.

Now she stared out at the red-tipped waves as they rippled to shore and lapped gently against the sand where she first had encountered Lochiel Montgomery. She looked thoughtfully at the small white scar in the palm of her hand and then angrily shook her head. She could not afford to think of the tall dark Scot. They had no future together. She had to find her brother and devise a way for them both to escape. But to where, she worried, and her tired mind, deprived of sleep for nearly forty-eight hours, could only conjure up the bleak pile of stones that loomed on the barren moor. She and Michael had to leave Kenlaren forever, she realized, and go where no one knew them so they could start a new life.

"Oh, Michael, where are you?" she screamed aloud, her voice picked up by the sea breeze. The library had been the first place she had looked. She had peeked in, sure that she would find him immersed in his precious books as though nothing out of the ordinary had happened, but the serene room had been empty, as was his bedchamber and the attic rooms where he had sometimes hidden as a child. Maybe he had returned to the university in Edinburgh, where he felt tall and proud? He was a scholar, after all, she had thought, but his horse munched placidly in the stable. She had tried to ignore the grim forboding that ached her exhausted body as she determinedly searched, but she found no trace of him anywhere.

"Michael? Michael?" she screamed over the moorland, her voice bouncing off and echoing through the gray granite blocks of the Devil's Stepping Stones. "Och, Michael-mine, I'll take care of you," she promised softly as she lay forward and entwined her hands in Dubh's mane, hugging his arched neck. She sighed and closed her eyes, lulled by the horse's steady rhythm, not heeding where he carried her.

Loch stared moodily out of the salon window at the brilliant sunset.

"Dashed morbid, if you ask me," remarked Robert, pouring himself a generous snifter of brandy.

"She needs time to mourn," replied Loch softly.

"Deuced depressing! I've a mind to trot upstairs and remonstrate with my young ward . . . forcibly drag her out of that chamber of death and into the world of the living," he said, purely to spark some reaction from the brooding Scot.

"She's not there," responded Loch. "She's off on the moors riding out her tears."

"Och, you're a wonderful, loving man, Lochiel Montgomery," laughed Iona, giving him a hug and rejoicing at the tenderness she saw soften his carved features.

"I say, what about me?" complained Robert petulantly.

"Och, and you are a wonderful, loving man, Robert Forsythe," she sang out, giving him a kiss on the end of his aristocratic nose.

"Can you believe the infernal gall of your cousin?" said Robert after kissing his wife soundly. "The absolute nerve . . . the temerity . . . the audacity of the bounder to march into Kenlaren as bold as brass?"

"Darling, I hardly think skulking in the wine cellar could be termed 'marching in as bold as brass,' " returned Iona affectionately before her face creased with anxiety.

"Penny for your thoughts, my pet?" asked Robert softly after a pause.

"How did Ross Montgomery get into the house without anyone's knowledge? What was he doing here?" fretted Iona. "Oh, my God! If we hadn't discovered him, he could have murdered us while we slept!"

"But we did discover him, so it's a moot point," comforted Robert, enfolding her in his strong arms.

"But what about Michael? Where is he? Oh, Robert, I have never seen such festering bitterness. I would never have guessed. It came as a total surprise. He always appeared so timid and mild," declared Iona. "Have you ever seen that side of him before?"

"Can't say that I have," replied Robert. "Sometimes pettish and arrogant, sometimes a bloody bore, but never violent. I wonder where the poor boy is hiding."

"You don't think he'll hurt Annie, do you?" she ventured, and her brother turned and gave her such a dark look she knew he was asking himself the same question. "Of course he wouldn't. It was, as Mrs. Wilson would say, 'all talk!' All bluff and bluster! He has had plenty of opportunity to harm her through the years and he never has," she reassured herself.

"I don't think he knew how much he hated until today," stated Loch.

"But he wouldna hurt her, he's her brother!" Iona protested.

"And David Gunn was his father!" snorted Robert.

"I think he needs another to do his hurting for him,"

mused Loch. "He tried to enlist Nevins and Ross Montgomery. . . ."

"Dash well didn't with his own father!" remarked Robert. "Did the gory deed all by himself."

"But he dinna mean to," insisted Iona. "He was just a poor, frightened little boy who had witnessed terrible things."

"And he still is a poor, frightened little boy," sighed Loch tersely as unease gnawed in his belly.

"By Jove! To think I so innocently walked into this gruesome situation that spring day. Those silent, sullen twin nephews of mine burning all my sister's possessions . . . and Oriana and I locked in the kitchen," Robert recalled, appalled as he thought of all he had recently learned. "I shudder to think what boredom and curiosity led me into." He poured himself another drink.

"Maybe we should go and look for Annie?" worried Iona, unable to stay still.

"There's no point trying to find her until she wants to be found," returned Loch harshly. "We maun just trust her instinct. That old crone taught her well," he added.

"They'll be no rest until she returns," sighed Robert, ringing a bell to summon Wilkes or Roderick as his stomach growled with hunger. "Well, I dash well hope that the confounded little minx hasn't decided to perform one of her extended disappearing acts! I say, Falconhurst, you and Oriana aren't by any chance on the outs, are you? For if you are, we may not see hide nor hair of her for months, and I do so want to get on with my honeymoon," he groaned exaggeratedly.

"I intend to marry her," stated Loch shortly.

"Deuced civilized of you to ask my permission, old chap," replied Robert mildly.

"But Loch, she's as stubborn and proud as you!" said Iona distressfully. "I doubt she'll return until she has everything sorted out and solved."

"Aye, but there is a difference. She knows I love her and I know she loves me. I have to trust that that fact will seep through her mourning shroud and she'll be flying into my arms by nightfall," he stated forcefully, as though the mere act of saying it would cause it to happen.

"Well, old boy, she dashed well better start flapping her wings," Robert later sighed heartlessly as the sun sank low in the sky.

"I need some air," snapped Loch, irritated by his nonchalant brother-in-law.

"Darling, you shouldna tease him," chided Iona as the door closed firmly behind her brother. "I have never seen him so vulnerable before. He's eaten up wie worry."

"And I am not?" hissed Robert, his lazy blue eyes hardening to a steely gray. "Would you prefer two unbearable bores fretting and fuming and pacing the carpet? Would it do anything to improve this harrowing situation? Oh, I am so sorry, loveykins, I didn't mean to bite your pretty head off like that," he apologized ruefully, noticing her dark eyes fill with tears. "We are all rather frazzled, it would seem, my pet." He enfolded her in his arms. "Well, very soon we shall be galloping away from this accursed Kenlaren. I wish I had never set eyes on this godforsaken place or the barbaric Gunns!"

"If it were not for Kenlaren and Annie Gunn, I would not be here in your arms," sniffed Iona, snuggling against his firm chest.

"Shameless hussy," reproached her fond husband, nibbling her velvet earlobe. "I hire what I am led to believe is a pure, unimpeachable, demure governess to teach decorum to my slightly wayward ward . . ."

"*Slightly* wayward?" laughed Iona.

" . . . my *slightly* wayward ward, and what does this governess do but seduce me," he sighed sorrowfully. "Come in," he called in answer to a discreet rapping. Then he lowered his head and kissed his wife lingeringly with many little grunts of appreciation, ignoring the polite coughs until Iona struggled free and turned blushingly to Wilkes.

"Aaaah!" she said lamely, trying to regain her composure.

"You rang?" answered the immaculate little man.

"Yes, Wilkes. I do believe with all this commotion of would-be assassins skulking, faithful housekeepers dying, and nephews' murderous tendencies . . . that I missed one if not several repasts," observed Robert blandly.

"Where would you like to dine, sir?"

"The small dining room will suffice," replied Robert.

"The kitchen will be grand," contradicted Iona firmly. "Robert, there are no servants but Roderick and Wilkes," she added gently, her dark eyes pleading for thoughtfulness.

"Quite so," muttered Robert. "The kitchen it is then."

"I would not advise the kitchen, Lady Iona, as there is rather an unfortunate aroma," recounted Wilkes.

"Aroma?" echoed Robert.

"Aroma," confirmed Wilkes.

"What is causing the unfortunate aroma?"

"Dead cockerels, Sir Robert," responded Wilkes, keeping his face emotionless despite Iona's muffled squawk of amusement.

"Dead cockerels?" echoed Robert with stupefaction.

"Dead cockerels, sir."

"Cocks? Roosters?"

"Cocks, roosters, chanticleers," enlightened Wilkes. "Male chickens, sir."

"I am quite aware of what a cockerel is, Wilkes," answered Robert. "But *dead* cockerels, you say?"

"Yes, sir. Dinner will be served in the small dining room within the hour. Will that be all, sir?"

"Yes, thank you, Wilkes," answered Robert, waving the small man from the room as Iona collapsed against him roaring with laughter. "Extraordinary conversation! Did you hear all that, my pet?" he uttered as she wept with merriment, nodding and unable to answer. "Dead cockerels, he said. The aroma of dead cockerels!"

"Chanticleer *morte!*" crowed Iona.

"Dash it all, I hope we're not dining on coq au vin!"

Lochiel strode through the orchard, appreciating the lush fragrances that had been released by the heat of the sun. Energy positively hummed about him in stark contrast to the previous days, when all nature had been in gray suspension. Now flocks of birds flew squabbling and bickering; rainbow butterflies languidly floated and drifted between the hot summer colors; bees busily buzzed as though making up for lost time; and ponderous hens clucked and stabbed at wasp-covered apples that lay fragrantly rotting beneath the laden trees. Where were the roosters, he wondered idly as he strode up the muddy, rutted lane toward the hidden meadow where Dubh ruled his harem. He smiled, hearing the furtive rustles of mice and voles, shrews and moles in the thick hedgerows, and he threw back his head and laughed with the hoarse cawing of the rooks that nested raucously against the bloodred sky. There was a jubilation in the air. A celebration, he decided. It was Lammas, the pagan festival of the harvest. A hot, ripe. lusty time for loving, Loch mused, stopping in his tracks as the great stallion Dubh proudly walked toward him carrying his golden mistress.

Annie felt Dubh's steady rhythm cease but she was loath to open her heavy lids. She rubbed her nose into the stallion's warm neck and stretched like a cat, loving the sensuous heat of the setting sun on her back. Lazily she wiggled her body to urge her horse to move, but he remained still.

"Go, Dubh, go," she whispered sleepily, and then started as a strong familiar body swung up behind her and took her possessively in claiming arms. She opened her eyes, staring up into Loch's shadowed face before grinning contentedly and snuggling into his chest.

"I am not a piece of furniture, infant," he scolded, touched at her trust.

"Not an infant," murmured Annie, wriggling her small bottom back until it pressed intimately against the center of him.

"Definitely not an infant," agreed Loch against her golden hair as she sighed deeply and stopped thinking, content to sink into the strong, rhythmic safety of the steady horse and the dark Scot.

"My two dark males," she whispered as she let go of her fears and worries and slept soundly.

Lochiel stared speculatively at the Elizabethan manor, the setting sun reflecting off the latticed windows, before changing Dubh's direction and heading toward the coast. He was loath to wake Annie, knowing she was totally depleted, and he guessed that upon waking she would tense with worry for her brother. He held her close, achingly aware of the tiny hand that curled about his large thumb as though she were fearful he might escape her, and they cantered across the treeless moor past the looming rocks of the Devil's Stepping Stones. He gazed up to the highest point, remembering the black-garbed figure who had roosted like a bird of prey defying and challenging the folks of Kenlaren village before being shot by Ross Montgomery. Loch had no doubts that the bullet had been meant for him. Was it just that very morning? So much had happened that it seemed a lifetime ago, he reflected. That wildly fired shot could have ended Annie's life. He shivered at the morbid thought and gathered her more tightly close to his heart. He turned his head away from the hulking gray reminders and looked west to the sea.

Loch cradled his woman in his arms as he stared down at the moonlit beach where he had first encountered the beautiful, wild child eight years before. He longed to lay her gently in the sand and claim her thoroughly, but knew he wanted her free and unfettered by worry for her brother. Regretfully he turned Dubh around and headed back to Kenlaren Manor, his body aching with fatigue and his stomach rumbling with hunger.

Annie opened her eyes as the sharp sound of cobblestones reverberated through her and Dubh clopped across the stable yard.

"Urgh! What's that foul stink?" she exclaimed, inelegantly wrinkling up her tiny nose. Loch shook his head and stared toward the open kitchen door at Roderick before swinging himself off the horse and holding his arms out to Annie. She looked at him sleepily, her small face screwed up with distaste at the rank odor, before giving a mischievous grin and toppling trustingly off the tall stallion. Loch caught her to his broad chest with a triumphant laugh.

"Mr. MacDonald, what is that disgusting stench?" he asked.

"Dead cocks!"

"Deceased roosters," corrected Robert in dignified tones accompanied by an undignified squawk of mirth from Iona as the married couple stood hand in hand at the open French doors.

"Dead cocks?" echoed Loch, striding toward them and looking down at Annie, who shook with laughter.

"Och, you wicked auld witch, you," giggled Annie. "Och, you dear, dear, dear Mrs. Wilson," she chuckled before going into peals of merriment as she looked up into Loch's suspicious expression.

"Why on earth would Mrs. Wilson kill all the cockerels and hide them under the floorboards?" asked Robert as Annie and Loch ate hungrily.

"I really dinna think you would care to know, Uncle Robert," returned Annie primly, taking a sip of wine. "It might put you off all manner of things," she added impishly.

"What things?" asked Robert. "That putrid aroma dashed well put me off my dinner, I can tell you! What else could it put one off?"

"Uncle Robert, I dinna think it a proper subject for a well-bred young lady!" simpered Annie wickedly. "Anyway, I dinna think she meant to leave them under the floorboards so long . . . or then again maybe she did," she mused aloud before taking a healthy bite of roast beef.

"You're not a well-bred young lady, minx!" stated her uncle, raising a blond eyebrow at her bare feet and trews.

"Och, clothes dinna make the man . . . or lady," she quoted glibly.

"Very true, but they certainly help," retorted Robert. "Now, I insist you tell me the purpose in killing all the cockerels!"

"You insist?" she returned impishly.

"Do you think that wise, Robert?" asked Iona.

"I most certainly do insist!" answered Robert sternly. "Do you know the purpose, Falconhurst?" he asked as Loch leaned back in his chair, evidently appreciating Annie's vivacious impudence.

"Och, I can hazard a fair guess but I'll not deprive your anticipation, Forsythe," laughed Lochiel.

"Come on, Uncle Robert, I am sure you can fathom it," said Annie challengingly as she bit into a crisp apple. "I shall give you a clue. Did each of the cockerels have their necks . . . er . . . knotted?" she asked, trying to be very serious but unable to suppress a giggle.

"Dead cockerels with their necks knotted?" mused Robert somberly as he shrugged and shook his head, unable to find a rhyme or reason for such a bizarre action.

"Was it to scare away the servants?" reasoned Iona.

"That was certainly a part but by no means the whole," replied Annie. "Och, not the whole, by any means!"

"Oriana, I am your guardian. I demand obedience!" stated Robert dictatorially. "Now, no more nonsense! Tell me why on earth Mrs. Wilson would kill the wretched birds and knot their necks?"

"To wilt manhoods!" declared Annie.

"I beg your pardon?" blustered Robert.

"To wilt a person's manroot," explained Annie. "Well, not necessarily your manroot . . . but someone's. It is a wilting spell to make a cock limp," she continued innocently, wickedly choosing to interpret her uncle's shocked expression as ignorance.

"Enough!" bellowed Robert, crossing his long legs.

"Dinna fret, it doesn't work unless you believe it will," she comforted, trying desperately to keep a straight face. "If you think your manhood will wilt . . . it will."

"Enough! I said *enough!*" roared Robert. "Falconhurst, control her!"

"Nay, Forsythe! I give my wee woman free rein!" laughed Loch, cupping Annie's glorious face and staring deeply into her warm, sparking, amber eyes. "Och, you've whiskey eyes, my love," he murmured, noting that despite the apparent sunniness there lingered a cloudy sadness barely beneath the surface. "It has been a long, long day and it is time for bed," he stated, swinging her up in his arms.

"I say! By Jove, old chap!" blustered Robert as Loch carried Annie from the room. "Iona? Shouldn't we do something about that—about them? It isn't quite the done thing, you know. Well, dash it all, I doubt if I could stop them even if I tried! Bloody good job that we are stuck in the middle of nowhere, isn't it?"

"Och, hush up, Robert!" ordered Iona irreverently before smothering his indignation with a very passionate kiss.

"I think we should see if Mrs. Wilson's spell was effective," she added thoughtfully.

"Anything you say, my pet," complied Robert.

Lochiel carried Annie into her room and laid her gently on the bed. He stood silhouetted against the window, gazing down on her as he marveled at such bravery, spirit, and strength in such a petite person. Annie stared up at him, committing each sharp angle of his chiseled face to memory and she wished she had time to soften each harsh line. Sometimes he was so aloof and unapproachable, his hawk-like face too well defined by the dark shadows of the past that accentuated his prominent cheekbones and stubborn jaw. How she loved him. She loved him so much it ached throughout her whole body. Tears burned as she remembered she had to leave him and take Michael far away from Kenlaren and possibly Scotland. She would take Dubh, she resolved, unable to bear the thought of parting with both of them. She had loved Lochiel Montgomery since that first distant day when she had been a child riding the stolen filly across the sand by the Solway. She had loved him when she had escaped him astride his own stallion, and suddenly she realized that Dubh had been a symbol for his dark master . . . a symbol, a promise of the sleek, virility of her future mate.

"What is it?" asked Loch softly, seeing the emotions play across her expressive face and a suspicious brimming of her thickly lashed eyes.

"I dinna want to sleep alone tonight," stated Annie, unable to admit how much she loved him. "I prefer the stink of dead roosters to the sickly stench of roses," she hissed angrily as a warm breeze wafted through the open window. She fought to harden herself as Loch sat beside her on the bed and smoothed back the tangled riot of curls. "I'm sorry . . . so sorry!" she cried as the events of the day, her fatigue, and the effects of his close proximity combined and she exploded into tears.

"Och, cry them out, Rob Roy," he crooned, gathering her into his arms and easily overpowering her struggles.

"I am not a sniveling . . . female! I am not a whining bairn! I . . . am . . . not . . . some . . . vap . . . or . . . ous

. . . chit!" hiccoughed Annie, trying desperately to stem the rising tide before losing control and weeping helplessly on his broad chest.

"Aye, I ken," grinned Loch lovingly, his own dark eyes suspiciously wet. "You are a courageous, wonderful woman. A positive giant among woman . . . in fact an Amazon!" he declared expansively. Annie sniffed and looked warily up at him, too proud to show her ignorance by asking what an Amazon was. "Och, Rob Roy, it is going to be a rare experience living wie you, my love!" He laughed joyously and gathered her even closer, kissing her hot, salty little face. Annie scowled at him even as her whole body was fired, racing her pulses and causing excitement to flow, aching the core of her.

"You look like a wee, outraged kitten," he remarked, planting teasing kisses on her mutinous little face and trying not to laugh at her confusion. "What's the matter, Rob Roy? You dinna ken whether to be angry or loving?" he asked huskily, noting her erect nipples that raised the thin cotton of her shirt.

"Loving? Nay lusting!" replied Annie.

"Loving," corrected Loch softly, unbuttoning her shirt and caressing her firm breasts.

"'Tis rutting, mating, covering, whoring!"

"When I was sick and you gave yourself to me . . . was that loving?" he asked gently, unbuttoning his own shirt and pressing her warm nakedness to his bared flesh.

"You said it was whoring!" stated Annie, fighting the exquisite feelings that flooded through her.

"I was very very wrong . . . and I want to spend the rest of my life undoing that hurt," he apologized huskily.

"How does one know what is loving and what is whoring? When we lie together and our bodies join . . . I'm not thinking of anything . . . not love . . . not anything but the wondrous excitement that is building and building almost to hurting," Annie strove to explain as Loch laid her back against the pillows and tugged her trews down her lithe golden thighs. "Maybe you could be any man and I am like my mother . . . a whore . . . able to have many men between my legs?" she wondered aloud fearfully.

Loch felt a wave of fury stab into him at the thought,

and he stared at her in amazement as he realized he was jealous for the first time in his life. He had never felt possessive about a woman before. He had rutted and sown his wild seeds and as long as the women had been compliant, undemanding, and free from disease, everything had been all right. Without question he expected fidelity, not because of any maudlin notions of love but because he didn't like to be made a fool of.

Annie stared up at Loch, feeling extremely vulnerable in her nudity and afraid of his sudden intense silence. Keeping her eyes pinned to his harsh, unapproachable expression, she blindly felt about for the bed covers, needing to burrow under. Maybe she *was* like her mother and he had just realized it? What had been said just that very afternoon about lunacy running in families? First her mother, and now her.

"Rob Roy?" called Loch tenderly, seeing the girl's eyes staring with terror into space. She forced herself to look at him and he tried to speak steadily although he felt like howling at the pain he saw reflected on Annie's face. "Could you have lain wie Vicar Nevins?" he asked, and he hated himself as he saw a great shudder shake her small naked body and her flesh goose-bumped with loathing. "Could you have lain wie Ross Montgomery? Niall Potter? Your Uncle Robert?" he probed mercilessly, and Annie shook her head violently from side to side. "Why not? They are men, after all," he added relentlessly.

"All save Uncle Robert are disgusting . . . unappealing," she whispered. "And Uncle Robert is my Uncle Robert."

"What of other men of your acquaintance?"

"What of them?"

"Aren't there any you wish to lie wie?" asked Loch, choosing his words very carefully, his lean face gaunt with tension as just the mere thought caused pain to churn his gut.

"No, only you," confessed Annie. "Always you . . . ever since I first saw you and stole your stallion. In the beginning I did not understand the feelings . . . but there was a deep ache . . . a pain that I held close to me. I dreamed of you, of both of us riding Dubh across the sand by the sea, over the moor wie the wind rushing by . . . and then I heard you were dead." She was unable to continue for a moment as tears welled and she buried her face against him and clung closely. "When I heard you were dead it was though a part of me died, and I knew that I had always loved you and had been waiting. All through the years when I put Dubh to stud and I watched him cover his mares . . . it was you I ached for. His thrusting rhythm and the sun shining on his black mane. . . ."

"Och, my wee Rob Roy," groaned Loch as her sensuality and courageous honesty touched him deeply and sparked a burning need.

Michael stood in the dark corridor outside of Annie's bedchamber and heard the age-old committment of two loving bodies. His young face was drawn and bitter as he recalled each of the humiliating times he had attempted to lose his own virginity. He stifled a sob and clenched his fists in fury as the memory of jeering laughter tormented his ears, and he crept downstairs to the sanctuary of his library. Quietly he closed the heavy door and leaned against it, allowing hot tears to course down his cheeks as his blurred eyes sought the comfort of the conforming rows of books in the cold, bluish moonlight. He sniffed and scrubbed the tears savagely away as he strode across the carpeted room to run his hands backward and forward along the firm spines, caressing the cool, bound volumes as he tried to erase the sensuous picture of Lochiel's and Annie's entwined bodies.

"Words! Words! Words!" he screamed, suddenly sweeping the unresponsive books from the shelves. Violently he cleared each of the rows until the walls were empty, and then he sat on the floor methodically tearing the pages out of volume after volume. Crying and laughing and occasionally reading aloud a verse or sentence, he savagely ripped the books to shreds until he had built a large pyre in the middle of the room in the very center of the ornate design of the carpet. Finally he stood back and surveyed the empty shelves before lighting a taper and deliberately torching the literary pile. He opened the door and giggled as the draught fanned the flames. As an afterthought he ignited the elegant draperies and wrenched the oil paintings of his frowning ancestors off the brocaded walls. He roared with laughter as their disapproving features bubbled and melted in the crackling heat.

Michael watched the flames leap higher and higher, and smile of pure triumph blazed across his face. He felt all-powerful, almost godlike, he decided, as he raised his arms as though to conduct the raging inferno.

Annie lay across Loch's broad chest, still intimately coupled, listening to the steady beat of his heart. How could she bear to leave him? She loved him with every fiber of her being and the thought of being without him caused a bleak numbness. But she had to find Michael and take him away where no one could find them. Poor Michael, so tormented and alone while she was so cherished and complete, she thought, burying her small nose in the warmth of Loch's bare chest and hugging him fiercely.

"We'll find Michael and take care of him together," murmured Lochiel as Annie's deep sigh echoed through him. She gasped and pushed herself back so she could look into his face. He clasped her small buttocks to keep his manhood nestled within her.

"How did you know what I was thinking?" she asked wonderingly.

"One minute I held a very contented, soft, purring kitten and the next a tense, uncomfortable, sharp . . . er . . . thing," he explained, firmly removing her pointed elbows from his chest.

"Thing?" she echoed indignantly.

"Your beautiful body is as expressive as your exquisite little face," he said, kissing the tip of her nose and running his hands down her silky back. "For a moment I was slightly offended, thinking you unappreciative of my lovemaking, but on realizing that was impossible as I rather pride myself on my prowess in that area I put two and two together . . ." he teased, trying to lighten her mood.

"Prowess?" interrupted Annie.

"Aye, prowess," agreed Loch roguishly, his ebony eyes glinting with mischief.

"That means you've been practicing!" accused Annie.

"Who with?" she challenged. Loch bent his dark head, intent on smothering her questions with seductive kisses as his manhood stirred and she wriggled delightedly against him.

Suddenly Loch raised his head and, with an oath, lifted her off him.

"What is it?" she cried, finding herself unromantically uncoupled and unceremoniously shunted aside as he leaped off the bed.

"Get dressed!" he ordered tersely, throwing a shirt at her and tugging on his tight riding britches. Annie stared wide-eyed, following his scowling gaze to the curls of smoke that crept under the door from the corridor.

"Fire," she mouthed fearfully, and she obediently pulled Loch's shirt over her tousled head. A bloodcurdling, maniacal laugh shattered the night's silence. "Michael!" she screamed, rushing toward the door.

"No! Dinna touch the door!" shouted Loch as he doused towels with water from the ewer on the washstand.

"But . . ." protested Annie, but he picked her up and strode to the open window.

"Thank God, you're as agile as a monkey," he muttered, placing her on the wide casement. "Climb down and rouse the others!" He gave her a swift, hard kiss.

"But . . ."

"Do as you're told!" he snapped harshly, wrapping a wet towel about his nose and mouth and striding back to the door. "Start climbing!" She stood watching him and he looked back at her, committing each line of the glorious lithe body to memory as she stood poised on the window ledge, the moonlight shining through the thin fabric of the shirt she wore.

Annie's heart raced triple-time and she cried out with alarm as he opened the door and let in the angry crackling roar of the hungry fire that seemed to be ravenously devouring the very core of the house. She stifled another scream as Loch strode into the corridor to be swallowed up by the dense swirling smoke. For a split-second she debated disobeying and following him, but then she resolutely turned and shinnied down the thick ivy vines. Reaching the ground, she felt about blindly in the darkness, grabbing fistfuls of pebbles that she frantically threw against the dark windows of the second floor bedchambers.

"Fire! Fire! Fire!" she screamed. The words caught in her throat as she looked toward the elegant French doors of the library and saw a grotesque, clawing shape silhouetted against the orange flames. As though sensing her gaze, the figure slowly circled and stared accusingly, the hands beckoning, reaching, stabbing toward her before crashing into the glass panes that exploded on impact, showering thousands of sharp fragments and freeing the ferocious flames that roared up the outside walls.

Annie stared in horror at the deformed, blackened figure of her brother which lay sprawled atop the rose bushes. Without thought, she slowly approached, her eyes pinned to his face, which smirked fiendishly, untouched by the fire except for several sooty smudges. His thick, wavy, auburn hair and amber eyes caught the reflection of the violently dancing flames, so he seemed alive despite his awkwardly twisted body suspended from the thorns.

"Michael?" she called urgently, not heeding the fiercely spitting sparks that hissed and pitted, stinging holes through her thin shirt. "Michael, wake up and take my hand," she implored, reaching through the sharp barbs that raked her bare arms as they possessively clawed onto the body of the youth. Frantically she clutched at the leg of his trousers, but the material crumbled to ashes in her hands. "Michael?" she screamed again. She fought her way through the full-blown roses on their long spiked brambles that whipped sharply and wrapped painfully about her flesh. "Och, Michael-mine," she lamented as she stared into his still face and saw death starkly imprinted.

Lochiel sat on the rolling lawn with Annie sheltered between his long legs, her back pressed against his broad chest as they watched Kenlaren burn noisily, lighting up the dark Lammas night until morning, when the hollow shell quietly steamed, the ribbons of smoke wending straight upward to meld with the gray sky. He had wanted to protect Annie, to carry her away out of sight of the raging inferno, but she had firmly and silently resisted, needing to witness the final demise of her family home. He sensed it was a way of putting her sad past in perspective. It was a way to say good-bye, not just to her brother Michael and her old nurse, Mrs. Wilson, but to her own childhood. Robert, Iona, Roderick, and Wilkes kept an understanding, respectful distance.

As the long night wore on and Annie kept her eyes pinned to the burning house, Loch stared down at the bright head between his encircling arms and wondered fearfully about the scars and sadness that might remain to shroud her vivacious spirit. Only once during the silent vigil had she made a sound.

"The roses are burning!" she had screamed, and he had followed her anguished gaze to the heavy blossoms that seemed to throb, getting larger and larger until they burst, their petals snaking into flames. Then the walls of Kenlaren collapsed with a long low rumble, entombing Michael and the accursed rose garden.

The sun climbed higher and higher, turning the sky from the morose mourning gray to a fresh innocent blue, and Annie sighed.

"It is over . . . finished," she said softly, taking her dry, burning eyes from the smoking ruins and tilting her head up to stare at Loch's firm jawline.

"Aye, and we're just beginning," he returned huskily, seeing the bright promise in her amber eyes. He placed a tender kiss on her sooty upturned nose as he rejoiced in her invincible spirit. Annie smiled tremulously before hugging him so fervently he lost his balance and rolled back in the dewy grass with her clasped in his strong arms.

"And we'll start now . . . today!" she stated vehemently, lying atop him and gazing into his glinting ebony eyes, recognizing the love lights that sparked and ignited delicious shivers of anticipation throughout her entire body. "We'll start now! This very second!" She stretched herself over the length of him, delighting in the feel of his taut, hard muscles.

"This very second?" repeated Loch as she wriggled sensuously. "I think I should like a wee bit more privacy," he suggested casually as he heard the low murmur of approaching voices. Annie pouted and ran the provocative tip of her tongue across her top lip as she rotated her hips seductively against him. She grinned impishly as she felt his manhood rise and press throbbingly, before she rolled off of him with a husky gurgle. "Och, you'll pay for that, my bonny minx," growled Loch as she smiled triumphantly, feeling powerful and secure in her ability to arouse him.

"Och, I dinna ken you were so prim and proper, Lord Falconhurst," she trilled saucily. "Are you sure you're not English?" she taunted, and lithely stretched, unaware of what a glorious picture she made with the morning sun flaming her riotous mane of hair and silhouetting her naked body through the thin, torn shirt.

Loch propped his dark head on his arms and lay back, grinning his appreciation of her long, graceful legs as Annie gave a piercing whistle to summon the stallion from the high pasture. A gentle summer breeze molded the tattered fabric to the inviting curves of her breasts and thighs as she stood above him poised like a young goddess. Sensing his searing gaze, Annie smiled wickedly down at him and he hummed, trying to appear nonchalant with a buttercup between his teeth. She giggled and stared suggestively at his groin, raising a mischievous eyebrow at his obvious arousal before tutting in mock disapproval.

"Och, my wee witch," he growled reaching out a rapid hand and grasping a small foot so that she toppled onto his broad chest. "Observers or not, you'll have to take the consequences of your rash teasing," he threatened as she molded her body to his with great satisfaction and offered herself without reserve.

"I say, Iona, wasn't that a pee-wit?" declared Robert loudly, tactfully changing directions and averting his eyes from the highly improper spectacle of his brother-in-law cavorting with his ward on the rolling lawns of the still-smoldering Kenlaren Manor.

Epilogue

Sir Robert Forsythe stood in the apple orchard clad solely in a charred nightshirt, trying to assume a dignified stance that befitted an English peer, and to ignore the decidely unladylike squawks of his curtain-draped wife, who sagged against him overcome with helpless laughter.

"By Jove!" he uttered for perhaps the tenth time, staring with suspicion at the warmth that oozed between his bare toes. "By Jove! I say! Dash it all! Jolly rude if you ask me! Bloody impertinent! Who does your brother think he is? Galloping off like that with my nearly naked niece and a herd of probably stolen horses . . . without a word! Without even a by-your-leave!" he blustered, no longer able to remain fashionably blaseé and understated.

"Hardly without a word, my love," corrected Iona with a gurgle of merriment. "He did say 'Cheerio, old boy!" She collapsed once more into whoops of mirth as she recalled the look of utter stupefaction on Robert's usually bland face when Lochiel and Annie had ridden off, followed by at least twenty mares and foals, with Roderick bringing up the rear, trying to look nonchalant in Mrs. Wilson's pinafore and donkey cart.

"Deuced ragmannered!" snorted Robert.

"But devilishly romantic," quipped Iona impishly as she envisioned the glorious sight of Lochiel and Annie together astride the giant stallion, her brother bare-chested with the petite golden girl between his brown arms and muscular thighs.

"The least they could have done was have the courtesy to allow us to accompany them . . . as chaperones, of course," stated Robert quellingly.

"Rather late for that, don't you think, my love?" suggested Iona with a suspicious quaver in her voice. She tried to look properly sympathetic to the dilemma of her near-naked husband, who seemed to recoil just from the feel of the raw earth beneath his bare feet.

"Excuse me, Sir Robert," ventured Wilkes's very correct tones. Robert turned and surveyed his tiny valet, who despite the fire that had incinerated everyone else's entire wardrobe, was as usual immaculately dressed from the crown of his hat to the polished tips of his shoes.

"Do you sleep fully dressed, Wilkes?" he remarked testily.

"Am I wrinkled, sir?" replied the diminutive manservant inspecting his impeccable attire solicitously and flicking at imaginary bits of lint.

"Take your garments off!" ordered Robert, feeling at a decide disadvantage.

"I dinna think Wilkes's clothes will fit you, my darling," giggled Iona looking mischievously from Robert's tall, imposing stature to Wilkes's immaculate tiny person.

"Draw the curtains a trifle, my pet," warned Robert, glancing pointedly at her inviting decolletage as the velvet drape slipped distractingly off one delectable shoulder.

"A double entendre in the midst of this frightful situation!" exclaimed Iona admiringly. "Robert, you are quite wonderful." She watched several fat hens peck hungrily about her husband's constantly wiggling toes, and held her breath so she wouldn't chuckle as one particular chicken cocked its head from side to side as though sighting her prey with beady eyes before attacking. Robert bellowed and leaped into the air.

"Confounded insolence!" he roared, losing his elegant stance and aiming a well-placed kick at the offending bird.

"Och, I'm sorry, Robert," howled Iona, unable to stand erect as she doubled over and screamed with laughter. Her long-suffering husband shook his blond head in despair, refusing to allow a smile to cross his handsome face although his blue eyes twinkled with humor.

"I beg your pardon, sir, but—"

"As you are of the female persuasion, my pet, it is quite impossible for you to appreciate the delicacy of being without one's trousers. *Sans culotte,* so to speak," interrupted Robert. "It makes a man feel decidedly vulnerable."

"Quite so, sir," acknowledged Wilkes, unbuttoning his frock coat.

"Never mind. Never mind," said Sir Robert graciously. "There is no earthly point in our both being in the same undignified state, is there?"

"Thank you, sir," responded Wilkes. "But I am loathe to . . ."

"I suppose there is nothing for it but to be . . . pococurante," sighed the hard-done-by aristocrat, offering his crooked arm to Iona as though they were about to enter a formal gathering.

"Pococurante?" echoed Iona before redoubling up with hilarity. Robert patted her hand indulgently, as though humoring a maiden aunt.

"Yes, my sweet, pococurante—or, if you will, devil-may-care. How about *sans souci?*" he offered expansively.

"*Sans souci?*" choked Iona.

"Sedate? Serene? Insouciant?" he continued, frowning with mock disapproval as his wife shook with mirth. "So what's it to be, my pet?"

"May I suggest either a very hasty retreat or a stiffening of the sinews, sir!" Wilkes burst out briskly, determined to speak without interruption.

"Stiffening of the sinews?" repeated Robert, at a loss.

"Imitate the actions of the tiger!" quoted Iona. "Wilkes is reciting Shakespeare, darling."

"What on earth for? And why the bloody hell would I want to be a tiger, Wilkes?"

"Your mother, the Lady Amelia, and your sisters, including the Mother Superior, have arrived," announced the gentleman's gentleman, allowing a trace of sympathy to flit across his placid countenance.

"I should never have placed our wedding announcement in the *Catholic Herald,*" mourned Robert.

"Oh, Boo-boo? Yoo-hoo? Where are you?" boomed several robust voices. Iona stared with absolute horror at the grim procession of black-clad women who marched across the stable yard, their rosary beads clicking. She emitted a very loud squawk and the velvet curtain floated about her shapely ankles.

"May I suggest insouciance?" proffered Wilkes without batting an eyelid at the exposed charms of his mistress.

"You may," consented Robert, striking a regal pose and draping a careless arm about Iona's naked shoulders. "Chin up, old girl," he directed, and he smiled benevolently at his collection of female relatives who gaped, unable to believe the Edenic scene.